Her Surrender

TARA CONRAD

HIS ONE HER ONLY PUBLISHING

Second Edition Printing 2022

Published by His One, Her Only Publishing

Cover art by Boundless Book Covers

Formatting by Mr. George Conrad III

Contents

To my Sir,

i've loved You for more than half my life. i hope to love You for many more years—there will never be enough. You are the heart and soul of this book. It's Your love that gave me the courage to write this story. You are my moon and stars. The breath I breathe. My world. i love You.

Author's Note

In the BDSM lifestyle, language carries special meaning. You may notice that words such as *i* or pet names for the submissive, such as *baby girl*, are written in lowercase, while words used to address the Dominant, such as *You* or *Sir*, are capitalized.

This is an intentional expression of respect and dynamic within the lifestyle, not an editing oversight.

I've chosen to honor that tradition in this story to reflect the authenticity of the relationship dynamic you'll encounter within these pages.

Prologue

HE'S GOING TO PROPOSE TO ME. I'LL FINALLY BE ONE step closer to becoming Mrs. Thomas Moore. Since Thanksgiving break is so short, I could talk my professors into letting me take my midterms a few days early, and I could change my flight to Missouri. Between classes and working, I've never been able to visit Tommy on campus. But that's all going to change with this trip home. He's not expecting me until Wednesday evening, so I can't wait to see his face when I show up at his dorm tomorrow morning.

Tommy's mom took off after he was born. He never knew who his father was. It was his aunt Delia who raised him. Right after we graduated from high school, she had a major heart attack and needed surgery. Although Tommy had a full-ride football scholarship to the University of Missouri, he didn't want to leave her until she'd recovered. Thankfully, the school was willing to hold his scholarship for him. While I'm in my first year of graduate school, Tommy's still an undergrad. He plans to spend five years at Mizzou to maximize his football eligibility. When I graduate, he will, too. Then, we can have our happily ever after.

My parents didn't want me to leave Northmeadow to live in New York City. They felt the distance would put too much of a strain on Tommy and me. Even though we talk almost every night and see each other on school breaks, the past five years haven't been easy, but they will be worth it.

It was a bit of a last-minute scramble, but I could make it to the airport with just enough time to clear security and board the plane. Before I left, I downloaded enough bridal magazines to keep me busy for the entire flight. I've been so busy scrolling through them that I don't realize how much of the flight has passed until the fasten seatbelt light turns on. An announcement plays through the plane's overhead speakers, alerting the passengers that we'll be landing shortly. I stuff the e-reader into my bag and look out my window. My heart beats wildly, knowing this trip home will change my life.

An hour later, I'm heading to Mizzou's campus in my rental car. Thankfully, it's not a long ride, and before I know it, I'm pulling up in front of the Rotunda building.

The campus is beautiful, but it's enormous. Although I know Tommy's dorm name, I have no idea where it is, and I don't want to waste time driving around. So, I'm thankful when I spot a group of what appear to be students walking down the sidewalk. I hit the button to lower the window.

"Excuse me?"

"Do you need something?" a girl in a Mizzou hoodie asks.

"Can you tell me where Center Hall is?"

"Take the main road through campus. It's the big red brick building in the middle." She points me in the right direction. "You can't miss it."

I find the dorm easily and park in a visitor spot. My hands shake as I drop the keys in my purse and make my way to the building.

When I get to the door, I try to open it, but it's locked. Putting my hand up to the glass to see inside, I notice a few guys sitting in a lounge area watching a football game on a large flat-screen TV. I knock on the door, hoping to get their attention. It takes only a second for one of the guys to come over.

"You looking for someone?"

He towers over me, and I have to lift my head to see his face. "I'm looking for Tommy Moore."

"You're in the right place." He steps aside and lets me in.

"Is he here?"

"What's your name?" he asks.

"Natalie." My voice is quiet, and I feel a bit intimidated being the only girl here with a group of guys.

"I'm Mike." He reaches out to shake my hand. "We're on the team together. Are you his sister or something?"

"No, I'm his girlfriend."

The room goes silent.

I know it's not a coed dorm, but I'm sure I'm not the first girl who's come by.

"I have his room number. If you can point me in the right direction."

"Is he expecting you?" Mike asks.

"No." I smile. "I flew in early to surprise him."

He glances back at the group, who are now whispering to one another, before shrugging and turning back to me.

"Come on. I'll bring you up."

Mike leads me down a hallway and opens the door to the stairwell. We begin the climb up when I hear a shuffle of feet and voices behind us. When I look over my shoulder, I see several of the guys in the lounge area are now following us up the stairs.

"Why are they coming?"

"Guess they want to see the big surprise, too."

I hoped this would be a private moment, but the best-laid plans and all. It doesn't matter. I'm so excited to see Tommy that I don't care who's following me.

We arrive on the third floor and walk down a long hallway. Doors line both sides, and bulletin boards hang on the walls announcing all the latest campus happenings. People are coming and going, reminding me why I'm thankful I don't live on campus anymore.

Finally, we stop outside Tommy's room. I find it odd that there's a tie draped over the doorknob.

"You sure about this?" Mike asks. "It's not too late to turn back."

The vibe I'm getting from these guys is off. Why do they care that I'm here to see my boyfriend?

"I'm sure."

"Hey Scott, you have your key?"

"I don't think this is a good idea, Mike," a tall blond guy behind me says.

"Key." Mike puts out his hand.

Scott pushes his way through the group. "Move. I'll do it." He grabs the tie off the knob before unlocking the door and pushing it open.

When I look into the room, the sight in front of me nearly brings me to my knees.

A blonde woman is on top of Tommy. "Yes. Just like that, babe. Harder."

Scott clears his throat.

Tommy pops his head up. "What the fuck?" he yells and pushes the girl off him.

She turns around, seeming not to care that she's naked in front of a group of men. When she sees me, she offers a smug smile.

"Ash?" She and I just talked yesterday. She knew I was coming —knew I'd find them. "How could you?"

I spin around and see Mike and a few guys laughing and elbowing each other. Scott stands in the doorway, clearly unamused by his roommate's behavior.

"I need to get out of here."

"You're an asshole, Moore." Scott throws the tie on the floor. "Come on."

I rush down to the main floor, needing to get as far away from Tommy as possible.

"I'm sorry you had to see that."

The realization of what I just witnessed hits me, and tears fill my eyes. I squeeze them shut. I can't cry. Not here.

"How long have you two been dating?"

"Eight years."

"Damn."

"Has she—" Do I really want to hear the answer? Deciding I need to. I continue, "Has she been here before?"

Scott looks as if he's asking if I really want him to answer.

I nod.

"Yeah, she's been coming to see him since he started here. He introduced her as—"

"Stop, please." It's too much. "I have to go." I push the door open and run to my car.

"You're in no shape to drive," Scott calls after me.

"I'll be fine." I look up and see Tommy rushing out the door.

I fumble through my purse, trying to find the keys.

"Natalie, wait," he yells.

Without waiting or looking back, I head straight to the airport and secure a seat on the next available flight to New York City.

The flight back feels like a blur. It's not until the jet's wheels screech down on the runway that the image of Tommy and Ashlynn together finally fades, and I'm brought back to the present.

I feel lost as I stand in the center of the bustling terminal, surrounded by noise and chaos. I watch the hurried travelers grumbling as they maneuver around me. Some rush to catch their flights, while others embrace each other as if celebrating a homecoming. But I am alone, left behind by my best friend and the man I was supposed to marry, feeling betrayed.

When I step outside, I'm hit by the cold night air. It helps snap me out of the haze I'm walking around in. There's a line of yellow taxis waiting for a passenger, or I can use the ridesharing app, but then I'll have to wait for a car to get here. Even though it'll cost a small fortune, I decide to take a cab. I'm desperate to get back to my apartment.

I open the door of the nearest taxi and slide onto the leather seat that's cracked and worn from use. Immediately, I'm hit with a strong scent of incense. The driver, an older Asian man, turns slightly in his seat. "Where do I take you, miss?"

I give him my address in the Village, and he types it into his GPS. Then, we begin the slow process of driving out of the airport.

"You've been crying," he says. His voice is soft and kind. "Are you okay?"

"Not really." I sniffle.

Opening the glove compartment, he grabs a small pack of tissues and hands them to me. I guess I'm not the first passenger he's picked up in this state.

"My name's Shusuke," he says as he glances in the rear-view mirror. "I listen if you want talk."

"Thank you, but not really."

I stare out the window, watching the cars pass by. Maybe I should call Lana and let her know I'm on my way home? I pull my cell phone out of my purse and turn it on. There's a barrage of alerts from missed calls and texts. Almost immediately, my phone starts ringing. Tommy's picture flashes on my screen. I send the call to voicemail, but he doesn't leave a message. The phone rings again. This time, I answer.

"What do you want?"

"Please let me explain," Tommy says.

"How can you explain my finding you in bed with my best friend?"

"It was a mistake. It won't happen again."

"I know it won't happen again." I let out a sarcastic laugh. "Because we're over."

"Natalie, wait—"

I disconnect the call.

The phone rings, but I'm not playing this game all night. Instead, I power off the phone and throw it back into my purse.

"That's who makes you cry?" Shusuke asks.

"Yes," I say softly. "It's my boyfriend—was my boyfriend." I try to take a deep breath, but grief weighs heavy on my chest. "I flew home early to surprise him, but instead, the surprise was on me." The fissure in my heart grows when I say the words out loud.

"You loved him."

"We've been together for eight years. I was supposed to marry him."

Shusuke takes the Queensboro Bridge, which is not the typical way a cabbie usually goes, but I'm glad. This is my favorite way to enter the city. The view of the skyline from the bridge, especially at night, is breathtaking. Once we cross and enter the city, I feel a weight lift. I'm back in my comfort zone—a place untainted by Tommy.

Fortunately, Shusuke knows all the side streets to avoid the traffic. I want to get home, crawl into bed, and pretend tonight never happened. Finally, the taxi pulls in front of my apartment. I gather my things to get out when Shusuke turns in his seat.

"Your heart is broken now. It is blessing when wrong person leaves your life. Don't let hurt turn to anger. Tonight is start of new journey. Now right person comes." He offers a kind smile.

His words play in my mind as the elevator carries me to my apartment. I'm sure he meant well, but I'm not taking a chance with my heart again.

I don't even know what time it is when I finally walk into the apartment I share with Svetlana. We met two years ago when we shared a dorm room on campus and became fast friends. Over the summer, right before we started graduate school, her dad rented us an apartment in the Village.

The lights are off, so I try to be quiet. I don't want to wake Lana and end up explaining why I'm home early. Right now, I just want to sleep. Tomorrow will come soon enough.

Using the flashlight on my phone, I tiptoe down the hallway to my bedroom. That's when I hear it. Lana's whimpering, begging someone to stop. A male voice yells at her to shut up.

Without a moment of hesitation, I dial 911.

"What's your emergency?" the dispatcher asks.

"There's someone in my apartment. My roommate's being attacked," I whisper into the phone and give them our address.

Although they tell me to wait on the line, I disconnect the call, intending to stop the attack. I grasp the doorknob and take a deep breath before I throw the door open.

Shining the light toward Lana's bed, I yell, "Stop! The police are on their way."

Lana's head flies up. "Natalie?" she shrieks. "What are you doing here?"

My cell phone isn't bright enough, so I flip on the overhead light. When I look over at Lana, I scream. She's naked and tied to the bed. A man I've never seen before is holding what looks like some sort of a gag in his hand. "You. Don't move," I yell.

He drops the object. It lands with a thud as he puts his hands up in surrender.

"Nat, this isn't what it looks like. Can you untie me?" she asks the man.

He looks between us before quickly untying her.

Svetlana climbs out of bed. "I thought you were in Missouri," she says as she slips her robe on and hurries over to me. "What are you doing home?"

"Are you okay? Did he hurt you?" I examine Lana for injuries before glaring over her shoulder at the man who's busy putting his shirt on.

We're interrupted by banging on the door. "NYPD, open up."

"Oh my God, you really called the police." Lana's voice is panicked.

"Of course, I called them."

They pound on the door again. "NYPD, open the door."

"Come with me." Lana grabs my arm. "We need to fix this."

Lana drags me out of her bedroom and into the living room. She makes quick work of the locks before opening the door.

"Good evening, officers. Please come in."

"We received a call about an assault in progress." The officer looks past me. "You, put your hands up and don't move."

I spin around and get a good look at the man. He's tall with creamy brown skin. His dark curls are pulled back into a neat ponytail. It's obvious he works out, as evidenced by the T-shirt stretching tight across his chest. But it's the color of his eyes that strikes me the most. They're a deep gray like clouds before a storm, and right now, they're fixed on me.

I collapse onto the couch from a mix of exhaustion and confusion.

Lana and the officers are talking by the door. I hear their voices but can't make out what they're saying. She turns and motions to the man, who cautiously walks across the room. Their conversation continues for a few minutes longer.

"Thank you, and sorry for the confusion," Lana says, shaking the officers' hands before they turn and leave the apartment.

"Do you want me to stay?" the man asks Lana quietly. "I can help you explain."

"I don't think that's a good idea. I'll call you in the morning."

"Okay, talk to you tomorrow," he says, kissing her forehead before leaving.

Lana locks up and then sits next to me on the couch. "I don't know where to start." She turns to face me, and the expression on her face changes. "You've been crying."

I'm overwhelmed. Thoughts and emotions run through my mind so quickly that I can't make sense of them. All I manage is a nod.

"What's wrong?" she asks. "Why are you home?"

"Tommy," I say, trying to change the subject. "What was going on back there?"

She glances down the hall before answering. "It wasn't what it looked like."

"Did he hurt you?"

"No. Well, not any more than I asked for." Lana giggles.

"What?" Why is she laughing after nearly being assaulted?

"I'm going to grab us a glass of wine. I think we're going to need it. What happened with Tommy?" she asks as she grabs a bottle of wine and pours us each a glass.

I sit back on the couch. "I got to his dorm and found him having sex with Ashlynn."

She hands me a glass of red wine. "Ashlynn, as in your best friend?"

"The one and only." I tip the glass and take a big drink.

Lana sits down. "Wow."

"Right now, I'm more concerned about what was happening here." I motion around the room.

"I wasn't expecting you to be home." Lana sips her wine before setting it down. "What you saw wasn't what you thought. I mean, it was, but not like you think."

"You were tied up and begging him to stop. It looked like he was hurting you."

She looks up and laughs. "Oh boy, I don't know where to start?"

"How about the beginning?"

"Have you ever heard of BDSM?" She blurts out the question, and I nearly choke on my wine.

"I've read about it in some romance novels. It's all that kinky sex and stuff." Once the words leave my mouth, the realization hits me. "Is that what was going on back there?" I set my wine glass down before I drop it.

"Yes," Lana says and slowly nods her head. "I grew up in the lifestyle. Papa's a Dominant, and Mama is his submissive."

I don't know what I expected her to say, but that wasn't it. "You mean to tell me your dad goes all *Christian Gray* and ties your mom up in the bedroom?" It's a lame joke, but it's all I can manage at the moment.

"Ha, ha. You're so funny." Lana laughs. "That's not exactly how it is in real life. My papa adores Mama, and she him. Their relationship has always been an example of what I hope to find someday." She beams as she talks about her parents.

This is all a bit TMI. "Why would you want to know what your parents get up to in their bedroom?"

"Eww." Svetlana pretends to gag. "We didn't talk about any of *that* stuff. BDSM is about so much more than kinky sex."

Lana explains that BDSM is often a lifestyle choice, not just something limited to what happens in the bedroom. The submissive, man or woman, takes care of the daily wants and needs of their Dominant. The Dominant ensures the safety of their submissive and will lavish their love and attention on them.

I've been to Russia with her to meet her family. I remember thinking their relationship seemed a bit old-fashioned, even more so than my parents'. Every day, Mrs. Solonik wore a dress and heels. Her hair and makeup were always perfect. She spent every minute doting on her husband, ensuring he had everything he needed—before he even asked for it. I found myself exhausted just watching her.

But I'll never forget the expression in Mr. Solonik's eyes when he looked at his wife—pure adoration. What really made an impression on me was his openness in showing Mrs. Solonik affection. He was generous with his kisses, caressing touches, and loving pet names. I remember wishing Tommy were half as affectionate with me. I couldn't even get him to hold my hand in public.

"What you walked in on tonight," she hesitates, "was a scene Brandon and I'd been planning for a while. You were supposed to be gone."

"Wait a minute. You do this BDSM thing, too?"

She nods. "I'm a submissive."

"How were we roommates for two years, and I never knew?"

"It's not a topic that's easy to bring up. Hi, I'm your new dorm mate. I like to get tied up and whipped."

We both laugh.

Lana explains how she first got into the lifestyle. She was eighteen when she went to her parents and expressed an interest. They had some serious conversations regarding what being in the lifestyle meant.

"Mama wasn't so sure, but I knew I was a submissive. She stressed the importance of being mature enough to put my needs second to someone else's. It isn't as easy as it sounds."

The way she talks about her relationship with her parents so casually makes my heart ache. I could never speak to my parents the way she's able to. My parents' view of sex is that it is something you only do after you're married—period, end of story. If they knew I wasn't a virgin, they'd go crazy.

"Mama gave me some books to read and introduced me to a trusted friend who was an experienced submissive. She was my mentor until I went to Moscow to study. That's where I submitted to a Dominant for the first time."

I'm stunned by my friend's confession but also curious. "Do you still happen to have the books she gave you?"

Lana raises her eyebrow. "Why?"

"I figure reading them might come in handy when I graduate." I shrug.

"I've been to Northmeadow." She leans back and crosses her arms. "I don't think your teen clients will be into BDSM."

I'll be working as a school therapist when I return home, but she's right. I highly doubt I'll encounter this topic there. "Maybe *I'm* curious," I say, trying to make light of it.

"I'll be right back." Lana walks down the hall and disappears into her bedroom. When she comes back, she's holding an e-reader. "They're loaded on here." She passes me the tablet. "Your turn. Tell me exactly what happened when you got to Mizzou."

The level of betrayal I feel toward Tommy and Ashlynn is indescribable. Maybe my parents were right when they said I shouldn't go to New York City, but would that have changed anything? Were they seeing each other even back then? The thought makes me sick.

Lana listens patiently as I tell her everything.

"Now I have to come up with an excuse to tell my parents," I say through a yawn. "There's no way I'm going back there until I have to."

Lana grabs our empty wine glasses and brings them to the kitchen. "Why don't you sleep on it first? We can come up with something later."

The sun is beginning to rise, and we haven't slept at all. Between being up all night and the wine, my head is spinning.

"You have to promise to tell me more about your being tied up by that hot guy." I grin.

"I just hope he's still interested. Someone scared the shit out of him by calling the police." She links her arm with mine, and we walk to our rooms.

I need to sleep off the worst night of my life.

The following day, I called my parents. As expected, they were upset that I wouldn't be home for Thanksgiving. I made up an excuse, telling them the counseling center I'm interning for asked me to fill in for someone at the last minute, and I couldn't say no. I need some distance from Northmeadow.

Tommy's been calling and texting every day, begging for forgiveness and making every excuse possible for his *indiscretion.* When the tone of the messages shifts to blaming me for coming to New York in the first place, I decide to change my number.

Funny, though, Ashlynn hasn't bothered to call. We've been

friends since we were born. We've done everything together, been through everything together. That pain hurts almost worse than Tommy cheating on me.

All of this has forced me to open my eyes to everything in front of me. For the past five years, I've kept one foot in Northmeadow, afraid to let go of everything familiar.

I pick up the picture of my brother Michael and his boyfriend Evan that sits on my dresser. I miss them so much. I can't believe they've been gone for seven years. I'm transported back to my junior year in high school when Michael told me about Evan.

"Nat, do you have a few minutes?" Michael asks from my doorway.

I look up and smile. Even though he's only a year older than me, my brother is my hero. I would do anything for him. "I always have a few minutes for you." Closing my math textbook, I jump up and follow Michael outside.

"Let's go for a walk," he says nervously.

He doesn't look at me, and his hands shake as we walk silently down the path into the woods behind our house until we come to the clearing we always played in when we were kids.

When we get there, Evan's waiting for us.

"I thought you'd never get here," Evan says, smiling.

Michael finally looks at me. "I have—we have something to tell you." Michael moves to stand next to Evan.

"Okay." I look back and forth between them.

"I don't know how to tell her," Michael says to Evan.

"I'll do it." He grabs Michael's hand and looks at me. "Natalie, your brother and I are together. I'm in love with him."

I'm surprised by this revelation.

Michael and I grew up with Evan. His family lives on a farm across town. We all played together as children, but as we've grown up, I've seen how they look at each other—it's different from just friends. Michael doesn't know that I know, but I've watched him sneak out his bedroom window late at night to meet Evan. I watched them embrace and kiss, but I didn't say anything. This was Michael's to tell me when he was ready.

"I know," I say with a big smile. "And I'm so happy you guys finally told me."

Michael stands there, his mouth hanging open.

"You know?" Evan asks.

"I've seen you two together," I say, looking at Michael, who's turned pale.

"Do Mom and Dad know?"

"I doubt it. They sleep like the dead."

We share a laugh.

"Are you going to tell them?"

"Yes." Michael shuffles his foot nervously. "We're telling all of them tonight. We want you to know first because things probably won't go well after that."

"I'm glad you told me." I reach out and hug them. "I'm happy for you both."

I run my finger across the picture of Michael's face. He was right. After they told our parents, nothing was the same.

As Michael and Evan come out to our parents, Mom cries hysterically. You would've sworn someone died. Dad yells so loud the dishes in the China closet rattle. Evan's dad passed away when he was young, so it's just his mom.

She's silent for a long time, watching the spectacle my parents are making. Finally, she speaks, "I'm proud of you, boys. There's liable to be a lot of hate coming your way. I'll always be on your side. I love you both so much."

My parents aren't as kind. "Get your things and get out," Dad yells.

Ten minutes later, I'm standing by my bedroom window with tears pouring down my face as I watch my brother walk away. Thankfully, Evan's mom welcomed them into her home.

My eyes fill with tears as I remember what came in the weeks to follow. It was their senior year. It should've been filled with happy memories. Instead, every day was a new level of hell. The entire school turned on them. They were called fags and fairies by kids in the hallway. Messages of hate were posted on their social media accounts. I was alienated from everyone except Ashlynn and Tommy, but I didn't care. I loved my brother and Evan.

Looking back, I think the breaking point for Evan was seeing his mom's car parked in their driveway. One day, when they came home from school, a message was written in soap on the windshield of his mom's car. It read, "You'd be better off dead." And "Fags not wanted here."

One month after they came out, Evan took his daddy's gun, went into the field, and shot himself. Michael wasn't the same after that.

I wasn't allowed to go to Evan's house. So, the only time I could see Michael was at school. I thought he was still living with Evan's mom. Michael never told me he had moved out and was living in a tent in the woods.

It was graduation night when I realized something was wrong.

"Aren't you going to Michael's graduation ceremony?" I ask my parents.

"No," Dad says and goes back to reading his newspaper.

The only reason I'm allowed to go is that it counts as service hours for school.

When I get to the school, I search for Michael, but he's nowhere to be found. It's not a big graduating class, so I know I didn't miss him. There's no way Michael would miss graduation. Something is terribly wrong.

I called the police, but they refused to file a report because he's over eighteen and not 'officially' missing. Instead, they tell me they'll keep an eye out for him.

The next day, an officer knocks on our door. Before he speaks, I already know. Michael's body was found near his tent in the woods, not far from Evan's house. The officers also found a note addressed to me.

I open the picture frame and carefully take out the worn paper.

Natalie,

I hope one day you'll forgive me for leaving you. The pain is too much. I can't do it anymore. I'm going to find Evan—going to find our happily ever after. Please don't be sad for me. I want you to get out of Northmeadow and live your life to the fullest. Find someone truly worthy of all the love you have to give. I expect you to make your mark on the world. I will always love you and will be watching over you.

Love, Michael.

Tears stream down my face as I sit silently, wishing my older brother were by my side. After re-reading his note, I take a deep breath and carefully fold it, tucking it away safely behind the picture.

"I'm going to make you proud of me, Michael," I say aloud to my brother, hoping he can hear me.

My past hasn't changed. I still have to go back to Northmeadow after I graduate. But right now, I'm living in one of the biggest cities in the world. It's time I embrace everything it has to offer.

I've been reading the books Lana gave me about the lifestyle. At first, I was so horrified that I turned off the e-reader and left it on my desk, where it sat for a few days, taunting me until curiosity got the better of me.

The other night, I turned it back on, determined to keep an open mind, and started reading. The more I read, the more intrigued I became. The ideas about sex are different from anything I've ever known. But the basic principles of a relationship and respect between two people are exactly how I was raised.

After I finish the last book, I search for Lana and find her in the kitchen cooking. Sitting on one of the stools at the island, I tap my fingers on the granite counter.

She turns around, spatula in hand. "You're driving me crazy with the nervous tapping. What's up?"

I'm not used to talking openly about sex, so it takes me a

minute to muster the courage before answering. "I was wondering if I could ask you some more questions? You know, about the books I'm reading."

"Sure," she says without hesitation before turning her attention to whatever she's cooking, which smells delicious.

"What're you making?"

"Piroshki. It's kind of my mama's recipe, except I cheated and bought the dough," she says with a smile. "But I don't think that's what you wanted to ask. Dinner's ready. We can eat and talk."

She grabs two plates out of the cupboard and dishes out the food. I get the forks and glasses, pouring a generous portion of wine for each of us before joining Lana at our small dining table.

I love it when she makes one of her mom's dishes. "Oh my god, Lana. This is amazing."

"Thanks, but you're avoiding."

"I want to learn more," I say quickly and take another bite.

Lana laughs. "That's what you were so nervous to say."

I shrug.

She grabs my phone and unlocks the screen. "Here's the club I go to. It's called Fire and Ice." She hands me the phone with a web page pulled up. "They have classes for people who think they might be interested. You should take one."

"I'm not ready for anything like that," I say. "Isn't there anything else I can read?"

She sets her fork down. "There are tons of books, but you'll learn more by taking the class and talking to real people."

"I'll think about it." I bookmark the site and go back to eating. But I know I have no intention of stepping foot in a club.

Natalie

PRESENT-DAY (A YEAR LATER)

It's mid-morning on Saturday, and I'm sitting cross-legged on the sofa, my face buried in my textbook. Looks like another weekend that I won't be going out. Although I decided to embrace city life, I also have to maintain my grades to keep my scholarship. It's a tricky balance to maintain.

"Are you still studying?" Svetlana grabs the textbook from my hand and reads the title aloud, "Love and Attachment: Adult Relationships." She raises her eyebrows. "You need to get out of this apartment."

"I have a paper." I jump up and swipe at the book, but she's taller than me and holds it out of my reach.

"You can study tomorrow. Tonight, I want you to come out with me."

"But—"

"Come on, Nat." She hands back my book. Her glacier-blue eyes plead with me to say yes.

I resume my sitting position on the sofa and flip through the text to find my place. "I'll go out next weekend, I promise."

"I need you to come out tonight." Lana flops down next to me.

"Why?"

"Well, you remember Brandon, the guy you called the cops on?" Lana smirks.

My cheeks heat from embarrassment. "How could I forget?"

"Thankfully, you didn't scare him away."

"That's good because he sure is hot."

"He is, isn't he?" she says, a huge smile on her face. "I've finally consented to be his submissive." She pauses, allowing me a minute to digest this new information. "We're doing a scene at the club tonight, and I really want you there."

Now she has my attention. I close my book and set it next to me to give Lana my full attention.

"You're doing a scene? Like getting naked in front of an audience?"

She nods slowly as if she's measuring my response.

"This is what you want?" I ask.

Being naked in a room full of people wouldn't be my first choice. I may not know much about her lifestyle, but I want to make sure she's a completely willing participant.

"I'm so excited about it, but please, I need my best friend there." Lana bats her eyes at me.

"I wouldn't miss it for the world."

She pulls me in for a tight squeeze. "I'm so glad you said yes. You're going to have a great time."

I'm unsure about having a great time. I plan to go, sit in a quiet corner, and watch Lana do her thing. Tonight should satisfy my curiosity, and then I can move on.

The rest of the afternoon is spent getting ready for our night out. We give each other manicures before I help Lana fix her long brown hair. She says her hair must be up and out of the way.

"There, all done," I say after putting in the last bobby pin.

"Thanks, I love it," Lana says as she checks out her hair in the mirror.

"I'm going to take a quick shower," I say and turn to leave, but stop midway. "What do you suggest I wear tonight?"

"I was hoping you'd ask. I have the perfect outfit for you," Lana says, giddy with excitement as she hurries into her walk-in closet. When she comes out, she's holding a hanger with a tiny black scrap of material on it.

"You're kidding, right?"

Lana's stunning. She's tall and fit, with curves in all the right places. Everything she wears looks fantastic on her. I'm five-two, and although I work out, my body looks nothing like hers. There's no way I can wear that dress.

"Nat, you're gorgeous." She pushes the hanger into my hands. "You're going to turn heads tonight."

"Do I want to turn heads?"

"You never know who you might meet," she says as she points me to my room, giving me a nudge forward. "Go shower and get dressed. Now."

"Are you sure you're not a Domme?" I call as I head down the hall. "You're awfully bossy."

My statement is met with Lana's laughter.

When I get to my room, I hold up the hanger and look at the dress—if that's what you can call it. It's black and made of stretchy material with a cutout that will expose my midsection. Two straps hold up the top section that wraps around the neck and crisscrosses in the back.

Peeking my head out, I yell down the hall. "How do I wear a bra with this thing?"

"You don't."

I roll my eyes, close the door, and toss the dress onto the bed.

Then, I strip off my sweatpants and t-shirt and step into the shower. My hands shake as I shave my legs, but surprisingly, I don't nick myself. Standing under the hot water, I let it cascade over me, hoping it'll soothe my frayed nerves.

After finishing, I wrap a fluffy towel around my body and stand in front of the bathroom mirror to dry my hair and apply makeup. I style my blonde curls so they cascade softly down my back.

As I walk across the plush carpet in my bedroom, I ignore the dress lying on the bed and instead open my drawer to grab a pair of panties.

I smile as I pull on a sexy thong. Tommy was a fan of sensible cotton bras and underwear. After discovering he was cheating, I emptied them all into the garbage. Lana took me shopping for some adult lingerie. It started as an act of defiance, but I've grown to love wearing something sexy under my clothes. It gives me a sense of confidence I didn't realize I'd been missing.

Holding up the dress, I give myself a pep talk before I step into the black fabric and drag it up my body. The material clings to my curves, leaving little to the imagination. Grabbing a pair of black heels from my closet, I slide my feet into them and slowly turn to face my full-length mirror.

Svetlana appears behind me. "I knew it! You look amazing!" She hugs me tightly.

I've never worn anything like this, but I like what I see.

Suddenly, this all seems too real. "What should I expect tonight?"

"The car's here," Svetlana says. "I'll tell you on the way."

"The car?"

"Brandon sent a car to pick us up. You ready?"

"Yep. Don't want to keep your man waiting."

Alex

It's the weekend, but I'm in the office handling a few things that can't wait until Monday. I'm in the middle of uploading files when my phone rings.

"Hey, man," Brandon says. "Where are you?"

"At the office."

"On a Saturday? You work too much."

"How did things go with Lana last night?"

Although Brandon and Lana have been playing together for quite some time, they've never formally signed a contract. He's wanted to make their Dom/sub relationship official for quite a while. But for some unknown reason, Lana's been dragging her feet.

"It went well. Can you meet me for a few drinks?"

I've been here all day, and I'm exhausted, but it sounds like Brandon needs to talk. "Text me a time and place, and I'll meet you there."

An hour later, I walk into the bar. I'm only a few steps in when a group of girls approaches me.

"Hey, handsome," the brunette says as she wraps her hands around my arm. "You here alone?"

"I'm meeting someone." I brush her off.

Brandon waves me over.

"Excuse me, ladies," I say and head over to Brandon.

"I bet he's gay," one of the girls says loud enough for me to hear.

"All the gorgeous ones are," another says.

I laugh at their assessment of me. I'm not here to find a date.

There's a beer waiting for me when I sit next to Brandon at the bar.

"You ready to tell me how it went last night?"

"Lana finally consented to be my submissive. After much negotiation, we signed the contract last night."

"Congratulations." I'm really happy for my friend.

"Lana and I are doing a scene at the club in two weeks. It'll be our first public scene, and I'd like you to be there."

"Wouldn't miss it." I slap my friend on the back.

The next few weeks pass by like all the rest.

Wake. Work. Sleep. Repeat.

It's finally Saturday, and I'm out for a run when I get a text from Brandon.

Brandon: Remember Lana's roommate?

Me: Yes.

Where's he going with this?

Brandon: She's coming to the club tonight. I need a favor.

Me: No.

Brandon: She needs an escort.

Me: The same girl who called the cops on you last year?

Brandon: Yeah.

Me: And you want me to escort her?

Brandon: Come on, bro.

Why me? Just what I want to do with my Saturday night. Babysit a college girl who'll be scared out of her mind.

Brandon: You know I'd do it for you.

Me: I'm not feeling well. I don't think I can make it.

Brandon: The fuck you aren't. You're out running right now. Tell me I'm wrong.

Am I that predictable?

Me: Fine. But you owe me.

Brandon: Thanks, man.

I slip my phone back into my pocket and finish my run. I can't believe I agreed to babysit tonight.

Natalie

THE CAR DROPS US OFF IN FRONT OF A NONDESCRIPT building. Fire and Ice is an exclusive club in Chelsea, nestled among traditional businesses. I'm surprised when Lana pulls the door open. I've walked by here many times and never realized there's a sex club here.

Once inside, we're standing in a pretty foyer that could pass for the entrance to any office. A few people are waiting in line. A stunning woman wearing a black latex one-piece that hugs her perfect body stands behind the counter, checking them in.

Feeling insecure, I tug at my dress, trying to give it some length that isn't there.

"Stop fidgeting," Lana scolds while holding back a smile.

"I'm so nervous, but I'm also a bit excited. Is that normal?"

"It's perfectly normal. Don't worry." Lana grabs my hand. "We're going to have a great time tonight."

Trying to distract myself, I shift my focus to the oversized dark wood doors that grant entrance to the club. They look like something from medieval times with their ornate hinges. There's an iron knocker on each door with the BDSM triskelion forged in the center. I recognize it from the books. It represents the three divisions of the lifestyle: bondage and discipline, dominance and submission, sadism, and masochism. It also stands for the motto of *safe, sane, and consensual.* Although simple in its design, the triskelion holds deep meaning for those in the lifestyle.

"When we get to the desk, you'll be checked in as my guest. Mistress Star will give you a colored wristband."

"What's it for?"

"The colors represent a person's role," Lana explains as she points to a sign on the wall.

The chart breaks it down by color—Dominant or submissive, partnered or single, there to watch or ready to play.

"You'll wear a purple band. It marks you as a first-time guest under a Dominant's watch, and no one can approach without his permission."

Although I don't know Brandon, and I haven't seen him since the night I called the police, I know Lana trusts him. I'm less nervous knowing I'll have a safety net tonight.

"Good evening, Lana."

"Good evening, Mistress. This is my friend, Natalie," Lana says. "She'll be our guest this evening."

"Brandon gave me her information." Mistress Star turns to me. "Has Lana explained our color system?"

"Yes, she has."

"Do you have any questions?"

"No."

"May I have your right arm?" I hold it up, and she puts on a purple band. "You understand you'll have a Dominant responsible for your comfort and safety tonight?"

"I do."

"Are you comfortable with that?"

"Yes, ma'am." It's clear they take informed consent seriously.

"You ladies can go right in. Brandon is waiting for you at stage three," she says, and then turns to me. "Natalie, I hope you have a wonderful evening. I'll be around all night if you have any questions or concerns."

Lana grabs my arm. "Come on. I'm so excited for you to officially meet Brandon."

As I take my first steps into the club, I'm surprised by what I see.

I imagined we'd be at a seedy nightclub, but it's nothing like that. The expansive main room has a modern, industrial vibe and is brightly lit from overhead. Soft instrumental music plays in the background. I expect to find people naked and engaging in sex acts. Instead, everyone wears casual clothes and seems focused on putting the finishing touches on the setup.

"Things don't start for a few hours. That's when the real fun happens." Lana waggles her eyebrows, making me laugh.

We walk across the room to where a man stands, his back to us. He's giving directions to several people who are setting up the stage. He must hear us behind him because he turns to greet us.

"Natalie, I'd like you to meet my Dominant, Brandon."

His unforgettable gray eyes meet me, but this time, they're soft—not frightened.

"It's nice to finally meet you," Brandon says.

"It's nice to meet you, too." My cheeks heat from embarrassment. "I'm sorry for calling the police."

"Already forgiven," he says with a kind smile. "It's good to know Lana has someone looking out for her."

Movement behind Brandon catches my attention. Two muscular men push a giant wooden X onto the stage. Cuffs dangle from the top and bottom.

"What's that thing? It looks like a torture device."

Brandon laughs. "It's a Saint Andrew's Cross. I'll secure Lana to it and use my whip to pleasure her."

"Your whip? Won't that hurt her?" Gruesome visions of my best friend being tied up, her body torn to shreds, run through my mind. I'm ready to grab Lana and get the heck out of here.

"I won't her hurt. Much." He winks.

I look at Lana, but she shows no signs of fear.

"Lana likes pain, and I know how to give her what she craves without hurting her." Brandon attempts to reassure me.

"It's okay, Nat. Brandon and I have already talked about everything we're going to do tonight. This is something I want."

"You're sure?" I'm not sold on the idea.

"Positive."

I know Lana knows what she's doing, so I guess I shouldn't freak out—yet.

Brandon looks over my shoulder, and his smile widens. I spin around to see what he's looking at and am captivated by what I see.

A tall, well-groomed man stands inside the doors, running his hand through his dark hair while he looks around the room. When he spots Brandon, he starts walking in our direction, exuding confidence with each step.

People smile and whisper to each other as he passes by, but he pays them no attention. I'm unable to take my eyes off him.

"Glad you made it," Brandon says as he shakes the man's hand.

"I wouldn't miss it," he says, then turns to Lana. "How are you tonight?"

"I'm fine, thank you," Lana answers, keeping her gaze downward.

I've never seen my best friend act so demure. It's an odd contradiction to the self-assured, outspoken girl I know. It leaves me wondering how she manages to separate these two opposite parts of herself.

"Natalie. I want to introduce you to my best friend, Alex."

Words abandon me as his soulful blue eyes lock on mine. It's as if he's peeled back every layer, leaving me laid bare beneath his gaze—exposed, as though he can see the truth I try to keep hidden.

"Alex is also a Dominant here. I've asked him to be your escort tonight."

"Oh," I say, surprised. "I thought I'd be staying with you and Lana?" I look at Lana, who's wearing a mischievous grin.

"We won't be available for the entire evening, and because you're a first-time guest, you can't be alone in the club," Brandon explains. "You're in good hands with Alex."

I have a feeling Lana knew about this all along. She and I will be having a chat later.

"I've heard a lot about you," Alex says with a grin.

"You have?" Once again, I look at Lana, who's hiding behind Brandon.

"I have. You're the girl who called the police on my friend here." He slaps Brandon on the back.

"Oh my God. I can't believe you told anyone about that." I promised Lana I'd be here tonight, but right now, I want to escape through the nearest exit.

"There's no reason to be embarrassed. I'm sure Brandon appreciated your desire to protect your roommate." Alex chuckles.

"Lana and I have to finish setting up our stage," Brandon interrupts the awkward moment. "We'll see you two later."

Lana waves before she walks away.

"How about I show you around before things get started?" He offers his arm.

"That sounds good," I answer, hesitantly linking my arm with his.

When I do, a current of electricity runs through my body. Does he feel it too? I glance at him, but it he feels it, his expression gives nothing away.

Natalie

"We'll start here. As you can see, all three stages will be used for scenes tonight."

The spaces aren't extravagant. Just simple areas set a step above the main floor. Alex and I watch Brandon walk up to the cross, checking the cuffs before picking up his whip and giving it a few practice swings.

"I'm assuming Lana told you what their scene entails?"

"We talked about it. But I still don't understand why anyone would volunteer to be whipped. Seems more like torture to me."

"People find enjoyment in many different ways. What one sees as torture, others see as the ultimate pleasure."

"If you say so."

"Come, there's more to see," Alex says, leading me to the next stage.

Stage two appears much less threatening. A black metal bed sits in the center. Beside it is a matching table. A short, older man with a darker complexion stands, arranging candles into color groups.

A second man with shoulder-length blond hair and crystal blue eyes smiles as he walks past us and steps onto the stage.

So, this is where all the good-looking guys hang out. I almost laugh out loud at my wayward thoughts.

He approaches the older man, who points toward the table, appearing to give him instructions. The blond man looks our way before whispering something in the other man's ear.

The older man turns and walks toward us. "Alexander Montgomery," he says, extending his hand. "It's great to see you."

"Good to see you, Anthony." The men shake hands.

While they talk, I watch what's taking place on the stage. The blond man fits the mattress with a black rubber-like sheet before he finishes setting up the candles. When he's through, he takes his place at Anthony's side, his head bowed slightly. I stare shamelessly at the two men.

"Natalie, I'd like to introduce you to Anthony and his submissive, Leopold. Tonight, Anthony will demonstrate his skills with wax on his canvas."

I look between the men, my interest piqued. "It's very nice to meet you both."

"I didn't realize you took a new submissive," Anthony says.

"I'm not—"

"Natalie's a guest of Brandon and Lana."

Anthony smiles knowingly. "Well then, I hope you enjoy yourself tonight."

"Let's let these two get back to work." Alex places his hand on my back.

His touch feels natural and familiar, as if we've known one another for much longer than a few minutes. As we turn to walk away, a group of women approaches Alex. They're smiling and giggling like schoolchildren.

"Hello, Sir." A pretty brunette bats her eyes at Alex.

I inch closer, feeling a hint of jealousy.

"Ladies," Alex says as he leads me away.

Glancing over my shoulder, I'm met with a glare from the brunette. Alex chuckles as he tightens his arm around my body. His territorial move makes my heart race.

The final area is sectioned off, and chairs are set up. On the stage are a few piles of artfully arranged rope. A man sits on the floor cross-legged in the far corner, his back to us. He appears to be meditating.

"Master Kiyoshi is a guest at the club tonight. He'll be closing the evening with a Shibari demonstration." "I've seen pictures of that online."

"You have?" Alex sounds surprised.

"The art created with humans and rope is beautiful." I debate telling him I like it so much that I have a secret board for it on Pinterest, but decide against it.

"I took the liberty of reserving us two seats." Alex's gaze meets mine, and once again, he takes my breath away. "Let's continue the tour before everything gets started."

We make our way toward a dining area. It's set apart from the rest of the club by a half wall.

"This is the café. It's for club members only."

Inside the café area, employees are hurrying about. Some are putting linens on tables, while others perfect the place settings.

As we move through the space, the club swells with bodies, the air humming with anticipation. I take in the way people transform themselves. Some are polished in near-formal attire, others I recognize from earlier now gliding past in seductive, club-ready outfits that shimmer beneath the lights. The shift makes everything feel more electric, and for the first time tonight, I don't feel out of place in this dress—I feel like I belong.

As we walk, a couple passes. A man holding a leash nods at Alex in greeting. At the other end crawls a man on all fours, his collar and hood giving him the uncanny look of a dog. Each time his handler pauses, the pet settles obediently at his side, patient and still. I've read about pet play before, but seeing it in person leaves me both unsettled and oddly fascinated. It's not something I'd ever want for myself, yet I can't deny the couple's quiet contentment.

Here, body shape and size don't seem to matter. Not everyone has a model's figure, yet they reveal themselves boldly, some in barely-there outfits, others with nothing to hide at all. What stands out most is the confidence. There is no whispering, no pointing, no judgment, only the freedom of unapologetic display. It feels foreign to me.

When I face a mirror, all I notice are imperfections, but watching them now, I find myself both envious and in awe of the ease with which they own their bodies.

We turn a corner and start walking down a quiet hall. Alex points out the doors on each side. "These rooms are available by reservation for members who want to do a private scene and for aftercare."

"May I see inside one?"

"Sure." Alex takes a card from his pocket and finds the first door that doesn't have a reserved sign. He swipes the card over the reader and pushes the door open. He steps aside, allowing me to enter first.

I step into the private room, my movements cautious, giving myself a moment to reconcile what I expected with what I see. I'd braced for something seedy, like the back room of a cheap motel, but this feels closer to stepping into forbidden luxury.

There are no windows, only the glow of a crystal chandelier overhead. Its light softens the shadows, painting the space in a romantic haze. Gray walls embrace the room in understated elegance. My heels click against the tiled floor as I drift toward a door left slightly ajar. Inside, a lavish en suite gleams, its deep soaking tub waiting like an unspoken invitation.

Back in the main space, the bed commands me. A black metal four-poster dressed in silky black sheets, a plush red blanket folded at its base, pillows aligned with precision. My fingers trail over the fabric, lingering on the smooth surface before I notice the vase of red roses on the bedside table, their fragrance rich, deliberate.

Every detail is precise, indulgent. This private room doesn't whisper secrecy. It hums with intention, with desire woven into every choice.

"It's breathtaking."

I turn, pulse quickening when I find Alex leaning in the doorway, hands buried in his pockets, eyes dark and unreadable.

"It is." His voice is deep, steady. But the way it rolls through me makes me wonder if he's talking about the room at all.

I drift further inside, drawn like a moth to a flame. Along one wall, soft downlights illuminate an array of leather instruments hanging from a wooden rack. My breath catches. "What are these?"

"Floggers."

The word alone makes me shiver. I reach out, fingers brushing over the leather tails. The texture sends goosebumps racing up my arm. "What...what do they feel like?"

"Anything you want them to," he answers, voice rougher now. "They can sting. Or they can caress."

Before I can second-guess myself, the question slips out. "Will you show me?"

For a moment, silence. Then he inhales sharply, eyes burning into mine. "You want me to show you how a flogger feels?"

I nod. My throat is dry, my heart a frantic drum. I can hardly believe I asked, but the need inside me drowns out reason.

Something shifts in him, restraint snapping into resolve. He pushes off the doorframe, rising to his full, commanding height. Calm, deliberate, he presses the button by the door—occupied. The soft click of the lock makes my stomach flip.

"They lock automatically from the outside," he explains, voice low. "From inside, you're in control. Turn the handle, and it opens."

"That's good to know." My words wobble, though I try to steady them.

Alex crosses the room in measured strides, his presence magnetic, overwhelming. My breath stalls as he reaches up, muscles straining against the black fabric of his shirt, and takes down a flogger. He runs the purple tails across his palm, slow, deliberate, his gaze locked on mine.

"Before we begin, we need safe words. Yellow if you're close to your limit. Red if you need me to stop immediately. Do you understand?"

I nod.

His eyes narrow, his authority unmistakable. "Say it, Natalie."

"Yes, I understand."

Approval glints in his gaze, sending heat rushing through me. I feel wild, reckless, like everything in my life has been leading here, to this impossible moment.

"I'll be gentle." He closes the distance, brushing his knuckles along my cheek. The tenderness is almost unbearable. "You're a courageous young woman." His hand slides down, threading through mine as he leads me to the bed. "Bend over. Hands above your head."

My body obeys even as my mind reels.

"Good girl."

The words shouldn't matter. They're simple, harmless. Yet they melt something deep inside me, stripping away defenses I didn't know I still clung to. Why does pleasing him feel so achingly important?

"May I lift your dress?"

The question pierces me. Shame should be gnawing at me, but it's not. Instead, I'm trembling with anticipation, heat pooling low and insistent. "Yes."

His hands skim the backs of my thighs, slow and reverent, before catching the hem of my dress. Inch by inch, he drags the fabric upward, baring me until my lace panties are exposed.

"You have a beautiful body."

The words strike something raw inside me. I've been conditioned to expect criticism, to brace for the list of flaws someone else always found. But when I glance back at him, I see nothing but reverence. No judgment. No cruelty. Just desire. Just truth.

"Hands above your head. Don't move." His voice tightens,

firm yet low, each word stroking over me like a caress. "Trust me and remember your safe words. I'm about to begin."

The soft hiss of leather cuts the silence a second before it kisses my skin. A sting blooms across the back of my thighs—sharp, shocking, yet oddly electric.

"How was that?"

"It stung." My voice shakes. "But it felt good."

"Do you want more?"

"Yes."

The word barely escapes before another strike lands, then another, each one unpredictable. Every lash ignites my nerves, sharp pain dissolving into dizzying pleasure. The contrast unravels me. It's an exquisite paradox that both terrifies and consumes me.

Again and again, the flogger sings against my skin, until I'm trembling, lost in the rhythm of sting and release, each strike a surrender I didn't know I was capable of giving.

Finally, the leather falls silent. "We're done."

Gently, he lowers my dress, the simple act almost intimate. I'm too stunned to speak, my body thrumming, my thoughts scattered.

"Are you okay?" His hand presses against my lower back, grounding me.

I straighten slowly, turning into him before I even realize what I'm doing. His arms close around me, steady, solid.

"That was amazing," I whisper against his chest.

His smile breaks, dazzling and warm. "I'm glad you enjoyed it. But we should head back out."

Reality intrudes like a distant echo, reminding me why I came. "I hope we didn't miss Lana's scene."

Alex

I TAKE MY TIME RETURNING THE FLOGGER TO ITS PLACE on the rack. What just happened?

Brandon called a few weeks ago and asked me to stop by tonight to see his scene with Svetlana. I hadn't been to Fire and Ice in a while. I agreed to come to support my friends. At the last minute, he asked me to escort Lana's roommate—the same girl who called the cops on him last year. I envisioned spending a miserable night calming a frantic girl. That thought was enough for me to almost not show up.

I never thought I'd be spending the evening with a beautiful young woman who's not only unafraid, she's curious. She asked me to flog her. The arousal on her sexy lace panties tells me she enjoyed it as much as I did. I busy myself, pretending to straighten out the floggers, giving my arousal time to calm down.

When I return to her, she readily takes my hand and allows me to lead her back to the club's main room. Lana's scene is just starting. She's naked and restrained to the St. Andrews Cross, her back facing the people gathered to watch. Brandon warms up his arm by taking a few practice strokes with his whip.

A few submissives notice me approaching and step aside, allowing me space to stand at the front. I raise my hand, signaling them to stay where they are. Natalie and I have a good view from here. I appreciate the submissives' respect and make a mental note to compliment them later.

Brandon pauses, and the overhead lights in the club go dim, leaving only the stage illuminated. Then, the room goes silent as everyone waits for Brandon's signature move, a loud crack of the whip signaling the start of their scene.

He begins with softer strikes, allowing Lana to acclimate to the sensations before increasing the intensity. As he does, Lana's skin turns a beautiful shade of red. Her cries are a mixture of pain and pleasure.

Over and over, the whoosh of the whip's thong fills the room before it connects with Lana's body. Brandon demonstrates his skill by creating an intricate crisscross pattern on his willing sub's skin.

Halfway through the scene, he stops and lays his whip on the table. Moving to the back of the cross, he leans close to Svetlana.

"What's he doing?" Natalie whispers.

"He's asking her color."

Natalie studies their interactions. She's most likely trying to connect how the man who was leaving welts on his submissive is now feathering kisses on her face and stroking her hair. Brandon and Svetlana may be in a room full of people, but right now, they're only aware of each other's presence. Watching their tender interaction spurs a longing I haven't felt in years. Although I'm a member of Fire and Ice, when I visit, it's usually to observe. I've had offers, sure, but I turn them all down. I haven't had a submissive or even desired one until this evening.

As we stand and watch the scene, I try to make sense of my emotions. The only reason Natalie came tonight was to watch Lana's scene. She's not in the lifestyle. But earlier, there was a connection. I felt it. Did she feel it, too? Should I ask her if she'd be interested in getting to know each other? If I do that, I'm opening myself up to the possibility of getting hurt. I'm at a cross-roads, unsure which way to go.

Natalie's soft voice pulls me from my thoughts. "She looks so peaceful."

I shift my attention back to the stage where the action has resumed. Lana's body is now relaxed in the restraints. Her earlier cries were only whimpers.

"It looks like she's starting to experience subspace."

"What's subspace?"

"When a submissive experiences extreme pain, it causes their endorphin levels to climb. That can give a person a sense of euphoria. Svetlana tends to be a take-charge kinda person," I say, and Natalie giggles quietly. "This scene, her submission in general, provides a safe space where she can give that control to her Dominant. It's a very freeing experience, I'm told."

"So, the intense pain becomes her release."

She's already figuring out the intricacy of the pain/pleasure response. That's an uncommon observation from someone inexperienced.

"Being in subspace makes Lana vulnerable," I add.

"How so?"

"Her ability to gauge pain levels may be compromised. Brandon's experienced and recognizes this. That's why he's decreasing the intensity. The scene will be over soon."

Natalie doesn't take her eyes off the stage.

When Brandon's finished, he sets his whip on the table. He moves closer to Lana and runs his fingers over his creation before leaning close, whispering to her while he unlocks the cuffs. Then, he lifts her into his arms. Lana curls into him, resting her head on his chest. We're all privileged to witness such an intimate moment—the intense bond shared between a Dominant and their submissive.

People move aside, allowing Brandon passage through the club.

"Where are they going?"

"He's taking her for aftercare. As her Dominant, his job

doesn't end with the scene. It's his responsibility to care for Lana while she comes out of subspace."

"I thought this was all about sex." Natalie quickly puts her hand over her mouth.

Her embarrassment at letting her unfiltered thoughts slip is adorable.

"Sex is a part of it, but this world is about so much more."

"I'm beginning to see that."

What else are you beginning to see? I study her face, looking for any clue as to what she's thinking.

Natalie

After Lana's scene ends, the lights in the club come back up. Alex and I stand off to the side while the audience begins to disperse into different areas of the club.

"Excuse me, ladies and gentlemen." Alex gets the attention of a small group walking past us. They stop, heads bowed.

"I appreciate the respect you showed earlier. Your actions didn't go unnoticed."

I'm impressed that Alex took the time to compliment these individuals. It speaks volumes about his character.

"Thank you, Sir," each one says before walking away.

"The next scene will start in a few minutes. Shall we head over to get a spot near the stage?"

"I'd like that." I've never seen wax play, and I'm curious how it works.

We take our place near the front. Anthony and Leopold are already on the stage. Leopold is wearing a black silk robe and is kneeling while Anthony speaks to him. I wish I could hear what he's saying. Leopold finally stands and unties his robe—it falls to the floor.

My mouth hangs open as I take in the tattooed perfection standing completely naked and unashamed on the stage. Anthony looks at his submissive appreciatively before kicking the robe out of the way.

"Lie down," Anthony instructs.

Leopold climbs onto the table and lies on his back. This time, the lights stay on, and New Age music plays through the club's sound system as Anthony lights the candles. With skilled precision, he picks up a yellow candle and drizzles the melted wax onto Leopold's chest. While he works, Anthony gazes lovingly at his submissive, offering caresses and kisses. Leopold looks like he's sleeping. His eyes are closed, and his hands rest at his sides.

"I never realized wax could do such amazing things," I say, unable to take my eyes off the men.

"There are many things that can be used in ways you've never imagined," Alex whispers in my ear.

I don't know what it is about this man, but his words make me want to experience everything this lifestyle offers—with him.

Over the next half hour, Anthony drizzles pink, purple, orange, and yellow wax across his willing canvas. The design, when finished, is a summer sunset. It's exquisite. Then, Anthony turns his attention to Leopold's erection, stroking it up and down. I've never witnessed anything as erotic as this, and I find myself aroused watching them. Leopold moans in ecstasy as his Dominant brings him to orgasm.

I glance at Alex and find him staring at me, his eyes filled with desire. Our gaze stays locked on each other until the applause from the audience interrupts the moment.

"We should head to Master Kiyoshi's stage and get settled."

"Okay." I struggle to get out even that one small word.

Alex takes my hand in his as though it's the most natural thing to do. We walk to the next area, where we meet Mistress Star.

"Are you enjoying your evening, Natalie?"

"Very much."

She glances down at our joined hands and smiles before showing us our seats. "I'm glad to hear that."

Alex points to the stage where Master Kiyoshi and a woman kneel, facing each other. "He chose a female submissive from the club to participate in his demonstration tonight."

"Wow, she's a lucky girl. She must be excited."

"I'm sure she is. Master Kiyoshi is well known for his Shibari skills. To be chosen by him is an honor."

Several moments later, the lights dim, and the muffled tones of conversation fade. Soft sounds of a bamboo flute fill the room. Master Kiyoshi rises and offers his hand to the submissive, helping her to her feet. Then, he removes her kimono. She's wearing a white bodysuit with a sheer flowing skirt.

I don't have a good poker face, which Alex must notice because he leans over and whispers, "Not everyone has to be unclothed to do a scene."

If I thought he was gorgeous before, he's even more beautiful when he smiles. And I can't help but return it with one of my own.

Our attention is drawn back to the stage when the lights go off, leaving the room dark. A soft spotlight illuminates the submissive standing in the center. Master Kiyoshi begins his work, moving gracefully as he wraps her body in colorful ropes. His movement mimics the flow of the music.

I've read accounts from those who've experienced Shibari. They describe the sensation of the ropes being wrapped around their body and the knots' tightness, allowing them to slow their breathing and relax into the bondage. Knots are often placed on erogenous zones or pressure points, amplifying the extreme sensations. The rope allows them to experience a deep, almost meditative state, something we're witnessing on the stage. The submissive's body is being manipulated into challenging positions. Rather than tensing, her body relaxes into the intricately bound jute.

When the Master ties off the last piece of rope, he steps back and examines his artwork. Once satisfied, he walks to the side of the stage and picks up a rope attached to the submissive. As he pulls it, the woman's body leaves the ground. Suspended in an arabesque position, her sheer skirt flutters around her seemingly weightless form. It's a breathtaking sight.

After allowing her to fly for several minutes, the Master gently lowers his submissive and begins the process of untying her. Rather than being hurried, she's released with great care and grace. While he works, Master Kiyoshi never breaks eye contact with the woman. Their connection is so strong it's almost palpable. Seeing how choreographed the scene was when they had just met was incredible. It speaks to his level of mastery.

Alex places his hand on my shoulder to get my attention. "How about we grab a table and get a bite to eat?"

I didn't realize how hungry I'd gotten over the last few hours.

"That sounds great."

We walk over to the cafe and are seated at an empty table. A male server brings us water and menus.

"What did you think about tonight?" Alex asks.

I take a sip of water while thinking about everything I've experienced this evening.

"Watching Lana get whipped, I know I should've been scared, but I wasn't." I gesture around the room. "All the rest of this, I was expecting to feel uncomfortable, that this was wrong. And maybe I'm crazy, but it feels so right. I'm surprised by my thoughts."

"Surprised? How so?"

"This is all foreign to me. If you knew how I was raised, you'd understand how much. When I walked in on Lana that night—" My face heats with embarrassment, and Alex chuckles. "I read all the books she gave me, but I still had a very different picture in my mind. Being here tonight, it's nothing at all like I imagined. Each couple we watched shared a genuine connection. There was nothing wrong about—"

A pair of arms wrap around my neck, and I nearly fall off my chair.

"I'm so glad you liked it." Lana's excitement pulses through her body.

"Great scene tonight." Alex stands and shakes Brandon's hand. "Grab some chairs and join us."

Brandon borrows two chairs from a nearby empty table and drags them over.

"Are you enjoying your evening?" Brandon asks.

"I've had a great time." I glance at Alex, and my stomach flip-flops. The man beside me is incredibly gorgeous, and I've been the lucky recipient of his attention all night. "I think I'd like to learn more."

"The club has intro classes during the week. You should sign up," Brandon suggests.

Lana told me about the classes a long time ago, but at the time, I wasn't interested. After tonight, I can't imagine just walking away.

Alex

THE FOUR OF US SPEND THE NEXT FEW HOURS TALKING and laughing. I catch myself staring at Natalie far too often. I didn't think I'd ever want a submissive again, but if she expressed an interest, I'd jump at the chance to be her Dominant.

"Oh, wow, it's almost two a.m. I promised Cinderella here I'd have her home early." Turning to Brandon, she asks, "Sir, do I have permission to leave?"

"You did great tonight." Brandon runs his knuckles lightly down Lana's cheek. "Go, get your friend home."

"Thank you for the tour, Alex."

I stand and kiss her cheek. "It was my pleasure."

The girls turn and head to the door. But my feet remain bolted to the floor, watching Natalie walk away.

"Go after her."

"I don't know if I can." My heart beats furiously, and my palms are sweating.

"You can't just let her walk away," Brandon says as he nudges me forward.

If I don't go now, I'll never get another chance, and I'll regret it. I hurry through the club and catch up with the girls as they sign out.

"Natalie," I call.

"Alex," she replies, turning my direction.

The sound of my name on her lips makes me feel like a schoolboy with his first crush.

"I'm hoping." I fumble for the words. "Can I give you my number? Maybe we could get together again?"

Star chuckles from behind the desk, obviously amused by my awkwardness.

"I guess that would be okay." She pulls her cell from her purse.

"May I?"

Natalie looks at Lana, who nods with her approval before she unlocks the phone and hands it to me. Opening her contacts, I add my name and number. Then I shoot myself a quick text, ensuring I have her number.

"Done." I hand the phone back.

She gives me an awkward smile and slips the phone into her purse. Did I read everything wrong tonight? I'm confused by her reaction. She seemed so receptive until now.

"I guess I'll talk to you soon."

"Yes, you will."

I watch the girls walk out the door and then turn to Star. "That girl is going to be mine."

Natalie

Alex calls me the next day. Honestly, I didn't think I'd hear from him, but I'm happy he called.

"Have you made a decision about the intro classes?"

"I'm going to call tomorrow and sign up for the next start date."

"I'm glad to hear that." His voice sounds hopeful. "I'd like to keep in touch if that's okay with you?"

"I'd like that too."

I call Fire and Ice on Monday and register for the six-week intro course, which starts the next night.

I'm nervous about going to the club alone and almost tell my driver to turn around at least a dozen times. When I arrive, I'm glad to see our group is small. There are only five of us. Mistress Star and Master Owen, the club's co-owners, lead the class.

The first part of the session is spent getting to know each other and getting to know ourselves. We talk about our personalities and our likes and dislikes. After taking a short break, Mistress Star introduces us to the distinct roles people can assume in the BDSM lifestyle. I thought the only options were Dominant and submissive, but I was wrong. A person can be a switch, top, or bottom. And that's just scratching the surface.

Some couples are twenty-four-seven, while others are only in the bedroom. For instance, some people sign a one-night agreement to play at the club. With so many options, there's a place for everyone.

We're sent home with some resources to read before class next week to help determine where each of us feels we might fit within the lifestyle.

From the start, I felt drawn to the role of submissive. It feels like I've been one my whole life, but for all the wrong reasons. What really made an impression on me and addressed any doubts I had was the short time I spent alone with Alex. I didn't have to think or worry. Alex had complete control, and I felt special for the first time in a long time. I was in a submissive role, but I still had a voice.

The following week's class focuses on vetting and safety. Given the potential for injury during a scene and the overall level of trust needed between a Dominant and submissive, vetting a new partner is a serious topic. It can take a potential couple of months before they're ready to sign a contract and begin their dynamic. That seems like common sense, but our lesson takes this topic to a depth I didn't consider. The handout we're given provides sample questions to ask a potential partner. I feel my face flush when I read some of the questions—they get very intimate.

It's week four of class. We now have a solid foundation with the basics of the lifestyle and a good idea of where we might fit in.

Although I'm not making any commitments, I'm enjoying learning about all this lifestyle offers. Mistress Star calls the class to order and takes her place in front.

"This week, you'll be paired with one of our club members for one-on-one instruction." She gives us our room assignment, and then I'm off to see who I've been partnered with. I'm shocked at who I find waiting for me when I open the door. "Leopold."

"The one and only," he says, pulling me in for a big hug. "I hope you're not upset you got paired with me."

"I'm thrilled to be with you." I was very impressed by his wax scene, and he's easy on the eyes.

"Me too. Come on and sit down so we can get started." Two modern armchairs are set up with a small table between them. "The first thing we need to do is list any questions you have. That'll give us a starting point." He picks up a pad and a pen from the table.

"I can't think of anything off the top of my head."

"That's okay. Tell me about yourself, and we'll go from there."

"There isn't much to tell."

I fill him in about the small town I come from, my brother, and how I ended up in New York City. Leo's laid-back demeanor makes him easy to talk to.

"What about you?" I ask. "How did you get involved in the lifestyle?"

A dark shadow passes over Leo's face. "Life hasn't always been good to me," he shares. "I met Anthony at one of the lowest points. He saved me," he says, meeting my gaze. "He taught me it was okay to trust again."

Leo reminds me so much of my brother. It feels like I'm talking to Michael again. It's both bittersweet and heartwarming.

Tonight's the last class. I'm sad that it's ending, but now I'm armed with a great deal of information.

"I hope to see you all at the club," Mistress Star addresses the class. "Don't hesitate to reach out to Master Owen or me if you need anything."

After we all say our goodbyes, Leo and I head out for dinner and drinks.

Now that class is officially over, I know Leo will ask about Alex and what direction he and I are headed. The problem is, I don't have the answer. Alex and I agreed to keep in touch during my classes, but decided we wouldn't see one another. It was a boundary I asked for because I know what my future holds, and I didn't want either of us to get too attached.

"Have you talked to Alex lately?" Leo asks as we drink our margaritas.

"We talk once a week and text almost every day."

"So, things are going well?"

"I guess so." I look down, fiddling with my hands.

"For a girl who says things are going well, your face tells another story. Start talking."

"Last night, Alex asked if I'd be interested in discussing a Dom/sub relationship."

"The problem with that?" He motions for me to keep talking.

"I have to go back to Northmeadow in a few months. I don't want to start something and then have to walk away."

"When you're discussing the contract, you can tell him you want a time limit. That way, there are no unrealistic expectations."

"That's an option, I guess." I play with the straw in my drink to avoid making eye contact with Leo.

"Wait a minute. The problem is you really like the guy and don't want it to end."

"Maybe." I shrug. "Doesn't matter, though. I'm sure he isn't interested in me as anything more than a submissive, and I don't want to put my heart on the line. So, I don't see any use in us getting involved."

"Have you ever heard of a plane?"

"If it were only that easy."

Leo rolls his eyes. "Girl, if that man were interested in me, I'd scoop him up and never look back."

"I bet Anthony would love to hear that," I say, laughing.

"My Master knows I'm completely faithful to him and him only. But he also knows a sexy man when he sees one, and Alex is *all* that. Don't let him get away."

Leo's words repeat in my head for the rest of the evening.

This is my last year of grad school. In a few months, New York City will become a part of my past. I haven't told Alex about my scholarship or the contract that ensures I return to Northmeadow. When I do, I'm sure it'll change everything.

Natalie

ALEX AND I HAVEN'T TALKED MUCH THIS PAST WEEK. Not only did I have a huge paper due, but I also picked up a few extra hours at the counseling center where I intern, so I've been swamped.

Thankfully, my paper has been handed in, and now I have time to breathe. I'm lying on my bed when my cell pings with a text.

Alex: Do you have plans tonight?

Me: I'm staying home and ordering a pizza.

Alex: Can I take you out for dinner?

I want to go out with him. Any sane woman would. But I can't get involved with someone right now.

Me: I don't know.

Alex: I'll pick you up at six.

I should say no. Just say no, Natalie.

Me: Sure. I'll see you then.

I set the phone down and rest my head in my hands. I can't believe I didn't say no, and now I'm going on a date with Alex. I know he'll ask if I've thought about his question. I haven't stopped thinking or dreaming about it. I think we'd be good together, and I'd love to explore the lifestyle with him, but I can't risk getting my heart involved in something that can never be.

When I check the time, there's less than an hour until he picks me up. I should text him and tell him I changed my mind. Instead, I'm trying on every outfit in my closet before settling on an ankle-length pink dress with open shoulders. I pin my hair up, leaving only a few loose curls that fall softly around my face. The doorbell rings just as I put on my lipstick.

It's been almost two months since the night at the club—the last time I saw Alex. My stomach flip-flops as I pad through the living room and open the door. Alex stands on the other side in black dress pants and a light gray button-down shirt. His dark hair has grown since I last saw him. He's even more handsome than I remember. In his hands is a bouquet of red roses.

"These are for you." He gives me the flowers. "You look gorgeous," he says, his eyes taking in every inch of my body.

"Thank you. Come on in. I'll put these in water before we leave."

Alex follows me into the kitchen while I grab a vase. I can feel his eyes tracking my every movement. Once the flowers are neatly arranged, I set them on the kitchen island.

Offering me his hand, he asks, "Ready to go?"

I thread my fingers in his as we walk to the door, where I get my coat.

"It's not too chilly, and the restaurant is only a few blocks away. Do you mind walking?"

It's mid-December, but the temperature is mild.

"I don't mind at all."

I enjoy the envious glances of the women we pass on the busy New York streets. Sorry, ladies, he's taken. *Woah.* Where did that come from?

Going out for dinner doesn't mean he's mine.

We stroll past Washington Square Park over to MacDougal St. We stop when we reach Italiano Desiderio.

"I hope you like Italian."

"I love it," I reply. "I've been dying to come here, but they're booked solid. How did you get a table?"

"I know the owner," he says with a grin as he opens the door. "After you."

When I step inside, the street noise disappears. The restaurant looks like a scene straight from Italy. The room is long and has a series of arches with ivy growing up the columns. Small lanterns hang from the branches, providing soft lighting for the room. Instrumental music plays softly in the background. If we hadn't just walked through New York City, I'd think we were in Venice.

We wait for the hostess, whose back is turned while she's talking to a server. When she spins around and sees Alex, her eyes light up.

"Mr. Montgomery, so nice to see you tonight," she says, batting her eyes at *my* date.

I don't know what it is that is making me feel so territorial.

"Thank you. Is our table ready?" Alex pays no attention to her blatant flirting.

The hostess glances my way, letting her saccharine smile falter. "Right this way."

I swear she's swaying her hips just a little extra as she leads us through the restaurant to a private room in the back, where there's a small table set for two. The lighting is soft and romantic. There's a beautiful garden space outside, the large windows lit up with soft twinkling lights. It must be incredible during the summer.

Alex pulls my chair out for me to sit before moving around the table and taking his seat.

The hostess hands each of us a menu. "Is there anything else you need?" she asks, placing her hand on Alex's arm.

He stiffens. "No."

She appears annoyed by his further attempts to thwart her flirting. "Your server will be with you shortly," she says before turning and walking away.

"This place is amazing."

"It is. Tony and Leo have done a wonderful job with it."

"Tony and Leo? Are they the same Tony and Leo from the club?"

I hear a man's deep laugh behind me.

"Tony, great to see you." Alex shakes his hand. "You remember Natalie?"

"How could I forget such a beautiful woman?" He leans down and wraps me in a hug. I look at Alex, who's shooting a death glare in Tony's direction, making Tony and me laugh. "I'm glad you two could make it tonight. If you allow me, I'd like to offer you a bottle of our finest champagne."

"Thank you. That would be perfect."

Tony motions to a nearby server, who hurries over and pours us both a glass of the bubbly drink.

"Please, relax and enjoy your meal. I'll be back to check on you later."

We're left alone to look over the menu.

"Would you be okay if I ordered for you?"

I lower my menu and look at him, not entirely surprised by his question. This is something Leo and I talked about—ways a Dominant might wish to take charge. He's asking me first, which is appropriate because he isn't my Dominant. But I'm curious to see how this will work.

"I think I'd like that."

"Thank you." Alex smiles and continues looking over the menu.

The server returns a few minutes later and takes our order. I'm impressed with the food choices Alex makes. I also notice the server doesn't seem thrown off by Alex's ordering for both of us. I wonder how often he sees something like this.

"May I offer a toast?" Alex asks. "Congratulations on being one step closer to completing your education."

I'm not sure if he's referring to the classes at Fire and Ice, being in my final year of grad school, or both. We raise our glasses, clinking the crystal together. I bring the flute to my lips and take a sip, savoring the sweet effervescence of the exquisite champagne.

"Have you given my proposition any thought?"

"I have. And I can see myself in this lifestyle."

"You can?" Alex seems intrigued.

"But I don't think the timing's right."

"Why not?"

I've practiced this conversation for weeks, knowing it was something we'd eventually discuss. But now that the moment is here, I've forgotten everything I practiced and struggle to find the right words. Without much thought, I lift my hand and start biting my fingernails. How do I tell him I'm not staying here permanently? Thankfully, our server arrives with our appetizer, a beautiful Caprese salad. I've been granted a reprieve, at least for a short while.

I pick up my fork and cut a piece of tomato and cheese. Alex's eyes follow my movements as I lift the food to my lips and take a bite. The fresh cheese, coupled with the tomatoes' sweetness and the acidity from the balsamic vinegar, explodes in my mouth.

Closing my eyes, I moan in delight. "This is one of my favorite dishes."

"I'm glad to hear that. But you didn't answer my question."

He doesn't miss a beat. "In a perfect world, I'd like to give the lifestyle, give us a try, but—"

"What's holding you back?"

"I'm not sure it fits with my previous obligations." I take another bite before attempting to change the subject. "Tell me more about how you became so successful in marketing."

Alex has mentioned that he owns his own marketing company. I hope to distract him long enough that he'll forget about me not answering. For the moment, he drops his line of questioning and tells me how he opened his firm five years ago with only a few small accounts.

"I struggled for the first few years. I was at the point I thought

I'd have to close until the right client walked in. I was incredibly lucky."

With how persistent he's been in getting me to go out with him, something tells me luck is only a small part of his success.

Our meal is served at a leisurely pace, with one decadent dish after another being brought to our table.

"I've never been to Italy, but this is how I imagine the food to be, fresh and rustic," I say as I take a bite of manicotti with truffle shavings.

"That's because it is. Behind the restaurant, Tony has a greenhouse. He grows as many ingredients as possible and makes all the pasta fresh."

"No wonder it's impossible to get a reservation here."

We're served the last course, espresso and cannolis. The dessert looks fantastic, but there's no way I can eat it.

"If you don't like cannoli, we can order something else?"

"I like it very much."

"Then why haven't you touched it?"

"I already overate." I try hard not to bite my nails. "With how I look, I can't eat stuff like this."

"The way you look?" Alex's eyes narrow. "What's that supposed to mean?"

"My weight. I need to watch everything—"

"Stop." He puts his hands flat on the table. "I will not have you talking about yourself that way. You're beautiful. Your body is beautiful."

My eyes are locked on his, ready to challenge him when a man clears his throat.

"I'm sorry for interrupting," Tony says hesitantly. "I can come back in a few minutes."

"No need," Alex says without taking his eyes off me.

"How was your meal?"

"It was incredible. I'm so full I can't manage to eat my dessert. May I have it wrapped?" I glance in Alex's direction.

"Absolutely." Tony smiles, clearly relieved that the tense moment seems to have passed.

"Thank you, Tony," Alex says. "Everything was perfect."

"Anytime. Natalie, I hope I get to see you again soon."

"I'd like that very much."

"Alex will give you my number. Call me anytime you want to come by."

I can see why Leo is head over heels for this man. Tony leaves the table, and our server takes his place to wrap my dessert.

Alex settles our check and offers me his hand. "There's a back exit we can take."

The tension from before melts away slightly, and we walk in silence until we return to Washington Square.

"Can we sit and talk?"

"Sure."

Alex leads me into the park to a bench, where we sit together and spend a long moment watching the people milling about before Alex breaks the silence.

"You said you're interested in the lifestyle, but it doesn't fit with your *obligations*." He searches for my face. "Can you tell me what that means?"

"I'm only in the city for school. The scholarship I was awarded came with a five-year work requirement. When I graduate in the spring, I have to return home."

"We still have plenty of time to try it out." Alex takes my hands in his. "When it's time for you to leave, we can re-evaluate if we want to continue together or walk away."

"You'd be okay with a time limit on this?"

"Yes. I'll take any opportunity to explore us as a Dom/sub couple." His smile reaches his beautiful blue eyes.

"Okay," I say, returning his smile with my own.

"Is that a yes?"

"Yes, Sir." I try out the word and am surprised by how natural it feels.

Alex sits up straighter. "Let the negotiations begin."

Natalie

"Last night was like a real-life fairy tale," I tell Lana as we sit at the table drinking coffee. "Alex is amazing."

Lana smiles proudly. "I knew you two would get along."

"How long have you known Alex?"

"A little while."

"How long's a little while?" I have a feeling there's more to this story than she's telling me, but our conversation is interrupted by the doorbell.

Lana jumps up. "I'll get it."

"Saved by the bell," I call. "But this conversation isn't over."

"Alex," Lana says a little louder than necessary. "I didn't know you were coming over."

"Is Natalie here?"

I'm here, but I'm not letting Alex see me like this. I'm wearing the sweatpants and T-shirt I slept in last night. My hair's thrown up in a messy bun, and I haven't even brushed my teeth yet.

"You bet. She's in the kitchen."

I start to get up from the table, hoping to sprint into my room and get dressed, but Alex's voice stops me before I make it to my feet.

"Good afternoon, Natalie."

"Hi. Can you excuse me for a minute? I need to get changed."

"You look perfectly fine to me."

I lift my head and raise my eyebrow.

"I'm going to shower and study," Lana chirps. "I'll leave you two alone." She hurries to her bedroom.

"I wasn't expecting you." My heart's beating rapidly. "Can I get you some coffee?"

"I'd like that," he says. "I brought a contract with me. I hoped we might go over it together."

I almost drop the mug I'm holding. "You have a contract already?"

"It's a standard contract that I made some adjustments to. Since this is your first time as a sub, I kept it very basic."

My fluffy socks cushion my steps as I walk across the kitchen and place the coffee on the table. "Do you take cream or sugar?"

"No." He looks up at me, his blue eyes dancing with excitement. "Thank you, baby girl."

Baby girl? Those words sound so intimate coming from him. I melt as I sit in my chair.

Alex slides a copy of the contract across the table to me and keeps one for himself. "We won't make any final decisions today. But I wanted to read it together in case you have any questions."

This is all new to me, but his statement puts me at ease. I lift the papers and sit back in my chair as I skim through them. Master Owen showed us examples of contracts during class, so I have some idea of what to expect. When I look up, Alex is watching me intently, his hands folded on the table. I imagine this is what he looks like when he's at work conducting a meeting with a client.

Alex was right. The contract reflects my newness to the lifestyle. It details how Alex, as my Dominant, will treat me respectfully and be responsible for my safety. As his submissive, I will treat him respectfully and conduct myself appropriately, as I reflect my Dominant. Although we won't be together twenty-four hours a day, the contract specifies daily check-ins and obligations. Another section details the rules and the consequences for breaking them. Some prohibited things are drinking to intoxication, disrespecting my Dominant, and orgasming without his consent.

"You want to stop me from biting my nails?" I ask, looking up at him.

"I'd like to keep that. We can discuss other, less destructive ways to deal with anxiety."

His reasoning isn't what I thought it would be. "Okay. I'm open to that."

"On page three, there's a list of things I'd like to do sexually. Can we discuss your experience level first and then review the list? After that, we can address your limits and remove whatever's necessary."

I flip to page three and start skimming the page. Blindfolds, crops, floggers, bondage, anal trainers, gags, and many other things are on the list. Talking openly about sex is still a new concept for me.

"I'm not a virgin," I say quickly. "I've only been with one person, and it was all very *plain*."

Alex laughs. "Plain?"

"Yeah, vanilla, I guess you'd call it. Tommy, my ex-boyfriend, did his thing and never, well, never made sure I got anything from it."

"He never gave you an orgasm?" Alex leans forward.

I shake my head back and forth slowly.

"baby girl," Alex says. "That will not happen between us. Part of my job, and it's a part I love, is to give you pleasure."

His words make me squirm in my seat. I've already had a small taste of how my body responds to Alex's touch from the night at the club. I can't imagine how much more exciting it could be as his submissive.

"I have a question."

"You can ask anything you want." His voice is calm and steady.

"Anal trainers? What are they?"

"I'm assuming anal sex is new to you?"

I nod in agreement.

"They're a series of butt plugs designed to stretch you so I can enter you without causing physical damage. If that's not something you're open to right now, we can take it off the list. I want to help you grow but not push you too far."

Anal sex is something I've always been curious about, but whenever I brought it up to Tommy, he shut me down. "We can leave it there as long as we go slowly."

"Deal." Alex smiles.

The way his face lights up when he smiles is a sight I don't think I'll ever grow tired of. We spend the next hour going over everything in the contract. The more we talk, the more comfortable I become. Alex doesn't pressure me or have expectations I feel are unreasonable.

"The contract will expire five months from now, in time for your graduation. We can reevaluate then."

The thought of parting ways already makes me feel sad. It's something I'll have to get used to, though. Whether I want to or not, I have to return to Northmeadow in May.

Alex looks at his watch. "I need to get going. I have to be in the office for a meeting."

"On a Saturday?"

"I try not to, but this is an important client, so I make myself available whenever he requests." Alex stands. "Take some time with the contract. Let me know if you have any more questions or changes, and we'll take care of it."

I walk him to the door. "Is there a deadline on when you need it back?"

"There's no rush. I want you to make a fully informed decision before we continue." Alex leans in and kisses my cheek. "But I do hope I hear from you soon."

Over the past few months, my life has changed dramatically. When I went to the club with Lana, I wasn't looking to meet anyone. And I certainly had no intention of becoming a submissive. But after reading the books and taking the classes, pieces of me I didn't know were missing started falling into place.

Now, here I am, considering signing a contract to be a submissive to a kind and thoughtful, not to mention incredibly gorgeous, man. Closing the door, I drop my forehead against it.

"Is he gone?" Lana asks, peeking out from the hallway.

"Yes, he just left. He had to work."

"And?" she asks as she walks into the living room and flops onto the sofa.

"He brought a contract," I sit next to her. "Will you look it over with me?"

"I'd love to."

Alex

I PICKED UP MY PHONE TO CALL HER ALMOST EVERY night this week, but stopped myself. As much as I want Natalie to sign the contract, I don't want to pressure her. It may be the hardest thing I've ever done, but I need to give her the time and space to make the right decision for herself.

Right now, I'm in my office reviewing some files from Maxim Solonik, Svetlana's father, and my biggest client. I owe him everything. I probably would've had to shut my firm down years ago if it weren't for him. I certainly wouldn't be where I am today. Opening the security software, I click the button to encrypt the information before saving it. While the files are saving, I recline in my black leather chair. My mind drifts back to my first meeting with Maxim.

Early in my college career, I decided to double major in marketing and bioethics. Climate change and eco-friendly business practices were beginning to grow in popularity, and I intended to take full advantage.

I'd been left some money when my grandfather passed away. Dad helped me invest it wisely, so I had a small nest egg. Fresh out of school, I said goodbye to my life in Seattle and set off in search of fame and fortune in New York City. I planned to take the city by storm, rebranding businesses and highlighting their eco-friendly efforts.

At the time, I felt office space was more important than living space. So, I used most of the money to secure a prime location and rented a cheap room in a hostel, certain it would be a temporary stop. I figured I'd have a steady cash flow for an apartment within a month or two.

Unfortunately, finding clients wasn't as easy as I expected. Not many businesses wanted to take a chance on the new kid in town. I signed on a few small clients, but they weren't bringing in enough to pay the bills. My ego had taken a hit, and I quickly ran out of money.

My father, who was still recovering from the loss of my mother, suspected I was in trouble and offered to help. But I was too proud to accept it.

I'll never forget that night. It was a Tuesday like any other. I stayed in the office late, trying to figure out how to afford the rent for the office, my room, and food for the week. But no matter how hard I tried, the numbers weren't in my favor. I would have to give up my room and live in my office.

I must've forgotten to lock the door. The jingle of the bells startled me. A man in an expensive tailored suit entered my office and walked directly toward me. He hadn't yet spoken, but something about the way he carried himself made me sit up and take notice.

"Can I help you?".

"My name is Maxim Solonik," he introduces himself and, as if he owns the place, takes a seat. "I have a business proposition for you."

Maxim told me about his company. He was in the Russian oil industry and sought to expand his operations in the United States by getting involved in the natural gas pipeline network. His company held technology that would prove helpful in advancing cleaner energy sources.

He had my full attention as we discussed his unique needs at great length. We talked until it got late, and Maxim proposed we continue our meeting over food and drink.

That night, he made a compelling case for why I should take him as a client. We shook hands and have been working together ever since.

Being young and naïve, I didn't ask many questions. All I saw was the chance to save my failing business. I didn't know or really care why he chose me or that our partnership would eventually extend beyond environmental technology.

Meeting him changed everything for me. His involvement ensured my business became more successful than I ever dreamed. And all these years later, it led me to the best thing in my life.

In the beginning, Maxim and I spent a lot of time together, both here in the States and at his home in Russia. We became more than business associates. We also became friends.

One of his trips to New York coincided with the first anniversary of my mother's death.

I'd always admired my parents' relationship as a married couple and a Master/slave. I wanted what they had, so when I turned twenty, I entered the lifestyle. It was everything I wanted and more. Until I witnessed my dad lose everything that mattered to him—my mom. In a reckless move, I left the lifestyle behind. I walked away from my submissive without so much as an explanation. My actions hurt her, something I've made amends for.

My mother's death wrecked me. It left me stumbling aimlessly through life. I refused to be involved with anyone for fear of falling in love.

That night, after I didn't answer any of his calls, Maxim showed up at the hostel. I was drunk, trying to numb the pain and loss. He stayed with me while my drunken self told him everything I'd been holding in.

Max didn't know my history with BDSM, or so I thought. The following night, he told me we were going out. He brought me to Fire and Ice and introduced me to a submissive. It was a one-night arrangement—no strings attached.

After the night was over, Maxim explained why he chose me.

"Alexander, many years ago, your parents visited a well-known dungeon in Russia. Your father wanted to learn how to wield a bull-whip. It happened to be the same dungeon Irina and I went to. I became your father's teacher."

I sat stunned, listening to his story.

"Over the years, we'd travel to the States, and your parents traveled to Russia to visit one another. They were very dear friends."

Max stayed in the States for several months and mentored me as I cautiously started practicing the lifestyle again. Because of his intervention that night, I not only found myself but also eventually found Natalie. I owe Maxim more than I can ever repay.

With the encryption done, I shut my laptop off and push to a standing position. My muscles are tight from sitting in one spot for so long. Before heading out, I check my phone one last time and finally see a text from Natalie.

Natalie: I've gone over the contract and have one request.

Me: What's the request?

Natalie: I'd like to add rope bondage. You know, like Shibari.

I can almost hear her voice asking the question, and I smile. She's adventurous. I like that. But there's one big problem. I don't know much more than the basics, but, for her, I'll learn.

Me: Done. Is there anything else you want to add?

Natalie: No, that's everything. I'm ready to sign.

I'm ready to sign.

I read the words over and over, not believing they're real. But, sure enough, the text stays on the screen. Having a submissive is a big responsibility, one I've screwed up in the past. I hope you have your shit together, Alex. You can't mess this up. Natalie deserves only the best.

Me: Do you have plans tonight?

Natalie: Lana's out with Brandon. I just made popcorn, and I'm going to watch a movie.

Me: How about I pick you up? We can grab a bite to eat and watch a movie together at my place.

Natalie: I'd like that.

Me: I'm getting ready to leave the office now. I'll be at your place in about twenty minutes.

Natalie: I'll be ready.

I send one last text to my driver, Viktor, before sliding my phone into my pocket and locking up. When I get outside, Viktor's standing by the passenger door of my black Model 3 Tesla.

"Where to, boss?"

Viktor wasn't with me when I picked Natalie up last time, so I gave him the address before getting in. It's a typical Friday evening in the city. Traffic is terrible, and we take longer than my anticipated twenty minutes. When we finally arrive at her building, Viktor waits in the car while I go in to collect my new submissive.

Natalie

I HAVE TWENTY MINUTES TO GET OUT OF MY COZY jammies and get ready to see Alex. You've got this, Nat. I rush around my room, looking for something comfortable yet sexy. Tonight's a big night. We'll sign the contract and officially start our Dom/sub relationship.

My hands shake as I put on my light pink strapless bra and slide on my cream, off-the-shoulder sweater. Then, I step into my favorite pair of jeans. I had my hair pulled up in two little buns. It's going to have to stay that way, or else my curls will be a frizzy mess. After putting on mascara and lipstick, I look at my reflection in the mirror. I'm unhappy with what I see, but the doorbell ringing interrupts my thoughts.

Tonight is going to be a defining night in my life. For the next few months, I won't be living only for myself. Alex will come first in everything I do. My words and actions will not represent just me but will now also represent my Dominant. With a final breath, I walk to the door and open it. Alex stands on the other side, wearing a black suit. The top button of his white shirt is open, and his red tie hangs loose.

"Hi."

"Hi," he says, his eyes taking me in. "You look beautiful."

"I'm a bit underdressed." I lower my gaze, both uncomfortable with the compliment and embarrassed by the outfit I chose. He puts his finger under my chin and lifts my face so I can't avoid his eyes.

"Don't look away when I compliment you." His tone is stern yet calm. "Let's try this again. You look beautiful, baby girl."

"Thank you, Sir," I say quietly.

"Are you ready to go?"

"I just need to grab my coat."

The warm spell we had a few weeks ago is gone, replaced with more seasonable chilly air. Like a true gentleman, Alex helps me into my coat before offering his arm. Together, we make our way toward a high-end car. A scary-looking man with large muscles and a bald head stands beside it. My body stiffens, thinking we're about to be mugged.

"What's wrong?"

I shift my gaze back to the man.

Alex chuckles. "I'd like to introduce you to Viktor."

Embarrassed by my actions, I debate running back inside. But then I remember I'm a reflection of Alex. "It's nice to meet you."

Viktor nods and opens the car door.

I've never been in a car like this. The seats are made of soft black leather and are heated, a nice addition given how chilly it is outside. Alex slides in next to me, and our legs brush against each other. A sizzle of electricity runs through my body.

Inside, the car is silent as Viktor weaves in and out of traffic. I steal a glance at Alex. His posture is tense. Is he as nervous as I am?

Viktor pulls the car into a lot under a building. Then, Alex leads me to an elevator. He punches in a code before pressing the penthouse button. I'm stunned silent. Why would a man who lives this lifestyle be interested in someone like me? The elevator doors open directly into Alex's apartment. He motions for me to step out first.

"Make yourself at home. Can I get you something to drink?"

"May I have some water, please?" I say almost absentmindedly. I'm distracted by the view from the floor-to-ceiling windows that line two walls. One overlooks his Upper West Side neighborhood, and the other offers a spectacular view of the Hudson River. "The view is stunning."

"The view *is* stunning," Alex says before going to the kitchen to get our drinks. "Come sit. We need to talk." The dark gray sofa is situated by a fireplace, which adds warmth to the room. When I sit down, Alex hands me a glass of ice water. I take a sip before setting it on the glass end table. I fidget with my fingers, bringing one to my mouth to bite my nail. Alex reaches out and takes my hand, placing it in my lap.

"Relax. There's no reason to be nervous."

"Where do we go from here?"

"Before we move any further, I'd like to review the contract one last time. Then, if you're sure you're ready, we'll both sign it."

"I forgot to bring my copy."

"I have one in my office. Wait here."

Alex walks down a hallway. His shoes make a loud clicking sound that seems to echo in the ample space. I silently chastise myself for forgetting something so important. It only takes a minute before he's back with papers and a pen in his hand.

"Here's a copy for you. You'll see, I made the changes you requested."

We take the next few minutes to review everything, ensuring it's written exactly as we both want.

"It looks good," I say, offering him a nervous smile.

"Are you ready to sign?"

Am I ready to sign? Lana and I talked about this for hours the other night. If it were anyone else, she would've advised me to wait—to vet him longer. Because she and Brandon know him so well and have vouched for his character and intentions, I feel safe moving forward so quickly. This is my opportunity to try something new and exciting—to live on my terms.

"Yes, Sir."

He rewards me with a smile that makes my insides quiver. Alex hands me a pen, and I sign both copies. When I finish, I pass the pen back to him, and he does the same. Then, he takes the contracts and sets them aside on the table. The energy in the room suddenly shifts. Sexual tension fills the air. Every time we're together, there's chemistry between us. But until now, we've been unable to act on it.

The first rule Mistress Star drilled into us was not to get physically involved with anyone we were vetting because it could cloud our judgment. Now, the vetting is over, and we can finally act on our feelings.

Alex brushes a strand of hair from my face and tucks it behind my ear. The small amount of contact sends chills down my spine. He leans in for a slow, gentle kiss. His tongue explores my lips before I open, allowing him access to my mouth.

When I do, it's as if a dam spills open. The connection we share explodes. Our kiss turns desperate. He lifts me so I'm straddling his lap.

"Do you feel this between us?" he asks breathlessly. "Do you want me as much as I want you?"

I nod in response.

"I need a verbal answer, Natalie."

"Yes. I want you."

The words no sooner leave my mouth than his lips are back on mine. Then, he stands, lifting me with him.

"Wrap your legs around me." I obey immediately, and he walks us toward his bedroom. He sets me down before stepping back and unbuttoning his shirt, throwing it over a nearby chair.

Following his lead, I pull my sweater off and drop it on the floor.

"You. Are. Beautiful."

Alex makes quick work of his button and zipper before pulling his pants and boxers off. When I see his erection, I gasp.

"This is all for you, baby girl."

With quick strides, he closes the gap between us, his body pushing mine back on the bed as he begins kissing me again. His hands reach around my back, unhooking my bra. He tosses it to the side. His mouth is on one breast, sucking and nipping before switching to the other one, paying it the same attention. Sliding his body down mine, he kisses a trail between my breasts and down my abdomen.

"I need to taste you," he says before unbuttoning my jeans and sliding them off.

Slowly and carefully, he removes my lace panties, feathering kisses along my leg as he does. Then, he spreads my legs and gives an appreciative groan when he sees I'm waxed and smooth, just as he specified in the contract.

"You're so wet for me already," he says before kissing my inner thigh, moving higher and higher. When he reaches my center, his tongue teases my clit, tracing light circles around it.

My hips move of their own accord. Alex pulls back. "Stay still."

"Yes, Sir."

He returns to his task and adds two fingers, sliding them in and out, matching the rhythm of his tongue. I've never had a man's mouth on me before. The feeling is exquisite. It doesn't take long before an orgasm washes over me, and I moan in pleasure. He continues to lick and suck until the waves of my orgasm subside. Then he makes his way back up my body.

"You taste even better than I imagined," he says before kissing me deeply, allowing me to taste myself on him. It's subtle and tangy, like nothing I've tasted before.

"Sir, I need you inside me." My voice is breathy.

He sits back on his knees. "You need to learn some patience."

His hand begins stroking his length, up and down. "Is this what you want?"

"Yes, please."

He leans in and drags his cock over my sensitive clit, teasing me before he lines himself up with my opening and slides in ever so slowly. Once he's fully sheathed inside me, he pauses, closing his eyes. "Fuck, you feel so good." Then, he moves slowly, not rushing our first time together.

I reach up and run my fingers through his dark hair before lifting my head to kiss him. Although this is only supposed to be a contractual relationship, my heart is already falling for him. Our bodies move together in a passionate rhythm. Alex's hands slide up my stomach to my breasts. He holds them in his hands, rolling my nipples before giving them a hard squeeze, eliciting a gasp from me.

"Did you like that?"

"Yes." My words are barely a whisper.

"These will look beautiful with clamps on them."

His words only heighten my quickly building arousal.

"I'm so close."

"Do not come yet," he orders as he increases his pace. "Open your eyes. I want you to look at me when you come—to remember who you belong to."

Our eyes remain locked on one another as Alex thrusts harder and faster.

"Come now," he orders.

An orgasm sweeps through my body. With one more thrust, Alex is coming inside me. He kisses me deeply as we ride out the pleasure together. When our orgasms subside, he drops his forehead to mine. The only sound in the room is our mingled breaths.

"We're so good together, baby girl. I'm glad you decided to give us a chance."

Alex rolls onto his back and pulls my body into his. I lay wrapped in his arms, my head on his chest, until I drift off to sleep.

Alex

OVER THE YEARS, I'VE ASSEMBLED TEAMS OF VERY talented individuals who design successful campaigns. Because of this, I've built one of the most sought-after marketing companies on the East Coast.

We've recently signed on with several large companies, which means I've been in back-to-back meetings all day. Where I don't work hands-on with each client, I oversee every project.

I'm sitting in my fourth meeting of the day when an email notification pops up on my phone. A quick swipe of the screen shows it's from Maxim. The subject line reads *New Client Coming Onboard.* This gets my attention, and I sit up straighter. Another client? I'm eager to open the email and read more about it.

"Mr. Montgomery, what are your thoughts on the new campaign slogan?" The team leader interrupts my reading.

"Everything looks good here." I gather the papers in front of me before pushing my chair back and standing. "If you'll excuse me, I just received an email that needs an immediate response. I trust you have this under control." Without waiting for his response, I leave the meeting room and head straight to my office.

Once I'm back at my desk, I type in the password to unlock my screen and open the email.

Alexander,
A colleague of mine, Mr. Nicholai Federov, requires your services.
He has technology that will be of interest to alternative energy
companies. I want to arrange a meeting with the three of us to
discuss how we wish to proceed. This client will require a great deal
of time, but it will be mutually beneficial. Attached you will find
the proposal. We will make time to speak next week.
Maxim.

Opening the proposal, I start reading it right away. Nicholai is involved with a company studying Neutrinovoltaic Energy, the latest in renewable energy resources. That's the official business that will go on paper. I have a phone call scheduled with Maxim next week. That's when he'll fill me in on how Nicholai fits into the more sensitive aspects of his business.

When I finally look up, it's dark outside. The sun has long since set. I got so involved in reading the proposal that I didn't realize how time had gotten away from me. Grabbing my phone off the desk, I text Viktor, letting him know I'll be out shortly. Then I reply to Maxim, acknowledging the receipt of his email.

My house is quiet and lonely when I return after a long day at the office. Coming home after work on Fridays to the smells of dinner cooking and knowing Natalie is waiting for me is something I quickly grew used to. She usually stays over on the weekends, something I've never done before—never shared my home with a submissive. When she's here, it's like we live in our own little bubble. Natalie was initially hesitant but agreed to it as long as we kept it to weekends only. She's holding back because she has to return to Northmeadow and doesn't want to get too attached.

Having her here for a few days at a time has helped us to work out some of the initial kinks. My little sub does well following the rules. I've only had to punish her once. Not biting her nails is a challenge for her.

She takes advantage of my fully stocked kitchen when she's here, ensuring we have a home-cooked meal that we sit and eat together. It reminds me of my childhood. The aromas coming from the kitchen as my mother lovingly prepared dinner for my father, of us sitting down to meals and talking about our days. I didn't realize how important those memories are and how much I desire that in my life.

My biggest concern is knowing Maxim is expanding his operations and wants me to take on another client. It'll bring in a lot of money, but it'll also mean sacrificing personal time. Natalie and I only have a few months together, and I don't want to waste a second of it—I'm torn.

I put my briefcase on the dining table and loosen my tie before walking to the windows. Looking out over the water, I recall the look on Natalie's face the first time she stepped into my apartment. Her green eyes shimmered as she took in the view. Something I had never stopped to appreciate before that moment. I'm guilty of taking for granted everything she saw that first night. I miss her presence here and want her back. That thought stops me in my tracks—Natalie's only temporary. The realization causes a stirring in my heart. I don't want her to leave. What is it about this woman that has me turned upside down? Maybe it's her innocence. Even though I've told her very little about my personal life, she's been open about hers.

Losing her brother to suicide greatly impacted her and is the driving force behind her career choice. She's also told me about her ex-boyfriend, the one who broke her heart but is also responsible for her new outlook on life. His loss is my gain.

I'm beginning to care about her as more than just my submissive, which terrifies me. I have to shut those feelings off. We agreed this was nothing more than a few months of fun before she returns home.

Natalie

The remainder of the semester flies by. Finals are over, and graduation is in two weeks. If you'd asked me last year, I would've said I couldn't wait to graduate. But now, everything's changed. I'm thankful that my schooling is complete and I'll be able to start my career. But at the same time, I feel like I've just started embracing life in the city, and it's ending already.

Then there's Alex.

We've grown close over the past few months. We see each other one or two days during the week and spend weekends together. Every Friday night, he comes home to find me kneeling inside his foyer. His eyes heat the second he sees me. I've learned to keep dinner on warm because we rarely make it to the table before we're naked, and he's inside me.

This wasn't supposed to be anything more than a few months of fun. A chance to try out something new—no strings attached. I should've known that wasn't going to be possible. I'm falling in love with him. Too bad he doesn't feel the same. I have to remind myself that his kindness and affection are part of the contract. Nothing more than his responsibilities as my Dominant. Our relationship, just like my time in the city, comes with a rapidly approaching expiration date.

"Nat, your phone's ringing," Lana calls from the living room. "Who is it?"

"It's Alex," she says in a sing-song voice before answering it.

I hurry down the hall and into the living room.

"Here she is." Lana hands me the phone. "Did you invite him to graduation?" she whispers.

I put my hand over the phone. "Yes."

She nods in acknowledgment. "I'm getting my bag. Brandon will be here any minute. I'll see you at the ceremony."

"Okay, have fun."

Lana's spending the next few weeks at Brandon's. The two of them have been nearly inseparable lately.

"Hello?"

"Hi, baby girl. Did I catch you at a bad time?"

"No. I was saying goodbye to Lana. She's headed to Brandon's."

"He told me she's staying with him for a while. Sounds like they're getting pretty serious."

I feel a pang of jealousy. I'm happy for my best friend but sad for me.

"Are you coming over this weekend?"

It's our last official week together.

"Yes."

"Why don't you spend the week with me?" His voice holds a glimmer of hope.

"I can't. I have to pack and get everything shipped home."

Although that's true, it's more of an excuse. Everything's pretty much already packed. There's no way I can handle spending the whole week with him knowing, in the end, I have to say goodbye.

"We can stay at your place. I can help you."

"I don't think that's a good idea."

"I had to try. I'll have Viktor pick you up Friday."

"I'll be ready."

I disconnect the call and already feel my heart breaking. How am I going to say goodbye to Alex?

Natalie

I fight back the tears as Viktor takes my bag and walks me to the car. It's a quiet drive across town, although that's no different from most days. Viktor doesn't talk much. He's all business. We pull into the parking garage and into the usual spot.

"I'll bring your bags up in a few minutes. I have something I need to take care of."

"Take your time."

The elevator takes me up to Alex's apartment. When the doors open, a trail of roses leads me into the bedroom, where I find a note.

Take a hot bath using the toiletries I left for you. You have one hour, then I expect to find you on my bed wearing only the item provided.

I pick up a red blindfold and run my fingers over the silky material, feeling a shiver of anticipation run through me. What has Alex planned for tonight? My heart pounds with excitement as I imagine the possibilities.

I turn on the hot water and pour some lavender body wash into the tub, watching as it fills with steamy bubbles. Slowly, I strip off my clothes and sink into warm water. The sensation is heavenly, and I close my eyes, letting out a sigh of contentment.

As I soak, my muscles gradually loosen, and my mind drifts. I rarely take the time to relax like this, but I realize how much I need it. When I finally emerge from the bath, I feel rejuvenated.

Drying off, I notice a note resting on top of a fluffy white bathrobe. I wrap myself in the robe, tying it around my waist, and read the card.

Make sure your hair is pulled back and off your shoulders.

I grab a comb and run it through my damp hair, braiding it before pinning it up into a bun. I can't help but wonder what Alex has in store for me tonight.

When I glance at the clock, I realize only five minutes are left. I quickly dry myself and lie down on the bed, feeling a rush of excitement and anticipation as I reach for the red blindfold. A thrill runs through me as I slide the silky material over my eyes.

Without my sight, my other senses are heightened. The air is still and quiet, and I try to steady my breathing, waiting for Alex to arrive.

I hear footsteps approaching from the hall. The door opens and closes, and I hear the lock click into place. The room fills with the familiar scent of citrus and sandalwood.

Alex.

Silently, he moves around the room, opening and closing drawers. The atmosphere is charged with excitement, and I can't help but wonder what Alex has in store for me tonight. I jump when I feel something soft being run gently up my leg.

"That tickles," I giggle.

"Shh. There will be no talking."

The same item, a feather, I think, is being dragged over my arms, leaving a trail of goosebumps in its wake.

"Spread your legs," Alex commands.

Without hesitation, I do as he instructs.

"Mmm...so beautiful."

Alex never holds back compliments about my body. At first,

they were hard to acknowledge. Slowly, I've been improving at accepting them.

Next, he secures a cuff around one ankle and then the other before attaching them to the hidden clips on his bed. My wrists are next. He ties them over my head and secures the rope to the headboard. I'm completely at his mercy, and I love it.

Following the same path the feather took, there's now what feels like a spiked wheel rolling over my skin. The sharp sensation is such a contrast from the feather. Alex continues dragging it to my abdomen before rolling it across my breasts. My nipples harden in response. The sensation stops as abruptly as it started.

Then there's silence, and I start to panic. "Alex? Are you still here?"

"I'm not going anywhere, baby girl."

Leaning over me, I feel his warm skin on mine. He kisses me before placing a set of headphones over my ears. The sudden hearing loss surprises me, and I pull on my restraints.

He moves one from my ear. "Color?"

"Yellow." I'm finding having both my sight and hearing taken away difficult.

"Do you want to continue?"

"I just need a minute."

He removes the headphones and gently touches my shoulder, kissing me deeper. I lose myself in the passion, and the anxiety dissipates. His hands leave my shoulders, but I can still feel the warmth of his body. I know he's close.

"Can I put the headphones back on?"

"Yes, Sir."

Once he replaces them, everything goes silent. My back arches when something cold swirls around my belly button and down my stomach before he drags it through my slit, where it leaves a trail of burning fire. I thought it was ice, but there was also warmth. The contrast in sensations is intense.

It's not until I feel him suck on my nipple that I'm sure it's ice, and it's been in his mouth the whole time. But just like last time, the object disappears. The silence from the headphones is replaced with soft music.

Alex places feathered kisses down my body, returning me to a state of relaxation. Then, his body is gone again, and I'm left anticipating the next experience. He doesn't make me wait long before I feel something warm and slick on my back entrance, and I tense. We've not had anal sex before, and although I'm open to the idea, I'm also nervous.

Before I have a chance to panic, Alex's fingers begin teasing my clit. My arousal intensifies as an orgasm quickly begins to build. At the same time, I feel something firm yet smooth penetrating the tight muscles. Alex increases the pressure on my clit as he gently eases a toy in and out, allowing my body to adjust to the new sensation. He doesn't rush.

By the time the plug is fully inside, I'm on the edge of an orgasm. He stops abruptly again, and I moan in frustration. I try to pull my legs together to quell the overwhelming sensations, but with the restraints, that's impossible.

The music changes. I don't recognize the song until I hear the lyrics. It's Eminem's "Lose Yourself." As if on cue, the toy vibrates a pattern in time to the music. I've never felt anything like this. My body is overwhelmed. It feels as though I'm on the edge of a precipice, but I'm unable to fall off the other side.

Alex's fingers begin to tease my clit again. I raise my hips, needing more, but his other hand pushes them down. When I think I can't take it anymore, his tongue penetrates my entrance. It's all I needed to send me over the cliff.

Before my orgasm ends, he slams inside me. At first, it feels like it's too much, and I don't think my body can handle it. Fully sheathed inside me, he doesn't move. Instead, he leans down and kisses me, distracting me from the pain.

Slowly, he begins to rock his hips, and what started as pain morphs into pleasure. The toy continues to pulse, and Alex picks up the pace of his thrusts. My second orgasm rockets through me, leaving me breathless. Alex removes the headphones and the blindfold. It takes a minute for my eyes to adjust, but when they do, I find him staring at me with an intense look on his face.

"You're changing me. You're making me a different man. A man who wants us to be more than just a contract."

As soon as the words leave his mouth, he explodes inside me. I follow right behind him. My body convulses with a climax stronger than I've ever felt.

Then, blackness creeps into my vision, and I'm floating in a quiet, peaceful bliss.

Natalie

The day I've dreaded since Alex and I finalized our contract has come—the end. He asked if we could sit and talk after my shower. Standing under the hot water, I close my eyes and allow it to wash over me while I try to imagine how our conversation will go.

When we signed the contract, we agreed that neither of us wanted a relationship. We were just two people having fun and exploring the lifestyle together. I'd get some firsthand experience, and Alex would have a sub to play with for a few months.

From day one, I began preparing myself to say goodbye. To walk away and leave him in my past. But then, last night, he said something that changed everything. He said he wanted something more than a contract. What am I going to do?

I graduate next week. There's a one-way plane ticket to Missouri sitting on my desk. No matter how much I want to continue exploring this dynamic, I'm tied to Northmeadow for the next five years. I don't have a choice. I signed away my options when I accepted the scholarship.

After I shower, I wrap a fluffy white towel around my body, blow-dry my hair, and put on some makeup. I look around and realize I have so much stuff here. It's a good thing I brought a bigger bag. I'm packing everything up now, knowing I plan to return to my apartment after our conversation today.

Alex wants me to spend the week with him, but I can't. I need some time alone to sort out all these mixed-up feelings. Slipping on a pale blue sundress, I look in the mirror. A sad reflection stares back at me. It's time to be strong, Natalie.

Barefoot, I enter the kitchen, where Alex sits at his table waiting for me. He looks up, a gorgeous smile on his face. His eyes hold so much hope. But when he sees me, his smile disappears.

Alex

I RETRIEVED TWO COPIES OF OUR CONTRACT FROM MY office. Today is the expiration date, the day to reevaluate where we want to go from here. I fully anticipated saying goodbye to Natalie today. I had no intention of this arrangement being anything more than a few months of playtime for her and me.

But something happened. Somewhere along the way, my feelings for her changed, and my heart softened.

Natalie's special. She isn't like any woman I've ever known. So much about her is pure innocence, yet she's wise. Despite having a strict, conservative upbringing, Natalie is curious and open to new experiences. Being a submissive comes naturally to her. She's genuine and beautiful, both inside and out.

I've grown to care about her, and after seeing the look on her face last night when I told her I wanted more, I think she cares about me, too. I can't let her leave without fighting to keep her.

I hear her footsteps as she approaches the kitchen. Excited to share my idea with her, I turn, but the breath is sucked from my body when I see her face. It isn't the face of a girl ready to fight for us. She's prepared to say goodbye. Natalie sits across from me and looks down at her hands.

"I know you're graduating next week and planning to return

home. But I don't want us to end. I want to try to make us work however that might look."

"Alex," she says, standing and walking to the windows. It's something she does whenever she's struggling. "Your life is here. Mine is halfway across the country in a small farm town. I don't see how we can be together." She rests her forehead on the glass.

I walk over to her and wrap my arms around her tiny frame. "We can do this in whatever way works for us."

Turning in my arms to face me, she asks, "How?"

"I see two options. First, I own my business and can visit you whenever I want. You'll get vacation days, and you can fly back here, too."

"I won't be making a fancy New York salary. Buying plane tickets to fly back and forth isn't in my future."

"Then let me buy out your contract," I blurt out. "You won't have to leave. We can be together."

Natalie frees herself from my arms. "I will not have my boyfriend, my Dominant, whatever you are, buying out my contract. I made a commitment, and I *will* see it through."

I'm losing this argument to the beautiful yet stubborn woman standing before me. But as much as I want to, I can't force her to stay. To choose me.

"I don't want to walk away from us either." Her emerald green eyes fill with tears. "I'm so confused right now."

"Natalie, please. Don't walk away from us."

She reaches out and cups my cheek in her hand. "These past few months have been the best of my life." A tear drips down her face. "But it's time to say goodbye. Will you take me back to my apartment?"

Reluctantly, I accept her answer.

Natalie

WE DRIVE IN SILENCE. A HEAVINESS HANGS BETWEEN us. I don't want to walk away from this. From Alex. But there will be hundreds of miles between us. How could we possibly make that work? I know firsthand the betrayal that can happen when distance is involved. Alex is different. I know that. But I promised myself I wouldn't put my heart on the line again.

"We're here." Alex puts the car in park. For the longest moment, neither of us moves. "We're so good together, baby girl. Please don't give up on us."

The longing in his voice shatters the last shards of my resolve.

"I'll try."

He turns and looks at me. "Will you let me buy out your contract?"

"No. I'm going back to do my job. I'll agree to try this long-distance. But I do have some requests."

"Can I come in? Then, we can discuss them inside."

We walk together to my second-floor apartment. I fumble in my purse for the keys when the door swings open.

Alex pulls me behind him. "Who are you?"

"Who are *you?*" a very familiar voice asks.

I stand on my tiptoes and peer over Alex's shoulder. "Dad? Mom? What are you doing here?"

"I decided to close the store for a few days. We wanted to surprise you by coming early." Dad looks from Alex back to me. "Looks like we accomplished our goal."

"That you did." I smile, trying to hide my shock.

"Are you going to introduce us to your friend?" Dad asks.

"Mom. Dad. This is Alex."

Alex reaches out to shake my father's hand.

"Nice to meet you, Mr. Clarke."

"I thought you'd appreciate the help packing your things." Mom reaches around Dad and pulls me in for a hug. "I'm sure you can't wait to get home."

My head is spinning. I can't even form a sentence.

After an awkward silence, Mom says, "Why don't you two come in? I'll put some coffee on." She walks toward my kitchen.

Alex looks at me, and I mouth the words *I'm sorry*. We were supposed to be alone to figure out how to move forward. My request was to keep our relationship a secret from my parents, at least for now. I know how they feel about the city and the people in it.

There's no possible way to explain how we met or that he's not my boyfriend but my Dominant. If things work out and we become a real couple, I'll figure out a way to tell them. If not, they'd never need to know. I'm not prepared for this. Tonight could very well end in disaster.

We go to the kitchen, where my mom fumbles around in the cupboards.

"Where do you keep your coffee pot, sweetie?"

I point to the Keurig on the counter. She looks at it and shakes her head disapprovingly. My parents resist anything new.

"I'll take care of it. Please, everyone, sit down."

While I make coffee, my parents start the inquisition.

"How do you know Natalie?" Mom asks.

"I met her through her roommate. I'm a friend of Svetlana's family."

Is that for real or just a story for my parents? I'll have to ask him about that when we're alone.

"What's the nature of your relationship with my daughter?" Dad asks as he leans forward.

I nearly drop the coffee cup I'm holding.

"Dad, please."

"It's okay. We've been seeing each other for the past few months," he answers calmly.

"You realize she has a boyfriend at home?" Mom asks.

"Tommy and I broke up a long time ago," I respond sharply. "Can we please stop this and just have a normal conversation?"

"Natalie tells me you own a pharmacy?" Alex smoothly changes the subject.

Dad's face lights up. He's proud of his business.

"Alex owns a marketing firm, Dad." I place a cup of coffee in front of my father. "Maybe he can give you some ideas for advertising?"

The tension between my father and Alex seems to subside, at least for now. But Mom's a different story. She sits back, her arms crossed over her chest. She's not going to let this go.

I'm in awe of Alex's composure. My parents' presence doesn't shake him at all. Actually, he and Dad seem to have hit it off quite well. While Alex and Dad talk, Mom and I discuss what must be done before next week's graduation.

"It looks like the evening's gotten away from us," Alex says. "None of us has eaten. I'd love to take you all out for dinner."

I smile at him, appreciating how accommodating he's being.

"Thank you, but we'll be eating in," Mom snips. "We're not much for the chaos out there."

I roll my eyes. "You're more than welcome to stay for dinner."

"I'm afraid I didn't make enough for a guest," Mom says as she stands and walks to the counter, where she turns the oven on.

I overlooked the covered baking pan sitting on the stove until now.

"Mom," I say, appalled by her rude attitude.

"It's okay, Natalie. I'm sure your parents want to catch up with you." He stands. "It was wonderful meeting you both."

Dad stands and shakes Alex's hand. "You, too."

"I'll walk you out." When we get back to his car, I say, "I'm so sorry. I had no idea they were here."

He pulls me close. "It's clear your parents care a great deal about you."

"A bit too much. They tend to go overboard. And that bit about my ex—"

"I'm not worried about it," Alex reassures me.

"I should get back upstairs before they come looking for me." I let out a sarcastic laugh.

"That's probably a good idea." Alex threads his hands in my hair as he kisses me goodbye. His kiss is passionate and purposeful. Without using words, his body tells me he doesn't want to let me go. "Text me your stipulations, and we'll figure it out."

"Yes, Sir. I'll try to call you tomorrow."

Alex gets into his car. I stand on the sidewalk and watch him pull away. Even though the air is warm, my body shivers at the loss of his presence. My fingers touch my lips, hoping that the memory of his kiss won't fade.

With a deep breath, I return to my apartment and my waiting parents.

Natalie

Even though I'm not a baseball fan, Yankee Stadium, the site of our commencement ceremony, is quite a sight to behold. Sitting in the bleachers, listening to the inspirational speakers, and then walking the warning track to the stage to receive my diploma is an experience I'll never forget. After the ceremony, I search the crowd trying to find Lana. She spots me first and runs over, wrapping me in a tight hug.

"Can you believe it?"

"We did it!" I squeal.

"My parents insisted that your parents ride in the car with them. Alex went with Brandon. He left Viktor to bring us home so we can change," Lana says without taking a breath. "We'll meet everyone at the restaurant."

"Sounds like a good plan." I hug her, suddenly feeling very emotional. "I'm going to miss you."

"You can always change your mind and stay. I know someone else who'd like that, too."

We start walking to the parking area to find Viktor.

"Alex doesn't want us to end. He asked me to stay."

Lana stops dead in her tracks. "And? What did you say?"

"I really like him, but I have to go back. I agreed to try something long-distance, although I don't think it'll work out." I resume walking, and Lana follows. "Please don't say anything about it in front of my parents. They don't need to know."

"I get it. It's too bad, though." Lana puts her arm around me. "Alex hasn't been interested in anyone for a long time. You and he are so good together."

"Alex has women falling all over him. Every time we're at the club, they practically drool when he walks in. He can have anyone he wants."

Lana laughs. "Subs have always tried to turn his head, but it never works."

"There's Viktor." I point in his direction.

We walk the final steps to the car and climb into the backseat. The drive from the stadium back to our apartment takes forever. Traffic is the only thing I won't miss. It's a quiet ride. Neither of us wants to continue our discussion with Viktor present. I stare out the window and get lost in my thoughts.

I can't deny the fun Alex and I have had. Not to mention, he's the hottest guy I've ever met. But where can we go from here? He's not going to wait five years for a girl he only sees now and then. I learned that lesson the hard way, and I don't intend to have a repeat performance.

We finally pull up to our apartment.

"Wait here, Viktor. We won't be too long."

Svetlana amazes me. When she's with Brandon, she's the perfect submissive. She's quiet, subdued, and waits for instructions. But in her day-to-day life, she's anything but submissive.

I've always been envious of her ability to take charge in any situation. But, since becoming Alex's submissive, I envy that even more. We walk into our apartment, and I flop onto our sofa.

"Why did I agree to this? Long-distance relationships don't work." The words slip from my mouth.

Lana sits down and puts her arm around me. "Is there anything I can say to change your mind?"

"You know I can't do that." Even if my heart feels like it's being torn in two, I rest my head on her shoulder. Lana's like the sister I never had. "If I don't go home, I have to pay back the scholarship, and I don't have that kind of money."

"Alex offered to pay for it. Why don't you let him?"

We sit quietly until the buzz of Lana's phone breaks the silence. She pulls it from her purse and glances at the screen.

"It's my dad. I told him we're almost ready to leave."

"Give me a few minutes to get changed."

Five minutes later, we're walking out the door and getting back into the car. This time, I'm thankful for the traffic. It gives me some time to clear my head before we get to the restaurant. With a final turn, the Russian Tea Room comes into view, and so does Brandon, who's outside pacing back and forth.

"You're finally here." He rushes over to Lana as we step out of the car. "I was going to send out a search party to look for you." He laughs.

"Sorry. That was my fault. I needed a few minutes."

"Are you okay?"

"Not really, but I will be." I try to force a smile. "I'm a bit overwhelmed with graduation and all the changes about to happen."

"I'm always here if you need to talk," Brandon offers.

I'm grateful for the friendships I've made here. They're something I'll treasure always.

Walking into the restaurant, I'm surprised to see it's empty except for our families.

Brandon moves closer behind us and whispers, "Mr. Solonik rented the entire place for the evening."

"Somehow, that doesn't surprise me." Lana threads her arm through mine. "Let's go celebrate."

I take a deep breath and put away my melancholy mood. I owe it to everyone here and myself to have a good time tonight.

Mr. Solonik stands as we approach. "Ah, our guests of honor are finally here." He stops and kisses us on both cheeks in greeting. "I am so very proud of both my girls."

"Thank you, Mr. Solonik."

"Natalia, you must call me Maxim. We are family now." He bends closer to whisper in my ear. "Lana tells me you have entered the lifestyle."

My eyes grow wide and dart towards my parents, who are beginning to walk toward us.

"Do not worry. Your parents know nothing, and it will remain that way unless you say otherwise."

"Thank you." I sigh in relief.

"Alex tells me—"

Maxim is interrupted by my mother. "Sweetheart, your father and I are so proud of you." She wraps her arms around me and squeezes tight. "The house has been so empty. We can't wait for you to come home."

I try to hide the conflict I'm fighting inside.

"Can we talk about that later? Tonight's for celebrating."

Mom steps back, crossing her arms in disapproval, while Lana shoots me a concerned look from behind her. Maxim's deep, accented voice fills the room.

"Irina and I would like to thank you all for coming to celebrate the girls' graduation. Let us sit down and begin the meal." He signals a nearby server, who turns and enters the kitchen. "I took the liberty of ordering the full menu for tonight's festivities."

"Isn't that wonderful," Mom says with a saccharine smile before taking my arm and leading me away. She whispers in my ear. "Is he always so loud and overbearing?"

The restaurant has been rearranged to make one long table. My parents are sitting at one end. I'm sure trying to stay as far away from the others as possible. There's an empty seat for me between Mom and Alex. When we reach the table, Alex stands and pulls my chair out.

Maxim has spared no expense. He really ordered everything from the menu, complete with a wine pairing for each. He encourages my parents to try tasting at least one of the wines, but they decline. They don't drink alcohol for any reason, something Maxim, being Russian, can't understand.

I try each of the wines with the various courses. I've grown to love both Russian food and wine since living with Lana.

Alex tries to engage with my parents throughout the meal. Dad seems to be enjoying their conversation despite Mom's disapproving glares.

Hoping to ease the tension, I turn to my mom. "Alex put together a small marketing campaign for the store," I say.

"We're doing fine on our own."

"Dad told Alex that business has been slow."

"It'll pick back up. It always does."

"Maybe Alex's ideas can help."

Mom shrugs.

From the look on Dad's face as he talks to Alex, he's excited about the idea. Hopefully, he'll get Mom on board. If only she'd give Alex a chance, I know she'd like him too.

The celebration continues late into the evening. Dessert is just now being served, a Russian Napoleon Cake. I take a bite of the flaky pastry and savor the rich flavors and the crème filling.

"The cake is delicious, isn't it?" I ask Mom.

"It's okay. Although I'm not sure why we couldn't have a more traditional cake."

It takes all my willpower not to roll my eyes. "It's a Russian restaurant, and this is a very traditional Russian cake." I don't understand why my parents, my mother in particular, can never enjoy anything without being critical.

While we eat dessert, a server places a shot glass in front of each of us. Another server follows behind, filling each with a clear liquid that I'm sure is Russian vodka.

"Can I have everyone's attention?" Maxim asks. "I want to propose a toast to two exceptional young ladies." He rounds the table so he's facing us. "Svetlana and Natalia, you have both worked diligently, and today, we celebrate that accomplishment. I know you will both meet success in whatever ventures await you."

He raises his glass, and we all follow. *"k uspekhu nashikh dvukh baryshen*. To the success of our two young ladies."

Cheers are called out from those around the table as we all take our shots. The burn of the alcohol in my throat causes me to cough. Alex laughs softly next to me. I've done Vodka shots with the Solonik's before, but I have the same reaction every time. Guess I'm a bit of a lightweight.

"Natalie, it's time we head home. We have a flight to catch tomorrow," Mom says as she stands. Dad follows her.

"You guys go ahead. I'm going to stay awhile longer."

"Don't be late, honey," Dad says before Mom can reply.

"I won't."

Maxim and Irina get up to say their goodbyes to my parents.

"I'll send a car to take you to the airport tomorrow," Maxim offers.

"We'll take a cab," Mom replies.

"It was a pleasure meeting you." Irina ignores Mom's icy attitude.

I watch my parents walk out the door and breathe a sigh of relief. Tonight could've gone much worse.

Alex

"Are you ready to go?" I ask Natalie. The party has wound down, and I want to be alone with her before she leaves for Missouri tomorrow.

"Can I say goodbye to Lana first?"

"Take your time." I know saying goodbye isn't going to be easy.

We walk across the room to where Lana and Brandon are standing. The girls embrace each other. Their tears are flowing freely.

"I can come by in the morning to see you off."

"That'll only make it harder to leave." Natalie wipes her face.

"Okay. But call me as soon as you land."

"I will."

Brandon leans in to hug her goodbye. Ordinarily, a Dominant wouldn't touch another Dominant's sub, but this is different. Brandon's like a brother to both Natalie and me.

"Keep in touch. Call us if you need anything."

Lastly, we make our way to Maxim and Irina. It's hard to watch Natalie in pain, especially knowing I could change this if only she'd let me. After the emotional goodbyes, we exit the restaurant. Natalie shivers in the cool evening air. While we wait for Viktor to bring the car around, I remove my jacket and help her slip it on.

It's after midnight when we finally get to my place. Natalie takes my hand and leads me to the bedroom. Tonight isn't about Dominance or submission. It's about showing Natalie I'm in love with her. Tears slide down her face as I help her undress. My hands caress her body, committing every curve to memory.

"No more tears, baby girl."

I make love to her slowly and gently, savoring every second I'm inside her. After we're both sated, I pull her close, and she rests her head on my chest. It doesn't take long until we both fall asleep.

"Alex, wake up." Natalie shakes me. "It's morning. We must've fallen asleep."

I open my eyes and find her rushing around the room, looking for her clothes.

"What are you doing? Come back to bed."

"I have to get back to my apartment. My flight's this afternoon, and my parents—" She checks her phone. "Ten missed calls."

Getting out of bed, I pull on my pants as she frantically swipes across the screen.

"I'm sending them a text."

"Natalie." I place my hands on her shoulders, stilling her movement. "Slow down and breathe. It's a short drive to your apartment. We'll get dressed, and I'll have you back to your place long before you need to leave for the airport."

She visibly relaxes as she leans into my touch. Unfortunately, the ringing of her phone interrupts the moment.

"It's my dad."

"Go ahead and take it. I'll finish getting dressed."

"Hi, Dad. I'm fine. I'm with my friends."

She looks at me for my reaction. I raise an eyebrow.

"We were up late talking. I meant to text you, but I guess we fell asleep."

I watch, impressed, as she slips back into her panties mid-conversation without missing a beat.

"Yes, I know what time it is. I'm already packed. I'm on my way home right now. Okay, bye."

"Are they always this overprotective?"

"They're used to being in a small town where everyone knows everyone. They tend to get a bit jumpy when they're here."

"Are you sure I can't talk you into staying?"

"I'm very sure. I'm going to miss you so much." Her green eyes fill with tears once again.

"We'll talk, and I'll fly out to see you in a few weeks." I kiss her trembling lips.

"Until we see if this will work, can we meet somewhere? I don't want my parents to know I'm still seeing you."

Her words sting, but I understand her hesitation. "I don't like it, but if that's what you need from me, we can do it that way. For now." I'll agree to just about anything not to lose her.

The beginning of our drive is silent. I'm at war with myself. I want to tell Natalie I've fallen in love with her, but I've never said those words to a woman.

"Alex. I'm sorry."

"You have nothing to be sorry for." I reach out and take her hand in mine.

"For not staying."

"There's still time to change that." I glance at her.

"I can't." She turns her head to look out the window.

We pull up to her building. I get out and walk around, helping her out of the car.

"We're going to make this work. I'm not letting you get away." I kiss her deeply, wanting to make sure she remembers the feeling of my body against hers. Willing her not to forget me—forget us.

"Thank you for last night." With those words, she begins backing away until just our fingertips are touching. "I'll text you when we land."

"I'll be waiting."

Then, she turns and walks toward her building. When she reaches the door, she looks back over her shoulder. Tears are streaming down her face.

It takes every ounce of discipline I possess not to go after her and carry her over my shoulder back to my apartment.

Instead, I stay rooted in place until she's out of sight.

Natalie

I nearly trip over a suitcase when I walk into my apartment. Mom and Dad, who are both sitting at the kitchen table, turn their heads when I walk in. I'm not used to having to answer for my whereabouts, but from the looks on their faces, they aren't going to let this go.

"I'm sorry I didn't call. We were all hanging out, and I guess we fell asleep."

"You had us very worried, young lady." Mom narrows her eyes. "We thought you might've been killed."

I let out a sarcastic laugh. "Alex was there. He'd never let anything happen to me."

"I'm not thrilled either, but she's here now," Dad says and pats Mom's hand. "Safe and sound."

Mom pulls her arm away. "Our taxi will be here any minute. I can't wait to get out of this place. Are you ready to go?"

"I have to grab something. I'll be back in a minute."

Looking around at the stripped-down room fills my heart with sadness. Everything that made it mine has been packed and shipped back to Missouri. All that's left is the furniture. One of the best times of my life is about to come to an end.

Sitting on the bed, I take a minute to reminisce about how

Svetlana and I first met. I was the quiet girl from a small town struggling to transition to one of the busiest cities in the world. She was a girl from another country, confident and sure of herself, and ready to experience a new culture.

We were randomly paired as roommates and have been best friends ever since. I write a quick note and leave it in Lana's room.

Lana,
Thank you for being the best friend I could've ever asked for. You've changed my life in so many ways. I'll be forever grateful to you. I won't say goodbye because our friendship will never end.
~Natalie

Then, I grab my backpack and take a final look around. I can't believe six years of my life have passed so quickly, and now I'm going home.

Home.

I've always considered Northmeadow home, but if that's true, why does it feel like I'm leaving home now? It feels like I'm returning to some place I'm afraid I'll no longer fit in. So many contradicting thoughts and feelings are a jumbled mess in my head. I slowly make my way back to my parents, who impatiently wait at the door.

"I'm ready," I say and muster a smile.

"Good," Mom says. "Let's go."

When we get outside, the cab is already waiting for us. Dad puts our luggage in the trunk, and the three of us pile into the back seat. I watch out the window as we pull away from my apartment and wipe a stray tear from my face.

"I know you think you don't want to leave this city, but it wasn't that long ago you felt the same about Northmeadow," Mom says.

I nod.

"This was just one chapter, and now it's over. It's time to turn the page and move on." She pats my shoulder as if her words magically make everything better.

"What if I'm not ready for it to be over?"

"Are you talking about that man?" Mom sighs.

"Yes."

"Honey, I understand why you *think* you like him. He's successful and, some would say, handsome. It feels good when a man like that pays attention to you, but he's not like us."

Dad leans forward and peers at me around Mom's shoulder. "Long-distance relationships are difficult, sweetheart."

"I know, but—"

Mom interrupts. "And a certain young man is waiting for you to come home."

"Who?"

"Thomas."

"Tommy Moore?" I roll my eyes. "We broke up, remember?"

"He comes into the pharmacy every week. Thomas has grown into a fine young man, and he can't wait to see you."

Thankfully, we pull up at JFK, and our conversation is interrupted.

I never told my parents why Tommy and I split up, and I don't plan to now. I never want to talk about that night again.

I sit in the back of my parents' car as Dad drives the familiar windy roads through the Ozark Mountains. We pass a herd of deer grazing on the side of the road. It's a sight that was once a part of my everyday life, but one I haven't seen in a long time. As we get closer to Northmeadow, familiar farms come into view.

Mr. Johnson is tending his cows in the field. When I was a little girl, I loved it when we drove by the dairy farms. Dad would slow the car just like he's doing now, so I could see the new calves in the fields grazing alongside their moms.

Then, the scenery changes from farmland to the town's streets. It's late Sunday afternoon, which means nothing's open. The roads are quiet and empty. It's a foreign feeling after living in New York City for so long—it's never quiet there. I pull out my phone to text Alex.

Me: We landed a little while ago. We're almost home.

Alex: Glad you got there safely, but I miss you already.

Me: I miss you too.

Alex: Will you be home at nine?

Me: Small town, remember? Everything's closed today. LOL, I'll be home.

Alex: Good, I'll video call you then.

Me: Can't wait. TTYL.

As we make the last turn for home, I shoot a quick text to Lana, letting her know I arrived safely.

Dad pulls into our driveway, and I look up. My mouth hangs open in shock. Strung from end to end on my parents' front porch is a large, brightly colored banner that reads *Welcome Home, Natalie.*

Bouquets of rainbow-colored balloons are tied across the rail. And, there, standing on the steps, is Tommy Moore. He's dressed in dark jeans and his old Northmeadow High Football T-shirt. His dirty blond hair is cut short, and he's wearing a huge grin.

"Surprise." My mother beams with pride.

I'm speechless, and not in a good way.

I'M FROZEN IN SHOCK AS TOMMY CONFIDENTLY STRIDES toward the car and opens my door. He reaches in, grabbing my hands, pulling me out, and into him.

"Welcome home, Natalie." He leans in to kiss me, but I turn my head just in time for the kiss to land on my cheek. "I've really missed you." He bounces back without hesitation.

"Umm. Wow. I don't know quite what to say."

Mom gets out of the car and hurries over to Tommy. "You did a great job with the decorations." She pulls him in for a big hug.

"Thanks, Mrs. C. I'm so glad she's finally home."

I watch their interaction. It's like a bad movie playing out in front of me. Except it's not a movie. It's really happening.

"I know you just got home, but can I steal you for a walk?"

"I don't think—"

"Of course you can," Mom answers for me. "It'll give you two kids a chance to catch up."

Tommy grabs my hand, but my feet are lead weights, unwilling to move. His hand holding mine feels wrong. It isn't the hand I want. It isn't Alex. Tommy gives a tug, forcing me to move, leaving my feet with no choice but to obey.

We walk behind my parents' house to a well-worn path alongside fields that used to be farmland. However, they don't look like they've been planted for many years. When we get to a familiar wooded area, I'm hit with an onslaught of memories. All the times Tommy and I snuck off here while we were in high school.

He was my first boyfriend, my first kiss, and the boy I lost my virginity to. Everyone expected we'd get married. Once upon a time, I expected that too, but then he shattered that dream and my heart.

Tommy stops walking and turns to face me. "Natalie, I know things ended badly between us."

"You could say that." The hurt I so carefully buried bursts through my chest, reopening old wounds. "At one time, it was you and me against the world," I yell. "Until I came home and found you in bed with my best friend. Seeing the two of you like that ripped my heart out."

He pulls my unwilling body against his. "And I'm sorry for that. I was lonely. It'll never happen again, I swear it."

"You think saying you're sorry will make it go away?" I pull out of his hold.

"It was a long time ago, Nat. I thought we moved past it."

"Tommy, I—"

"You're back now. We're together again." His voice is desperate, pleading. "Things'll be different this time."

"What you and Ashlynn did is unforgivable. We are not *together*, and we never will be." I start walking home.

"Natalie, wait."

I spin around and cross my arms in frustration. "What?"

Tommy reaches into his pants pocket and pulls out a prescription bottle. He takes out a tiny white pill and swallows it.

"What did you just take?"

He leans up against a nearby tree. "After we broke up, I got hurt in a game. I couldn't play anymore and lost my scholarship." Tommy holds up the bottle, giving it a shake. "Now and then, I need a little something to take the edge off, so I have these guys."

My parents mentioned something about Tommy getting hurt,

but I didn't want to hear about him, so I never asked for details. "Have you seen a doctor? I don't think popping pills is a good long-term solution, do you?"

"I've seen a doctor, more than one doctor." He pushes off the tree and closes the distance between us. "There's nothing else they can do. Let it go. I'm fine."

"Whatever you say. I'm going home."

"I'm right behind you."

When we get back to the house, my mother's just putting dinner on the table. "I had your Aunt Delia stop by and throw a casserole in the oven. You two are just in time."

"I'm not hungry. I think I'll go and unpack."

"You'll do no such thing, young lady." My mother scolds me like I'm a child. "You have a dinner guest."

"*You* have a dinner guest," I answer, a hint of sarcasm in my voice.

"Natalie, you'll not speak to your mother like that," Dad says. "You will apologize right now."

In a matter of seconds, I feel myself shrinking back into the subservient girl I was before I went away. The perfect daughter who did as she was told and would never defy her parents.

"I'm sorry for being disrespectful."

Dinner is excruciating. It's my turn to be the silent one, the outcast at the table. Tommy and my parents carry on as though they haven't missed a beat. It's like they've been talking all this time, pretending we're still a couple. Although I didn't think Tommy would ever leave, dinner finally winds down. He says his goodbyes, promising he'll see me soon.

After Tommy leaves, Dad retires to the living room to watch the nightly news while Mom and I clean up.

"It's so good to have you home, honey," she says as she puts the last plate in the cupboard. "And seeing you back with Tommy, well, everything's perfect now."

"Tommy and I aren't together." I fold the dishrag and set it on the counter. "We broke up a long time ago. I've moved on."

"You left him." Mom reaches behind her, untying her apron. "You should be thankful he still wants you. Most girls around here would jump at the chance to be with Thomas."

"They can have him." I check the time on my phone. It's eight forty-five. "I'm feeling a bit off. Probably jet lag. I'm going to get to bed early."

"Please be smart, Natalie. That man from the city is not right for you." She kisses my cheek. "I love you and want you to be happy. I'm sure you'll see reason after having a good night's rest."

"Night, Mom." I don't argue. She isn't ready to see things my way.

"Night, Daddy." I kiss him on the cheek as I pass through the living room on my way upstairs.

Once I'm in my room, I close the door and lean against it. I feel like I've entered a time warp. I haven't been in my bedroom in nearly two years, yet everything is exactly where I left it. The flowered sheets and pink ruffled bedspread from when I was younger still dress my twin bed. I pick up a pillow and smell the familiar scent of the laundry detergent my mother makes. She must've made sure the sheets were freshly washed.

My stuffed animals and dolls sit neatly on my chair in the corner. I walk to my dresser and run my fingers over the pictures taped to the mirror—pictures of my youth. Carefully, I pull one off to look at it closer.

It's a picture of Tommy and me on the first day of our senior year in high school. He was so handsome, tall, and muscular from working out. I remember how lucky I felt to be dating the starting quarterback. Tommy has his arm around me, and I'm staring up at him, a girl head over heels in love. I set the picture on my dresser and pull another down. This one's from the end of my senior year. I'm standing with a group of my friends, including Ashlynn. We're all in our caps and gowns.

Each of us was young and naïve. And with very different dreams for our futures. None of the girls in this picture ever left Northmeadow. We've led very different lives. I'm not the same girl

I was then. Will they like the person I am today? Will they accept me back into their circle? Do I even want to be accepted by them?

My phone buzzes in my pocket, bringing a smile to my face. I set the photo on my dresser and take out my phone to answer the call. Cell service is spotty here, so it takes a second for the image of Alex to pop up on the screen. He's sitting in front of his windows with the city lights illuminating the night sky behind him.

"Hi," I say, and sit down on my bed. "Nice view."

"I thought you might be missing it tonight."

"I can't believe how much I miss it already."

"Do you miss anything else?" He raises an eyebrow.

"Hmm—let me think," I tease. "I miss Lana. And there's this guy. I forgot his name." I flash him a cheeky grin.

He puts his hand over his heart in mock surprise. "You forgot me already?" I could never forget Alex, and that's part of the problem. If this long-distance thing doesn't work, I don't know how I'll be able to get over him. "How was your flight home?"

"Pretty uneventful. Mom talked my ear off. She made sure I was up to date on all the Northmeadow gossip." I roll my eyes, and Alex laughs.

"What are your plans for tomorrow?"

"For starters." I flip the camera so Alex can see my bedroom. "I need to make this room fit for an adult. Other than that, not much."

Conversation has always come easily for us, but tonight, I'm at a loss for anything to talk about. The divide I was afraid of is already rearing its ugly head. This is why I didn't want to tell anyone about us. I don't see how we can make it work.

"Natalie, stop biting your nails," Alex reprimands.

"Sorry, I didn't even realize I was doing it."

"What's bothering you?" He leans forward, bringing his face closer to the camera.

"Nothing."

"That's not true. Talk to me."

I look down, trying to figure out how to put my feelings into words. "I'm terrified of the distance between us. I don't see how we're going to make this work."

"Right now, we take it one step at a time," Alex reassures me.

"How can I be your submissive when we don't live in the same city, the same state?" I quickly catch my error. "Sorry for raising my voice, Sir."

"I forgive you. We *will* make this work. I told you we can fly to see each other whenever we want."

I remain silent, trying to process his words. He makes it sound so easy, but selfishly, I want more than a weekend visit now and then. I want the whole experience. I'm not ready to face what that means, so I attempt to change the subject.

"May I ask you a personal question, Sir?" In the few months we've been together, he hasn't told me much about his life or family. I know it isn't typically shared in a contractual relationship. Still, I'm hoping we're at a place where he'll share it with me.

"You can ask me anything." He sits back and relaxes.

"How did you get involved in the lifestyle?"

"My parents. My dad and mom were involved in the lifestyle. Until she passed away."

"I'm sorry." I didn't know he'd lost his mom. My heart hurts seeing the pained look on his face and knowing I'm not there to comfort him. "How old were you?"

"I was twenty-two. She died from breast cancer." He shakes his head. "I knew from an early age I had dominant traits."

I'm starting to think everyone but me was raised in this lifestyle.

"Were you able to talk to your father about it?"

"Yes, my father supported my interest. We lived just outside Seattle, where there are several very active BDSM communities in the area. My father introduced me to his friends. I developed a great respect and appreciation for their ideals and what they stood for. I enjoyed being a part of the lifestyle for several years. Until Mom died. After seeing what Dad went through losing her, I decided I wasn't interested in a relationship in the lifestyle or otherwise."

"What changed your mind?"

"A few months after I came to New York. Maxim walked into my office and hired me to do a marketing campaign for him."

"Maxim? Lana's dad?"

"Yes, Lana's dad. After I took his account, we spent quite a bit of time together here and in Russia." He closes his eyes as if lost in the memories. "Maxim was the one who reintroduced me to the lifestyle. Helped me find my way."

"Why me?" I don't understand what this amazing man sees in a twenty-four-year-old girl from a small town in Missouri with no real experience in this lifestyle. "Why do you want to do this with me? Especially now that I'm so far away."

"I'm drawn to you. There's a connection between us. Do you feel it, too?"

"I do," I say softly.

What scares me is that I feel it too much. I fell in love with him even though he told me this wouldn't become anything more.

"Do you still consent to move forward? I don't know what it'll look like. I wish I had all the answers, but I don't." He shrugs, and I glimpse something I've never seen before in him—uncertainty.

Even though I don't see this working out, I can't say no. I don't want to say no.

"Yes, I consent to that."

"I have some ideas for our Dom/sub dynamic. I emailed you a copy. We don't have to do everything all at once."

I reach over the side of my bed and grab my bag, pulling my laptop out. Once it's fired up, I open my email to see what he sent. There's a list of suggested rules and modifications to our Dom/sub contract. We read through the list and agree on a time for me to call him each morning to let him know my plans for the day. Every night, at nine, we'll video call each other. Alex promises to fly out one weekend a month. My schedule and finances will determine when I can visit him in New York.

"This is a good starting place," Alex says. "Then we can see where it goes on its own.

Having these rules in place makes our relationship feel more stable. I close my laptop and yawn.

"You look tired, baby girl."

"I am. It's been a long day. I don't want to, but I really should go. I have to work at Dad's store for a few hours tomorrow."

"I have a full day, too. I'll call you tomorrow night."

"I can't wait. Night, Alex."

"Sleep well, baby girl."

Summer has flown by, and as per usual here, nothing interesting has happened. I've been able to sneak away to see Alex twice. Saying goodbye was awful and gets harder each time.

It's August now, and in Missouri, which means oppressive heat and humidity, made worse by the lack of air conditioning in my parents' house. Although I've just showered, I'm already sweating, and my curls are a frizzy mess.

Come on, hair, not today. I struggle to pin up the unruly strands. In an hour, I'm meeting with Mr. Meadows, the principal of Northmeadow High, who also happens to be my new boss.

Finally, I get my hair secured in a loose bun and put on some makeup. I'm attempting to look polished and professional. I'm not sure why I'm going through the trouble. I'm only going to sweat it off.

Since my job at the school doesn't officially start for a few more weeks, I've picked up as many shifts at Dad's pharmacy as possible. Between that and the small amount of money I saved while I was away, I managed to pick up a used car. A 2002 silver Honda Civic I've nicknamed Rhonda the Honda. She's not fancy and doesn't even have power windows, but she runs and gets me where I need to go. Best of all, she's mine.

My next goal is to get an apartment. Living with my parents long-term isn't an option. I can already feel myself shrinking back into the teenager they still see me as. Suddenly, I'm under their thumb again, every move scrutinized, every choice met with commentary.

They mean well, but it feels suffocating. The constant questions, the endless advice about what I should or shouldn't be doing. It grates on me, like I'm being measured against standards I never set for myself.

The worst part is the tug-of-war inside me. A piece of me craves the safety of being cared for, of not having to do everything on my own. But the larger part, the restless, aching part, wants freedom. Independence. Space to make mistakes without a lecture waiting for me at the kitchen table. The tension is already straining our relationship, and I'm terrified of resenting them when all they're really trying to do is help.

I smooth my hands over my outfit and give myself a final once-over in the mirror, silently reminding myself I'm not that kid anymore. Then I grab my bag, head out the door, and slide behind the wheel of Rhonda.

Aside from the years I was gone for school, I've never lived outside Northmeadow. As I drive through town, I realize absolutely nothing has changed. The same mom-and-pop shops with their run-down storefronts line Main Street. There are no chain stores or restaurants. The residents fought hard to keep them out of town. It's both positive and negative. Small, local-owned businesses have kept their doors open, but just barely.

The summer months bring tourists from Finn Lake. It's that revenue most businesses rely on to get them through the rest of the year. Year-round residents who don't own a business in town work on their farms, often struggling to make ends meet. It's a stark contrast to New York City with its booming companies, crowds of people, and overabundance of money.

I make the turn into the parking lot of my old high school. It feels odd to pull into a spot designated for faculty. Resting my head against the seat, I close my eyes and take a few calming breaths.

When I graduated from high school, I was the only one in my class leaving the state for college. Heck, I was the only girl pursuing a college degree. Most were content to stay here, marry a local boy, and have his babies. Once upon a time, I planned to marry a local boy, but not until after I had a chance to experience life outside Northmeadow. See how well that worked out, Natalie? This town was once my home, and this was my dream job. I wanted to serve the youth in my community. But things have changed—I've changed.

I can't help wondering if I could've served the youth in New York City with the same satisfaction. None of that really matters, though. I'm locked in this position for the next five years. "Six years flew by in the city. These will go by just as fast." I say the words aloud, trying to convince myself they're true.

But the excitement I once felt when I imagined this moment is gone. Taking a deep breath, I turn off the ignition, grab my bag, and step out of the car. Using the side-view mirror, I straighten my black skirt and silky white blouse. Despite everything, I want to make a favorable impression.

Instinct urges me to use the student entrance, but I continue past and walk to the building's front instead.

I've never stopped and looked at the historic building that houses the school. I shield my eyes from the sun and look up at it. Four sections make up the three-story stone structure. Each floor holds four sets of four windows that sit in perfect symmetry. Drawing the eye to the center of the building are four large columns that flank the sides of the main entrance. The building is typical of classical revival architecture. Something I learned about during my time in the city.

One by one, I walk up the granite steps until I reach the main door and pull it open. It's a lot heavier than it looks. Stepping inside, I'm hit with a sense of déjà vu. The familiar school smell brings me back to my student days. It feels like I walked these halls yesterday instead of six years ago. The building is empty, except for a few custodians who appear to be freshening up the paint on some lockers while others clean up the desks. The click of my high-heeled shoes echoes in the hallway as I make my way to the main office.

"Excuse me, miss. Can I help you?" a male voice calls from behind me.

Startled, I turn around. An older and slightly rounder version of the Mr. Meadows I remember from my high school days stands with his hands on his hips, wearing track shorts, a tank top, and a baseball cap. Guess I'm a little overdressed.

"I was just heading to your office." I walk back toward him.

"And you are?"

"Natalie Clarke."

Do I have the wrong day for our appointment?

His forehead wrinkles, and his eyes narrow as he takes in my appearance. "I didn't recognize you."

"I guess it has been a few years."

An awkward silence lingers between us. The warm feelings I initially had when I walked in have disappeared, replaced with an icy unwelcomeness. Ms. Campbell told me she was getting a lot of pushback from adding a therapist to the faculty.

"Your office is this way. Follow me." He turns and takes long strides down the hallway.

I do my best to keep up with him, but I fall behind. Besides being nearly a foot shorter, I also have a skirt and heels to contend with. We pass classrooms that were once a daily home for me. I peek into them, hoping to rekindle the feeling of belonging. Instead, I'm left feeling like an outsider—an intruder.

"This is your office." He waves his hand at the open door.

"You'll notice your window has been frosted. Something about maintaining privacy."

"That's perfect, thank you." I smile.

"It wasn't my doing," he says sharply. Digging into his pocket, he pulls out a key. "This belongs to you."

I reach out to take the key, which he hesitantly hands over before taking the first step into my office. The walls have recently been painted a crisp, clean, and oh-so-plain cream. The smell of fresh paint lingers in the air. Scuff marks from the many shoes that have walked in and out of the room mar the tile floor.

A standard high school-issue metal desk sits in the center of the room with a chair on each side. The wall behind the desk boasts a large window overlooking Main Street. It offers the natural light this otherwise poorly lit room needs. I'm surprised at how spacious it is. With a bit of creativity, I'll be able to transform this bare space into something special.

Mr. Meadows walks past me, heading straight toward the chair behind the desk.

"Let's go over the paperwork, shall we?" he says as he lowers himself onto the padded leather chair.

Feeling intimidated, I sit across from him in the simple wooden chair. The same as those found in the hall outside the principal's office. The cushion is worn and has long since disintegrated. I add it to my mental list of things that need to be redone. I'm unsure where to put my bag, so I hold it on my lap and fidget with the straps. It'll help keep me from biting my nails.

Mr. Meadows opens a red binder that's sitting on the desk and takes out a stack of papers. He flips through them, mumbling to himself before he glances up at me.

"Looks like your clearances have come back and are in order. Did you bring a copy of your licensure?"

I reach into my bag and pull out a folder containing my paperwork.

"Here you go."

He quickly skims the paper. "This looks like it's okay. I need your signature on a few pages, and then we'll be done." He slides a stack of papers and a pen across the desk.

Seeing no other choice, I set my bag on the floor to free my hands. I pick up the first paper and begin to read through it.

Tap. Tap. Tap.

The impatient rhythm of Mr. Meadow's pen tapping on the desk urges me to move quickly. I glance up and see Mr. Meadow looking at his watch. Sensing his impatience, I try to read as fast as possible without missing anything important. Don't bite your nails. I struggle to keep my nerves in check.

"Ms. Clarke." His voice is sharp. "These are just your standard employment papers."

"I'm sure they are, but I'd feel more comfortable reading through them before signing. I'm sure you understand."

"As long as this doesn't take too long." He looks at his watch again. "I have another appointment in ten minutes."

I nod in understanding and skim the last few pages, barely reading them. The final paper restates the requirement of remaining employed by the Northmeadow School District for five years, at which time a new contract may be negotiated. Terminating employment before five years will result in immediate repayment of all scholarship money. With trembling hands, I grab the pen and sign my name.

"Very well then," Mr. Meadows says as he grabs the papers and taps them on the desk. "Your schedule and employee handbook are in here." He points to the red binder before making his way to the door.

I follow after him. "Am I able to redecorate the office?"

He spins around with a less-than-amused look on his face. "Isn't it to your liking?"

"It's fine, but it's kinda plain. I was hoping to make it a bit more inviting. Maybe add some artwork to the walls, an area rug, and bean bag seating. To help the kids feel more comfortable."

He crosses his arms in front of him and tilts his head as if trying to figure me out. Ticking from the clock, usually unheard, echoes in the absence of other noise.

"You can do as you see fit." He lowers his hands and begins to walk away, pausing to add, "But it will need to come out of your pocket. We don't supply a *decorating* budget."

"I understand. Thank you." It feels as though I've won a small victory.

He shakes his head and mutters as he walks down the hall. I close the door and lean against it. It doesn't surprise me that Mr. Meadows isn't thrilled with my being added to his faculty. He made that known the day I was offered the scholarship.

It was one week before my high school graduation. Our community was still suffering the devastating effects of both Evan and Michael's suicide the year before. The world was changing, and Northmeadow wasn't immune to those changes. Our young people were experiencing problems the older generations either didn't face or refused to acknowledge, and it was taking its toll.

After losing my brother, I decided I didn't want to work at Dad's pharmacy like we'd planned. Instead, I wanted to pursue psychology with the hopes of working with young people and preventing another tragedy. My sights were set on New York University. In my opinion, it would give me a chance to experience life outside of Northmeadow while getting a solid education. After graduating, I would return, marry Tommy, and work with our young people.

I applied and was accepted. Even though I was eligible for financial aid, it wasn't enough to cover the expenses. My parents weren't supportive of my going away to school and refused to help. I'd just about given up on my dreams until I was summoned to a meeting in the principal's office. When I arrived, Mr. Meadows was there along with Ms. Campbell, the district superintendent. I sat across from them, not knowing the importance of this meeting for my future.

"How are you today, Natalie?" Ms. Campbell asks.

"Today's a pretty good day."

"I'm glad to hear that." She smiles. "I'm sure you're wondering why I've asked you here.

"Yes, I am."

After Michael died, Ms. Campbell stepped in as a sort of counselor. She allowed me to talk about Michael and Evan without fear of judgment for my feelings—feelings I could not express at home. I had the best childhood, filled with so many happy memories. The four of us were very close. My parents were never wealthy, but they made sure Michael and I never wanted for anything. My parents' relationship was one I always looked up to. They demonstrated love and respect for each other, but they turned ice-cold after Michael died.

I was lost without my brother, yet I was forbidden to discuss anything about him at home. My parents took his pictures down and even emptied his room. It was like he never existed. I don't know how I would have gotten through that first year without Ms. Campbell's help.

During our meeting, Ms. Campbell told me she'd heard whispers from the student body about other issues, including violence and recreational drug usage. Other young people were struggling with issues related to their sexual orientation—something our conservative religious town found abhorrent.

Our conversation was raw and honest, and has remained with me through the years.

"Natalie, as you're all too aware, our young people are struggling," Ms. Campbell says.

"Yes." I look down, trying to hold back the tears threatening to fall.

"Your generation is dealing with issues most of us." She gestures between Mr. Meadows and herself. "Just don't understand."

Mr. Meadows sits back in his chair and crosses his arms. I sense a growing tension between the two adults in the room.

"Would you be willing to share with Mr. Meadows why you're so passionate about pursuing higher education?"

I'm uneasy sharing something so personal with him, but Ms. Campbell gives me an encouraging nod to ease my hesitation.

"I want to study to become a therapist. I don't want anyone else to go through what Michael and Evan did." I pause and swallow over the growing lump in my throat. "I don't want anyone else's family to lose someone they love. I don't share the beliefs of my family or community. I believe the heart can't help who it loves."

Mr. Meadows mumbles under his breath, earning a disapproving glance from Ms. Campbell.

Ms. Campbell sits forward on her chair. "Natalie, if we don't do something, we will lose more youth to tragedies I believe are avoidable."

Mr. Meadows shifts, clearly uncomfortable with the conversation.

Ms. Campbell turns her attention to him. "Jacob, will you excuse us for a few minutes?"

A vein pulses in Mr. Meadow's neck, the only outward sign of his anger. Finally, he walks out of his office, closing the door a little too forcefully.

"Natalie, I know you applied and were accepted to New York University."

"Yes, ma'am."

"Have you replied to your acceptance letter yet?"

"Not yet. But I'm going to have to decline."

"The school board has talked and agreed. We're prepared to make you a generous offer." Her face lights up with excitement. "We're offering a scholarship to cover the full cost of your education in exchange for your agreement to work in the district for five years."

It took a few minutes for her words to sink in fully. "You'll pay for everything?" I ask, still not believing what I think I heard.

"Yes. Tuition, books, room, and board." She pulls a paper from a folder I hadn't noticed lying on the desk. "It's all right here. If you agree, you only need to sign the contract." She hands me the paper.

At the time, I had every intention of living in Northmeadow

and marrying Tommy. However, he'd be away at school on a football scholarship, and now I'd also have the opportunity to get my degree. It was a dream come true. Since I was eighteen, I didn't need my parents' permission and didn't think twice. I signed the contract right then and there.

Ms. Campbell has had a significant impact on my life. We've kept in touch over the years. She's the only person, aside from Lana, who knows everything that happened with Tommy. I've told her about Alex, although I've been hesitant to tell her everything. She knows I've been secretly seeing Alex all summer, something neither Alex nor Ms. Campbell is thrilled about. They both think I need to tell my parents the truth. Of course, that's much easier said than done. They don't have to live with them.

I grab my bag off the floor and dig through it to find my cell phone. After taking pictures of my office, I send the images and a text to Lana.

Me: Before pictures. Drab and boring, a typical US high school office.

Lana: Looks similar to my school in St. Petersburg. Please tell me you can change it?

Me: Online shopping is calling my name, LOL. How's it going with the job hunt?

Lana: I have another interview today. Fingers crossed, I get hired soon. Guess what.

Me: What?

Lana: I was going to call you tonight, but I can't wait. Brandon asked me to move in, and I said yes.

Me: OMG! I'm so happy for you.

Although I'm happy for my friend, I'm sad for myself. If I'd stayed in the city, would that be Alex and me?

Lana: How's everything there?

It's awful. My parents are smothering me. My ex-boyfriend won't leave me alone, and the man I love is halfway across the country.

Me: Everything's good. Did you get the invitation to the birthday party my parents are throwing for me?

Lana: I did, but we won't be able to make it.

Me: I knew it was a long shot. It was supposed to be a surprise party, but Dad spilled the beans.

Lana: I wish we could fly in. I'm sorry. Is Alex going to be there?

Me: I didn't invite him. They still don't know I'm seeing him, remember?

Lana: Oh yeah. I'm about to walk into an interview. I'll call you tonight, and you can try to explain why you won't tell them.

Me: Good luck.

I sink into the chair behind my desk. It's much more comfortable than the other one, and I set my phone down. The red binder draws my attention.

Opening the cover, I flip through the pages, beginning to familiarize myself with policy and procedure. When I look at my phone, I see that two hours have passed. After I mark my page, I close the binder and slide it into my bag.

With a final look around the room, I lock up and head home to do some shopping.

Natalie

THE MINUTE I WALK THROUGH THE DOOR, I KICK OFF my heels and throw my bag on the couch. Moments like this, when both my parents are working, and I have the house to myself, remind me how much I miss living on my own. Another thing I miss—coffee shops. If I want an afternoon pick-me-up, it's either the diner or homebrewed.

Opening the cupboard, I pull out a paper filter and push it into the plastic receptacle of my parents' ancient Mr. Coffee machine. After spooning in the grounds, I turn it on and wait. "Maybe I'll get them a Keurig for Christmas," I say aloud. "As if they'd ever use it."

My parents prefer the tried-and-true way of doing things. They finally retired the stainless-steel stovetop percolator just before I left for college. But of course, they didn't throw it away. Now it sits proudly on the windowsill above the sink, reimagined as a vase for fresh-picked flowers. In their world, nothing really leaves the house. It just gets promoted to a new job.

While the aroma of coffee fills the kitchen, I busy myself putting away the dishes Mom left on the plastic drying rack. I always hated handwashing. It was such a treat when Lana and I got our apartment, and I finally had a dishwasher. Mental note—when apartment shopping, make sure there's a dishwasher.

Ten minutes later, the coffee is finally ready. I pluck my favorite mug off the accordion rack under the cupboards and pour the liquid gold. Add a little sugar and creamer, and the coffee is perfect. Then, I grab my things and go upstairs. Setting everything down on my desk, I strip off my work clothes, exchanging them for shorts and a tank top that exposes my now-toned abdomen.

Several months ago, Lana and I decided to use the gym that NYU provides for its students. We started getting up early to work out before class. The physical changes have helped me view my body more positively.

Since being home, I haven't exercised at all. I'll have to get back to it, or I won't be wearing clothes like this for long.

The unpacked boxes in the corner of the room draw my attention. I hoped to have my own place by now, but that hasn't worked out as planned. I've saved enough money to pay for a few months' rent. Unlike in Manhattan, where there's always real estate available, I haven't been able to find an apartment in North-meadow. But I'm not giving up. Something has to open up, eventually.

Meanwhile, somewhere in this mess are books and decorations I want for my office. The goal for this afternoon is to go through the boxes and find everything.

As I stare at the task ahead, I realize I should've done a better job when I packed. At the time, my only thought was to get everything in a box and shipped. I feel overwhelmed looking at the pile of twenty boxes.

Nothing's going to get done just standing here. So, I grab the nearest box and start rummaging through it. As I do, I separate things into two piles—one for my office and the second to be repacked. I'm retaping the boxes when my phone chimes. Alex hasn't texted all day, and I'm anxious to talk to him, so I grab the phone quickly.

Unknown: I'm picking you up at five.
Me: I think you have the wrong number.
Unknown: Is this Natalie?
Me: Yes
Unknown: Then I have the right number.
Me: Who is this?
Unknown: It's me.
Me: I'm gonna need a little more to go on than *me.*
Unknown: Tommy

I roll my eyes. Oh my God, go away already.

Me: How did you get my number?
Tommy: Your mom.

She and I will need to talk about not giving out my phone number.

Me: I'm not going out with you tonight.
Tommy: Yes, you are. Be ready by five.
Me: No.
Tommy: I've already talked to your parents. We're going out tonight.

Already talked to my parents. Is he for real?

Me: I'm not in grade school. You can't ask my parents for a play date with me.
Tommy: Already did. You'd better be ready.
Me: I'm not going out with you.
Tommy: See you soon.

I drop my head in my hands. How do I get rid of him? He obviously doesn't understand that we're over.

Done.

Never getting back together.

I decide not to waste all afternoon arguing with him through texts. I have more important stuff to do. I'll deal with him if he shows up. Until then, I have money to spend and shopping to do.

The sound of gravel crunching in the driveway grabs my attention. Checking my phone, I see it's four fifty-five. Wow, I didn't realize I was shopping for that long. Curious to see who it is, I pad across the worn-out carpet on my bedroom floor and pull aside the ruffled purple curtains to look outside.

Tommy's beat-up red Chevy pickup is in front of my house. I race across my room and slam the door. This is ending right now. I take the steps two at a time, intending to stop Tommy before he makes it onto the porch. He can turn that truck right back around because I'm not going anywhere with him.

What I can't see from my room becomes apparent when I open the front door. Tommy's helping my mom out of the passenger seat. Mom looks up. The smile fades from her face when she sees me.

"You aren't going out dressed like that?"

"I'm not going out."

"You and Tommy have a date." She smiles at him.

Tommy leans against the rusty old truck. He wears a smug look as he listens to our exchange.

"Tommy told you wrong." I cross my arms.

"Excuse us a minute, dear," Mom says to Tommy before she hurries up the steps and grabs my arm, forcing me to follow her into the house. "Stop acting like an ungrateful child. That young man out there is crazy about you."

Sure that I've misunderstood her because we've already gone over this at least a hundred times, I ask,

"Excuse me?"

"You don't live in the big city anymore," my mother says, her voice raised. She narrows her eyes. "You need to get off whatever high horse you climbed on while you were off playing house." She uses air quotes to emphasize *playing house*. "You're back home, where you belong, and you need to start acting like it. Now, march upstairs and put on something presentable. You will not keep him waiting."

My mouth hangs open. I'm speechless. I've only been home for a few months, and already I find myself fighting the same battles I'd gone through in my teenage years.

Mom was always strict, but after Michael died, her actions

became suffocating. She refused to acknowledge that I was an adult and could make my own decisions.

"Now, Natalie." She crosses her arms and taps her foot on the hardwood floor.

In moments like this, I wish I were more like Lana—unyielding, confident enough to stand my ground, especially with my parents. It was easier in the city, with Alex at my side, bolstering me in ways I didn't even realize until now. But here, it's just me and them. And I'm all they have left.

My greatest weakness has always been this. My inability to bear disappointing them, even when it costs me pieces of myself. So, instead of screaming or fighting back, I do what I've always done. I fold. I slip seamlessly back into the role of the dutiful daughter.

Climbing the stairs to my childhood bedroom, I can feel the independence I fought so hard to claim draining out of me. The self-confidence I built in the city fades with every step, and the worst part is knowing I'm powerless to stop it.

Tommy

I FOLLOW CHARLOTTE CLARKE'S GAZE TO HER FRONT porch, where Natalie stands in tiny denim shorts and a cutoff shirt. Her body is smoking hot and on display, especially when she crosses her arms, pushing her tits up higher. Even the daggers she shoots my way do nothing to dispel the arousal in my jeans. Tonight's going to be more fun than I anticipated.

Charlotte and Natalie argue while I lean against my truck, amused by the scene. I know I have her parents on my side, which means Natalie will come around. She'd never defy her parents.

While I wait for Natalie to come back out, my hands shake, and sweat forms on my forehead. Yesterday, I saw the doctor and convinced him I'm still suffering. He's a pain in the ass, nagging me to try physical therapy and acupuncture. This time, I could use living in Northmeadow and its lack of resources as an excuse, with the promise I'd look outside of town for something. I'll spout whatever shit he wants to hear to get a new prescription.

I grab my Oxy bottle and swallow two pills, craving the high they give me. I need to feel good tonight because I'm taking Natalie to the county fair. We used to go every year. I'm sure this will remind Natalie how much she loves me, and if I'm right—

and I know I'm right—before the night's over, I'll be buried balls deep between her legs, just like old times.

Natalie doesn't keep me waiting long. Within a few minutes, she's walking down the porch steps in the same denim shorts, but she now wears a black t-shirt instead of her half-shirt. I open the door and offer my hand to help her into my truck. My little wildcat refuses my help and climbs in on her own. Smiling, I close the door behind her, walk around to the driver's side, and get in.

The fair hasn't changed. Food vendors are set up, creating a virtual maze offering anything fried and on a stick. Natalie's favorite was always the stuffed pretzel stand.

"Can I have two steak and cheese stuffed pretzels?" I ask the kid behind the window. He takes my money and hands me paper-wrapped food.

"Here ya go," I say and proudly hand one to Natalie.

"Thanks," she answers quietly and takes the offered food.

"We'll sit over here and eat." I lead her to an empty table.

She nibbles at the pretzel while staring off into the crowd.

"It must be nice to be home," I say, trying to get her attention. She's acting distant, and I don't know why.

"It's great," she mumbles.

"I'm glad you're back," I say, placing my hand on her thigh.

She pulls her leg away. "Tommy, don't."

"You never had a problem with me touching you before."

"You lost that right when you started screwing my best friend." She stands up, throwing away her uneaten food. "I've moved on. I'm seeing someone else."

"Excuse me?" Charlotte didn't tell me this. What the hell?

"I have a boyfriend. Someone I met in the city."

I stand up, knowing I have to plan my next move carefully. It's obvious those people have poisoned her mind, but I'll fix it. I'll fix her.

"Come on." I take her hand. "Let's go ride some rides."

She tries to resist, but I leave her no choice. She's forced to follow me. We stop at the ticket booth, where I buy a few books of tickets.

"Tommy, I don't want to go on any rides," she protests.

"Loosen up. It'll be fun."

Natalie is compliant, something I've always loved about her. Anything I wanted, she always did. I'm confident tonight won't end any differently. We're riding the Ferris Wheel, and it's our turn to be stuck on top.

The entire fairground, surrounded by the mountains, is in full view, but I'm only looking at the view sitting next to me. I put my arm around Natalie and pull her close. This time, she can't resist. She's always been afraid of heights and has nowhere to go. With my other hand, I turn her face to meet mine and kiss her.

"Tommy." She pushes against my chest. "Stop."

"Be quiet. You're going to make a scene."

"If you don't stop. I'll scream."

"Relax," I say and drop my hand.

Patience, that's what I need. Patience and a few more pills. I pull the bottle out of my pocket and pop another pill, knowing it will keep my frustration to a minimum.

The sun has set, and although we're walking around, Natalie's still tense. I thought by now, she'd have calmed down and started to enjoy our date. I don't know what's going on with her. I should slip one of my pills into her drink. That'd calm her down.

It's not helping that her phone's been going off for the past hour. I can't see who it is, but I'm happy when she finally powers the damn thing off and sticks it in her back pocket. Now, she can focus on us. I pull out my bottle and swallow another pill.

"Are you in pain? Maybe we should go home?"

"I'm fine."

"Then why do you keep taking pills?" She stops walking and puts her hands on her hips.

"Leave it alone, Natalie," I say, a warning tone in my voice.

"But—"

I grab her arm and drag her to a dark area behind the livestock building, caging her against the brick wall. I'm thankful there's no one around because my temper has reached the boiling point.

"When I say leave it alone." I get up in her face. "I mean it. Leave it alone. Got it?"

She nods. Something about the fearful look in her eyes turns me on. I kick her legs apart and push my erection against her.

"See what you do to me?"

"Please just take me home, Tommy," she whispers. "It's been a long day, and I'm tired."

"Let me kiss you." I press my body harder against hers.

"No." She tries to turn her head.

"Wrong answer, sweetheart." I lean in and take what I want. My tongue forces its way into her mouth, deepening the kiss. She squirms around, trying to get out of my hold. "Don't fight me. You know you want this." I lean in to kiss her again when a light shines on us. I back up to see a security guard holding a flashlight.

"What's going on back here?" he asks.

"Sorry, man," I say, pulling Natalie close. "My girl just came back from school, and well, I guess I got a little carried away."

"Is that true, miss?" he asks Natalie.

I squeeze her waist tight in a warning.

"Yes, sir," she says sweetly. "This is really embarrassing. We're leaving now. I'm sorry."

"Go on. Get out of here, you two," he says and laughs.

I knew she wouldn't rat me out. It's the proof I needed that she's still mine.

She'll soon forget the city and the people in it. I'll have her back in my bed in no time at all.

Alex

I'VE SPENT THE ENTIRE DAY IN MY OFFICE SETTING UP the framework for Nicholai's account. I don't have all the specifics yet, but I know enough of the basics to get started. To my employees, it'll look the same as any other ad campaign.

In reality, it's a complicated structure. Everything needs to be encrypted to ensure the underground aspects of Nicholai's dealings remain hidden. I'm the only one here who has access to the data.

I check my phone and see Natalie still hasn't returned any of my texts. She met her new boss earlier and was supposed to tell me how it went, but I haven't heard from her all day. I text Viktor and ask him to get the car ready before slipping my phone into my pocket.

After giving the office a final once over, I lock up and head outside, where Viktor's leaning against my car, waiting. When he sees me approach, he moves to open the door, but I wave him off. I'm grateful for his service, but my pensive mood makes me want to seek solitude.

After sliding into the car, I pull my phone from my pocket. Still nothing. This isn't like her. She usually has her phone on and responds right away. I refresh the screen like a schoolboy desperate to hear from his crush.

Fifteen minutes later, my message is finally read. The three dots dance on the screen, letting me know she's typing.

Natalie: Not a good time. I'll call you tomorrow.

Not a good time? What's that about?

Me: Is everything okay?

Another half-hour passes, and my text isn't read. I'm pacing back and forth in my apartment. It's late, and I'm concerned. No longer willing to wait, I pull up Natalie's number and hit the call button. The phone rings and rings before going to voicemail. I leave a message.

Natalie. What's going on? Is everything okay? Call me. I need to hear your voice.

And then I wait. Nine o'clock comes and goes with no call. My phone doesn't ring until the following morning. Natalie's uneasy during our conversation. Something about it doesn't sit right with me.

"My texts went unanswered all night. Where were you?"

"I was at the fair with some friends," she says hesitantly. "The reception was terrible."

"I see."

"I turned my phone off, and I guess I forgot to turn it on until this morning."

"I'm on my way out for a run. I'll call you later." My tone is cold, and I don't wait for her to say goodbye before disconnecting the call.

I understand Natalie's struggling to fit back in with her town while balancing our relationship.

I've never lived in a small town and feel like my hands are tied, especially when she won't talk to me. When she won't tell me everything. I don't want to fight with her and make things worse. If Natalie's not going to tell me, I'll try Svetlana. Maybe she knows something.

Me: Have you heard from Natalie?

Lana: Not since yesterday afternoon. Why?

Me: She blew me off last night. We just talked, but something's off.

The message shows it's read right away, but her response takes longer than I think it should. I pace back and forth in my kitchen, waiting for a reply. I hold off going for my run as long as possible, but Lana isn't returning my text. I need to go now to run off some of this frustration. Something's going on, and I intend to get to the bottom of it.

I turn the music app on and put my earbuds in. Then, after securing the phone in my back pocket, I ride the elevator down and set off on my run. After I'm a few miles in, I get a text notification. I stop running and pull my phone out.

Lana: She told me everything was okay yesterday, but I get the feeling she's having a hard time readjusting to being home. She isn't saying much, though.

Me: I have that feeling, too. I wish there were something I could do to make it better.

Lana: I'm assuming she didn't mention anything about her birthday party next weekend?

Of course, she didn't tell me. She's still keeping us a secret.

Me: Birthday party?

Lana: I'll take that as a no.

Me: I know it's her birthday Saturday. But she didn't mention a party.

We've only been together for a few months. Most of that time, it was strictly a contractual relationship. I thought she understood I was serious about making us work.

Knowing her past and the damage her ex did by cheating on her, I anticipated she'd struggle with our physical distance. Reluctantly, I agreed with her about keeping us a secret at least until she felt more secure.

I've flown in twice to visit her. We stayed a few hours away from where she lives. I thought things were going well, and we were making progress, but she's still holding off on telling her parents about us. I'm done being patient. If we have a future, we can't be a secret anymore.

I finish my run and take a quick shower before calling Svetlana. She gives me the information about the party and her word that she won't tell Natalie about my plans.

After our call, I make the necessary arrangements for a flight to Missouri on Saturday morning.

My little sub will be getting a surprise visit. It's time to discuss what the path forward will look like.

Natalie

Between what happened with Tommy at the fair and Alex's distant behavior, my nerves have been on edge all week. Today I have my birthday party. It was supposed to be a small get-together, but it turns out my mother has invited half the town.

It's already mid-morning, and I still haven't been able to reach Alex. I'm supposed to call him every morning to check in, but all my calls go straight to voicemail. I wonder where he is? I've been dragging my feet getting ready, hoping to speak to Alex before we have to leave, but I'm running out of time.

Going through my closet, I settle on a pale-yellow sundress. I slide it on before fixing my hair. It's going to be hot today, so I grab a hair tie and pull my hair into a ponytail.

Knowing there probably won't be cell service at the lake, I dial Alex's number one last time. The call goes straight to voicemail again. I've already left two messages, and as much as I want to hear his voice, I can't bring myself to leave a third. I don't want to come across as desperate or clingy, like I'm asking for more than he's willing to give.

I collapse onto my bed as a feeling of dread washes over me. Have I messed everything up by not telling him about Tommy? Maybe this is his way of telling me it's over between us? I knew this wouldn't work. Distance makes it too easy for people to grow apart. And this time, I have no one to blame but myself.

"Natalie, we're ready to go," Dad calls from downstairs.

"Be right down."

Alex said he wants this with me, but he's used to far more than I can ever offer him. Dragging myself off my bed, I stand in front of the mirror.

You're nothing but a small-town girl. You'll never be anything more. You had your fun in the city, but now you're home, back where you belong.

I don't want my parents to be right about Alex, but what if they are? Maybe today needs to be the day I stop resisting and start reacclimating myself into Northmeadow? Grabbing my phone, I slide it into the pocket of my dress before I leave the safety of my room. I make it down the steps just in time to hear my mother call for me from the kitchen.

"Natalie, come give me a hand, dear."

I enter the kitchen and gasp. "Did you buy everything in the store?" I laugh.

"I want the party to be perfect." Mom's eyes gleam with excitement. "Everyone's so happy you're home. They can't wait to see you."

It's been a long time since I've seen her excited about anything. She may be overbearing, but she has put a lot of work into this party. For her sake, I'll try to put my issues aside and share in her joy.

The half-hour drive to Finn Lake is a familiar one. Although we weren't rich, my parents did better financially than many others in Northmeadow. They gave Michael and me a good childhood, including a few weeks each summer spent in a rental cottage at the lake.

Every year, I'd beg my parents to stay longer. Being by the water was magical. But each time, they'd pat me on the head and tell me we had a fine home. Then we'd pack up, leave the water behind, and go back home.

Then, like with everything else, after Michael died, we stopped going.

Before I realize it, Dad turns the car onto Lakeshore Drive, and the pavilion comes into view. It's always been a popular spot for summer parties, even though it's nothing more than a concrete pad and a few wooden posts that hold up a metal roof.

"Who did all this?" I ask when I see the decorations.

"Your mom and Delia Laurel came down early this morning," Dad says.

It doesn't surprise me that Tommy's Aunt Delia had something to do with it. She and Mom have always been close.

"It looks great, Mom."

"Thank you, dear," Mom says and smiles proudly.

She's outdone herself, even if it looks more like a party for a ten-year-old. Purple streamers are draped from each post. A Happy Birthday banner with pastel flowers hangs over the entranceway and waves in the gentle breeze. Purple and pink helium balloons are anchored to each picnic table. Guests are already gathering. They smile as they greet each other, the ease of familiarity written in their actions.

"I told you we should have gotten here earlier, Stanley," Mom scolds Dad.

"Yes, dear," Dad says, appeasing her.

He silently exits the car and begins to unload the food.

I jump out of the backseat. "Let me give you a hand, Dad."

"No, you don't," Mom says as she climbs out of the car. "This is your party. Go, say hi to your friends." She gives me a gentle nudge forward.

I cautiously approach the pavilion, trying to stay hidden

behind some trees as I search the sea of faces. People I once knew and who once knew me.

"Well, look who's back," a female voice says from behind me.

My stomach turns at the sound. It's a voice I'll never forget and hoped never to hear again. Slowly, I turn and take in the tall, curvy blonde standing behind me, her hands on her hips.

"Finally realized Northmeadow is where you belong?" she asks mockingly.

"Why are you here, Ashlynn?"

"Your mother invited me." She walks past me, hitting my shoulder on her way. "Didn't think we'd ever see you back again."

Ashlynn and I were inseparable growing up, which didn't surprise anyone since our mothers were best friends. They grew up together, got married within weeks of each other, and were pregnant at the same time. Everyone just assumed we'd follow in their footsteps.

When we were thirteen, Ashlynn's mom died in a car accident. After that, her father struggled with depression and alcoholism. Mom stepped in and filled her best friend's shoes, helping raise Ashlynn through her teen years. My mother loves her like a daughter. I never had the heart to tell her what happened between Ashlynn, Tommy, and me.

"I guess you thought wrong." I attempt to keep a bored tone in my voice while I look over her shoulder for someone, anyone else I recognize—anything to get away from her.

"Don't worry. Your *boyfriend* will be along shortly."

"My boyfriend?" She can't possibly know about Alex.

"Don't act so coy, Natalie." She cocks her hip to the side and places her hand on it.

Then it dawns on me who she's referring to. Seriously, is everyone in this town delusional?

"If you're referring to Tommy, he and I ended a long time ago. I'm sure you remember the circumstances." Just thinking about that night, about their betrayal, makes me feel sick.

"Somebody had to be there for him after you walked away."

"I guess if you like being sloppy seconds, he's all yours," I snap back.

Before Ashlynn can respond, Mom walks up carrying a box filled with party favors, interrupting our conversation.

"I see you found Natalie."

"Yes, I did, Mrs. Clarke," Ashlynn replies in a sickeningly sweet voice.

"It's so nice to see my two girls together again. I'm sure you'll pick up right where you left off." Mom places a kiss on Ashlynn's cheek. "That's the beauty of friendship," she says and walks away.

"Let me give you a hand with those." I move quickly to catch up with her.

I refuse to play Ashlynn's petty games.

Despite my initial reservations, I'm having fun getting reacquainted with old friends. The only thing that could make today better would be having Alex by my side. Would he get along with these people? Would they like him? The lives my friends here lead are so different from my friends' lives in the city.

Even though I shouldn't be, I'm shocked to see that most of my old girlfriends are married and either already have children, are currently pregnant, or both.

While holding one of their infants, a beautiful baby girl, I can't stop my mind from wandering. If I'd never left, would Tommy and I be married with our own baby? I look up and spot Tommy watching me from across the pavilion. When his eyes meet mine, I see a flash of sadness and quickly break eye contact.

Did he share the same thought, or is he finally accepting we're over? When I look up again, the sadness is gone, replaced with something dark and unfathomable. It causes the hairs on my neck to stand on end. I pass the baby back to her mother just as Reverend Miller and his wife, Hannah, approach.

Much to Mom's dismay, I stopped going to church when I moved to NYC. I was sick of the gossip and hypocritical attitudes I'd witnessed growing up in the church. Organized religion no longer holds any appeal to me. I don't share the same beliefs as my parents. Looking back, I realize I never did. So far, I've gotten a pass on not attending church, but I think my time is about to expire.

"Natalie, it's so good to have you home." Hannah reaches out and hugs me.

I've always liked her. She's a genuinely kind woman who manages to steer clear of the gossip and judgments the people in this town are so good at dishing out. I still don't understand what she sees in her uptight, fire-and-brimstone husband.

"Thank you. It's good to be home." That's the answer everyone expects, so that's the one I give. It's easier that way.

"We haven't seen you at Sunday service," Reverend Miller says, a look of disapproval permanently inscribed across his stern face.

Reverend Miller placed me on the spot, and I'm unsure how to respond to him. My hands fidget at my sides, and I desperately struggle not to bite my nails—to follow my Dominant's rule.

Hannah puts her hand on her husband's shoulder. "Dear, she's only been home a few months. I'm sure she's still trying to get settled in." She offers me a kind smile.

"Mhm." Reverend Miller nods. "Tomorrow's Sunday. I take it you're settled in now and can attend service?"

"I'll do my best," I reply quietly.

The wind blows, and a familiar scent of citrus and sandalwood permeates the air. "Excuse me, please." I quickly walk away, searching for the source of the fragrance.

I look around but drop my shoulders. Don't be foolish, Natalie. He's not here. I take a few tentative steps before movement outside the pavilion catches my eye.

Standing up against a large River Birch Tree with his hands in his pockets is Alex. Not trusting my eyes, I slowly begin to walk toward the figure. As I get closer, my heart rate speeds up. The realization hits me. He's really here.

He takes his hands from his pockets and opens his arms to me. Without thinking, I run into them. My head settles on his chest as I savor the feeling of his arms wrapped tightly around me. After a few minutes, I pull back and look at him.

"How? Why?"

"Happy Birthday, baby girl." He leans in and kisses me.

"How did you know?" I ask, then answer my question at the same time as Alex.

"Lana."

We share a laugh. Then, his brows draw together, and his mouth tenses. "We have some things we need to talk about."

I drop my gaze and kick my sandaled foot in the loose dirt. He places his finger under my chin, returning my gaze to him. "Don't avert your eyes, Natalie. Talk to me."

"Well, well. Who do we have here?"

My body stiffens at the sound of Tommy's voice. I move out of Alex's embrace and spin around, ready to tell him to get lost. But Alex is already stepping forward, his hand extended.

"I'm Alexander Montgomery, and you are?"

"Thomas Moore, Natalie's boyfriend," he replies, keeping his arms crossed tightly in front of his body.

Alex drops his hand and looks between Tommy and me. The look in his eyes is a mix of hurt and confusion.

I ball my hands into fists at my sides, willing myself not to explode and cause a scene.

"For the millionth time, you are *not* my boyfriend," I snap.

"Very true, sweetheart." Tommy reaches out and grabs my arm, pulling me to his side. His grip is tight and will leave a bruise. "After all this time, we're so much more than that, aren't we?"

Alex's gaze turns cold. "Take your hands off her."

"Or what, city boy?" Tommy puffs up his chest.

I twist my arm from Tommy's grasp. "Tommy, knock it off." I move to Alex and place my hands on his chest. "Can we go somewhere and talk?"

"I think that would be a good idea," he says, not breaking eye contact with Tommy.

The two men stare each other down for what feels like an eternity before Tommy drops his shoulders and takes a step back. "I'll be waiting for you, *sweetheart.*"

Ignoring him, I thread my fingers with Alex's and lead him away from the pavilion and my guests, who've stopped what they're doing to watch this scene.

"Natalie," Mom yells from behind me. "Come back here."

I glance over my shoulder. "I'll be back in a bit."

"Let her go, Charlotte," Dad says, taking Mom by the arm and leading her away. I'm grateful for his intervention.

Alex and I walk silently along the graveled path that winds its way around the lake. Anger rolls off him in waves. I stop when we come to a clearing with a bench overlooking the lake.

"Want to sit here?"

"Yes." His answer is cold and clipped.

I've sat on this bench many times. It's a favorite place for me, tucked far enough away from the swimming areas and houses to give the illusion of being isolated, far from everything and everyone. The view of the lake with the backdrop of the Ozark Mountains is breathtaking. A slight breeze causes the water to lap gently against the rocky shore. The sound has always been calming for me. Right now, I hope it's equally calming for Alex.

After sitting for a few minutes, both of us staring at the lake, Alex adjusts his position and leans back on the bench, but his gaze remains fixed ahead of him.

"Alex." I place my hand on his arm. "Tommy's not my boyfriend."

He turns his head. A storm brews in his dark blue eyes. "Care to share why he seems to think otherwise?"

I sit back and throw my hands in the air. "I don't know."

How am I supposed to explain something I don't even understand? "I've told him repeatedly that we ended a long time ago. I even told him I moved on with you. He doesn't seem to get it, and my mother keeps encouraging him to come around." I blow out a frustrated breath.

"Were you with him when I called the other night?"

"Yes. I didn't want to be, but there's no arguing with my mother. Tommy was in a bad mood, and I didn't want to cause a scene when you tried calling. I didn't know what else to do." The words spill from my mouth without a breath in between.

Alex sits up and puts his hands on my shoulders. "Natalie, you have to communicate with me. Talk to me. Trust me." His voice softens. "Without communication, this relationship won't work."

"I know."

Seeing the disappointment on his face and knowing I had caused it is too much for me. I try to turn away, but Alex doesn't let me.

"Do you trust me?" he asks.

"Yes, but—"

"You either trust me, or you don't." He searches my face for an answer.

"I trust you."

"Good. Now, tell me everything."

I begin recapping the events of the past few weeks, this time telling Alex the whole story.

"Apartment hunting has been useless," I say and slump back on the bench. "There's absolutely nothing available. So, it looks like I'm stuck at my parents' house for the foreseeable future."

"How does Tommy factor into this?"

"My parents are insisting I go out with him. When I try to refuse, they start freaking out. They say as long as I'm at home, I need to follow their rules. Which leads me back to problem number one. I can't find an apartment."

"Where did he take you the other night?"

"The fair." Then I tell him everything that happened that night.

"I'm going to kill him." The anger in Alex's voice startles me.

"I don't want any trouble, Alex. I feel like no one is listening to me and what I want."

"And what is it you want?" He pulls me onto his lap.

"I want you."

He presses his lips to mine and pulls my body against his. I can feel his hardness between my legs.

"I think it's time we tell your parents about us, don't you?

I reach between us and cup his erection. "Right now, there are other things I'd rather do."

"As much as I'd love to stay hidden in the woods with you." He stands and sets me on the ground. "I think we should get back to your party."

"I'd rather stay here with you." I hold on to him.

"We have the rest of the weekend," he says with a mischievous glint in his eyes. "Let's go."

We follow the path back to the party. I get more nervous with each step, knowing we have to face my parents and their questions about why Alex is here.

In a perfect world, they'd welcome him, and all would be well. But I know this world is far from perfect. I only hope they don't cause a scene in front of everyone.

Natalie

With my hand tightly gripping Alex's, we return to the pavilion. My eye is immediately drawn to a picnic table where my mother sits next to Delia. The two women are deep in conversation. Tommy sits across from them, listening carefully. When he spots us, he points over Mom's shoulder. She jumps up and stalks toward us, a grimace on her face.

"Natalie, may I have a word?" Mom asks, not even attempting to hide her disapproval.

I squeeze Alex's hand tighter. "Whatever you have to say, you can say in front of Alex."

"I don't think that's a good idea."

She's infuriating. The last thing I want is a big scene in front of everyone, but she doesn't seem to care.

Thankfully, Alex steps in.

"It's okay, Natalie. I see your dad over there. If you don't mind, I'll say hi to him while you talk with your mom."

I nod, letting him know I'll be okay. He kisses my forehead and, with his hands in his pockets, strolls over to where Dad and his buddies are fishing.

"What is he doing here?"

"He came to celebrate my birthday." I try to keep my voice quiet, hoping not to draw attention to our conversation.

"I don't know why you thought it would be okay to invite that man."

"That man has a name. It's Alex."

"He has no business being here." My mother responds sharply.

"Alex is here because I want him here." I pause and readjust the volume of my voice. "I don't want to argue about this in front of everyone."

"Fine. We'll continue this discussion with your father and Thomas later."

I walk away before I explode on the spot. Needing somewhere to calm down, I look around and find a small grove of trees that'll provide shade and protection from my guests' prying eyes and ears. Leaning against a tree, I look up. The sun shines brightly in the vibrant blue sky. White, puffy clouds float with a freedom I envy. The view is a necessary distraction, giving me time to re-center myself.

When I feel more in control of my emotions, I push off the tree and head toward the lake. But I notice Alex isn't there anymore.

I look around for him and freeze when I spot him on the other side of the pavilion. The anger I had just worked so hard to dispel is back with a vengeance.

Ashlynn is talking to *my* Alex, her hand on his shoulder and her head thrown back in laughter. Alex stands stiff, not returning her overly friendly behavior but not being outright rude, either.

This party has turned into a disaster of epic proportions. No longer caring if I make a scene, I quickly race across the pavilion to where they're standing and stop behind her. My hands are on my hips, ready for a fight.

"Excuse me," I snap.

The polite and quiet girl has stepped aside, allowing space for a woman on a mission—a woman who wants to rip out Ashlynn's eyeballs for even looking at Alex. Ashlynn turns with a satisfied smile on her face. She knows exactly what she's doing, and I just played right into her hands. Alex removes her hand from his shoulder, walks over to me, and wraps his arm around my waist.

"Is everything okay with your mom?"

"Yes," I say, my sights fixed on Ashlynn. "Why are you over here?"

"Natalie, relax," she says in a condescending tone. "I'm just introducing myself to your friend."

"Ashlynn was telling me stories about the two of you in high school."

"Oh, I bet she was. Did she also tell you—"

"Natalie," my father calls from across the pavilion. "Time to sing Happy Birthday."

"It was nice meeting you, Ashlynn." Alex flattens his palm on my lower back and leads me away.

"How could you talk to her?"

"Relax, baby girl. I know who and what she is. She can try all she wants, but I'm all yours." He flashes me his panty-melting smile as we make our way to where my mother and father stand, a gigantic cake on the table in front of them.

Knowing she's touched Alex makes me want to throw up, but his reassurance helps me see reason.

When we near the table, Dad lights the candles, and my guests break out in the birthday song. Closing my eyes, I make a wish and blow out the candles. My wish has already come true, and he stands next to me with a smile so bright his eyes light up. I love this man with all my heart and want to spend forever by his side.

Thankfully, Ashlynn leaves while I'm opening my presents. My mother sent her off with an extra piece of cake to bring to her father. But Tommy remains lurking along the outskirts of the pavilion. I do my best to ignore him as I introduce Alex to all my old friends.

Together we share laughs over stories from my high school days. Alex doesn't have much in common with these people, but somehow, he blends seamlessly into this part of my life. Seeing him comfortable here, I'm encouraged.

Maybe we can make this work.

With the afternoon winding down, the last guests leave, and we begin to tackle the clean-up. Despite my mother's less-than-welcoming attitude and Tommy's refusal to leave, Alex stays by my side and helps with everything.

"Looks like we got it all," Mom says. "Let's go, Natalie."

I look between her and Alex. "Alex is in town for the rest of the weekend. I'm going to stop by the house and grab some clothes. I'll be staying with him."

My mother's face turns red, and her nostrils flare. "You are an unmarried woman. You will not be spending the night with him."

"Mom, this has to stop. I'm a grown woman, not a child."

Mom stands silent. Her arms are by her side, and her body is tense with anger. Dad walks over to us with a less-than-pleased look on his face. Behind them, Tommy sits on top of a picnic table. He shakes a few pills into his hand and swallows them, silently watching the confrontation.

Alex moves to my side. "It was a wonderful party, Mr. and Mrs. Clarke." He turns to me. "Are you ready to go?"

"I am."

Leaving the stunned trio behind, Alex and I walk hand-in-hand to his car.

"If we hurry, we can get to the house and grab some stuff before they get home."

Once I'm in the safety of his car, I'm able to take a deep breath. That wasn't easy, but it went better than I anticipated. Alex pulls out of the parking lot, and I look out the window. My parents appear to be arguing, my mom's hands flailing in the air. And Tommy is shooting daggers in our direction. Dread fills my stomach.

We may have avoided a confrontation this time, but we aren't going to be able to avoid it forever.

Alex

I'M THANKFUL TO BE DRIVING NATALIE AWAY FROM that scene. It's clear her parents, especially her mother, don't want me around. Her father's been friendly with me, but I have a feeling that it won't last much longer.

Dealing with them is going to be a tricky situation. I don't want to step in and take over. Enough people are trying to do that already. Natalie must be allowed to use her voice—to make her own decisions. But if they try to silence her in front of me, I'll have no choice but to step in. I'm hoping that won't happen.

There's also Tommy. If he comes near her again, so help me, he won't live long enough to be able to regret it.

"I'm very proud of you, baby girl."

She looks at me, a sad smile on her face.

"I'm tired, Alex. I'm sick of having this same argument with them."

"We're going to figure this out. Together."

"When I didn't hear from you. I thought the worst. I thought you were done with me."

"I could never be done with you." The words *I love you* sit on the tip of my tongue, but I hesitate too long, and the moment passes.

I pull in front of her house instead of in the driveway. With our head start, we got here first. Parking on the street ensures we won't get blocked in.

"Wait here. I'm just gonna run inside and grab a bag." She gives me a quick peck on the cheek.

I watch her run up the front porch steps and disappear into the house. It's been nearly a month since I last saw her, and I miss her in more ways than one. Although we video chat and play, I miss the feeling of her body beneath mine. But before we can get to that, she has a punishment coming for lying to me earlier in the week.

After being hurt, having a long-distance relationship is hard for her. However, honesty and trust are two crucial elements that our relationship must have. Now that I'm here, I see the extreme stress she's under and realize my punishment will need to change somewhat, but I can't let her totally off the hook.

While I wait, I get out and walk around the property. Her parents have a rather large house. At one point, I'm sure it was a beautiful home, but today, it sits in a state of disrepair. Like they've given up. The paint on the white wood siding is peeling, and the black shutters are faded. Their front porch is quintessential farmhouse style and wraps around the side of the house. Near the steps and door, the boards look to have been recently replaced but were left unstained.

The flower boxes that hang from the porch rails catch my attention. I recognize the petunias. They were one of my mother's favorites.

Walking around the side of the house, I spot a rusted swing set. It must have been Natalie and her brother's. The vision of a young Natalie, her blonde pigtails flying in the air as she swings back and forth, brings a smile to my face.

I imagine our little girl with Natalie's blonde curls and my blue eyes, giggling as I push her on a swing.

Our little girl? The thought catches me off guard.

Beyond the swing set is a large vegetable garden. Between the flower boxes and vegetables, someone is clearly skilled at garden-ing. I wander back to my car, taking another look at the house. A little TLC and it could be beautiful again. My phone buzzes with a text alert.

Brandon: Just checking to make sure you made it in one piece.

Me: I did.

Brandon: How's it going?

Me: She's not happy, man. The old boyfriend is still sniffing around, and her parents are smothering her.

Brandon: Lana's told me a bit.

Me: Speaking of parents, they just pulled up. Gotta go.

Natalie steps through the front door as her parents pull into the driveway. My instincts tell me things are about to explode. I hurry to meet Natalie at the steps. Her eyes lock with mine.

Just keep looking at me, baby girl. We've got this.

Her father's the first out of the car. "Alex, son. I don't know how they do things where you come from, but girls don't just run off and spend the night with strange men around here."

"Mr. Clarke. With all due respect, Natalie's a grown woman. She's fully capable of making decisions for herself." I hold my hand out, allowing her to make the choice. She willingly threads her fingers with mine.

"Natalie, you're making a mistake," her mother pleads. "People will talk."

"Do you think I'm the only girl having sex with her boyfriend?"

"Watch your tone, young lady," her father corrects her.

"Mom, Dad, I love you both," she says, her grip tightening on my hand. "I'll see you in a few days."

I'm filled with pride, seeing the woman at my side stand up for herself. Taking the bag from her, I lead her to my waiting car, help her in, and shut the door. Her parents stand side by side, their postures stiff.

"I'll have her home Monday," I say as I put her bag in the trunk.

As if unable to watch, Stanley Clarke turns his back while his wife holds her hand over her chest. This might have been the first time Natalie has ever willingly defied them.

I don't want her relationship with her parents ruined, but they have to allow her the space to make her own choices, and right now, I'm her choice. When no other words are exchanged, I get in the car, and we drive away.

After a few minutes, I reach across the console and hold Natalie's trembling hands. With us being apart, I've missed the feel of her soft skin and how her tiny hand fits inside my grasp. She's mine to care for—to protect.

"I know that was hard for you. I'm so proud of you."

"That was the hardest thing I've ever done. I wouldn't have been able to do it without you by my side."

"I'll always be by your side."

I turn on the radio and allow the soft sounds of music to fill the car.

"Where are we staying?"

"Water's Edge Bed and Breakfast."

When I googled the Northmeadow area, I was surprised to find there were no hotel chains within a fifty-mile radius. A few motels were on the outskirts of town, and several lake houses were still available to rent for the weekend. But then I found this bed and breakfast. It looked like the perfect place for a romantic weekend getaway.

"Mrs. Wilson's place." Natalie smiles.

"You're familiar with it?"

"I've seen it from the outside, but I've never stayed here."

Perfect. A first, we'll share in her hometown.

Hopefully, it's a first of many.

After the half-hour ride back to the lake, we pull into a small gravel parking lot. The pictures online don't do this place justice. The three-story log cabin structure is ideally situated just steps from the lake.

Lining the expansive porch are wooden rocking chairs that sit under large ceiling fans, giving the place a homey, inviting feel. Just inside the foyer is the check-in desk. Behind it sits an older woman. Her white hair is pinned neatly on her head.

"Hello, ma'am. I called earlier in the week and reserved a room."

She stands up and peers at us over her silver-rimmed glasses that sit low on her nose. "Your name?"

"Alexander Montgomery."

There's no computer to check for the reservation. Instead, the woman has a spiral-bound notebook in front of her. She flips through a few pages. "There you are." Glancing up, she looks between us. "Two nights?"

"That's correct."

"Here's your key. Your room is on the third floor. It's the second door on the left," she explains and points behind us. "Unfortunately, we don't have an elevator. Enjoy your stay."

"Thank you, we will."

I smile politely and place my hand on Natalie's back as we make our way to the ornate oak staircase with a hand-carved knotty pine railing. As we walk away, I can feel the woman's eyes boring into our backs. The judgmental attitudes in this town are unbelievable. Having always lived in a bigger city, I've never experienced anything like this. I'm getting a taste of what Natalie has lived with all her life.

As we climb the two flights of steps, we admire the candid photos of couples and families enjoying the bed and breakfast and the small beach. They add to the charm of the place.

We make it to the third floor and walk down the hall to the door of our suite. I place the key in the lock, and with a click, it opens. Natalie ventures in first.

"I've always wondered what these rooms looked like."

The woodsy feel of the outside has been carefully balanced to create a warm, country atmosphere. Our room overlooks the lake with large windows and a balcony. The doors are open, allowing the evening breeze to flow through the room. The hardwood floors creak as we walk into the room. I set the bags down, and we begin exploring. A small table and chairs are situated to the side under one of the windows. They have the same carvings as the handrail on the steps. When I look more closely at the intricate design, I see the carvings mimic the mountains and lakes in the region. They are indeed a piece of art.

A four-poster canopy bed is along the side wall, with sheer curtains flowing in the breeze. A handmade quilt stretches across the bed, with various pillows arranged neatly at the top. Next to the sides of the bed are tall, mahogany-stained tables, each holding a small lamp.

The back wall is home to an expansive wood armoire, allowing guests a place to unpack. The antique furniture and country décor add to the quaint and welcoming feeling one expects from a bed and breakfast.

On the other side of the room, there's a sitting area with a vintage sofa arranged across from a large stone fireplace. That must be incredible on a chilly winter night. The table in front of the couch is constructed from a reclaimed crate. A large vase of lilacs sits on top of it. Their fragrance fills the room.

Natalie walks onto the balcony, and I follow. "When I was growing up, we spent every summer in a rental cottage." She points off to the right, where I can see the lights from a few small cottages in the tree line along the lake. "Michael and I would see couples standing on these balconies, and we'd make up stories for them. I always thought it would be romantic to stay here."

I love hearing stories about her childhood.

Natalie sighs. "Things were so different back then."

I move beside her and look at the lake illuminated by the bright moonlight.

"Are you happy here?"

"Yes. No. I don't know. Nothing is like I remembered it. Maybe I changed too much while I was away?"

"You don't have to stay. You can come back to the city with me and get a job there."

"You know I can't do that."

I push off the rail and stand in front of her. "I can get you out of the contract. I'll pay the money for the scholarship. You can come back home with me."

In my mind, this is easy. With a quick phone call, the money will be transferred, and this can be done.

"We've already been over this. You are not paying my way out of it." She laughs and shakes her head. "That would make me nothing more than your whore."

"Natalie." I reach out to her, but she steps out of my grasp.

"No, Alex."

"You are not a whore, and I will not tolerate you speaking about yourself like that."

"What else would you call it if I allow the man I'm sleeping with to pay my way through life so that I can leave town with him?"

Her words take me aback. I'd hoped I was more to her than just the man she's sleeping with.

"I'd call it a man who's in love with you and would move heaven and earth to be with you."

I walk toward her slowly, closing the gap between us.

"A man who's in love with me?"

"Yes. I'm in love with you, Natalie Clarke. And I want you to come home."

Her shoulders relax, and her eyes soften. "Alex." She walks into my arms. "I love you too."

I wrap my arms around her, needing to feel her body next to mine.

"I don't want to sound ungrateful, Sir. But I can't accept your offer. I'm sorry."

Although I hate her answer, I respect her decision.

My arms don't want to let go, but there's a matter that needs to be taken care of before we can move on. I take a step back, breaking our connection.

"We need to address the issue of your lying to me earlier this week."

She looks down. "Yes, Sir. There is that."

I walk back inside the room and over to my bag. Unzipping it, I pull out a black leather riding crop. "Come here."

Although hesitant, she enters the room and stands before me. When I point down, Natalie lowers herself to her knees. My cock comes to life, watching her willingly submit to me.

We don't need anyone watching what's about to happen, so I shut the balcony doors and draw the curtains closed. Holding my palm out, I hit the crop across it, allowing the sound of the sharp crack to fill the room.

Natalie gasps. The crop's painless across my palm, but will cause a stinging bite when used on the delicate skin of her ass. The punishment won't be too much, but it will remind her of her responsibilities in this relationship.

"Natalie, this lifestyle and commitment between us require

nothing less than complete honesty. If we can't trust one another. If I have to question your honesty," I motion between us. "This won't work." Her gaze drops to the floor. "When we entered this relationship, we discussed punishments and why they're necessary. Do you understand why you're being punished?" Another silent nod. "You need to use your voice, baby girl."

"I lied to you about where I was and who I was with."

A Dominant is only as good as his word. No matter how much I hate giving out punishments or how difficult it will be, it's my responsibility to follow through. If I don't, what's the sense of having rules?

I sit on the nearest chair and hold the crop across my lap. "Stand and strip."

Natalie gracefully gets up. Although her hands tremble, she unzips her sundress before slipping the thin straps off her shoulders. The dress slides down her body, exposing her sun-kissed skin inch by inch. My sweet, innocent sub acts like a sexy minx, even though she's stripping for punishment.

Natalie turns and looks back at me. Her emerald eyes smolder with desire as she unclasps her white lace bra, letting it fall to the ground with her dress. My eyes follow her hand as she slides it down her body to her lace thong. The fabric glides down her legs. She bends over, her ass on full display, as she picks them up from the floor. Slowly, she turns to face me again. With a mischievous smile, she tosses her panties to me.

I catch them and bring them to my nose, inhaling her sweet scent. "These are coming home with me."

She runs her tongue along her lower lip.

I take a minute to appreciate her body before calling her to me. "Come here." My voice is sure and steady, betraying none of my emotions. "Lie over my lap."

She folds her body across my legs. I run my hand over the globes of her ass before dragging my finger between her legs. She's wet—aroused.

"You will receive ten strikes."

Without warning, I raise my arm. The swoosh of the crop fills the air, followed by the sound of it cracking across first one side of her ass, then the other. She whimpers from the sting of the leather. After three more strikes, she begins to cry. I don't know how thick the walls are in these rooms.

"You need to remain quiet. Or I'll have to gag you. Do you understand?"

"Yes, Sir," she says through her tears.

I've disciplined my past subs, but never felt anything when they cried. Natalie's cry and knowing she's in pain twist my heart. I know my submissive earned her punishment, but the man in me wants to throw the crop down and gather her in my arms. The depth of my feelings is as terrifying as it is thrilling. She's obedient and doesn't make another sound as I continue, alternating sides of her ass.

After the last strike, I drop the crop and inspect her red skin. It's a beautiful sight. My skill ensures no permanent damage, but she'll remember this when she sits down tonight. I help her up, and she curls against my chest, crying softly.

"I'm sorry I lied to you, Sir. It won't happen again."

"I forgive you, baby girl." I use my thumbs to wipe the tears from her face before pulling her in for a kiss.

With her punishment over, I can concentrate on giving her pleasure. I place her gently on her feet.

"Don't move."

That command used to be difficult for her. She was always concerned with covering her nakedness, ashamed of her body. Now, my beautiful sub stands proudly before me, allowing me an unobstructed view.

"Yes, Sir."

Reaching into my bag, I pull out a wrapped gift. When she sees it, her eyes light up.

"Happy Birthday."

"May I open it now?"

"Yes."

She wastes no time ripping the shiny paper.

"Oh, Sir, it's beautiful," she says as she runs her fingers over the length of soft jute I had dyed purple for her.

"When we first negotiated our contract, you said you wanted to include rope play."

"Yes."

"You probably thought I forgot about it."

"I did." She giggles.

"Other than a few rudimentary ties to restrain a sub, I didn't know anything about Shibari," I confess.

But, over the past few months, I've been taking online instructional classes with Master Kiyoshi.

"Most were video lessons. Last month, he visited Fire and Ice. I was fortunate to be able to attend and get some hands-on learning."

"Oh," she says quietly.

"Look at me." I place my finger under her chin, raising her face. "They were private lessons between the Master and me. I'm not an expert, but I'd be honored if you'd allow me to show you what I've learned."

She stands on her tiptoes and kisses me. "I couldn't think of a better present, Sir. Thank you."

"What are your safewords?" I ask, making sure they're at the forefront of her mind. An injury can happen too easily, even with simple bondage.

"Yellow and red, Sir."

I begin at the top of one arm. Using a single column to make a diamond pattern with the rope, stopping right before her wrist. With a separate piece, I do the same on her other arm. With both arms harnessed, I stop to check in.

"Does everything feel okay?"

She closes her eyes as if doing a mental inventory. "Yes, it feels good."

I return to my bag and pull out more rope. "Give me your hands."

She raises them, and I position her palms together. Using a double-column tie, I wrap the jute around her wrists twice and loop it through the middle. It's only a beginner's harness. But with each twist of the rope, I feel Natalie's body relaxing, submitting to my control.

This experience may be my present to her, but she's gifting me something even more special—freedom over her willing body.

Having that control over her is an incredibly intimate connection I've never shared with another. When I finish tying, I check to ensure the rope is taught but not tight. Then, I check in one final time.

"Is everything still okay? Nothing's too tight?"

She tries to pull her hands apart, testing the tension. "It feels good."

Grabbing the rope, I lead her to the bed.

"Lie on your stomach."

I help her onto the bed and stretch her arms above her head. Using the rope's tail, I thread it through the thick wood spindle of the headboard and tie it off. I tug at it to ensure it won't slip. Satisfied with my work, I walk to the bottom of the bed. Natalie wiggles, trying to turn her head, but comes up short.

"Good try, baby girl." I chuckle, watching her squirm.

I'm standing just out of her line of sight while I pull my shirt over my head and toss it on the chair. It lands next to her discarded panties.

"You need to stay quiet."

"Yes, Sir."

Moving closer to the bed, I push her up on her knees, legs spread wide. Her head and chest remain on the bed with her arms stretched out before her. I stand back for a second to admire her positioning.

"You're wet for me already."

"Very."

The desire dripping from her words only encourages my already throbbing dick. But as much as I want to sink into her tight, wet center, I still have other plans. My dick will have to wait. I pull one last item out of my bag and turn it on. A vibrating hum fills the air.

"What's that?" she asks as she tries to look over her shoulder.

"Have you ever used a magic wand?"

"No, Sir."

"Well, then, I'm happy to introduce you."

I crawl onto the bed, kneel behind her, and place the wand directly on her clit. She's already aroused from the crop and gasps at the intense sensation. Her first orgasm will be quick.

"You are so fucking beautiful."

The words barely leave my mouth when she throws her head back in ecstasy. Her legs collapse from under her. I use my free arm to hold her up while I keep the wand firmly in place, not allowing her body a chance to come down from its high.

"Alex, I can't," she pants.

"Relax, you can." I turn the wand on high and continue massaging her overly sensitive center. "I want to see you come again."

Her breathing increases as her body prepares itself for a second release.

"Come for me, Natalie." Her back arches, and her body explodes with another orgasm before going limp in my arms. I quickly release her arms and untie the rest of the rope. Climbing into bed, I gather her against me and pull the blankets over our bodies.

"I love you, baby girl," I whisper to her while she experiences the freedom of subspace.

Natalie

I'VE SLIPPED FREE OF MY BODY, DRIFTING IN A SEA OF shimmering colors that swirl around me like liquid light.

Weightless.

Untethered.

Every worry dissolves, every sharp edge softens until there is only stillness.

I'm free.

Whispers reach me, tender words of love threading through the haze, wrapping around me like a lullaby. I cling to them, wanting to stay here forever in this place where nothing hurts and everything feels infinite.

But slowly, inevitably, my lashes flutter, and the world begins to pull me back.

The room is dark and quiet. My head rests on Alex's chest. His arm is around me, holding me close. It takes a few minutes for the fogginess to clear. When I'm able to push up on my elbow, I study Alex. Even in sleep, there's an inherent strength on his face.

My fingers trace the dark stubble on his jaw from not shaving before my gaze travels down his chest. I admire the defined muscles in his abdomen and the trail of dark hair, where his jeans sit low on his hips. I struggle between wanting to open his pants and give him pleasure or letting him sleep.

"Welcome back, beautiful," he whispers.

"Hi." I lean in, kissing him.

"It's nice to have you back."

"That was an incredible experience."

He rewards me with a sexy smile, and I find myself aroused again. I can't believe this man is here with me and that he loves me. As I lower my hand to unbutton his jeans, my stomach grumbles.

"I guess I'm a little hungry."

"I think we missed dinner."

I continue to reach for his button. "I'd rather have you."

He grabs my hand. "And I would love that, but first, you need to eat. I know it's late, but is there any place we can get some food?"

"What time is it?"

Alex grabs his phone off the bedside table. "It's almost eleven."

"There's a pizza place down the road that might still be open."

I pull up their page on the web browser. Alex calls and places an order.

"They were about to close, but took the order as long as I agreed to go right over to pick it up." He throws his legs over the side of the bed and gets dressed.

I lean on my elbows, allowing the sheets to slide down, earning a throaty growl. When Alex is dressed, he comes back to the bed. Leaning over, he takes a nipple into his mouth, nipping and sucking before letting go.

"I'll be back in a little bit."

I let myself fall back onto the pillow and blow out a frustrated breath. How can I be so turned on after all the orgasms he already gave me? Alex is a generous lover. He always places my needs first. When he gets back, I'll give him the pleasure he deserves.

After he leaves, I jump in the shower to clean up and then slip into one of his T-shirts. I find a switch that illuminates the balcony with soft lighting. While I wait for Alex to return, I sit on one of the wooden chairs and allow the warm breeze to dry my damp hair.

Tommy

I PULL INTO HER PARENTS' DRIVEWAY, BUT I'M TOO late. Charlotte tells me Natalie left with Alex about ten minutes ago. She isn't sure where they're staying, only that Natalie said she'll be home Monday.

That guy isn't going to stay in a cheap motel. Other than a lake house, the only place to stay is at Old Lady Wilson's, so I take a chance and drive there.

Sure enough, there's a fancy rental car parked in the lot. I pull my truck into the driveway of an empty cottage next door. The moon is bright tonight, but the trees lining the property will keep me hidden. I open the glove box, pull out my gun, and make sure it's loaded. Then, I set it on the seat next to my night vision binoculars. Reaching into my pocket, I pull out my pill bottle and swallow two pills. I'm craving their high more and more.

I don't have a plan yet, but I'll be damned if I let this guy waltz into town and take Natalie away from me. It takes a few hours before movement in the lot catches my eye. Alex gets into the car and pulls away. Once I'm sure he's gone, I grab the binoculars and tuck the gun into the waistband of my pants. A path leads through the trees to a few outbuildings that allow me to stay undetected while also looking for any sign of Natalie.

I'm about to give up hope when the lights of a third-floor balcony turn on, and Natalie walks out. Looking through my lens, I see her hair's damp, and she's wearing a man's T-shirt that hangs to her mid-thigh. From the way her nipples poke through the fabric, I know she's not wearing anything underneath, and that makes me hard as fuck. Using the camera feature in the binoculars, I snap some pictures. I'll be getting off to these tonight.

While I'm figuring out my next move, Alex pulls back into the parking lot. I move further behind the building to stay hidden and continue watching. A few minutes later, he walks onto the balcony. Natalie stands up and wraps her arms around him. Her ass peeks out from underneath the shirt. I take more pictures before going back to my truck.

I need to come up with a way to get rid of him once and for all.

When I return to our room, the balcony door is open. I set the pizza box and sodas on the table before crossing to the doorway, where I pause, watching her. Natalie sits curled up in a wooden chair, legs tucked beneath her, the night breeze tugging at her damp blonde curls. She brushes a strand from her face, eyes fixed on the darkness beyond.

My chest tightens at the sight. She's hurting. I can see it in the slope of her shoulders, but she's so much stronger than she knows. And I've only got two days to make her believe it.

"Hungry?"

The sound of my voice startles her. When her eyes reach mine, she runs her tongue across her bottom lip before untucking her legs and standing. Slowly, she walks across the spacious balcony wearing only my T-shirt.

"Starved."

The meaning behind her answer is not lost on me as she wraps her arms around my neck and kisses me. My cock stirs, but once again, it'll have to wait.

"Let's eat out here. It's a beautiful night."

Natalie steps back. "Yes, Sir. I'll go make your plate."

She gives me a sexy pout as she walks past me, swaying her

hips. I smack my little temptress on her ass, making her giggle. While she makes my plate, I lean on the balcony rail. It's easy to see how Natalie got lost in her thoughts.

Unlike the noisy city, the only sounds I hear are the chirp of crickets and the occasional croak of a toad. Replacing the artificial city lights is a beautiful night sky with thousands of twinkling stars. It's so different from my daily life, but the tranquil feeling of being immersed in nature is something I could quickly get used to. Maybe we'll have to look at getting a place by the water?

We.

That's something I never imagined I'd be saying, but I've been thinking in those terms more and more.

My mind drifts to the night I first met Natalie at Fire and Ice. I've always had experienced subs. I never thought I'd be attracted to someone new to the lifestyle. I wasn't even looking for a submissive, but then *she* came along.

Natalie's special. She's the perfect mix of naïve and curious. She has a playful side I adore. It sets her apart from others who believe being in a Dom/sub relationship has to be all rules and formality.

Quite the opposite. In addition to following the protocols of our lifestyle, I enjoy laughing and having fun with her. Unknowingly, she's challenged me to be a better Dominant and a better man. I was running from my past, from love—until her. She changed my life.

Her smile, the one that lights up her emerald eyes, melted the ice that had formed a prison around my heart.

I see a future with her. A forever with her.

Natalie interrupts my thoughts. "I have your dinner, Sir."

I sit in one of the Adirondack chairs and take the offered plate. Before she goes back in, she drags over a small white table and sets my soda can on it.

When she returns, she sits next to me, tucking her legs back under her. My shirt rides up, exposing the top of her leg, and I see she's naked underneath. Natalie looks at me and bites her lower lip, my lust reflecting in her eyes. For a brief moment, I consider putting my plate aside and fucking her on the balcony, but she needs to get some nourishment before I bring her back to bed and have my way with her.

It isn't until I take my first bite that my sub begins to eat. The mood shifts from the lightheartedness we shared just a few minutes ago to one filled with tension.

While she eats, Natalie's gaze again drifts back toward the water. When she's stressed, she tends to withdraw. I desperately want to know her every thought.

"What are you thinking about?"

She sets her plate on her lap. Her brow creases with worry.

"It's harder being back here than I thought."

"Harder, how?"

"When I first left for school, I was an insecure girl who'd lived a very sheltered life. I mindlessly did as I was told. It was all I knew. I did a lot of growing up while I was away. A lot of changing."

My heart aches to see the conflict on her face, but I stay quiet and let her finish.

"For the first time, I could live life on my terms and make my own decisions. Coming back home—" She looks down at her lap. "I feel like I'm losing myself, my voice, and I don't know how to stop it."

I can make this situation go away for her, but she won't let me. It's frustrating, but I understand why. She's an independent woman who went to New York City with a plan for her future. Unfortunately, life had other plans for her. Now, she's stuck in a situation where she's unhappy.

It would be easy to buy out her contract and bring her home with me. She could have a career there, and we'd come back here to visit. It would be a win for everyone. But if I force that on her, I'll be just like everyone else in her life. As difficult as this is, my role as her Dominant is not to take away her voice.

"What can I do to help you?"

"I don't know that there's anything you *can* do. Other than being here for me."

"I'll always be here for you." I set my plate on the table and turn to face her.

"As your Dominant and the man who loves you, I'll stand beside you. I'll fight for you. I'll support your decisions and catch you if you fall."

"Alex—"

"You're my world, baby girl. My whole universe. There's nothing you could say or do that would change my feelings for you." I reach over and cup her face in my palm. "I love you, Natalie."

At this moment, I finally understand the love my parents shared and why my father didn't regret a second of loving my mom, even though she left him too soon.

I want the same with Natalie and am willing to risk everything to get it.

Natalie

Last night, something shifted between Alex and me. Barriers we'd both erected from our pasts began crumbling. When we finally finished eating, he took me to bed and made love to me all night. We fell asleep, our bodies entwined, just before the sun rose over the horizon.

By the time we wake up, it's nearly noon. We dress in a hurry, hoping to make it in time for lunch downstairs. And we do. Mrs. Wilson is just putting the food on the table as we walk into the dining room. A young couple follows shortly after and joins us at the table. As soon as the food is served, Mrs. Wilson excuses herself, leaving us to eat.

"Do you two live around here?" Alex asks.

"Alma and I were just married two days ago. We're on our way to California."

"Miguel was offered a job there," Alma explains. "So, we're having a cross-country honeymoon." She smiles lovingly at her husband.

The couple tells us they're only twenty years old, high school sweethearts who decided to throw caution to the wind.

"We have a few weeks before my job starts, so we decided to

drive across the country. We've been stopping in small out-of-the-way towns along the way," Miguel says.

We enjoy chatting with the couple as they tell us about their experiences so far. Throughout lunch, they continually touch each other, their love sweet and uncomplicated. After they finish eating, they quickly excuse themselves from the table.

Even as they walk away, the young bride leans into her husband's embrace. They don't have a care in the world, only excitement at starting their new life together.

A pang of jealousy stabs my heart, and I find it hard to swallow my next bite of food. I had a high school sweetheart. A boy I once shared dreams with. Someone I was supposed to marry. Until he betrayed me.

Watching them walk away, I wonder what my life would look like today if things had worked out as initially planned. Tommy and I would be married right now. I'd be living the life my parents arranged for me. That thought makes me pause. Would I have resented my life because it wasn't mine, but one forced on me since childhood?

The day I found Tommy and Ashlynn together, I lost two people who'd meant the world to me. But it was also the catalyst for my change. For me to figure out who I am and what I want, I found myself.

After returning to New York, I took Michael's advice. I allowed myself to start living my life rather than just going through the motions. I stopped worrying about pleasing others or what they thought about me. Instead, I chose to do things that made me happy. For the first time, I was content with who I was.

What I thought was the worst thing that could happen to me turned out to be the start of this incredible new journey. The one that eventually led me to the man sitting next to me.

Alex places his hand over mine. "How about we grab one of the boats and spend the day on the water?"

"You know how to row a boat?"

"Nope." He flashes me his sexy grin. "Do you?"

I return his smile with one of my own. "Of course I do."

"Well then, baby girl." He stands and pulls my chair out for me. "Why don't you show me your skills?"

We walk through the yard of the bed and breakfast, stopping to admire the lush flower gardens before making our way to the beach. Families are set up on blankets, some under umbrellas that shield them from the hot sun. Children splash and play on the water's edge.

"Do you want children?"

"Someday, sure," Alex says. "What about you?"

"Yes, I'd love to be a mother."

He wraps his arm around my waist, and I imagine a time in the future when we're here playing with our children. The thought fills me with warmth. We make our way to the dock, where Alex makes the arrangements, and then we're led to a waiting rowboat. Alex takes a tentative step down and quickly grabs the dock to steady himself from rocking back and forth.

Having done this before, I'm sure of my footing and step safely into the boat. I go to sit in the rowing seat, but Alex scoots me out of the way.

"I've got this. How hard can it be?"

I gladly move to the bench in front and kick my feet up. I can't wait to see my city boy in action. The employee unties us from the dock and gives us a little push. I bite my lip, holding in my laughter as Alex struggles. We go in circles for a few minutes until he gets a feel for the oars and the boat's movement.

"I'm impressed, Mr. Montgomery. You catch on quick."

"I'm a man of many talents," he smirks. "Which way are we headed?"

I point out the direction to take. "There's a quiet cove with a sandy beach where we can relax."

Alex rows us across the lake with what looks like practiced ease. Finally, we enter the shallow water of the cove. I slip off my sandals and hop out, pulling the boat onto the sand. Alex climbs out behind me, ensuring the boat is far enough out of the water that it won't float away.

The beach is a small, secluded area surrounded by trees. It's a spot not many people know about, so I'm confident we're not likely to see any other people while we're here. Alex sits on the sand, and I lie with my head on his lap. The August sun shines warm, making the water look like crystals dancing across the surface. Small waves lap gently on the rocks. The sounds of birds chirping fill the air. For the longest time, we simply enjoy the sounds of nature.

"I told my father about you," Alex says while he plays with my hair.

"Oh?" I'm surprised by his revelation.

Alex has told me a little about his family. But, with us not being a typical couple, I didn't know if we were something Alex would talk to his dad about.

"He'd like to meet you." He stops moving his hand and looks down at me, a hopeful expression on his face.

What must he think about how we met? Has he met all of Alex's subs?

As if he's sensing my wayward thoughts, he adds. "Even though my father lives in Seattle, we're close. He knows the nature of how our relationship started."

"Have you introduced him to your other subs?"

"No. I've never brought anyone to meet my family." He looks down at me. "I told him you're more than just my submissive, that I'm in love with you."

I sit up. Alex only told me last night that he loves me. I'm still getting used to this new part of our relationship. But knowing he's already told his father his feelings makes this between us feel like so much more.

"I'd love to meet him."

Alex lets go of the breath he's holding. "I'll arrange a trip to Seattle."

"I'd like that very much."

Alex reclines back on his hands, a carefree look on his face. Then, he begins telling me about his childhood.

"I'm an only child. My parents had just about given up on having a baby. And then, surprise, I came along."

I like this youthful side of him.

"My mom had a free spirit. She believed in letting children play and explore." He stares off as he speaks. "She encouraged me to pursue anything I was interested in. That's how I got involved in martial arts and became interested in Eastern philosophy. Many of those principles I carry with me today."

I can easily see that in the way he approaches life. He's disciplined, yet I also recognize his mother's free spirit.

"Mom would've adored you."

"I wish I could've met her."

We sit in silence for a while. Alex appears lost in his memories. I recline between his legs, my back against his chest, as he wraps his arms around me. Inside, I feel warm and content. The doubts I once had about our relationship fade with each day that passes.

Alone on the beach, we continue to share stories of our childhoods. We've come from very different worlds, but somehow, fate played a role and brought us together. The sun is beginning to set, casting vibrant colors over the horizon.

"We should start heading back," Alex says as he stands and dusts the sand off his shorts. He offers me his hand, helping me up. "I don't want to get stuck on the lake in the dark."

"You aren't scared, are you? There hasn't been a monster sighting in—"

Alex scoops me up and tosses me over his shoulder. "Shall we get in the water and find out?"

I hit his back with my fists in mock protest. "Put me down." I barely manage to say between fits of laughter.

"As you command." He motions like he'll toss me into the water before gently setting me on my feet in the boat. "You should've seen your face." He laughs, and the sound is music to my ears.

I sit while Alex pushes the boat back onto the water. He climbs in, trying to be careful, but we rock back and forth anyway. Good thing we're still in shallow water, or we'd both be soaked right now.

We arrive back at the dock just as the last of the sun begins to fall below the horizon. The attendant sees us approaching and jumps up from where he's sitting. I toss the rope, and he ties us to the cleat. The boat rocks back and forth again as Alex stands. I hold my breath, hoping he doesn't end up in the lake. Instead, he easily climbs onto the dock. With a grin on his face, he offers me a hand, pulling me up next to him.

"Let's find a place to eat and celebrate not capsizing."

"Good morning, beautiful," Alex says from the table, where he's sitting with a cup of coffee in his hand, his laptop in front of him.

"You're up early." I sit up and rub the sleep from my eyes.

"I have a meeting with a client when I get back today." He sets his cup down and comes over to sit on the bed. "I was getting some last-minute details in place."

He bends over and kisses me. I wrap my arms around his neck.

"I don't want you to go."

"My offer still stands."

All it would take is one phone call. I could be on a plane going back to New York with him today. He's waiting for me to say yes, but I can't. When I accepted the scholarship, I also accepted the commitment that came with it. It's important to me that I honor my commitment. But it doesn't make saying goodbye any easier. I can't say the words, so I shake my head.

"Come shower with me." He pulls off his shirt as he walks to the bathroom.

I climb out of bed and follow him, appreciating the view of his muscular back and how his jeans sit low on his hips. A part of me still can't believe this man is mine. I'm waiting for the bubble to burst. For him to decide I'm not what he wants.

Alex turns on the hot water, and steam quickly fills the small bathroom. Turning to face me, he grabs the hem of my shirt and pulls it over my head. His knuckles graze my nipples. They harden in response.

I step into the shower, and he follows, closing the glass door behind him. Water sluices over his muscular body. He stares at me like a predator about to pounce on its prey. In one move, he lifts me, and I wrap my legs around his waist. Then his mouth is on mine, his tongue seeking entrance.

The kiss is different—desperate. He walks us until my back is against the tiled wall, then slides his hard length into me. His movements are rough, almost primal, as he tugs at my hair, forcing my head up and giving him access to my neck. My orgasm builds, and I tighten my legs around Alex's waist, encouraging him to go even deeper.

I can't hold back any longer. An orgasm rips through my body, and I ride wave after wave of intense pleasure. Alex increases the intensity of his thrusts until he comes with a deep growl in his throat.

He lowers his forehead, resting it against mine. "Change your mind. Come home with me."

The desperation in his voice is almost my undoing. Instead, I unwrap my legs from his waist and slide down his body until my feet touch the ground. Reaching around him, I grab the small bottle of body wash and pour some into my hands. I wash his body, gliding my hands over the taut muscles in his abdomen and chest before moving lower. I leave no part of his body untouched.

After our shower, we dress and pack in silence. The ride back to my parents' house is tense. I spend most of the drive worrying about all the possible outcomes of the conversation that'll happen later. My heart is heavy. Saying goodbye gets harder with each visit. Knowing I'll have to face my parents tonight makes this goodbye the hardest.

"Stop biting your nails."

"Sorry, Sir." I put my hands under my legs.

"I can reschedule the meeting and stay with you. You don't have to do this alone."

"I appreciate the offer. But I have to do this myself."

We pull up to the house, and Alex shuts the car off. Neither of us moves, not wanting the weekend to end—not wanting to say goodbye.

Reluctantly, I turn to him. "If you don't go now, you'll miss your flight."

"That wouldn't be such a horrible thing."

I lean over the center console and kiss him. "I love you." My voice cracks. Reaching into the backseat, I grab my bag and turn to get out of the car. Alex reaches out and grabs my arm.

"Are you sure you won't change your mind?" His eyes plead with me.

"Call me when you land?" I open the door and step out.

"I will," he says, a sad smile on his face.

I close the car door and step back.

Watching Alex drive away, I feel small and alone.

The minute his car is out of sight, the tears I've held back roll down my cheeks.

Natalie

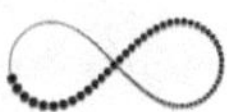

Insecurity about not pleasing my parents has plagued me all my life. My earliest memories revolve around trying to be the perfect daughter. It got worse after Michael died. I felt I owed it to my parents always to say and do the right thing. To do what they wanted, even if it meant I hid what I felt inside.

It wasn't until I found out Tommy was cheating on me that I realized I wasn't living. I was merely existing, continually trying to please someone else. The encouragement Michael left for me in his note, urging me to live my life to the fullest, finally made sense. So, I started fresh and created a new Natalie—the Natalie I wanted to be. And I was happy with that person.

I neglected planning how to continue being that girl once I returned to Northmeadow. I ignored it. It was easier to pretend my time in the city wouldn't end. But unfortunately, it did end, and I'm already losing the independence and confidence I had just a few months ago. I've regressed to the insecure girl who ignores her wants and desires in exchange for her parents' approval.

I love my parents. That doesn't change just because I have different thoughts and desires. Somehow, I have to make them understand that. When they get home, I need to be the woman who isn't afraid to stand up for herself. But will I be able to do this? Will my parents understand? Wiping the tears from my face, I walk up the sidewalk and into the house.

My parents are both at work, so I have the afternoon to myself. I go upstairs to my room and sit on my bed. I need a plan. Somehow, I have to get them to let go of the notion that Tommy and I are a couple. I need to convince them to keep an open mind about Alex. If they do, I know they'll see what I see. But how do I do it?

I grab my phone and call Lana. She'll know what to do.

"Hello?"

"Hey, girlie. Thanks for telling Alex about my party."

"Phew," she laughs. "When I didn't hear from you, I assumed you were mad at me."

"I could never be mad at you."

"How did your parents take him being there?"

"Not well. Mom freaked out when she saw him. They were even more furious when I left with him for the weekend. I haven't seen them since. That's why I'm calling. I need your help."

"Anything. You name it."

We spend the next half hour planning how to approach my parents. The goal is to focus on the positives. To show them Alex is a wonderful, caring man. That he's a hard worker and success-ful. He might live in a big city, but where a person lives doesn't have any bearing on their character. That thought is ridiculous. What matters is how he treats me and how we feel about each other. I need them to see how happy Alex makes me.

"Thanks, Lan. I knew you'd be able to help."

"Call me later and let me know how it goes, ok?"

"I will. Love ya."

After I unpack, I decide to make good use of my time and cook dinner.

"Maybe that'll ease things up later," I say to no one as I walk downstairs and into the kitchen. I take my phone out, tap my screen for the music app, and turn the volume up. Singing my favorite songs, I look through the kitchen for dinner ingredients. I decide on steak, fresh potatoes, and a salad from the garden.

I have many fond memories of gardening with my mother.

During the summer, our backyard was transformed into a thriving vegetable garden. Each day, Mom would don her coveralls and slip on her green garden gloves. She'd spend hours keeping the garden weed-free while Michael and I played.

Throughout the summer, we had fresh vegetables with our dinner every night. Then, in the early fall, we'd help her harvest what we hadn't used and preserve it, ensuring we had homegrown food all winter.

Because of my mom's love of gardening, I also grew to love it. While I lived in the city, I wasn't able to garden. Outdoor space comes at a premium. Lana and I had a small balcony where I managed to grow a few herbs, but it wasn't quite the same.

The afternoon has gone by quickly. It's almost time for my parents to get home, so I fire up the grill and start cooking. While I sit in one of our old lawn chairs, I practice what I'll say to them. I imagine how it might go and prepare answers to what I think they'll ask. The conversation plays over and over in my head. This has to work because I don't know what else to do if it doesn't.

The food is nearly done when I hear my parents' car pull into the driveway. I listen for them to come into the house. When they finally reach the kitchen, I open the door and peek in. "Dinner will be ready in a few minutes."

There's no response.

As soon as the food is done, I carry it inside. The salad I'd left on the counter is now on the table. My father sits in his usual chair, a muscle twitching in his clenched jaw. Mom sits to his right, her mouth drawn in a tight line, her eyes narrowed. With shaking hands, I set the food down and take my seat. I thought I was ready for this, but now I'm not feeling quite as confident.

Dad says grace and then quietly makes his plate and begins eating. Mom continues to glare at me.

"I hope you guys like it." I try my best to sound cheerful, hoping it'll break the suffocating tension in the room.

"Do you know how you've caused people to talk this weekend?" Mom asks, disapproval dripping from every word.

I sit up straighter and pull my shoulders back, steeling myself for the conversation.

"Surely I'm not the first unmarried girl who's spent a weekend with her boyfriend?"

"You're ruining your reputation in this town. You're ruining *our* reputation." She folds her hands in front of her. "And you're going to ruin your chances with Thomas. Then where will you be? Who will you marry?"

I laugh out loud. Mom and Dad stop and stare at me like I've gone mad.

"Ruin my chances with Tommy? Mom, do you hear yourself? I've tried to tell you I'm not interested in Tommy, but you won't listen. You aren't hearing me."

"What can you possibly say to make this okay?" Mom asks.

I look back and forth between them. This is the moment I've practiced for all day. When they meet my gaze, disapproval is evident in their eyes. My instincts try to force me to back down and cave to their demands. Why was I so stubborn when Alex asked to stay? I wish he were here now. But, no, this is something I have to do for myself.

I can do this. It's now or never. "I've been seeing Alex since I came home from school."

They remain stoic.

"The trips I've been taking weren't for work. I was with Alex."

Their angry stares pierce through me. But they say nothing.

"Alex is a good man. He's a hard worker, and he treats me well. He makes me happy. I plan to continue seeing him. I'm in love with him."

"That's enough." My father slams his hands on the table, startling me. "You're not to see that man again."

"What? You can't be serious?" I raise my voice.

"Natalie." Mom's tone is condescending. "I understand you think you love him, but he isn't right for you. Once you are away from him, you'll see that too."

It feels like I've been punched in the stomach. I struggle to take my next breath. Is this how Michael felt when he told them he loved Evan? The flicker of hope I had inside, the one that believed they'd see reason, maybe even give me their blessing, has extinguished. I'm alone in the darkness.

"So that's it?"

"I'm done talking," Dad says. "Whatever you think you had with him is over." He picks up his fork and resumes eating as if nothing happened.

They expect me to do as I'm told, with no questions, no arguments—it's what I was raised to do. It's what I've always done. But I can't do that anymore. I refuse to be that person again.

This is about my future—my happiness.

I'm sure they believe what they're doing is best for me. Maybe they're trying to save me from heartache? But, where I appreciate that they care about me and want to protect me, I'm an adult now. I have to be allowed to make my own choices. I don't want the same things they want for me.

Why are they refusing to support me? Just once, I'd love for them to cheer me on. Celebrate with me when I succeed and be there when I fail. Somehow, I have to make them see reason.

"I love you both very much. You've always been there for me. You've guided me, taught me, and raised me well. We've been through a lot, especially losing Michael." The ache in my soul comes back just as strong as the day we lost him, and I struggle to continue. "I thought being the perfect daughter would make our family whole again, but it hasn't. While I was away, I learned a lot about myself. Who I am and what I want. I understand Alex isn't your choice for me, but who I love isn't your choice. That doesn't mean I don't respect you or your input. I do." I pause to swallow the lump in my throat.

"Even if you disagree with my choices, I need you both to see me as a capable adult and at least try to respect them. All I'm asking is that you give Alex a chance. Spend some time with him and get to know him. He's wonderful—"

"That's enough. This is my home. As long as you live under my roof, you will obey my rules." Dad's voice is stern and leaves no room to argue.

I can't believe this is happening. My parents did the same thing with Michael. They shut off and refused to give even an inch. The next thing I say takes even me by surprise.

"I think it's best for all of us if I leave."

It's a move I've been planning to make, but I didn't envision it would happen like this. My father nods in agreement, ending the conversation.

No one speaks through the rest of dinner. The only sound in the room is my parents' forks and knives clinking off their plates. How can they carry on as if nothing happened? Is this my punishment for not obeying? My appetite is gone—nausea bubbles in my stomach. Instead of eating, I push the food around.

After Dad finishes his dinner, he walks into the living room and sits on the couch to read the evening newspaper. Mom goes to the kitchen to clean up. I decide to follow Mom, hoping if it's just her and I alone, we can talk. Maybe we can come to a better resolution.

"Mom."

"No, Natalie. You heard your father. The conversation is over." She turns her back on me.

It feels like I'm reliving the night Michael left home, except this time, it's me who's going. My knees buckle, and I grab the counter for support. I don't want to lose my family, but I refuse to give up Alex. It shouldn't have to be a choice. Why can't I have both? I put my dishes in the sink and quietly walk through the living room. Dad doesn't even look up from the paper.

One by one, I walk up the steps, noticing every creak and crack. I pause when I reach the top and look at the scene downstairs. My parents continue their nightly routine as though nothing's happened.

Once I get into my room, I grab my laptop and sit on my bed to start the search. But like every other time I've looked, there isn't anything available to rent in Northmeadow. I check the listings for a short-term rental at the lake, but with Labor Day in two weeks, everything's booked solid.

I don't know where to look next, so I call Alex. His plane should've landed by now, but my call goes straight to voicemail. I leave a message asking him to call me as soon as possible.

My next call is to Lana.

"How did it go?"

"Awful," I say, barely keeping my composure. "Dad said as long as I live in their house, I have to follow their rules. They actually forbid me to see Alex."

"You've got to be kidding. I'm sorry they're being awful."

"Trust me, I know. I told them I was moving out, but there aren't any available apartments. I even checked the lake for a rental, but there's nothing. I don't know what to do."

"Let me think. What about a hotel?"

"I didn't think about that."

I do a quick search for a hotel that's nearby. Rhonda's old and not in great condition. She won't make a long commute to work every day.

"I think I found something. The Lakeview Motel. They have cheap rooms, and they rent by the week."

"That sounds perfect."

"It does. Thanks, Lana."

"Anytime."

We hang up, and I make an online reservation. My savings will be enough to cover the room until school starts.

My phone ringing wakes me up. I rub my eyes and strain to read the time. It's three a.m.

"Hello?" I answer, my voice groggy.

"I'm sorry to wake you, baby girl."

"I'm glad you did. You didn't just get home, did you?"

"My flight was rerouted because of a storm." He yawns.

"Oh no, you missed your meeting?"

"I ended up having it online in a quiet corner of the airport café."

"I'm sure that wasn't," A yawn interrupts my talking, "ideal. I'm glad you're home safe."

"I got your message. How did things go with your parents?"

"I told them everything. I asked them to give you a chance, but they refused. They forbid me from seeing you as long as I live in their house. So, I told them I'm moving out."

"I'm so sorry, Nat." He pauses before hesitantly asking. "Do you need money?"

"I appreciate your generosity, but I have some saved. I could find a small place. The rent is cheap, and they don't require a security deposit." For now, it's best he doesn't know it's a motel room.

"That's one positive thing about not living in New York. It's late. Go back to sleep. I'll call you tomorrow."

"Yes, Sir." The words fall easily from my lips. "Alex?"

"Yes?"

Silence hangs between us as I go to war with myself. Will you rescue me? Will you buy out my contract and bring me back to New York? The words dance on the tip of my tongue, but won't come out. Instead, I say, "Thank you for coming this weekend. I love you."

"I love you, too, baby girl. Sleep well."

Natalie

AFTER HANGING UP WITH ALEX, I COULDN'T FALL BACK to sleep. Every time I closed my eyes, the scene at the dinner table replayed like a bad movie on repeat. My alarm didn't have the chance to wake me since I was already out of bed packing my things.

Today's the day I move out. This whole time, I had the silly notion it would be a happy occasion. I thought I'd have the support of my family, but that's not how it's turning out.

After I shove the last of my clothes in, I zip my suitcase and move it to the floor. Then I pull the sheets and blankets up, leaving my bed neatly made. Some habits are hard to break. Most of my things will have to stay here until I find an actual apartment.

Although this option isn't ideal, it's making it possible for me to move out right away. I stuff some essentials in another bag and then grab my suitcase and walk down the steps, setting it by the front door.

Dad's already left for work. Moms in the kitchen, going through her weekly cleaning routine. Before I leave, I have to try one more time.

"Mom."

She turns around, her reply curt. "What?"

"I found a place to stay. I'm taking some things with me today." My voice cracks as I speak. "But I'm going to leave most of my stuff here for now. I hope that's okay."

For a brief second, Mom drops her mask, and I see the sadness in her eyes. But just as quickly, it's gone. "That'll be fine."

She doesn't even ask where I'm moving to. I step closer, hoping to hug her goodbye at least, but she turns her back on me. "Mom, please," I beg. "I don't want to leave things this way."

"Are you ready to cut that man out of your life?"

"No."

"Then, I think it's best if you leave now."

"Yes, ma'am."

Walking away, I look around the house. A lifetime of memories washes over me. My first day of school. Mom braiding my hair, and Dad tying my saddle shoes. Christmas mornings, when Michael and I would sneak down the steps to peek at our presents.

Although tears fill my eyes, I don't let them fall. Everything happens for a reason.

I grab my things and walk out the front door with my head held high.

The mid-morning sun shines brightly as I drive the half-hour to the Lakeview Motel. My commute to work just got longer. Hopefully, Rhonda makes the drive every day without any issues. I pull into a guest parking spot and turn off the car.

There are only two other vehicles in the lot. That doesn't surprise me, as the place isn't exactly a five-star establishment. The planters contain the dead remains of the summer's flowers, and cigarette butts litter the walkways. The outside looks rundown, but it's all I can afford.

"It's only for a few weeks." I remind myself as I get out of the car and go to the main office to get my key.

When I open the glass door, I find myself standing in a dingy, smoke-filled room. To my right are two wooden chairs with torn vinyl seats and a small table littered with magazines. In front of me, there's a tall counter with dark brown paneling. I walk up and peer over it.

A man sits, his back to me, a cigarette in his hand. He's watching a Cardinals game on a flat-screen TV that hangs on the wall. The volume's so loud he hasn't heard me come in.

"Excuse me," I shout to be heard over the television.

The man spins around in his chair. His eyes open wide when he sees me.

"Hello, little lady. How can I help you?"

He stands and takes a puff of his cigarette. The smoke blows in my direction, and I cough. Do I really want to stay here, or will I be safer sleeping in my car?

"Hi," I say, trying to sound more confident than I feel. "I booked a room online last night."

He nods and types on an old desktop computer behind the counter.

"Natalie Clarke?"

"Yes."

"I put you in room seven. You're staying for one week?"

"Your webpage said the rooms could be rented long-term?"

"That's correct." He takes a final puff of his cigarette before snuffing it in the ashtray on the counter.

"Do I pay online for additional weeks?"

"No need." He checks the game over his shoulder before returning his attention to me. "Stop in here, and we can process the payment."

Keys hang on a pegboard next to his computer. I guess this place doesn't do key cards. He grabs the key that hangs under the number seven and walks around the counter, dangling it in the air.

"Can I show you to your room?"

"I think I can find it on my own."

This guy's creeping me out a bit.

"Suit yourself. If you need anything, there's a phone in your room. My name's Marshall. Press #11 to call me."

"Thanks." I take the key and walk out of the office.

I stop by my car, grab my suitcase, and then make my way to the red metal door with the number seven. The lock takes a little jiggling to get it to move, but finally, it clicks open. Pushing the door open, I take my first steps into my new home.

As soon as I enter the room, I gag from the overwhelming musty smell. Clearly, this room hasn't seen the light of day in a long time. The heavy drapes are closed, keeping the room dark. A shiny gold floor lamp, typical cheap motel style, stands in the corner.

I switch the light on and then close the door behind me. This will stay locked at all times. When I go to latch the security chain, I notice it's missing a screw. I'll have to ask Marshall to get it fixed. In the meantime, I grab one of the chairs and wedge it under the doorknob—a little extra security.

Hesitantly, I step further into the room. The carpet is worn and stained, probably where most of the smell comes from. I don't want to know what's stained it. There's a double bed on the wall to my right. Walking by, I run my hand over the ugly floral bedspread. On the wall over the bed hang two pictures, each in a cheap plastic gold frame. The photos must be from the 1980s, with bright colors and geometric patterns. The amount of dust on them must be from the '80s as well.

Across from the bed is a wooden dresser. Sitting on top of it is an old television. Good thing I don't watch much TV.

The last place to explore is the bathroom. I'm almost afraid to look, but curiosity gets the better of me. Pushing open the squeaky door, I walk into the small space. The first thing I notice is there's no window, only an overhead light with one light bulb burned out. I have to close the door to access the white pedestal sink. On the wall above it hangs a cracked mirror held together by a strip of tape. Opposite the sink is a toilet, and on the back wall is a walk-in shower—no tub.

"That's okay. I can live with only having a shower," I say aloud.

Closing the door to the bathroom, I go back into the main room and sit on the bed. It takes a few minutes for me to get my thoughts together and come up with a plan. First things first. I need some cleaning products to disinfect the room, and then I'll buy my sheets and a new comforter. That should help the space feel more like home.

This room needs some fresh air and sunlight. I head to the window and pull open the drapes. Dust flies everywhere, making me sneeze. But now, the bright midday sun is shining in the room. It makes the place feel better already. The hand crank on the window is stuck. I struggle with it for a few minutes before it finally gives way, allowing the window to open and fresh air to flow into the room. I make a mental note to buy an air freshener.

It's not the apartment I shared with Lana in the city, but it's not that bad. I can make it work until I find a real place.

I pull up Alex's contact on my phone. He won't like this, but I know he'll at least try to respect my decision. I tap the video call button and wait for him to answer.

"Hi. I didn't expect you to call so soon."

"I told you I'd call when I was settled."

Alex gives me a quizzical look. "It's barely been two hours. You've moved in already?"

"Well—" I hesitate. "I didn't find an apartment, exactly."

"Natalie, turn the camera around. I want to see where you are."

"Yes, Sir." I take a deep breath, tap the icon to reverse the camera, and pan around the room.

"Where the hell are you?" Alex yells.

His tone catches me off guard. He's never yelled at me before.

"It's a little motel outside of Northmeadow." I flip the camera back to me.

"A motel? It looks like a dump. Is it even safe?"

"Safe enough." I shrug.

"Safe enough? I'm getting you a room somewhere better."

"It's only for a few weeks. I'll be okay, I promise."

The heated discussion continues with a lot of back and forth. I know Alex has the means to get me something better, and although he begs me to see reason, he doesn't force his will on me. That's one of the things I love about him.

Alex never uses his authority to take away my voice. He's reasonable and fair and understands the importance of allowing me to make this choice. He doesn't like it, but he respects it— respects me.

"It's only for a few weeks, a month tops. I'll keep looking for an apartment. I promise."

"Fine. But promise me you'll keep the door locked and chained."

Neither of us wants to say goodbye, but he has to get back to work, and I have to run into the office for a few hours to do some last-minute prep before school starts.

"I have meetings the rest of the afternoon. I'll text you if I'm running late."

I see the stress on his face. This new client account is taking up a lot of his time.

"I'll be here when you get home." I smile, hoping to ease some of his worries. "Talk to you later." I reluctantly tap the screen, making Alex's image disappear.

So much has changed over the past few days. Alex showing up at my party was the best thing that could've happened to me—to us. I don't know how I would've found the courage to tell my parents everything without it. Keeping him a secret was hard on our relationship. Looking back, I see how unfair it was to him. It makes me even more thankful that he stuck around and gave me a chance.

When I left New York, I was uncertain if Alex and I could have a future together. Now, I can't imagine a future without him.

Alex

I KEPT MY COMPOSURE, MOSTLY, UNTIL WE HUNG UP. Now, I'm pacing around my office, talking to myself like a man gone mad. A motel? There are tons of tasks begging for my attention, but I can't focus on any of them. My mind is in Northmeadow with a certain young lady. I need to talk to Brandon. He's not in the office this week, so I call him.

"Hey, Alex. What's up?"

"What the hell is she thinking?" I yell.

"Slow down. Who are we talking about?"

"Natalie. She had a fight with her parents."

"Lana told me about it."

"She can't find an apartment. So she's staying at some cheap motel." I rub the back of my neck.

Brandon's like a brother to me and always manages to talk me off the cliff. Right now, I need his advice because I'm teetering on the edge.

"Let me get this straight. The town she lives in is so small that there are no apartments for rent?"

"It's hard to imagine. But I checked for myself while we were talking. There's really nothing."

"Shit. That *is* a small town."

"What do I do? Because right now, I'm ready to get on a plane and drag her back here."

"You need to give her some space."

"Space?" I ask, raising my voice once again. "How do I take care of her by giving her space?"

"Relax. You told me her parents were smothering her, trying to dictate her life?"

"Yes." I tap my fingers on my desk.

"Now you want to go there and bulldoze her with your agenda. That makes you no different from anyone else in her life. As her Dominant, that isn't your role. I promise it'll backfire on you."

I think about his words for a minute. As much as I hate to admit it, he's right.

"I don't know what to do." I drop my head into my hands.

"Are you in love with her?"

Brandon knows my history. He knows I didn't want to get involved with a sub, let alone fall in love with someone. When I took Natalie as a sub, he was happy for me. We've been so busy going in opposite directions at work. When I'm in the office, Brandon's traveling, and he's in the office when I'm traveling. And when I'm alone at night, he's with Svetlana. I haven't had the chance to tell him about my feelings for Natalie. Do I tell him now?

"Yes." A single word.

"I'm happy for you, brother."

"Thanks. But what do I do? How do I fix this for her?"

I'm out of my league. I'm a Dominant. I know how to make a submissive bend to my will—and enjoy it. What I don't know is how to be a Dominant and a boyfriend at the same time. The rules are different, and I'm struggling to keep up.

"Right now, the best thing you can do is to be there for her. Listen when she needs someone to talk to. Support her, but unless it's something you've already agreed on, you can't control her decisions."

We talk until my secretary buzzes that my next client is on the line and ready for our conference call.

"I have a meeting I need to be in. Thanks, Brand. I appreciate your help."

Natalie

I CAN'T BELIEVE LABOR DAY WEEKEND HAS COME AND gone, and I spent it holed up in my room. The hot, humid summer air is already starting to change, ushering in the crispness of Autumn, which is spectacular in Northmeadow.

The leaves on the trees color the mountains in shades of red, yellow, and orange. Being gone for so long, I forgot how beautiful it is, and can't wait to see nature's show.

Living at the motel isn't all that bad, either. Now that I have everything clean and smelling fresh, it feels like a home. Marshall even let me get a small fridge and a microwave for my room. I can't make gourmet meals, but it beats eating out every night.

With the change of seasons also comes the start of school.

My alarm goes off as planned, allowing me enough time to shower before leaving for work. As usual, the water is lukewarm, but that's something else I've gotten used to, and now I take a very efficient shower.

After I wrap myself in a towel, I grab my phone and read the messages from my friends back in the city, wishing me good luck. I love that they haven't forgotten about me. With my phone in hand, I walk to the full-length mirror I purchased. The bathroom's cracked mirror is useless. It's the one thing Marshall hasn't fixed. I grab my comb and run it through my hair before applying some product. Then, I take my time applying makeup while texting Lana in between.

Dropping my towel to the floor, I slip into a lacy bra and panty set. I snap a picture and text it to Alex. He loves it when I send sexy pictures of myself. I'm wearing the outfit I picked out weeks ago—a black pencil skirt and a soft blue blouse. When I turn to face the mirror, the image reflecting back at me is that of a professional woman, put together and confident. If only my hands would stop shaking.

The time on my phone reads seven-thirty. If I don't get on the road, I won't make it on time. I grab my bag, slip into my black heels, and walk out the door. The holiday weekend has brought a lot of people to the motel, although I'm not sure why.

When I got home yesterday, the lot was full, and I had to park at the far end. I make my way across the parking lot when I spot Marshall leaning against the brick wall outside his office, a cigarette in his hand. I laugh when I think back to the day I first met him. Over the past few weeks, I've gotten to know him better. We've shared lunches at the picnic table in the grassy area outside his office a few times.

He's in his mid-thirties and has never been married. Marshall bought this place a few years ago, hoping to make it a place tourists want to stay rather than a place they settle on when everything else is booked. He intended to fix it, but it's more expensive than anticipated. I've offered to speak to Alex for him and see if he can do anything to help marketing-wise. But Marshall refuses to accept a handout.

"You're all dressed up today," Marshall calls across the parking lot.

"First day of work."

"Knock 'em dead, kid."

"Thank you." I smile and get into my car.

The drive into Northmeadow feels like it takes forever. I miss the convenience of hopping on a subway or being able to walk wherever I need to go. Despite continually checking the listings for an apartment in town, there's still nothing available. I've even looked into renting a lake house, but most owners are closing them up. I'm already dreading this drive when winter comes. My phone rings just as I pull into the busy school parking lot. I smile when I see who it is.

"Alex. I didn't think I'd hear from you until tonight."

"Did you think I'd let you start a new job without wishing you good luck?"

Although I can't see him, from the tone of his voice, I know he's smiling. I let my head fall back on the headrest and close my eyes.

"I'm so nervous. I hope I can do this."

I've studied and trained for this job for the past six years. I know I have the right skills, but self-doubt has crept in again.

"Take a deep breath and relax." His voice is deep and sexy, causing my thoughts to drift elsewhere. "I know you and how invested you are in this. You're going to do terrific. They're lucky to have you."

"I have to get inside before I'm late. Love you. Talk to you later."

After hanging up, I step out of my car and walk through the busy parking lot toward my old high school. This time, it's not as a student but as a faculty member.

The parking lot is buzzing with activity. Students are milling about, greeting each other before filing into the side entrances of the building. No one seems to pay me any attention as I walk past them to the teacher's entrance.

I climb the main steps and pause before opening the heavy wooden door. When I take the next step, my heel catches in a crack, and I trip over the threshold. I stumble right into Mr. Meadows.

"Oh my gosh, I'm so sorry."

"Good morning, Ms. Clarke." Mr. Meadows frowns as he gives my appearance a once over. "I guess you didn't take my advice on your style of dress. In the future, remember this is a small farm town, not the fancy city."

A few students walking by snicker. My cheeks heat with embarrassment at his public reprimand.

"Yes, sir. I'll try to keep that in mind."

I didn't think my outfit was too fancy until I looked at the other teachers' clothes and realized I didn't fit in.

The male teachers, including Mr. Meadows, wear khaki pants or jeans with a polo-type shirt. Some female teachers wear slacks, the polyester variety, with a blouse buttoned up high. Two female teachers are wearing skirts that go to their ankles. My clothes aren't revealing by any standard, but I stand out compared to my colleagues' overly conservative outfits.

When I was a student, I never paid attention to what my teachers were wearing. When I interned in the city, my current outfit was standard. I'll have to stop by my parents' house after work and grab some of my old clothes.

I mumble an awkward good morning to the faculty members standing nearby, watching the encounter before lowering my eyes and walking away. I hear my name whispered, but I refuse to turn around. The last thing I need is for them to think they've got to me.

Ms. Campbell tried to warn me. She suspected I might not receive a warm welcome. She'd heard whispers that my support of Michael and Evan wasn't forgiven or forgotten. I listened to what she said, but convinced myself that enough years had passed. There was no way the community could still hold that against me. Guess I was wrong.

As I walk the long hallway, weaving my way between students, many thoughts race through my head. I remind myself that none of that matters. It doesn't change my reason for being here. I'm here for one reason—to help the kids who feel they don't have a voice.

When I get to my office, I reach into my pocket, grab my key, and place it in the lock. But when I turn it, I realize the door is already open. That's odd. I'm sure I locked it when I left yesterday.

Pushing the door open, I'm met with the sweet fragrance of flowers. On my desk sits a beautiful bouquet of red roses. I grab my phone from my bag before tossing it onto my chair. Snapping a picture, I send a text to Alex.

Me: Thank you for the flowers. They're beautiful.

Alex: They are beautiful, but they aren't from me.

If they aren't from him, then who are they from? I search the bouquet for the card.

Natalie,
Roses are beautiful, but they're nothing compared to you. Good luck on your first day. I'll see you tonight.
Love Tommy.

Furious, I rip up the card and dump the flowers into a trash can in the hallway.

Alex: Was there a card?

Me: Yes.

Alex: And? Who are they from?

Me: Tommy. They're in the trash. I'll call you later.

After recovering from the shock of the flowers, it's time to put my game face on and get to work. Today and every day this week, I'll be stopping in several classrooms to introduce myself to the students and tell them about the new counseling programs available.

After each classroom visit, I leave pamphlets that the students can take and read on their own time. It's important they know I'm here for them, no matter what they want to talk about.

When I return to my office, I leave the door open and sit at my desk. I'm very proud of how the room turned out. I still have the chair with a worn-out cushion, but now it has a brightly colored rainbow-shaped pillow. The other side of the room is much less formal. The old floor is covered by a circular rug with the yin/yang symbol. A few tie-dyed bean bag chairs are arranged on the floor around the rug.

Against the far wall, under the windows, is a small bookshelf. My psychology-themed books are on the top two shelves. The bottom shelf has various fidgets, including Rubik's cubes, stress balls, adult coloring books, gel pens, putty, and other sensory things. In the far corner is a white noise box that quietly plays the sound of ocean waves in the background.

I've tried to create a relaxed and welcoming environment. I hope my future clients feel the same way.

I'm looking over some files I was given for students who are considered high risk when there's a knock on my door. I look up and spot a female student standing in the doorway. I close the file I'm reading and set it aside.

"Come on in. Grab a seat wherever you're comfortable."

She closes the door behind her before taking tentative steps into my office. Her eyes open wide when she notices the bean bag chairs. "May I?"

"Absolutely. I'm Natalie."

"My name's Mary," she says quietly.

Mary. She looks very familiar, but I can't quite place why.

"It's nice to meet you."

"Thanks. My brother said you'd be nice and that you're safe to talk to."

"Your brother? May I ask his name?"

"Billy Simmons. He was two years behind you in high school."

Oh my goodness, this is little Mary Simmons, although she's not little anymore.

"I remember your brother. How is he?"

"He's doing well. Now."

"Please tell him I said hi. And thank him for the good reference."

"When I get to talk to him again, I will." Mary looks down at her lap and fidgets with her fingers.

It's clear she's nervous, so I get up from behind my desk and walk over to a bean bag chair.

"Mind if I sit?" She shakes her head, and I sit easily despite wearing a skirt. It's a skill I perfected while working at an after-school program in the city. I grab two plastic containers of putty from the shelf.

"Want one?"

"Sure," she says, smiling.

I toss one, and she catches it easily. We work the putty through our fingers while chatting about what grade she's in her favorite subject—the easy stuff. After getting a little more comfortable with each other, I ask, "What's brought you in today?"

She stops playing with her putty momentarily and looks up at me. "Do you know about my brother and everything that happened to him?"

"No. Are you comfortable telling me?"

Mary explains that when Billy was sixteen, he told their parents he was gay.

"They freaked out." She stands up and begins pacing the room. "They told him he needed to be cured of his evil ways, so they sent him away to get conversion therapy."

Flashbacks of the night Michael and Evan came out play in my head. Now's not the time to get lost in those memories. I stand up from my bean bag and walk over to my desk, leaning against the edge.

Mary's still pacing, her face red with anger. She has a death grip on the putty. "Two years," she says louder. "Billy was there for two years while they did unspeakable things to him. As soon as he turned eighteen, he signed himself out. He wasn't the same for a long time after that." She quickly wipes her tears.

"I'm very sorry that happened."

Mary stops, squares their shoulders, and looks me straight in the eyes. "I was born female, but I don't identify as one. I have a girlfriend I love. Eventually, I want to have gender reassignment surgery. Other than Billy and my girlfriend, you're the only one who knows. I'm sick of pretending. Sick of hiding. I'm ready to come out." The words spill out in a single breath.

"Thank you for trusting me with your story," I say gently. "I'm glad you're ready to share it, and I'll support you through that process. But maybe we can take it step by step. Talk it through first, put together a plan. Would that feel okay?"

Mary grabs the rainbow pillow from the chair before sitting down. "Yes."

"Good." I smile and settle behind my desk. "Before we dive too far ahead, there's a little paperwork we need to complete. We've got about ten minutes before lunch is over. We can get started now, and then I'll set up a regular time for us to meet. I'll let your teacher know and make sure you're excused from class."

Mary nods, and we begin the intake paperwork. I pause, looking up to meet their eyes. "What pronouns feel right for you?"

"They/them," Mary replies without hesitation.

"Thank you for sharing that with me." My voice softens. "It matters to me that I address you in the way that feels true to who you are."

Mary shifts slightly in their chair, lips pressing together before they answer. "I guess I'm not really used to that," they admit quietly, eyes flicking to the floor before meeting mine again. "But, thank you." Their voice carries a vulnerability that tells me the acknowledgment means more than they expected.

We manage to get halfway through the forms before the bell rings.

"I'll get the info to your teacher. And just so you know, everything we talk about here stays confidential. The same goes for your teacher excusing you. She can't share anything. Your parents won't be informed without your consent."

"Good. I don't want them to know I'm talking to you yet."

"Understood."

We say our goodbyes, and Mary slips back into the hallway. I watch as they merge into the stream of students, shoulders relaxed, steps lighter.

To everyone else, they're just another face in the crowd. But I know the weight of what they've just shared, and the courage it took to say it out loud.

My first day is busier than I ever imagined it would be. Besides Mary, three other students stopped in and signed up for counseling appointments. A few others stopped by and asked for more information on available services. After the final bell, I pack up my stuff and make sure to lock the door.

Before I go back to the motel, I need to swing by my parents' house. I'm glad they aren't there, and I use my key to let myself in. I grab some clothes and throw them into a small suitcase. I hate putting these back on. It feels like a huge step backward, but I have to choose my battles. Then I hurry out. I'm not ready for another confrontation with my parents.

After leaving their house, I stop at a grocery store to grab a few microwave meals and sodas. They don't make the best dinners, but it's much cheaper than eating out. I'm trying to save every penny I can to put toward an apartment when one opens up.

When I get back to my room, I put the groceries away. Even though it's early, I'm exhausted. I change into comfy pajamas before I microwave some dinner.

For the rest of the evening, I work on the intake paperwork for my newest clients. The district has finally gone digital, so I can access the kids' files from home instead of staying late at school. Good thing I have a mobile hotspot on my phone because the rooms don't have Wi-Fi.

I'm startled when my phone rings. I didn't realize it was already nine. I swipe to accept the video call request, a pattern that's become familiar over these past few months.

"Hey, baby girl."

"Hi, handsome," I reply and blow him a kiss.

"How was your first official day?"

"Great. I had a total of four students sign up for counseling. Can you believe it?"

"Of course, I believe it." His eyes fill with pride as he speaks.

"I know, but I wasn't sure." I lean back on my pillows. "The adults in this town are so close-minded. I wasn't sure how much of that had been passed down to the kids. But I think I have an opportunity to help them."

"I'm very proud of you."

"Thank you, Sir." Knowing I've pleased him fills me with pride. "How was your day?"

"Busy." Alex takes a deep breath and rakes his hand through his hair. His face is etched with concern.

"What's wrong?" I ask, suddenly filled with worry.

"It's the new account I've been working on."

"Did something happen?" I sit up, alarmed. I know this account is important to his firm.

"No, it's all good. It's just that this account comes with some travel obligations."

It isn't unusual for Alex to travel, especially for his important clients.

"Where do you have to go?"

"Russia."

"Did you just say Russia?"

Turmoil swirls in his blue eyes. "Yes."

"When do you leave?"

"In two days."

"How long will you be gone?" I ask quietly, afraid of his answer.

"I'll be there until mid-December."

Until December? That's nearly three months. He's never had to travel for that long.

Alex is quiet, watching and waiting for my response. I see how much he's struggling with this, so I try to put on a brave face.

"I'm sad you'll be gone for so long, but I know this is a huge opportunity." I try to find a positive in this situation. "And you'll be home before Christmas."

Over the next two hours, I ask him all about his upcoming trip. He seems to relax a bit as he tells me more about it. On Maxim's insistence, he'll be staying with the Solonik's.

I stayed there when I visited with Lana. Their home is as grand as a hotel. The trip will be long, but this account is huge for him. It'll be the second largest account his firm holds, Maxim's being the largest.

Alex tries to explain the company's new energy-efficient technology. I don't understand what it all means or why a Russian company wants to advertise in the U.S. When I asked, Alex told me there are confidential parts of the business. Proprietary stuff, I guess.

"It's going to mean a lot more travel. I'm hoping you'll accompany me on some of the trips."

His eyes hold so much hope as he waits for my answer. I want to say yes, that I'd follow him anywhere, but my schedule isn't as fluid as his.

"If it's a school holiday or I can get some time off, I'd love to travel with you."

The smile he gives melts my heart. Unfortunately, it's gotten late for both of us. This is the part I hate the most—saying goodbye. Each time, it gets more and more difficult.

After we hang up, my brave façade slips away. Being a few states away is hard enough, but at least we get to see each other every few weeks. This will be different. He'll be on the other side of the world, and we won't see each other for three months.

I grab Alex's T-shirt, the one I kept from our last weekend together, and hold it close as I fall asleep.

Alex

I left for Russia two weeks ago. Although it killed me to put more physical distance between us, especially with how much Natalie's struggling, I had no choice. My business with Maxim and Nicholai can't wait. Natalie was understanding, although I could see the sadness in her eyes.

The eight-hour time difference has made things more challenging. Daily contact is important to both Natalie and me. We have our video calls when Natalie gets home from work, which is about midnight. I'm trying to keep things creative, so every afternoon, I text her a sexy challenge for our call that evening. It's not the same as being together in person, but we're doing our best to make it work.

"Hi, baby girl," I say when the video comes to life.

"Hello, Sir."

She obeyed today's challenge and is kneeling beside her bed, wearing only a tiny pair of red lacy panties.

"You look gorgeous."

"Thank you, Sir."

"You may get up and sit on the bed. There are some things I want to talk about."

Natalie stands and readjusts her laptop before crawling across the bed. I'm treated to a fantastic view of her breasts through the camera lens. I groan, wishing I were there. Natalie giggles before she sits and gets comfortable.

It's nearly impossible to keep my focus with her half undressed. The sight of her bare breasts, nipples peaked and aching for attention, derails every rational thought. I hadn't considered how hard this would be when I told her to strip down. Now I see the truth. I've set myself up for a battle of my own. Whatever words I'd meant to say blur at the edges, and what's left is a lesson in self-restraint I hadn't bargained for.

"Obviously, we both want to continue working on our dynamic. So, I've been trying to come up with things we can do even while we're so far apart. I want to add some daily tasks to keep us connected."

"I like the sound of that."

"I've come up with a few activities we can do individually, and then we can talk about them on our video calls. I'd also like to know if you have anything you want to add."

"This is a great idea."

"I found a journaling app. I'd like you to write in it every day. I can access it from here and will write back to you."

Finding a solution to address Natalie's emotional struggle was a challenge. We're in nearly opposite time zones, so often, when she needs me, I'm not available. I'm hopeful that having a place to write her concerns, struggles, and victories will be an avenue to increase our communication.

"I haven't been exercising like I should since I've been home."

"I've been lax with it as well. Especially since being over here."

Natalie asks to add daily exercise to our tasks. It was never a rule, just something she and I used to do together. We write up a plan that we both promise to stick to. Then, I send her the link to the journal.

"I didn't realize there was anything like that available."

"I'm hoping this will become an important tool in keeping us connected."

"I don't know how you came up with this idea, but it's perfect."

"You know what else is perfect?"

"What, Sir?" She bites her lip.

"You. Now, take off your panties, and let me see you."

I stroke myself while I watch Natalie. My body is jealous of her fingers. It wants to be the one touching her soft, wet skin. To be the one giving her pleasure. Natalie throws her head back as her orgasm hits. My body follows. As good as it feels, it's not the same as being with her.

Natalie

ALEX'S IDEA OF USING THIS JOURNAL APP IS PERFECT. So often during the day, I want to grab my phone to text or call him. Then I remember the time difference. Having the journal makes it feel like I have more access to Alex while he's gone. I open the app on my laptop and type a note for him.

I'm really missing you today. Work is a double-edged sword. The kids seem to be embracing my services with open arms, but I'm not making any friends with the staff. But that's okay. Who am I kidding? It's not okay. It's lonely—I'm lonely. I'd like to have even one person here to talk to. Maybe someone to sit with at lunch. I've taken to staying in my office and eating at my desk instead.

I have to remind myself that I'm here for the kids, not the staff. I think I'm making a difference with them, especially with M. They're strong and brave. They know what they want and are not afraid to go after it. I love their tenacious spirit.

You asked if things were any better with my parents. Mom calls once a week. I'm hopeful our relationship is beginning to heal, even if just a little.

Tensions are still high with Dad. He and I haven't talked much. He's furious that I chose to defy him, but I haven't lost hope that he'll come around. I've tried to bring up the subject of you and me. When I do, Mom shuts it right down. I'm trying not to push but not to let it be forgotten, either.

One good thing. She's stopped bringing up Tommy. Hopefully, she's realized that's a dead end. I know they'll come around and see what we have is real.

I have to get back to work. Lunch is over. I love you.

~Natalie

I close the app and sit back in my chair. This separation was a bit rocky at first, but Alex and I have fallen into a routine uniquely our own. The journal has been a big part of that. I can write to him whenever I need, and I know he'll read it. Getting his notes back is equally exciting. It's adding another dimension to our relationship. It's helped make the distance a little easier. But I still can't wait until he's home and we can be together again.

The rest of the afternoon goes by slowly. I don't have any more appointments today. I'm sitting in my office, finishing some paperwork, waiting for three-thirty when my phone rings.

"Hi, Mom," I answer cheerfully.

"Natalie, your father isn't feeling well. We had to close the pharmacy counter early, but we didn't want to close the rest of the store. Can you come in and work until close?"

"Yes, of course. Is Dad alright?"

"I think he has the flu. He's been working himself too hard."

My father never gets sick, but I'm thankful Mom reached out to me. This is the first time since I moved out that they've asked me to work. I'm sure this is a good sign.

"I'm done here in half an hour. I'll come right over."

"Mrs. Smith will stay until you get there," Mom pauses. "Thank you, Natalie."

"You don't have to thank me. Please tell Dad I hope he feels better."

The phone disconnects. I hold it in my hand, savoring the brief moment where it felt like things were okay between us, like nothing bad had ever happened. I drop Alex a quick text letting him know I won't be able to call him after work. I'm going to miss talking to him, but I'm also glad for something to do. It gets lonely sitting in that motel room every night.

Finally, the bell rings, ending the school day. I grab my stuff and am one of the first out of the building and to my car. The pharmacy is only a few blocks down the street, so it doesn't take me long to get there. Dad's store is small, unlike the two-story Duane Reade pharmacies all over New York City.

Clarke's Pharmacy is more of an old-fashioned operation. My parents know all their customers by name and still offer personal lines of credit to them. Dad carries only the tried-and-true essentials. He rarely orders anything new. *'The people in this town don't like to try new things. They stick to what they know works,'* is the motto he lives by.

While that may be true, Dad seems to ignore the fact that Northmeadow sees a lot of tourists during the summer. In my opinion, many sales opportunities are missed because of that.

Coming to the pharmacy is almost like coming home. I grew up helping my parents in the store, so much of my life is connected to it. My Grandpa Clarke opened it when he was about my age. My father followed in his footsteps. He always hoped Michael would continue the family tradition, but Michael wasn't interested.

I was their Plan B, but they discouraged me from becoming a pharmacist because I'm a girl. I didn't fight them. I wasn't interested in that career path anyway. That's where Tommy came in.

My parents focused on their future son-in-law, encouraging him to pursue a PharmD so he could take over the store for them. I don't know what their plans are now that Tommy didn't finish school.

The bells on the door jingle when I pull it open and step into the store. Mrs. Smith is in a tizzy and barely gives me time to get behind the register before rushing to gather her things.

"It's about time," she says.

"I got here as soon as I could."

I try to stay out of her way as I watch her hurrying about.

She stops and gives me a cross look. "You wouldn't understand, Natalie," she says as if reading my thoughts.

"What do you mean?"

She crosses her arms.

"Things like making sure to be home and having dinner on the table for your husband as soon as he's home from work. Old-fashioned values that your generation has written off."

Her words sting, but I bite my tongue. Arguing with her will do no good. I remain quiet while she grabs her purse, says a quick goodbye, and hurries out the door.

I lean back against the counter. Mrs. Smith's words play over and over in my head. Alex may not be my husband, but I understand and embrace putting him first. It's the heart of my relationship with him. Everything I do as a submissive is meant to put Alex's needs ahead of mine. Our relationship isn't that different from so many of the relationships in this town—my parents included. I laugh out loud. Except for what we do in the bedroom, *that* is much different.

An idea pops into my head. Maybe this is the angle I need to take with my parents. All they've ever wanted is for me to be in a relationship that mimics theirs. Being with Alex isn't how they assumed it would happen, but if they see it in action, it could change the game. I'll ask Alex if he's willing to come in for a weekend when he gets back from Russia. We can plan to spend some time with my parents. It'll give us a chance to show them that part of our relationship—the *old-fashioned* part. If they see the similarities, they won't have an argument against it anymore. This could be the key to getting them to accept us.

The store is pretty much dead. Only two customers come in.

Finally, it's nine o'clock, time to close up. I lock the front door and grab the register drawer. As I walk to the back of the store, I peek down the aisles, ensuring everything is neat and organized for the morning. Then, I lock the drawer in the safe and let myself out the employee door around the back.

Tommy

I'VE BEEN WATCHING NATALIE FROM A DISTANCE FOR the past few weeks. She doesn't know I have a second car, which allows me to stay undetected. It's been easy to learn Natalie's schedule. She's so predictable. In the morning, she goes to work. A couple of times a week, she stops at the grocery store before going back to that dump of a motel where she's staying.

Speaking of the motel, I stopped by last week—uninvited, of course. I was outside Natalie's door, about to let myself in.

"What the hell do you think you're doing?" A male voice asked from behind me.

I spun around and quickly slid the lock pick into my back pocket.

"I'm a friend of Natalie's. I stopped by to see if she was home."

"I've seen you sitting across the street watching her. And picking a lock isn't the usual way to see if someone's home."

"I was just trying to surprise my girl. You know, trying to be romantic."

"If I see you here again, there won't be time for a nice conversation like this. It'll be a one-way conversation." He pulled a gun from his waistband. "Now, I suggest you get the hell off my property."

I lifted my hands. "No harm done, man," I said and slowly backed away.

He screwed up my plans for her at the motel, but at least I still have her parents in my corner. Charlotte called me earlier to let me know Natalie was working at the pharmacy tonight, just in case I wanted to stop by to see her.

As a matter of fact, I do want to pay her a visit. I park across the street from the pharmacy, in the lot for the grocery store, and wait. It's almost nine. Natalie will be getting ready to lock up soon. This is my chance. The streets are deserted as usual, but that works in my favor tonight.

Even still, I'm careful to check my surroundings before getting out of my car and crossing the street. I walk around the back of the pharmacy to the employee entrance, waiting for Natalie to come out.

My prescription ran out, and the damn doctor won't give me another one. He had the nerve to accuse me of being an addict. Suggested I seek treatment for my *problem*. Screw him. I'll find another doctor who'll give me what I need. I've done it before. It takes time, though.

The problem is that I took my last pill earlier today, and it's worn off. The withdrawal is making my eyes water and my hands tremble. Sweat is pouring off me even though I'm not hot. I need some pills to hold me over for a few days. Stanley always spots me a few until I get a new prescription, but he's not here tonight. Natalie will do it. She'd never tell me no.

Movement catches my eye. The door is starting to open. Quietly, I move in closer. She doesn't hear me. She's focused on locking the door. I walk up behind her and place my hands on her shoulders. She screams, and I put my hand over her mouth.

"Relax, it's just me," I say, trying to calm my girl down.

She spins around to face me. "You almost gave me a heart attack."

"I'm sorry." I reach out and tuck a loose curl behind her ear.

She tries to move away, but I place my arms on both sides of her head, caging her against the door.

"I need to get some pills."

"Dad's not here tonight. You'll have to come back in the morning." She tries to duck under my arms, but I don't let her move.

"I can't wait, Nat. I need them tonight." I rock back and forth on my feet, fighting waves of nausea.

"I've already closed up and can't fill a prescription even if I wanted to." She pushes at my arms, but I don't budge. "Please let me go."

"My prescription ran out. I need a few pills to hold me over."

"I can't help you, Tommy." She squirms, trying to get away. "Please just move out of the way and come back in the morning."

Why is she making this more complicated than it has to be?

"I'm not asking, Natalie. Open the damn door and get me some pills."

I know I'm scaring her. I don't want to do that, but I need her to cooperate. I place my hands on her shoulders and turn her to face the door.

"Unlock it." I hold her firmly until she puts the key in the lock and pulls the door open.

With my hands on her shoulders, I force her body forward. She reaches to turn the lights back on, but I stop her.

"No lights. We don't need any unnecessary attention, do we?"

She shakes her head but doesn't make a sound. I guide her to the pharmacy area.

"I don't know Dad's code for the lockbox."

Natalie must think I'm stupid. She's worked here since she was a kid and knows how to access everything. Hell, she could be the damn pharmacist if she wanted to.

I lean close and whisper, "Don't play dumb, sweetheart. I know you know the code." Her body is trembling. She's afraid. I have to admit, her fear turns me on. I lean in and kiss her neck.

She tries to pull away, and I snicker. "Open it and get the Oxy." She doesn't move. "Now."

I give her a small push forward, encouraging her to comply.

Slowly, she punches in the code to the lockbox where Stanley keeps the pain meds. She moves her head slightly, eyeing the silent alarm button only a few feet away.

"Don't even think about it, Natalie. Just take out a few pills and hand them to me. Then we can both go home." I'm beginning to run out of patience.

Without turning around, she says, "You aren't going to get away with this. There are cameras."

"I knocked them offline, and you aren't going to say anything." I know exactly how to play her. I know her weaknesses. "If you do, your parents will get some rather revealing pictures."

"What pictures?"

"Pictures, I know you don't want your parents seeing."

"Where did you get—"

"Don't worry about where. Just know I have them, and I'll use them."

She reaches into the safe and pulls out the bottle. "Three pills, Tommy. That's all you're getting."

"Four. Or your parents get the pictures."

"Fine." With how quickly she's complied, I know I got lucky.

She's hiding something.

There's gotta be dirt on either her or that guy that's hanging around. I'll call my buddy in the police department and have him do some digging for me. Natalie hands me the pills before replacing the bottle and closing the safe.

"I gave you what you want. Now get out."

I'm not taking any chances with her pressing the alarm.

"We'll leave together."

She shakes my hand off her arm and rolls her eyes.

I can't wait to get her back under me in bed. I like this feisty, grown-up version of her. She was always a good lay, and now she'll be even better.

"After you," she says, holding the door open.

I walk past her, not letting her get too far from me. She locks up again and looks around.

"How did you get here? I don't see your truck."

"I walked. You're going to drive me home."

I'll get a ride back to get my car tomorrow. Right now, I have the chance to spend more time with Natalie, and I'm not going to pass that up.

"I'm not driving you anywhere." She crosses her arms. "You walked here. You can walk home."

"Not a chance." I grab her hand and drag her to her car. "My place is on your way."

"Fine." She pulls her hand free. "I'll drive you home. But this is it. You need to leave me alone."

I raise my hands in mock surrender. "Whatever you say, sweetheart."

If she thinks we're through, she has another thing coming.

We're just getting started.

Natalie

My hands tremble as I drive Tommy to his house and drop him off. I make it a mile down the road before I pull over and vomit. There's no way that just happened. I lean my head on the headrest and take a few breaths, trying to calm my racing heart.

Tommy threatened to show my parents pictures of me. Alex and I have exchanged photos in texts and video calls, but I don't see how Tommy could have gotten access to them. Either way, I can't take the chance. I can't tell my parents what happened and risk Tommy showing them anything Alex and I have done. They'd never understand. I'd lose any chance I might have of getting them to accept him.

Once I'm calmer, I pull back onto the road and finish driving to the motel. By the time I make it home, it's late, and I'm mentally and physically exhausted. I text Alex, knowing he'll be getting up any time now. I let him know I'm home safe and will talk to him tomorrow. I can't tell him what happened tonight, either. He's got a lot on his plate with work. I don't want to add to his stress.

My stomach is in knots, so I don't bother eating. I get into pajamas and crawl into bed, hoping to sleep off the night's events.

Alex

I missed talking to Natalie last night, but I'm glad she could work at the pharmacy. Mending her relationship with her parents is important to her. Hopefully, this is a good sign.

I've been up for a while. I took an early morning run and had a shower. There's some time before I need to be in Maxim's office, so I leave Natalie a note in our journal.

baby girl,

I missed talking to you last night. This distance is killing me. I can't wait to be home and have you in my arms. The things I want to do to you. Next time I have to be gone for so long, you're coming with me.

Have you heard about the days you requested for Christmas? I'll book the flight as soon as you get word. My client just got here, so I have to cut this short.

Be naked and ready for my call tonight.

I love you.
-Sir

Natalie

FARMING IS A BIG PART OF NORTHMEADOW'S ECONOMY, so the schools close for two weeks, giving the students an extended Thanksgiving holiday. This allows the kids to be home to help harvest the fields and prepare their family's farms for winter. Vacation is coming at the perfect time because I'm exhausted. I've been plagued with nightmares since my run-in with Tommy.

In every dream, he has a gun pointed at someone, but I can't see their face. I wake up just as he pulls the trigger. Part of the problem is that I'm keeping the encounter bottled up. I still haven't told Alex what happened. I don't want to waste the precious time we get to talk. And I don't want him worried about me.

I can't tell my parents about it because Tommy can do no wrong in their eyes. I fear that if I bring up what happened, it'll only make things with them more tense. The ice is just starting to melt, and I don't want to refreeze the situation. I need to shake the whole thing off. Tommy's addicted to pain meds, and although the other night was unsettling, he'd never harm anyone.

Thanksgiving is in a few days, and I have no plans. Lana and Brandon invited me to spend Thanksgiving with them, but I couldn't bear the thought of going to NYC without Alex being there. While I'm lying on the bed watching a rerun of *Friends*, my phone rings.

"Hi, Mom. How are you?"

"I'm doing well. Busy getting ready for the holiday. Dad and I would like to invite you home for Thanksgiving."

I sit up, shocked by the invitation. Although we've been talking, it's been superficial conversations. I wasn't expecting this.

"Why don't you come early on Wednesday. We'll bake pies, and you can spend the night."

"Thank you. I think that would be nice."

After we hang up, I write a note to Alex.

Sir,

I'm in shock. Mom called and invited me home for Thanksgiving. Can you believe it? I'm going to spend the night on Wednesday. This has to be a step in the right direction. A sign that they're beginning to accept me—and soon us.

I wish you were here. Only two more weeks. I'm counting the hours.

I got the vacation days I requested, so I can fly out and spend Christmas with you. I can't wait!

i love You.
~Natalie

I close my laptop, but I'm too excited to sit still. So, I get up and take a shower.

When I was growing up, we affectionately called the day before Thanksgiving 'Pie Day.' Michael, Mom, and I would make apple, pumpkin, and pecan pies. Dad would beg Michael to go to Northmeadow High's big football game, but he always said no. He wasn't into sports. Michael was content to spend the day making intricate designs with pie crust. Together, the three of us made not only delicious but also beautiful pies for our holiday meal.

I haven't been home for Thanksgiving in years. I'm excited to have this back.

Natalie

After another restless night's sleep, this time more from excitement than fear, I give up on sleeping and get up. I grab a bowl of cereal and then take a quick shower. I have some time to kill before heading to my parents' house, so I busy myself with checking emails and then packing my overnight bag. The holiday is going to be near perfect. The only thing missing is Alex. I wish he could be here to spend the holiday with us. Next year.

Dad's still at the pharmacy when I get there, so there's room in the driveway, but I don't want to take his spot, so I park on the street. My nerves kick in full force when I shut the car off. I haven't been back home in almost four months. I decide to go into the house with no expectations and take things as they come. Hopefully, everything will go smoothly. I knock on the door before opening it.

"Hi, Mom, it's me," I call.

"Come on in. I'm in the kitchen."

I drop my bag by the door and head straight in. The scent of spiced pecans cooking makes my mouth water.

"It smells delicious in here." I kiss Mom on the cheek.

She's standing at the stove, wearing her ruffled apron with pumpkins on it. Tomorrow, she'll wear her turkey apron. The sight brings back many happy memories.

She points to a chair at the table. "I've made you an apron. I hope you like it."

Walking over to the chair, I spot the apron. It's made from the same fabric as Mom's.

"You didn't have to do that," I say as I hold it up.

Mom's a terrific seamstress. It's an exact replica of hers. But she *really* didn't have to do this. I'm not much for wearing aprons.

"Don't be silly," she says as she pours the cooked pecans onto the waiting wax paper. "The fabric was your grandmother's. She made my apron when I first got married." She wipes her hands off on a dish towel. "I've saved it all these years waiting for you to be married. But, well, never mind that. It's time you had your own."

"Thank you. I love it." I may not love the apron, but I love the thought and time she put into it. "Can you help me tie it?"

We keep busy in the kitchen the rest of the afternoon, making tomorrow's desserts. Each pie is made from scratch, the crust is decorated, and the pastry is baked to perfection.

In my naivety, I assumed today would be like old times, carefree and easy. But instead, there's an unspoken tension lying just beneath the surface. Conversation is limited, interrupted by uncomfortable periods of silence. I try to ignore the awkward moments, choosing to focus on the spirit of the day. Like when I was a child, I sample the filling for each pie before Mom pours it into the shell.

Michael and I used to fight over who got to lick the mixing bowls. He'd always tease me, reminding me he was the firstborn, so he was entitled to lick the bowl. I'd cross my arms and pout. Then, Mom would get me a second spoon so Michael and I could both scrape the mixing bowls clean. Days like today make Michael's death hurt all over again.

"One day, you'll be doing this with your children," Mom says with a dreamy look.

"I don't think that'll be happening any time soon."

"Well, you aren't getting any younger," Mom says as she puts the last pie in the oven.

"Alex and I have talked about having children."

"Alex? You're still seeing him?"

"Yes, I am." I put the bowl in the sink. "He's in Russia for work right now, but he's planning to spend a weekend here when he gets back. Maybe we can all get together for dinner?"

Mom ignores my question. "We need to clean the kitchen before your father gets home. You know how much Dad hates a mess."

I won't force the issue. I put it out there, and now she can think about it. We clean in silence, getting it done in record time. Per family tradition, Mom calls and orders Chinese takeout. Then, with the table set, we wait for Dad to get home.

He strolls into the house twenty minutes later, food bags in hand. Dad's talkative tonight, something I wasn't expecting.

"How's the job going?".

"Things are going really well. I have a nearly full caseload."

"I'm glad to hear it. You've worked hard for this."

"Alex told me he sent you his marketing plans for the store. Did you have a chance to look at them?"

"I got them. But it's not something I'm interested in."

"Is there something you'd like changed? I can ask Alex—"

"I've run this store on my own for over thirty years. I don't need some young hotshot coming in thinking he knows better than I do."

"I understand.".

I was hoping that bringing up something Dad was invested in and that Alex could help with would be a safe topic. But, obviously, I was wrong. Thankfully, the rest of dinner goes by without any more issues.

After we clean up, Mom cooks popcorn on the stovetop. Then, we settle in for another family tradition that started when Michael and I were little.

The town would start putting the Christmas decorations on the lampposts downtown before Thanksgiving. The stores put out their Christmas displays and turned on their Christmas music. We got our parts for the yearly nativity in Sunday school and started rehearsals. Christmas was all around us, making it easy for Michael and me to catch the Christmas spirit.

We'd come home and beg our parents to put up the Christmas tree. Every year, they'd tell us a firm *no*. We had to celebrate Thanksgiving before we could move on to Christmas. But on the night before Thanksgiving, Mom would make popcorn and homemade hot chocolate while Michael and I spread blankets on the living room floor. Then we'd all sit down and watch *Miracle on 34th Street*.

It was just a little taste, enough to get Michael and me through what we thought was the boring holiday that stood between Christmas and us.

"The parade is even better in person," I tell them when we get to that part of the movie. "Maybe you guys can come to New York next year, and we can all go together?"

"I don't think so," Mom answers. "I've seen enough of that city for a lifetime."

"I know it isn't your favorite place. But the parade is something extraordinary. We can have Thanksgiving dinner at Alex's apartment, maybe start some new traditions."

"The answer is no. Dad and I aren't looking for new traditions."

"What happens when Alex and I have children? Won't you want to visit the city and spend the holidays with us?"

Dad lets out a frustrated breath. "I see you haven't gotten over your ridiculous notion of a future with that man."

"It's not ridiculous. We're hoping you'd both be open to spending time with us when Alex gets home." I hesitate before continuing. "I love him. We both want you to be a part of our lives."

"Please don't ruin tonight with any more nonsense," Mom says. "This conversation is over."

They're infuriating.

Even though it's still early when the movie ends, Mom and Dad say goodnight. They'll be up before the sun to start cooking the turkey.

"I'll be up shortly. It's a beautiful evening. I'm going to sit on the porch for a little bit."

It's unseasonably warm, and Alex told me to call after the movie, even though it's the early morning hours in Russia.

"Don't be up late," Mom reminds me. "Tomorrow's going to be a busy day."

"I won't." I shake my head as I walk out the front door. Some things will never change, I guess.

Alex's voice is groggy when he answers the phone. I know I woke him up.

"You should go back to sleep. I can call you later."

"No, I want you to tell me about your day."

I try to condense everything into as short a story as possible. I can hear how tired he is. He has a big day ahead of him, too. Even though Russians don't celebrate Thanksgiving, the Soloniks are having a special dinner to commemorate the day for Alex.

Irina's never made a turkey before, but she bought one and plans to cook it herself. She even has Alex's mom's recipe for the stuffing. They're such a thoughtful family. Part of me wishes I were there with him.

After we say our goodbyes, I head to bed, my heart heavy. I'm envious of Lana's family. I'd give anything for my parents to be half as open as Maxim and Irina.

Is it possible to love my parents and, at the same time, wish I had a different family?

Alex

After hanging up with Natalie, I try to fall back to sleep, but that doesn't happen. So, I head to the kitchen and grab a very early breakfast. Maybe I'll get a run in before everyone gets up? Not wanting to wake anyone, I pad through the house quietly. As I move down the hallway toward the kitchen, I spot the library door cracked open. The light is on.

I get closer and peek inside. Maxim is sitting in one of the brown leather wingback chairs in the center of the room. In front of him is a wooden table with an open bottle of vodka sitting on top. A shot glass is in his hand.

"Come in, Alexander." Maxim's voice echoes in the silence.

"I'm sorry. I didn't mean to intrude."

"Get a glass and sit down."

"Yes, sir." It's way too early to drink. The sun isn't even up. But the pained look on Maxim's face implores me to do as I'm told. Walking over to the bar at the back of the room, I grab a shot glass before returning to the chairs and sitting down. Maxim picks up the bottle of vodka and fills our glasses. We share a shot.

I've never seen Maxim like this. His eyes are red, not from alcohol but from tears. Something has gravely upset him, but I'm afraid to ask questions.

"Today would have been Jelena's twenty-fifth birthday."

"I'm sorry, Max."

"As a parent, it is a wonder to see how different your children are. Svetlana was always spirited. She loved to steal the show. But Jelena was quiet. Content to stay in the background."

I listen as Maxim continues.

"I used every contact I had to find my Jelena. I went days without sleep trying to find my little girl. But Jelena was young and still a virgin. She was a sought-after prize and was sold right away." His haunted eyes fill with tears. "By the time we found the man who bought her, it was too late. They raped and tortured my daughter before they killed her."

I can't imagine the heartache of losing a child, but how Jelena died is unimaginable. No parent should ever have to experience that. Maxim avenged his daughter's brutal murder by taking the lives of the men responsible for her death.

"Did you know opening Jelena's Hope was Svetlana's idea?"

"I didn't."

Maxim explains how a young Svetlana approached him with her desire to help other people who were trafficked. "She wanted to make sure they could heal. As difficult as she can be at times, *moya babochka* has a good heart."

When Lana first came to live with me, I seriously doubted my sanity. Saying she was challenging is putting it mildly. She was infuriating. It took some heart-to-heart conversations with Pyotr to see past her prickly exterior to the scared little girl underneath. That's when I started to see her differently. But it was Brandon who really made a difference for her.

"Alami, that bastard, knew we were coming for Jelena. He had eyes all over and got a tip that my men were coming for him. We missed it, Alexander." His face twists in pain, and he pours himself another shot. "Jelena died because of me."

"That's not true, Max. You did everything you could."

"Some of them are in horrible condition," Max continues. "This is the most dangerous time for a recovered victim. They struggle with finding the will to live again. We lost one young woman in the very beginning. I will never forgive myself for that."

"I see." I know my response is lacking. I'm struggling to keep up and process all this information.

"I know we are fortunate that we were at least able to bring her body home. Many families do not get that much closure. That is why I vowed to hunt the scum that preys on innocents until the day I die. It will never bring back my Jelena, but I will ensure her death was not in vain."

My respect for Maxim grows exponentially. "I'll always be available in any way to help you win this war."

I'm honored Maxim chose me.

This is a fight for a worthy cause. One that's part of making the world a safer place.

Natalie

At seven a.m., my alarm goes off. With my eyes still closed, I reach out, trying to find my cell phone to turn the noise off. I'd hoped to sleep in on my vacation, but that's not happening today. Instead, I sit up and stretch. I don't know if it was the comfort and safety of my old bedroom, but for the first time in weeks, I slept all night and didn't have any nightmares.

Climbing out of bed, I throw on sweatpants and a T-shirt, my chosen outfit for the day. As soon as I open the bedroom door, my mouth waters. The fragrant aroma of the turkey has already filled the house. I hurry downstairs to the kitchen, knowing I'll find a familiar sight.

My parents have music on and don't hear me outside the room, so I'm able to watch them quietly. It's like a vignette from my childhood. Dad sits at the kitchen table, cutting the ingredients for his famous stuffing. Mom's at the stove working on her cranberry sauce. In past years, neighbors have placed orders for it ahead of time. I can almost see Michael's ghost at the counter with the Kitchen Aid, making homemade whipped cream for the pies.

Michael loved baking and had an exceptional talent for decorating his baked goods. He'd spend hours in the kitchen making decorated cookies in all shapes and designs. He made several birthday cakes for kids' parties. His dream was to open his own bakery. Before I get too emotional, I make my presence known.

"Morning," I say and head straight to the coffee pot.

"Good morning, Natalie," Mom chirps.

"Morning, Dad." I set my cup on the table and kiss his cheek.

"Morning," he grumbles. "You overslept. We've been up for hours working on dinner."

I shrug, refusing to engage.

"There are fresh biscuits and sausage gravy keeping warm on the stove."

"I haven't had that in years." I lift the lid off the pan to take in the aroma of the delicious Southern goodness. I grab a few biscuits and ladle a generous helping of gravy over them before sitting down to eat.

"Can you give me the recipe for this, Mom?"

"Sure, dear."

"I'd like to make this for Alex," I say and quickly take another bite.

"When you're done, can you start setting the dining table?"

"Sure."

"I got everything out. Do you remember how to set up the centerpiece?"

"Of course I do."

We never had company for Thanksgiving, but it didn't matter. It was one of the few days of the year we ate in the formal dining room. Mom would take out her China and set an elaborate table for the holiday. The focal point of the centerpiece was a wicker cornucopia she and Dad made when they were first married.

When Michael and I were kids, our parents made a big deal of filling the empty horn. Each year, Mom would sit down to tell us the history of the cornucopia and how it symbolized abundance. She'd have a bowl full of vegetables, flowers, and decorative gourds we spent all summer growing. Michael and I would take turns stuffing the horn full until the bounty of our work began to overflow onto the table. Then, we'd take turns saying things we were thankful for.

It's a memory I treasure deeply.

When I'm finished eating, I wash my dishes and go to the dining room. On the table is Mom's China, but with many more settings than we need for the three of us. I peek my head into the kitchen. "Don't you have too many plates out?"

"No, dear. We're having company."

"Company?" We've never had company for Thanksgiving.

"It's a tradition we started while you were away."

"Who's coming?"

"Reverend Miller and Hannah, Ashlynn and her dad, Delia, and a few others who don't have a family to spend the holiday with," Mom says. "You'll need to change your clothes before we eat. Put on something a bit nicer."

"Please tell me Tommy isn't coming."

"Delia and Tommy are with us every year. You will be on your best behavior."

I can deal with Ashlynn being here. My parents don't know anything about why we're not friends anymore. But Tommy. They know I don't want to be near him, yet they didn't mention he would be here. They should've said something, given me the choice. I guess it's partially my fault for not asking, but I had no reason to believe Thanksgiving had changed so much.

Today's a day for being thankful, not for fighting. I repeat my mantra while I set the table. I will not let Tommy's presence ruin this holiday for me.

The afternoon has flown by while we've been busy with the preparations. By the time I look at the clock, it's after two. We always eat early, so it comes as no surprise when the doorbell rings, announcing the first guests' arrival. I look down and realize I haven't changed yet.

While Mom answers the door, I race up the steps and find a dress that should be more appropriate. I make quick work of washing up before I get dressed and fix my hair. The doorbell rings again just as I'm coming down the steps.

"Can you grab that?" Mom calls from the other room.

"Sure." I open the door and freeze.

Delia and Tommy are standing on the other side. Even though I knew they were coming, I'm still shocked at their presence.

"Hello, Natalie, dear." Mrs. Laurel smiles and walks past me, carrying her casserole dish.

Tommy remains in the doorway, holding a bouquet of roses. He's smiling from ear to ear, clearly amused by the situation.

I, however, am not amused.

"Aren't you going to say hi?" Tommy asks.

"Hi," I say sharply and turn to walk away, but Tommy grabs my arm.

"That's not a very polite way to welcome a guest. These are for you." He pushes the flowers toward me. When I don't reach out to accept them, he squeezes my arm tighter. "Take your flowers like a good little girl."

Grudgingly, I take the bouquet before walking into the kitchen. Tommy follows close behind.

"Look at the beautiful roses. Are they from Tommy?" Mom asks.

"Yes," I say and drop them on the counter.

I start to walk away, but Mom stops me.

"Natalie, don't be rude. Put your flowers in a vase and set it on the buffet." She makes her way to Tommy and kisses him on the cheek. "That was so thoughtful of you."

Everyone's already seated at the table when I walk in and set the vase down. Our guests murmur their appreciation for the *romantic gesture*. I struggle not to roll my eyes.

Moments later, Dad comes into the room carrying a silver tray with the golden-brown turkey proudly displayed. He sets it on the table and then takes his seat at the head of the table. Mom sits to his right, leaving one empty chair for me next to Tommy. He's wearing a smug look on his face as I sit down.

"Let us join hands as we say a blessing for the meal," Reverend Miller says.

My stomach turns as I place my hand in Tommy's. He finishes his lengthy prayer, and there's a chorus of 'amens.' I quickly pull my hand away, ready to start the meal, when Tommy stands.

"Before we eat, there's something I'd like to say."

This time, I roll my eyes, earning a reprimanding glare from my mother.

Tommy turns to me. "Natalie, you and I have known each other for as long as I can remember. And I think I've loved you for just as long."

There's no way he's doing this. My heart rate skyrockets, and my eyes dart around the room, looking for a quick escape.

"I know we've had some problems. Every couple does." He glances at Ashlynn.

She looks down, her eyes filled with tears. Does she actually care about him?

"Things were rough when you went away for school. But since you've come home, any doubts I had are gone. It's clear what I want." Tommy reaches into his pocket and pulls out a small velvet-covered box.

Looking around the table, I realize no one's surprised at the scene unfolding before them. Reverend Miller and Hannah are holding hands. Mom's dabbing at the tears in her eyes, but there's a smile on her face. Nausea bubbles in my stomach, my palms are clammy, and sweat forms on my brow.

Tommy gets down on one knee.

"Natalie Clarke, will you do me the honor of being my wife?" He opens the box and takes out a ring. "Marry me?"

I can't move—can't breathe.

I don't know what to do.

I thought Tommy understood there isn't an *us*.

When I moved out, I assumed my parents understood it was because I was serious about Alex. When they invited me home for the holiday, I figured they'd finally accepted there'd be nothing with Tommy. Even if they weren't ready to accept Alex yet. But looking around the table now, it's clear no one has moved on except me.

"Tommy, I—"

He grabs my hand and tries to slip the ring on my finger.

"No." I pull my hand away. "I'm not marrying you."

He gets up quickly, trying to keep a smile on his face, but I see the anger boiling over in his eyes.

"Natalie, how dare you?" Mom snaps.

When I'm finally able to move, I jump from my chair, horrified at the situation.

"How dare I? How dare you. All of you." I point at the shocked faces around the table. "You all knew about this, didn't you?"

My parents' guests squirm in their seats.

"I've tried telling you, Tommy and I aren't a couple. We haven't been for years. We haven't been since he cheated on me."

Mom gasps.

"Natalie, don't," Tommy whispers in my ear. "Shut up and put the ring on your finger."

He grabs my hand, but I pull away.

"Don't touch me. I'm done. I refuse to do this any longer. I've kept the truth to myself for too long, but it's time you all hear it. I was in my first year of grad school and finished my midterms sooner than expected." I look pointedly at my parents.

"Do you remember I was supposed to come home? Instead, I called and told you there was a last-minute change of plans, and I had to work."

They stare at me but don't react.

"I was here. I flew in a few days early and went to Mizzou. I wanted to surprise Tommy. So, I went to his dorm. God, I was so excited. Until I opened the door."

The pain of that moment rips through me as if it happened yesterday. At this moment, I have a decision to make. I can tell everyone I caught Tommy and Ashlynn together.

But what will that do?

What good will come of it?

I let my gaze wander to where Ashlynn sits across from me. She looks at me, her eyes wide and pleading. I could be vindictive and hurt her as badly as she hurt me, but I don't want that. There's been enough hurt.

I just want to be heard.

"I found him in bed, having sex with another girl."

Our guests begin to whisper amongst themselves.

"I couldn't handle the betrayal, so I found the next flight to New York, and I left." I begin to back away from the table. "These past few years, I've tried to protect Tommy. I didn't want to ruin his precious reputation, so I kept it to myself. I thought it was the right thing to do." I let out a sarcastic laugh.

"Instead, everyone turned on *me*." I hit my chest. "My own parents refuse to accept I've moved on and that I'm in love with someone else. A man who's kind and treats me well. Someone honest and trustworthy who would never hurt me. A man who loves me. I naively thought I'd find support from my friends, and I thought my parents would be happy for me." I turn to face them.

"But you're content to trick me. To make a fool of me."

"Natalie, you will stop this instant," Dad yells.

"I'm sorry, Daddy, but this is too much. I can't do this anymore."

I turn and nearly trip over my chair as I hurry to leave the room.

"Natalie, child." Reverend Miller stands up, blocking my path. "Let's sit down and discuss this calmly."

"Move out of my way." My voice comes out in a roar.

He must sense the depth of my fury because he steps aside, clearing the path to the door. Tommy's right on my heels, and before I can get to the door, he grabs my arm. His voice is low, so only I can hear.

"If you walk out, I'll show them the pictures."

I pull free from his grip. "You know what? Do it. Get it over with. I don't care anymore."

"Natalie, if you walk out that door again, you won't be asked to come back," Mom says in an even, calm tone.

I look up and see my parents standing in the archway that separates the dining room from the living room.

"I wasn't planning on coming back."

I grab my purse from where it hangs by the door and, with hurried steps, rush out of the house. I'm thankful for the forethought of parking on the street. My tires squeal as I pull away.

I can't believe I was so stupid to think everything was okay. I thought my parents had accepted my choices, even if they disagreed. By the look on everyone's faces when Tommy stood up to make his awful proposal, they all knew what was happening. This was planned behind my back. Did they think I would say yes just because everyone was sitting there? That I'd cave to the pressure?

"Ha. They probably did," I say aloud.

Well, this time, they got the message. And, come to think of it, so did I.

But I'm not that girl anymore.

Alex

I'VE BEEN CALLING NATALIE ALL NIGHT, BUT MY CALLS keep going straight to voicemail, and my texts are all unread. I tried Lana, but she hasn't heard from Natalie either. She was supposed to call me after her family had dinner.

That was five hours ago.

Where are you, baby girl?

I traded sleep for pacing the house all night, waiting for her call. A new day has dawned, and I still haven't heard from her. I'm on the other side of the world and completely helpless. It's a feeling I'm not used to and one I don't like.

It's only seven in the morning, and I'm already on my third cup of coffee. Between my anxiety and the caffeine overload, I can't sit still. I pace back and forth in the dining room, willing my phone to ring.

"Alexander, you look terrible. Did you not sleep well?" Maxim asks as he walks into the room.

I run my hands through my disheveled hair.

"Natalie never called. Her phone's going straight to voicemail." My words come out hurried. I recheck my phone—nothing.

Maxim, never one to rush a response, pours his coffee and then sits in his chair at the head of the table.

"Have you tried calling her parents?"

"I called her father's cell. He didn't answer, and their landline is unlisted." I don't stop moving while I speak.

"Alexander, sit down," Maxim says with authority. "You are going to wear out my floor."

Although sitting still feels like an impossibility, Maxim's command leaves no room for argument. I sit at the table and pour myself another cup of coffee. The kitchen door opens, and Maxim's staff serves our breakfast. As delicious as the kasha smells, my stomach is in knots. I can't eat.

Maxim pulls his phone from a pocket inside his suit jacket and types out a message. After setting the phone on the table, he begins eating.

"I don't know what to do." I drop my head in my hands. "I need to go to Missouri. I need to find her, but I can't leave yet."

Maxim continues eating his breakfast, seemingly unfazed by my rambling. I dial Natalie's number, and again, no answer. Hanging up, I put the phone back on the table.

"I shouldn't have come. I shouldn't have left Natalie alone."

Maxim's phone vibrates. He lifts it and looks at the screen, but his face gives nothing away. A few seconds later, my text alert sounds. I rush to check it, hoping it's finally Natalie, but it's a text from Maxim instead.

"Her parents' phone number," he says calmly.

"How did you?"

"I have my sources, Alexander. Call them."

Pulling up the keypad, I input the numbers and tap the green call button. The line connects and begins to ring.

"Hello?"

"Mr. Clarke?"

"Who is this?"

"It's Alex Montgomery. I'm trying to find Natalie. Is she there?"

There's no response. I pull the phone away from my ear to check the screen, ensuring the connection didn't drop.

"She's not here."

"Do you know where—"

With a click, the line goes dead.

"He hung up on me." My hands shake from a mix of fear and anger. "What do I do now?"

Maxim stands, his demeanor eerily calm. "I am going to my office to make a few calls. We will find Natalia."

With confident strides, he walks away. And once again, I'm left alone with my thoughts. I know Maxim's reach is long. I'm hoping it's long enough to find Natalie. Because as much as I want to get on the next plane back to the States, I can't. I have a meeting with Nicholai in an hour.

I don't know Nicholai's story, but I assume it's similar to Maxim's, making these two men a formidable force in their fight against trafficking. Today's meeting is to set up the framework for a second treatment center in another part of Russia. Identifying a victim and getting them to safety is only the first step.

Yesterday, after our Thanksgiving meal, Maxim and Irina took me to Jelena's Hope. It's the first time I've been at their facility. What I witnessed will not soon be forgotten.

The people brought to the center are often severely injured physically, which turns out to be the easiest of the wounds to heal. The mental and emotional trauma is the most difficult to treat. It's often a long and bumpy road to recovery. These concerns need to be addressed before they're reunited with their families.

Sadly, some of the victims don't have a family. Worse yet are the ones whose families choose to no longer accept them. Maxim and Irina ensure they're set up with a new life and a support system. They'll never be unwanted again.

As we walked through the facility, I pictured Natalie working alongside Irina, helping to heal the broken. Her caring nature and her professional skills would be valuable.

I finish my coffee before going to my room for a hot shower.

There's work to be done, so I need to put on my game face. When I'm dressed, I leave my room on the second floor and take the grand staircase to the first floor. Maxim's office is down a hallway near the front of the house. I arrive at a closed door. Usually, Maxim's guard, Timur, is here, but since he isn't, I knock.

"Come in."

Maxim's office is impressive. The exterior wall is lined with windows that overlook the front of his property. Larch wood, native to Russia, was used to build the massive desk in the room's center. Behind it are built-in bookshelves filled with centuries-old books on Russian history. A pair of ornately carved, neoclassical armchairs that date back to 1820 sit opposite the desk.

"Viktor is on a plane heading to Northmeadow. He will call as soon as he locates Natalia," Maxim reassures me.

I lower myself into one of the armchairs and allow myself to breathe. Viktor's been loyal to me for years. I'm confident he'll find her and keep her safe. But it does little to stop the ache in my heart that I can't be there myself.

"Thank you." The words don't seem enough, but they're all I have.

The office door opens, and Maxim's guard announces Nicholai's arrival.

Nicholai's an older man. I'm guessing close to Maxim's age. He always arrives in a tailored suit and carries the same air of power and danger as Maxim. During our first few meetings, he was guarded, distrusting. We've spent a great deal of time together over the past few weeks. I've earned his trust, and he's beginning to open up.

Although I've seen a kinder side of Nicholai, make no mistake, he's a dangerous man—I wouldn't want to be on his hit list. His bodyguard steps aside when Maxim approaches. I follow, shaking Nicholai's hand.

"Good to see you this morning, Mr. Federov."

"Nicholai, please," he reminds me again.

"Let us sit down and get to work," Maxim says, nodding to

Timur, who closes the office doors. Nicholai's guard remains inside by the door.

I'm forced to set my personal issues aside for the time being and give this project my full attention.

With innocent people's lives at stake, every minor detail of this account is essential and must be done correctly.

Natalie

ONCE AGAIN, I FIND MYSELF RUNNING FROM TOMMY and the mess he's created. My only thought is getting away—putting as much distance between them and me as possible. Not wanting to be found, I turn off my phone and drive without conscious direction. But I find myself pulling up at Finn Lake. It doesn't surprise me. I'm always drawn to the water. Tourist season is over, and with it also being Thanksgiving, there's no one here.

I set off on the path I've come to so many times when I needed to clear my head and think. When I come to the bench, I nearly collapse from physical and emotional exhaustion.

The rhythmic sound of the water lapping on the shore has always helped ground me, but today, it does nothing to calm the thoughts rushing through my head.

Hours pass while I try to make sense of what happened, but I'm no closer now than when I got here.

What sort of alternate universe is Tommy living in to imagine that I might accept his ludicrous proposal? It seems like he's not the only one living there, either. I keep replaying the scene and come to the same conclusion each time. Except for Ashlynn, who looked just as shocked as I, no one else was surprised. They all knew what Tommy had planned. I've never felt so betrayed—so unseen.

"Michael, why did you leave me?" I yell. "I need you, and you're not here."

I drop my head in my hands and cry until my tears run out. A chill runs through my body, and I reach for my jacket. That's when I realize I don't have it. I didn't grab any of my things in the rush to leave.

With the sun now setting, it's getting too chilly to stay outside. I push my weary body to a stand and walk back to my car, shuffling my feet through the leaves that litter the path on my way.

Then, I begin the long, lonely drive back to my motel room.

Natalie

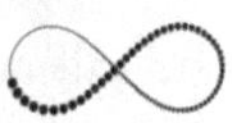

Although it's three in the afternoon, the curtains are still drawn tight. I was up all night, and now I'm exhausted. My hair is a mess, and I haven't bothered to get dressed. I'm lying on my bed, hoping sleep will pull me under, when banging on the door startles me.

"Natalie, are you in there?" I recognize the voice immediately. What's Viktor doing here? I jump out of bed and hurry to unlock the door, throwing it open. "Is Alex okay?"

Without waiting for an invitation, Viktor walks into my room.

"I've got her. She's right here, sir. It's for you." He hands me the phone.

"Alex? Are you okay?"

"Am I okay? Where have you been?"

"I've been in my room."

Then it dawns on me that I never turned my phone back on after leaving my parents' house yesterday.

"I've been worried sick about you. Are you okay?"

"Yes. No." Fresh tears fall, making it hard to speak.

"Put Viktor back on."

Even though I know Alex can't see me, I nod and pass the

phone back. Although I can't make out his exact words, it's clear from the volume of his voice that he's upset. Unable to handle more yelling, I drag my feet across the carpet and curl into a ball on the bed.

"She looks unharmed." Viktor's silent as he listens. "I'll stay with her and find out." He nods while Alex continues to vent. "Sir, if I may, please calm down. I'm here, and I won't leave her." More silence. "I'll have her call you as soon as she calms down."

Finally, he disconnects the call and slides the phone into his pocket.

A few minutes pass as he stands, arms crossed over his broad chest. His form is large and imposing in the small room. Then, he swipes his hand across his shaved head, looking uncertain, before grabbing a chair from the table and dragging it next to the bed.

Viktor sits silently beside me, his presence steady and unspoken. He places a hand gently on my arm, a quiet reassurance that I'm not alone.

The sound of the microwave beeping wakes me.

"Good evening, sleepyhead," Viktor says before opening the microwave and removing what smells like chicken soup. He places a bowl on the table. "Come over here. You need to eat."

I sit up and throw my legs over the side of the bed. My head pounds from all the crying I've done over the past twenty-four hours.

"What time is it?"

"Nearly nine," he says as he pulls out a chair for me before he goes back to the microwave to put another bowl in. "You cried yourself to sleep. By the way, you look like shit." He chuckles.

"Thanks, you're too kind." I roll my eyes as I stand up and walk to the mirror. I do look like shit.

What used to be a bun has fallen out, and now my hair is poking up in all directions. My face is blotchy. My eyes are swollen and bloodshot. Whatever. I continue my trek to the table and sit. "I'm not hungry." I push the bowl away.

"You can eat on your own, or I'll feed you. Alex's orders."

"He's so bossy, even from halfway around the world."

The microwave beeps again. Viktor grabs his bowl and sits across from me. My stomach betrays me by growling loudly.

"Eat." He points to the bowl of soup. "And start talking. What happened?"

Grudgingly, I pull the bowl to me and take a few spoonfuls of the warm chicken noodle soup before I gather the courage to relay the disaster that was Thanksgiving.

Viktor listens intently, and although his face shows no signs of emotion, his tightly clenched fists give away his anger. When I finish, he picks up his phone.

"Who are you calling?"

"Alex."

"Let me tell him, please."

I don't want to tell the story again, but he needs to hear it from me. Viktor hands me the phone. It's already ringing.

"Thank you," I whisper.

Viktor offers me a rare smile. "I'll just be outside."

"Hello?"

"Alex."

"It's me, baby girl."

Unlike earlier, his voice is now calm and gentle.

"Yesterday was awful." I struggle with the still-raw emotions. "And then I left. I turned my phone off because I didn't want my mom or dad calling me, and I forgot to turn it back on." He stays quiet for so long that I think the line may have disconnected. "Are you still there?"

The sound of his breathing is the only thing I hear.

"I'm sorry doesn't feel like enough. I feel useless. You need me, and I'm stuck here."

"Please don't do that."

I don't want him to feel responsible for this mess. It's not his burden to bear. The fault lies solely with the individuals sitting around that table yesterday.

"You're mine to protect. And I'm not there when you need me."

The pain in his voice is palpable, even through the phone.

"You're here now."

"No, I'm not. I'm half a world away." There's a raw edge to his words.

I close my eyes, fighting the tears threatening to spill once again.

"I know you're not here physically, but at least we can talk. And you'll be back soon."

"I'm assuming I can't talk you into going straight to New York?"

"You assume right. I have to work. But I'll be there in three weeks, and then I'm all yours until after the new year."

He sighs deeply. "Viktor will be staying with you until then."

"That's not necessary."

"This is non-negotiable. I can't do what I need to here, while I'm constantly worrying about you there. Viktor will be by your side until you get back home."

My Dominant is back, and I don't miss his use of the word *home*.

"Yes, Sir."

There's no use arguing with him, and honestly, I'm not sure I want to. I've been looking over my shoulder since that night at the store with Tommy. Something I still haven't told Alex about. It might be nice to have Viktor around for protection and some company. Glancing at the clock on the nightstand, I see it's nearly midnight, which means it's eight in the morning in Russia.

"It's late. You've been on the phone with me all night."

"I can stay on the phone as long as you need me, baby girl."

I smile, knowing I'm the luckiest girl on earth.

"I appreciate that, but it's late for both of us."

"Let me talk to Viktor. He has my card. I want him to get the room next to yours."

This isn't going to go over well.

"He'll have to stay in my room for the weekend." I hold my breath, waiting for the explosion on the other end.

"That's not going to happen," Alex growls.

"Marshall closed the motel for the weekend so he could take a much-needed vacation. He won't be back until Monday."

With tourist season over, the motel is a ghost town. Marshall knew I had nowhere to go, so he let me stay and left me his number for emergencies. I hardly consider this worth interrupting his time off.

"He'll sleep in the car."

"Don't be ridiculous." I let out a sarcastic laugh. "He'll stay in my room."

"Natalie—"

I ignore the warning in his voice and open the door. Viktor is outside, leaning against the wall. I motion for him to come back in and put the phone on speaker. I know I'm pushing Alex on this, but I'm not letting Viktor sleep in his car.

"Alex would like you to stay in Northmeadow until I leave for vacation," I say, addressing both men.

"Not a problem, boss. I'll—"

I raise my hand, interrupting him.

"The motel office is closed for the weekend. You and I'll be roomies until Monday." I sit down and cross my legs in mock victory.

Viktor's mouth hangs open. His eyes grow wide.

"Viktor," Alex yells. "Take the phone off speaker, now."

I swear the walls in the room shake. Maybe I shouldn't have pushed him *that* far. Viktor shoots me a warning look as he grabs the phone from my hand and once again steps outside the room. I've just managed to upset two powerful men.

Oh well, what's done is done. While they hash it out, I decide to take a much-needed shower.

After I dry off and get dressed, I crack open the bathroom door, trying to gauge the situation. Viktor turned the chair to face this direction. He's sitting back, legs spread, arms crossed over his chest. Cautiously, I step into the main room. I give a slight shrug and attempt a smile.

"It's a good thing that man of yours is in another country. Let's hope, for both our sakes, that he calms down before he gets home." He shakes his head, clearly not amused.

The past forty-eight hours hit me all at once. Exhaustion permeates my entire being, and all I want to do is sleep.

Knowing I'm safe with Viktor, I ask, "So, what side of the bed do you want?"

Viktor cocks his head to the side.

"Neither. I'll take the floor."

"That's ridiculous."

"Maybe so, but I want to remain alive and keep my job."

Remain alive? He's a bit overdramatic.

But I concede and am happy he at least lets me give him a pillow and blanket.

Natalie

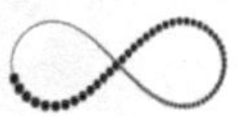

FIRST THING MONDAY MORNING, VIKTOR'S STANDING outside the motel office waiting for Marshall to arrive. He's now my neighbor in room six, which means I'm alone tonight. Alex video calls to ensure I'm appropriately punished for my behavior the other night.

"Undress for me, slowly," Alex instructs.

Climbing off my bed, I turn the laptop so Alex can watch as I strip. I remove each piece of clothing as slowly and seductively as possible.

"Pull a chair over and sit."

While I'm getting the chair, I hear the sound of his zipper. When I turn around, he's sliding his hand up and down his hard length. Unable to take my eyes off him, I stumble when I go to sit on the chair.

"Open your legs. I want to see you," he demands.

I do as I'm told, even though I don't see how this is supposed to be a punishment.

"Touch yourself."

I drag my finger through the wetness between my legs and rub small circles on my already sensitive center. Watching Alex stroke himself intensifies my arousal. With my free hand, I pinch my hardened nipple and moan at the sensation.

"That's it, baby girl." Alex encourages me. "You look so hot right now."

"I'm so close."

"Keep your eyes open and look at me."

"Yes, Sir."

Alex increases his pace as he chases his release.

"Alex, I'm going to—"

"Stop," he commands.

My hand stills, and I watch as he brings himself to orgasm, ribbons of cum landing on his shirt. He doesn't speak until the last of his contractions stop.

"Do not touch yourself until I give you permission."

I'm so close it's painful. My thighs squeeze together, trying to take the edge off. I'm ready to drop to my knees and beg Alex to let me finish, but I know he won't allow it. Denying an orgasm is my punishment.

"My little sub, you need to learn not to push me, especially in front of another man."

I lower my gaze. The knowledge that my actions disappointed him hurts more than being denied pleasure.

"I'm sorry, Sir."

"Look at me."

I raise my eyes to meet his.

"I forgive you." The edge that was in his voice is gone.

Punishment within a relationship is something I've had to get used to. I try to avoid it, but I know it serves a purpose. Alex is an experienced Dominant. His discipline challenges me, but doesn't push me past my limits.

The most beautiful part is the complete forgiveness Alex gives me. There are no arguments or grudges held. It's just over.

The hardest part is forgiving myself. That's still a work in progress.

Tommy

Natalie's behavior on Thanksgiving has anger pulsing through my veins like red, hot lava.

"What the hell was she thinking telling me no?" I pound the steering wheel.

The box with her diamond ring lies like a lead weight in my pocket. She left me standing in front of everyone, looking like a fool. I haven't figured out exactly how, but she'll pay.

For now, I'm back to following her from a distance. Since that motel guy found me outside her room and threatened me at gunpoint, I've had to watch my step. I found a secluded area where I could park my truck so it wouldn't be seen.

It's a half-mile walk through the woods until I'm across from the hotel, where I sit hidden in the tree line. I use my binoculars to keep an eye on her room. I'm gonna need a new plan soon. It's getting too cold to stay outside.

Natalie's been a naughty little girl, a thought that makes me hard for her. While her *boyfriend* is out of town, it seems she's keeping company with another man. He follows her around like a lost puppy. They do everything together, and I've got the pictures to prove it. I'll make sure her boyfriend knows what she's up to when his back is turned. She'll have no one to turn to, and she'll be forced to come back to me. I pull the ring out of my pocket.

"Then I'll slip this onto her pretty little finger, and she'll be mine once and for all."

It's my lucky night. The curtains are still open in her room. She and that guy are sitting at the table playing happy little family. I use the zoom lens on the built-in camera to snap some pictures before packing up and trekking back to the truck. It gives me time to think about all the changes since Natalie's tantrum.

Stanley hired me to work full-time at the pharmacy. That puts me one step closer to our original plan. I was supposed to follow in Stanley's footsteps and become a pharmacist. Natalie was going to have my babies and work part-time at the store. When her parents were ready to retire, the store would be given to us. That was until she screwed everything up when she took off for New York.

This arrangement works in my favor, though. Stanley was concerned that his new security system went offline a few weeks ago. So, I played hero by setting up new firewalls and security codes. Which means I have access to them, and her folks are none the wiser.

It's a handy bit of information to have since I haven't found a doctor who'll give me another prescription. I drove three hours to Kansas City to see a new doctor. But as soon as he accessed my records, he refused to give me meds. Said I had to go for some tests and other shit. Fuck that.

Instead, I found a seller online and got some pills. But they come at a high price. Now that I'm working at the pharmacy and have been given the code for the safe, I can grab a few pills now and then.

So far, Stanley hasn't caught on, and I plan to keep it that way.

Natalie

It took a week to get past the awkwardness of having Viktor around all the time. Once I broke through his tough exterior, I learned he's a lot of fun, and we've fallen into a comfortable pattern. Although I've tried to explain to both him and Alex that it's unnecessary, Viktor insists on driving me to work every morning and even stands guard outside my office door. After my punishment the other night, I learned my lesson about pushing Alex too far.

Every evening, Viktor and I eat dinner together and play a highly competitive game of rummy. It's not his typical assignment, I'm sure.

This morning, I woke to find a voicemail from my father telling me I have one week to remove my belongings from their house, or they'll be put in the trash.

Mondays are bad enough without adding this to the mix. How am I going to move everything out this week? Where am I going to store my stuff?

Like clockwork, I receive a text followed by a knock on my door—Viktor's right on time. Usually, I am too, but today I'm running behind. I unchain the door and let him in.

"Good morning," he says and hands me a cup of coffee.

He brings one every morning. The man is a saint.

"You're going to make some woman very happy," I say as I reach out and take the cup.

His mouth twitches with amusement.

"Have a seat. I'll be ready in a few minutes."

"No problem." He lowers himself onto the chair and pulls out his phone.

"Can we stop by my parents' house after work today?" I lower my mascara wand and glance at him in the mirror.

"Why?"

"I have to get some things."

"We'll go shopping. I have Alex's card for anything you need."

After I finish applying my lipstick, I take a seat opposite him.

"There's nothing I *need*, exactly." I play with my coffee cup nervously. "My dad called to let me know I have until the end of the week to move out my stuff, or else they're getting rid of it."

"Well, isn't that fucking fantastic of him."

I shrug, unsure what else to say.

Everything I'd once thought about my parents lies scattered in a debris field, and I've yet to sort through the remains. Is there any truth to my memories, or have they been this way all along? Perhaps because I never challenged them, I didn't see it. I'm not ready to face what I might find, so I place everything in a neat little box in the back of my mind. My primary focus is on making it through the next few weeks until I leave for New York. Maybe I'll be strong enough to face the hurt once some time has passed.

"Would you mind going with me and giving me a hand? It's just some clothes, books—"

"You don't have to ask. We'll go and get everything you need." He offers me a reassuring smile.

"Thanks."

"Just doing my job."

"Well, I appreciate you just doing your job."

"Right." He stands and heads for the door. "You ready to go?"

I laugh at his reaction, knowing he's operating in uncharted territory. I know Alex threatened Viktor within an inch of his life about being here alone with me. It's a little much, but Alex is my overprotective alpha Dominant. And secretly, I do love it.

"I'm right behind you." I slip on my winter coat, grab my bag, and follow him out the door.

Winter seems to have settled early this year. Snow flurries are dancing in the cold breeze. I reach into my pocket for my mittens and pull them on.

"Cold?" Viktor asks in a playful tone.

"Freezing." I almost forgot how much I hate the bitterly cold Missouri winters. And it's only the second week of December, not even really winter yet. "Don't tell me. You aren't cold?"

"This is nothing compared to a Ukrainian winter," Viktor says as he opens the door for me. "I've already warmed the car. Can't call my boss and tell him I let his woman freeze to death now, can I?"

I punch him lightly in the arm as I get in. Shaking his head, he rubs his arm and laughs before shutting my door.

Viktor seems to be in a good mood this morning. There's something I've been wanting to ask him about, but every time I go to say it, I chicken out. Since we're in the car, where I can't back out once I start, I decide it's now or never.

"Viktor?"

"Yes?"

"Would you help me with a surprise for Alex?"

He glances my way, lifting an eyebrow. "Depends on what you're planning."

"I want to change our plane tickets. I have some personal days that I took off. I'm hoping we can leave for the city a few days early so I can get everything ready for Christmas before Alex gets home. But you can't tell him. Can we do that?"

Viktor's face remains stoic. His eyes focused on the road ahead. I bite my nails, nervous he's going to say no. I need him to go along with this.

"Yes."

"Yes? I'm so happy I could hug you right now."

"You'll do no such thing." The edge of Viktor's mouth turns up in a small smile. "I'll change our flight this afternoon."

The adrenaline rush from the mix of excitement and nervousness makes it hard to sit still. For the rest of the drive, I make a mental list of everything that needs to be done. I'm going to have to call Lana and enlist her help. This is Alex and my first Christmas together. I want to be sure it's extra special.

When we pull up at the school, there's a group of kids outside with boxes of lights and ornaments. Some are already decorating the trees that line the sidewalk. Others are taking selfies.

"What are they doing?" Viktor asks.

Memories of my last year in high school rush to the surface.

"The Santa Parade is this weekend. Every year, the senior class decorates the trees for the parade. Businesses up and down Main Street do the same."

He nods as he continues to watch the kids stringing lights and garlands. It's clear they're having a terrific time, and as much as I'd love to sit here and watch them, I can't. I have to get into my office before the bell rings, and I'm late. I don't need to give Mr. Meadows any ammunition to use against me. I reach for the handle on the door, but Viktor grabs my arm.

"Wait." He motions over my shoulder.

Turning to look out the window, I see Tommy leaning against his parked car across the street.

"What's he doing here?"

"Don't know." Viktor turns off the car and unbuckles his safety belt.

My eyes stay fixed on Tommy while I wait for Viktor to come to my side. Tommy crosses his arms over his chest, undaunted by my staring. Viktor opens the door and steps into my line of sight. But I still hesitate to get out.

"It's okay. He won't get near you."

Viktor's reassurance is enough to give me the courage to leave the safety of the car. But I still grasp his hand for support. His body tenses at the contact.

"Thank you," I say softly.

I can feel Tommy's eyes boring into my back the whole walk up the steps and into the building. Viktor talks to me the entire time, reminding me to be brave and not look back. I'm relieved when we get inside the door.

Tommy's appearance this morning spooked me, and I've been jumpy and distracted all day. Since his proposal, he's becoming more and more unraveled. Now, I hear he's working at my parents' pharmacy.

After everything that's happened, I know I shouldn't care, but I do. My parents are hard workers, and I don't want them to lose everything because they refuse to see what's right in front of their faces. This time, it's on them. I can't—no, I won't step in and fix it.

"Miss Natalie." Mary's voice cuts through my wayward thoughts.

"I'm sorry, Mary," I say, embarrassed by my lack of professionalism. "Can you repeat what you said?"

"Is everything okay?"

I school my features, hoping to relieve some of the worries I see on their face.

"I'm just getting excited for Christmas. Do you have any plans for break?" I ask, switching the focus back to them.

"Oh yeah, big plans." They huff a laugh. "Billy's coming over. He'll leave his boyfriend home because, well, you know why." Mary rolls their eyes.

I know exactly why Billy won't be bringing Todd with him. Mary continues to tell their story matter-of-factly.

"It's all about appearances. Mom will be busy trying to make the perfect dinner. Dad will be watching TV until Billy gets there. Then all hell will break loose. They'll start screaming at each other. I'll go to my room, and then Billy will leave." They look at me with grief-filled eyes. "I miss him."

"I understand." My heart goes out to Mary.

Even though there's a five-year age gap between the siblings, they grew up close. Billy always looked out for Mary. He still does. A few months ago, Billy gave Mary a cell phone so they could talk to one another, and he tries to visit as often as he can. He's an essential part of their support system.

"Last session, we discussed how and when to tell your parents. We listed the pros and cons of telling them now or waiting until after your birthday. Have you thought about it at all?"

"I've thought a lot about it. Heck, I can't stop thinking about it. I can't go through the things Billy did. I decided it was best to wait until after my birthday. It's only a few more weeks." Mary looks down at their hands.

"That's a very mature decision."

When Mary first started sessions with me, they were fueled by anger and on their way toward a head-on collision with their parents. However, Mary has made a lot of progress over the past few months and is doing a great job responding rather than reacting. Mary accepts that they can't change what their parents do when they tell them about their gender identity, but it will change how Mary responds to them.

"I'd like to take your suggestion about inviting them to a session. Can we still do that?"

"Yes, we can. You'll need to sign a few papers permitting me to talk to your parents."

"Thank you for helping me. At least I'll be eighteen, and they won't be able to force me into therapy, too," Mary says with a sad smile.

We spend the rest of the half-hour session making a safety plan. Something they may need after they tell their parents.

If they kick Mary out, which is highly probable, I want to ensure they have somewhere safe to stay and can finish high school.

"Did you talk to Billy?"

"I did. He's glad I'm waiting to tell them, too. He and Todd said I can live with them as long as needed. They're already getting a bedroom ready."

I'm relieved to know Mary has somewhere to go. Over the coming weeks, we'll talk more about how they want the session to happen. My role will be to facilitate, ensure it remains productive, and be there for Mary in the aftermath.

Unfortunately, stories like Mary's are all too familiar in this community. But, unlike in generations past, these kids have access to the whole world via the internet and social media. As a result, they've seen ways of life different from what Northmeadow offers. Many of them hope to take advantage of the opportunities that await them because they know they won't have the support of their parents. Something I'm all too familiar with.

I see myself in so many of these kids. But unlike when I was in high school and felt alone, these kids have found each other. They've been my teachers in many ways, as they model bravery and self-confidence. They still have a long road ahead of them, and I refuse to lose any of them like I lost Michael and Evan.

When the dust settles, they'll need someone in their corner, and that someone will be me.

Natalie

THE ENERGY THROUGHOUT NORTHMEADOW HIGH HAS been building all week in anticipation of the upcoming holiday break. The students only have one more week of class, but today is my last day. After the bell rings, Viktor and I are going to the airport to catch our flight to New York City. I'm trying to finish all my paperwork when there's a knock on my door.

"Come in."

The door opens a crack, and Ms. Campbell peeks her head in. "Am I interrupting?"

"Not at all." I close the file and push it to the side. "Have a seat."

"I wanted to see you before the holiday break." She takes a seat across from me. "I'm very pleased with the work you're doing. I know it isn't easy around here. But you're doing great."

Ms. Campbell's one of my only allies in this place. Her compliment means the world to me. I sit back in my chair and let my guard down for a few minutes.

"It hasn't been easy. You're right about that. But the kids make it worth it."

"I hope I'm not overstepping. But with everything that's

happened with your family, I wondered if you had plans for the holiday? If not, I'd like to extend an invitation to my home for Christmas."

"Thank you so much." Her offer genuinely touches me. "I have plans already, though."

"Do those plans involve that handsome man you keep telling me about?"

"They do. I'm leaving today to spend the holidays with him."

"I'm glad you're getting away. But I'll miss seeing that hot man standing outside your door every day."

We both laugh.

Ms. Campbell blushes as she stands and walks to the door. "I won't keep you. Have a safe trip and a wonderful holiday."

"Same to you."

I'm anxious for the day to end, but I swear the clock moves more slowly than usual. Having difficulty focusing on paperwork, I walk across the room to the window and look out. Snow is falling softly. It's beginning to coat the decorated trees in white, making it look like a Winter Wonderland. A few people walk down the street. It's clear from the packages in their hands that they've been shopping. Tommy's appearance last week still has me shaken, but today everything appears normal.

My cell phone dings. Confident that everything outside is status quo, I walk back to the desk to see who's texting.

Viktor: I'm not in the hall. I ducked out a few minutes early to warm the car up. I'll be out front.

Me: Thank you. As soon as the bell rings, I'm outta here.

Viktor: Text me when you're on your way.

Even though my mind is already on vacation, I force myself to sit and finish my notes. I refuse to bring any work home over the holidays. With the last file done, I place them in the bottom drawer of my desk, making sure it's locked.

Almost as if on cue, the bell finally rings. I toss my phone into my bag and take one last look around the room. Then, I turn off the lights, locking the door behind me. I'm in a hurry to leave and begin my vacation.

I start walking toward the side entrance, texting Viktor as I go. A few students call out goodbyes. I wave and keep moving. I'm trying to get out of the building as quickly as possible. When I push the exit door open, I slam into a solid wall of muscle and let out a shriek as two large hands rest on my shoulders.

"I'm sorry I startled you," Viktor says, "Tommy showed up."

I look around Viktor's imposing frame, and there, in front of the school, is Tommy. He's sitting in his car—watching.

"He wasn't out there a few minutes ago. Why is he doing this?"

"He's trying to intimidate you. But we aren't going to let him. We're going to walk to my car like nothing's wrong."

"Right, focus on walking to the car parked behind Tommy's. Got it."

This time, Viktor grabs *my* hand. "I'm right here. I won't let anything happen to you."

I squeeze his hand tight as we start walking to the car. Viktor's calm and cool, the exact opposite of how I feel. He chats with me as though we're out for a casual afternoon stroll.

"Do you have everything you need, or do we need to make any stops before we get on the highway?"

It takes a second to slow down my irrational thoughts and answer. "I packed everything last night."

"Good, then we can leave right away. We'll stop to eat once we're farther from here."

My gaze drifts to where Tommy's parked.

"Eyes on me. Not him."

Out of the corner of my eye, I see Tommy get out of the car. He's walking straight to us. My heart beats so loudly, I'm shocked Viktor can't hear it.

"Get in the car, Natalie."

I'm sick of being ordered around. Everything moves in slow motion as I step out from behind Viktor's protective stance and confront Tommy. "What are you doing here?"

"I want to talk to you."

"You did enough talking with that ridiculous proposal. Don't you think?"

"Get in the car now," Viktor orders.

Ignoring Viktor once again, I step closer to Tommy. "This time, you're going to listen to me." I point my finger at him. "I'm done being a pawn in whatever game you're playing. It stops now."

"Sweetheart, you're just upset. You need to calm down." Tommy reaches out to grab my arm.

"Do not touch her." Viktor steps between us.

"Back off," Tommy sneers.

I place my hand on Viktor's arm. Our eyes lock in a silent battle before he steps aside.

"Once upon a time, you were my everything. I was in love with you. Until I walked into your dorm room and saw you and Ashlynn together. God, Tommy, you broke my heart." I close my eyes for a brief second. "I was lost and angry. So very angry. I hated you. I hated you both."

"I said I was sorry. It was a mistake. What else do you want from me?"

I put my hand up to silence him. "I forgave you long before you apologized."

Tommy smiles and puffs out his chest.

"It wasn't about you. I forgave you for myself." I watch the smile disappear from his face. "That afternoon, when I ran, I thought my life was over. I couldn't figure out how to pick up the broken pieces of my heart. I should thank you. That day marked a turning point for me. It ended up being the best thing that ever happened to me. It forced me to change how I viewed life. It was when I decided to start living for me." I point to my chest.

"There will never be an *us* again. I respect myself far too much for that. Whatever this is you're doing, hanging around watching me. It stops now. You're never going to win me back. You and everyone else in this town need to back off and let me live my life."

Having said my piece, I turn my back on Tommy and walk away.

"You're going to regret this, little girl," he sneers.

I spin around to face him. "You don't scare me, Thomas Moore."

Without another word, I get into the car. Tommy stands on the sidewalk, legs spread, arms crossed. His eyes are dark as he stares at me through the window. Viktor starts the car, and we drive away.

Like so many years before, I don't bother looking back. Except this time, my heart isn't broken. I'm proud of the stand I just took for myself.

Anger rolls off Viktor in waves. Neither of us says a word until we're out of Northmeadow and onto the highway.

"I didn't appreciate you ignoring my directive back there. But the way you stood up to him. I'm proud of you."

"Do you think he got the hint?"

"Let's hope so."

It isn't until the plane's wheels leave the ground that I breathe a sigh of relief.

Holding up my ear pods, I ask, "Do you mind?"

Viktor looks up from whatever he's reading on his phone. "Not at all. Try to relax."

And for the first time in weeks, I feel like I can actually do that.

I put the earbuds in and open my playlist before lying my head back and closing my eyes.

Natalie

I thought the Branson Airport was busy, but JFK is bursting at the seams. By the time we disembark and get our luggage, it's after midnight. Between the nap on the flight and the chilly New York air, I'm now wide awake.

"Do we need to get a ride?"

"Nope. Alex's car is here."

"You left the car parked here while you were in Northmeadow? It's going to cost you a fortune."

"It's going to cost Alex a fortune." Viktor laughs. "He made it clear. Your safety is worth more than any dollar amount."

The knowledge that Alex cares so deeply about me that he'll do whatever it takes to keep me safe makes me feel cherished.

We finally get to the car and get on the road for the last part of our trip home. While Viktor drives, I pull out my phone and double-check the list I made. I need to get a tree, decorate, bake, and do all my shopping before Alex gets home on Wednesday. That only leaves me five days. I sure hope Lana's up for the task.

When I look up, I'm surprised we're heading toward the Queensboro Bridge. I'm about to say something, but Viktor beats me to it.

"Alex told me this is your favorite way to drive into the city."

I'm amazed that Alex doesn't miss the smallest detail, even from so far away. The skyline, with all its twinkling lights, is a breathtaking sight. I have to hold in a squeal of excitement as we cross the bridge into Manhattan.

I'm almost home.

That's an unexpected feeling, but not an unwelcome one. I've spent so much time focusing on settling back into Northmeadow that I haven't let myself think about returning to the city or calling it home again.

But as we drive through the brightly lit streets, my mind paints a picture of me living here with Alex. Of being his submissive full-time. Of us getting married and having a family.

Slow down, Natalie.

Alex said he loves me and mentioned wanting something long-term, but he's never talked about marriage. Don't imagine things that aren't going to happen. You'll end up hurt, again.

We make our final turn into the parking garage. I look at Viktor, unable to hide the smile on my face.

"Thank you. For everything."

"You aren't getting rid of me yet." He gets out of the car.

"What do you mean?" I follow him. "I'll be fine here."

"If I leave you alone and word gets back to Maxim, well, I'd rather avoid that unpleasantness."

"What does Maxim have to do with anything?"

He hesitates for a minute before responding. "He signs my paycheck."

With a click of a button, the trunk opens. I reach to grab my suitcase, but Viktor removes my hand.

"I've got them."

Although his voice holds no humor, I laugh anyway and raise my hands in surrender. It's not a battle I choose to fight. But I do manage to close the trunk before hurrying to the elevator. Without having to wheel a suitcase, I have the advantage of speed. We are just walking into the apartment when my phone rings. Alex is requesting a video call.

"Shit," I whisper.

Viktor laughs. "Didn't plan for this part, did ya?"

I have to think quickly and come up with a story. I decline the video request and answer it as a voice call.

"Hello, Sir." The pitch of my voice is higher than I'd like. I hope it doesn't betray me.

"Why isn't your camera on?"

"My phone's acting up. The camera won't turn on."

Viktor shakes his head as he walks past me.

"Use my card and have Viktor take you to get a new phone."

"Okay, I'll do that."

"Finally, I don't get an argument." Alex's laughter is a warm, rich sound that makes me miss him even more.

"What do you have planned for today?"

"Maxim and I are meeting with Nicholai. We're finalizing the details of his account."

"I'm glad to hear that. I can't wait until you come home." Being here without Alex is making me miss him even more. I'm counting the minutes until he gets back.

"Me either," Alex says softly. "I asked Brandon to put up a job listing for a management position. My attention needs to be focused on Maxim and Nicholai's accounts. And having another manager will free me up to spend more time in Northmeadow with you."

"Really? You'd spend more time in Northmeadow?"

"I was thinking about buying a house for us there."

"I don't even know what to say."

"Nicholai just arrived. I have to go," Alex says, cutting our conversation short.

He's thinking about buying a house in Northmeadow? I'm on cloud nine as I walk to our bedroom, where Viktor has already put my suitcase on the bed. I take a few minutes to unpack, filling the drawers and closet space Alex left empty for me. Then, I change into my pajamas and crawl into bed, but I can't sleep. The energy in the city is contagious.

Even though it's nearly two in the morning, I call Lana, knowing she'll be awake.

"You're back," she squeals so loud I have to pull the phone away from my ear.

"I am. Are you free for breakfast and shopping tomorrow?"

"Absolutely. I'll meet you at your place."

"Sounds like a plan. I can't wait to see you."

We chat for a few minutes until Brandon calls for her.

"Gotta go. I'll see you in the morning."

<h1 style="text-align:center">Natalie</h1>

SSOMETHING, OR RATHER SOMEONE, JUMPING ON THE bed startles me awake.

"You're home." Lana giggles. "I missed you so much."

"Oh my God, you scared me. What time is it?"

"It's after one. Viktor told me to let you sleep, but I'm starving and couldn't wait any longer."

"I can't believe I slept so late." I jump out of bed. "Give me a few minutes to get dressed, and we'll head out."

I grab jeans and a sweater from the closet and go into the bathroom. While I get ready, Lana sits cross-legged on the bed, telling me about her new job. After I slip on my black Chucks, I turn to her, "Ready to go?"

Lana pulls her phone out. "I just have to let Brandon know we're headed out."

"He can come too."

Her fingers fly across the screen. A few seconds later, she gets a reply.

"He said no. It's a girl's day, and he'll see you soon."

I grab her hand. "Let's go, then. We have a lot to do."

It's been a long time since I've spent a day in the city with Lana. I can't contain my excitement any longer.

"We're on our way out," I call to Viktor, who's in the office.

We're about to step into the elevator when Viktor appears behind us.

Lana spins to face him. "Girl's Day, Vik. I have my car."

"No can do, ladies."

Lana rolls her eyes. "You're kidding, right?" He opens his mouth to speak, but she holds up her hand, stopping him. "Never mind, I know you don't kid around."

Watching their interaction is comical. Lana's so bossy with him. My laugh slips out at her comment on his inability to joke around.

"Viktor knows—"

"Knows how serious keeping you safe is." He raises his eyebrows.

I'll keep his secret. It's the least I can do for everything he's done for me over the past few weeks.

Our first stop is the Christmas tree lot on the corner. Lana and I pick the perfect tree and pay the delivery fee. It'll be waiting for us at the apartment when we get back.

"I'm starving. I need food," Lana says.

The next stop is a corner café. Viktor refuses to join us at our table. He's back to his serious, all-business demeanor.

Lana and I place our order at the counter and find a table in the corner.

"How was Tony and Leo's collaring ceremony last night?"

"I wish you could've been there. It was amazing."

"I'm so happy for them."

We stop talking when the waiter arrives with our sandwiches and coffee.

"I hope we get to the club while I'm here. I miss seeing everyone."

After we finish eating, we get down to business.

"Where do you want to start?" Lana asks.

"I thought we could head to the Holiday Shops in Bryant Park. We can figure out where else to go after that."

We walk around the market, marveling at the products made by talented artisans. I find a handmade ornament with two penguins kissing under the mistletoe that I have personalized for Alex and me. It'll look adorable on our tree.

When we're done at the market, Viktor drives us downtown to do more shopping. We spend the rest of the afternoon filling the trunk with packages and bags.

When we leave the last store, Viktor asks, "Where to now, ladies?"

I can tell he's holding back from rolling his eyes. He's been a great sport today.

"Can you drop me off at Fire and Ice? I told Brandon I'd meet him there. Wanna come? Leo and Anthony will be there."

"I'd love to, but I need to get home. I have a lot of wrapping to do."

I might have gone a little overboard with the presents. When we pull up at the club, I hug Lana.

"I missed this. I'll call you after Alex gets home, and we'll make plans for Christmas Day."

"Something tells me you might be a little tied up." We share a laugh.

Lana grabs her bags and, with a wave, heads into the club.

Viktor and I head back to the apartment.

Alex

I can't wait to see Natalie's face when I show up in Northmeadow tomorrow. Before I can get on the plane, I have to finish the most important task on this trip—picking up Natalie's engagement ring.

My driver pulls the car to a stop in front of a small jewelry store. According to Maxim, Yegor is the best jeweler in St. Petersburg. I take a minute to get my emotions under control. This ring is a symbol of both my past and my future. The conversation with my mom when she gave it to me is as clear today as it was all those years ago.

"Alex, I want you to have this." She slid her engagement ring *from her finger and placed it in the palm of my hand.*

I tried to give it back, tried to make her put it back on.

"You're going to beat this, Mom."

"Alexander." She placed her frail hand on my arm. "I'm tired. My body can't fight anymore. Listen to me, please."

Reluctantly, I sat quietly as she spoke.

"Your father gave this to me when I was a young woman—a symbol of his promise to love and care for me. He and I have discussed this. I want you to have it. One day, you'll meet someone. Someone who'll turn your world upside-down. A woman who'll love

you just as much as you love her. When you're ready to make the promise of forever, put this ring on her finger. Love her the same way your father has loved me."

I put the ring away and tried to forget about it. For so many years, it only represented what I'd lost—what Dad lost. Mom wasn't supposed to give up. She was supposed to keep fighting and beat cancer.

It took me a long time to accept that she didn't quit. That everything happened the way they were supposed to. It took Natalie coming into my life to understand what my parents shared and what the ring truly symbolized.

Before I left for Russia, I took the ring out and visited my mom's grave for the first time since she died. I apologized for being angry with her for leaving us. After nearly ten years, I finally made peace with my mother's death.

My parents' love story will always be a part of the ring, but I decided to redesign it, adding our love story to it.

I take a deep breath, trying to hide my nerves as I walk into the jewelry store. Yegor greets me with a kiss on both cheeks. He speaks very little English. Thankfully, I speak enough Russian to conduct a conversation. He motions for me to sit in a high wooden chair in front of the glass showcase before holding up a finger, letting me know he'll be a minute.

I perch on the edge of the chair and watch him walk into the back room. When he returns, he's holding a small jewelry box. He stands across from me and places it on the glass.

"Your ring, *Gospodin* Montgomery." He pushes the box to me.

With shaking hands, I carefully lift the lid and pick up the ring. Even though I drew up the design, what I see is nothing short of amazing.

Yegor has transformed my mother's solitaire round stone into a heart set on a platinum band twisted like a vine. One row of the vine is lined with diamond pieces that were removed from the original stone. The other is lined with black diamonds.

"It's exquisite."

"I'm pleased," he says, bringing his hand over his heart. Another man, a young version of Yegor, joins us.

"The ring is beautiful, sir."

"Your father did an amazing job with it," I say, still in awe of the ring.

"It will look beautiful on your *nevesta's* finger."

I pause at his words. *Nevesta—my fiancée, my future wife.*

I examine the ring one more time before setting it back in the box.

Yegor speaks his native tongue, but I don't understand enough to keep up. His son translates for me.

"I see many beautiful stones come through here, but none more beautiful than my wife. Treasure yours, and you will share many happy years."

"I plan to do exactly that."

Once the transaction is complete, I leave the store, knowing I'm the luckiest man on earth.

Alex

SIXTEEN HOURS AFTER TAKEOFF, THE PLANE'S WHEELS hit the ground at JFK. I have a two-hour layover until my flight to Missouri leaves. I'm exhausted from the long plane ride, so I grab a coffee and find a quiet corner to wait.

When I turn my phone on, I see three missed calls from Natalie. I can't risk her hearing the background noises and questioning my whereabouts, so I settle for texting.

Alex: I'm in a meeting. I'll call you later.

I don't like being dishonest with her, but it's the only way to keep my surprise. It'll be worth it when she's in my arms. A few hours and another flight later, I'm finally at the Branson Airport, weaving through people to get to the rental car counter.

While waiting in line, I text Viktor, asking if Natalie's at the motel. I'm expecting a return text, but instead, my phone rings.

"Hello?"

"Hey, boss." Viktor's voice is uncharacteristically nervous.

"Is Natalie in her room?"

"Why?"

"Because I want to know where she is."

He hesitates a bit too long for my liking. "Not exactly."

"Viktor." My voice rumbles. "Where's Natalie?"

"She's safe, boss. She's just busy right now."

"Busy?"

What's going on? He knows better than to evade my questions.

"Where the hell is she?"

"Shit. She wanted to surprise you. We're at your place."

"Natalie's in New York?" I laugh out loud. People look at me like I'm crazy and try to avoid me as they walk past.

"Alex, you okay?"

"I wanted to surprise her. I'm in Missouri."

Viktor lets out an audible sigh of relief.

"Guess my plans are changing." Excusing myself from the rental car line, I walk the opposite way and get in line at a ticket counter. "I'll book a flight and see you soon. And Viktor?"

"Yes, boss?"

"Don't tell her I'm coming."

With my new ticket, I get ready to board a plane back to New York. But first, I text my flight information to Viktor and instruct him to make sure she stays home.

One way or another, I'm surprising Natalie today.

Natalie

The apartment smells so yummy from the chocolate chip cookies in the oven. Viktor said he would help me with the decorating, but he got a phone call, and his mood went sour. He's been hiding in the office ever since. It's taken longer than I thought, but finally, I'm hanging the last wreath above the fireplace. The only thing left to do is for Alex to put the star on the tree when he gets home.

Climbing off the chair, I look around at my work and smile. Everything's perfect. When the timer on the oven goes off, I pull out the last tray of cookies. They look delicious, and my stomach growls in response. I didn't realize how late it got. I'm hungry, but I don't feel like cooking after baking all day. I'll grab Viktor, and we'll get some dinner. I walk down the hall and knock on the closed office door.

"Come in."

I take a few steps into the room. "Let's go out and get a bite to eat."

"You can order in," he says without even looking up.

"I'd like to go out."

"No."

"No?" I cross my arms, annoyed. "Why not?"

"I have things to do. Just order something in, okay?"

I'm confused by his cold response. What's gotten into him? I don't stick around long enough to find out. I storm out of the room, slamming the door behind me. Part of me wants to go out despite his refusal. The heck with him. But I know word will get back to Alex, and that'll end badly. I go back to the kitchen and grab my phone.

Opening the food delivery app, I scroll through my options and settle on Chinese takeout. Despite his bad mood, I order dinner for Viktor and me.

While I'm waiting for the food to arrive, I grab my book and get comfy on the couch. I'm in the middle of a page when Viktor walks into the room.

"I'm going down to my apartment."

"I ordered dinner for us. It'll be here shortly."

"I'm not hungry. I'll see you in the morning."

"Whatever," I mumble and go back to reading. I don't know what's wrong with him today.

A half-hour later, I hear the elevator signal its arrival. I'm not expecting company, and the delivery person doesn't have the code to get up here. I pull up Viktor's contact on my phone just as the elevator doors open. It takes a moment for the message to travel from my brain to my legs. When it does, I jump off the couch and run to the foyer. My eyes didn't deceive me. Alex is standing there holding a food bag in one hand and his suitcase in the other.

"Did someone order takeout?" he says with a huge grin.

"Alex? It's really you."

He sets the bag on the credenza and drops his suitcase before opening his arms.

"It's me, baby girl."

I run into his embrace. "You weren't supposed to be home for two more days."

"And *you* were supposed to be in Northmeadow."

He doesn't give me time to respond before his mouth lands on mine, his tongue parting my lips. He lifts me as we kiss, and I wrap my legs around his waist. Alex carries me into his bedroom and kicks the door shut behind him.

"I've missed you so much," he says, lowering me until my feet touch the floor.

"Why didn't you tell me you were coming home early?"

"Why didn't *you* tell *me* you were coming home early?"

The amusement in his eyes a moment ago quickly shifts to something dark and hungry.

"We'll talk about that later. Right now, I need to be inside you."

I don't waste a second before tugging my shirt over my head. Reaching out, I begin unbuttoning his dark blue dress shirt. My hands explore the toned muscles of his abdomen before moving lower to undo the button and zipper on his pants.

"Natalie." My name falls from his lips like a prayer.

My hands slide his pants and boxers down, freeing his erection as I lower to my knees. Alex stares at me with lust-filled eyes. I fist his hard length, earning a low growl of approval. It's a powerful feeling knowing I'm causing this reaction in him.

My tongue circles his velvety soft tip, teasing him. I look up and see his head thrown back and his eyes closed. Starting at the base of his cock, I flatten my tongue and drag it up his swollen length. When I reach the tip, I blow across it before running my tongue through his slit, tasting his salty essence. Alex grabs my hair, tilting my head up.

With our eyes locked on each other, I open my lips and slide my mouth down to the base. My hands cup his balls and massage them gently as I move up and down his shaft in a steady rhythm.

"Your mouth feels amazing. I'm not going to last long." His body trembles as he fights not to lose control.

Without warning, I take him deep into my throat. His grip on my hair tightens. I relax, allowing him to take control of the pace. Within seconds, his balls draw up, and I know he's close.

"Fuck." He loses himself, shooting waves of cum down my

throat. I greedily swallow everything he has to give before dragging my tongue up his length one last time.

Alex grabs my arms and lifts me so I'm standing in front of him. I unhook my black lace bra, tossing it to the side. The move only intensifies his desire. I step backward, and Alex advances on me like a predator stalking its prey. I keep moving until my legs hit the bed, and I fall back.

Leaning up on my elbows, I watch him as he slides my pants down my legs. His breath catches when he sees I'm not wearing panties. He spreads my legs and drops to his knees.

"My turn." He gives me a wicked grin.

Alex wastes no time as he drags his tongue slowly along my slit. My back bows off the bed from the intense sensation. He licks and sucks like a starving man, and I'm the meal that'll save him. He knows exactly how to play my body, and my orgasm builds quickly.

"Alex," I whisper his name as waves of pleasure pulse through my body.

He doesn't stop until I'm lying limp on the bed.

"I've missed you," he says before flipping me over on all fours.

He rubs himself back and forth through my wetness, teasing me. He's rock hard again.

"I need you."

"Where do you need me?"

"Inside me, please."

I'm already wet and needy. My body is ready to make up for our time apart.

"As you wish."

He lines his erection up with my opening, and with one thrust, he's fully sheathed inside me. Then, he grabs my hips, his fingers digging deep. Alex isn't gentle. He takes me hard and fast.

Reaching his arm around my body, he rubs my clit, intensifying the pleasure. His fingers pinch hard, and my orgasm crashes into me. His movements become frantic until I feel him explode inside me.

"I missed you so fucking much."

He lies on his back, and I curl up against him, my head on his chest. I lose track of time as we lie together, touching and talking to one another.

"We should go heat up dinner," Alex suggests. "Then I'm bringing you back to bed. I have a lot of time to make up for."

Alex

I wake Natalie a few times during the night. We've been apart too long, and I can't get enough of her. Between our marathon sex and the jet lag, it isn't surprising that, although it's nearly noon on Christmas Eve, I'm just waking up. Natalie's still asleep next to me, snoring softly.

Careful not to wake her, I get out of bed and throw on sweatpants and a T-shirt. Barefoot, I pad down the hallway and into my gourmet kitchen. I haven't eaten at home in months, ever since Natalie returned to Northmeadow. I'm thankful Natalie got here early and restocked the kitchen because I plan to start our day with a home-cooked meal.

Bacon sizzles in the frying pan while I flip the French toast. I'm in my own little world until I feel two slender arms wrap around my waist.

"That smells delicious," she says, resting her head on my back.

"I was hoping to surprise you with a late breakfast in bed." I put my free arm around her, pulling her to my side.

"I don't think we would've gotten much eating done there."

"Why don't you make the coffee while I finish cooking?"

Seeing her in nothing but my T-shirt makes me want to go all caveman, tossing her over my shoulder and dragging her back to bed. That needs to wait because today, I have other plans.

Natalie's setting the coffee mugs on the breakfast bar while I fill our plates. Then, we sit and enjoy our late breakfast. There's so much I've missed about her, but I missed these simple moments the most.

"I didn't get a chance last night to tell you how beautiful the decorations are." I've always lived alone and never decorated for Christmas. But Natalie's transformed the apartment into a Christmas wonderland.

"Oh, that reminds me." She sets her fork down and reaches for her phone. "I told Lana I'd call her today and let her know what time they should come over tomorrow."

"I already talked to Brandon. We're all set for tomorrow. As soon as we finish eating, we're heading out."

Her eyes light up. "Where are we going?"

"You're not the only one who can plan a surprise." I motion to her almost empty plate. "Eat up."

After we finish our last few bites, Natalie starts gathering the dishes.

"I'll get them. You go start getting ready."

"Are you sure?"

"Positive. And leave your phone at home. We're going off-grid."

While she heads to the bedroom, I throw the dishes in the sink. I'll deal with them later. Then, I text Viktor and ask him to have the car waiting. Thankfully, Natalie isn't a girl who needs hours to get ready. Ten minutes later, we're dressed and in the elevator.

"Now, will you tell me where we're going?"

"Nope." I laugh, knowing how impatient my sub can be.

I'm thankful we got out so quickly. With the holiday, the traffic downtown is worse than usual. When we near our destination, I see the recognition in her eyes.

"Are we going to Radio City?" She beams with excitement. "Did you know I've never been to the Christmas show?"

"I know. A little elf told me."

Natalie's green eyes are wide and sparkling with pure joy as we walk into the historic building.

"There's so much to see. I don't know where to look first." Her eyes dart from the terrazzo floor to the majestic chandeliers that hang from the four-story-high ceiling. "Wow," she murmurs.

I take her hand and lead her into the auditorium that's already filled with people. She spins around, taking in the three levels of mezzanines before turning toward the Great Stage.

I understand her excitement. Although I've been here many times, the opulence of this building never grows old. There's always something new to discover.

For the next hour and a half, the stage comes to life with Christmas magic. Natalie's totally immersed in the show, and I'm totally engrossed in watching her. When the curtain closes, she grabs my face and kisses me.

"Alex, that was incredible."

"I'm glad you liked it. Let's go. There's more to do."

"More?"

Our next stop, the Rockefeller Christmas Tree, is right around the corner. It's still daytime, but the tree is lit up with thousands of colored lights. Tourists from all over the world are here taking in the splendid sight. Being a New Yorker, sometimes I forget the magnificence of the city. But not today. I pull out my phone.

"I thought you said we're off the grid today," she says with a hand on her hip.

I show her my screen. "Airplane mode."

She laughs softly before cuddling close for our selfie.

For the next few hours, we pretend we're tourists visiting many of the iconic Christmas sites in the city to take selfies. We stop at the oversized Christmas ornaments before going to Fifth

Avenue to see the holiday window displays. They are all incredible, but Macy's outshines them all.

Natalie and I take selfies everywhere we go. I want to have the pictures to look back at and show our children one day when we retell our love story.

"I'm told you've been missing New York pizza," I say as Viktor approaches our favorite pizza place.

"You have no idea. Pizza isn't the same anywhere else."

We're seated by a window in the front, where we're treated to a view of people bustling about doing last-minute shopping for tomorrow. When we finish, I check the time on my phone. "If we don't get going, we'll be late."

"Late for what?"

"You'll see soon enough. Come on."

Hand-in-hand, we walk the few blocks to Central Park, where the final surprise waits. I'm filled with a mix of nervousness and excitement, knowing what lies ahead. I haven't decided exactly when to ask her. I'm counting on fate to lend a hand.

When we round the corner, a white horse standing in front of a white carriage comes into view. Both the horse and the carriage are decorated with red bows. When the driver sees us approaching, he climbs down from his seat. Natalie squeezes my hand tightly.

"Mr. Montgomery?"

"Alex, please." I shake the man's hand.

"My name's Seamus and this is my horse, Storm," he says with a lilting brogue. "We're ready to go if you are."

I look at Natalie. "Are we ready?"

She returns my gaze, her eyes sparkling with excitement. "I'm so ready."

I help Natalie into the carriage and then climb in behind her. The sun is setting, and the air has a chilly bite. Once we're seated, I pull the woolen blanket over her lap. The carriage starts moving and enters Central Park just as the Christmas lights turn on.

"I've walked through this park so many times. But something

about tonight feels different—magical." She rests her head on my shoulder.

I pull her close as we listen to the clip-clop of the horse as she prances her way through the park's lit-up trees.

Snow begins to fall in delicate flakes as we approach Bow Bridge. On one side, a group of carolers sing, their voices enchanting a small, attentive crowd.

"Can you stop right up there?" I ask the driver.

He nods.

When the carriage stops, I hop out first and help Natalie down. Taking her mittened hand in mine, we walk onto the bridge and listen as the carolers sing, "I'll Be Home for Christmas." My free hand is in my pocket, holding the ring box while I say a silent thank you. Fate has done her job and provided me with the perfect moment. Without letting go of Natalie's hand, I turn to face her.

"Natalie, last year, I was asked to escort a young lady for the evening at the club. I wasn't looking forward to it and almost didn't show up. I'm so glad I went because that night changed my life. It was the night I met you." I pause, swallowing over the lump in my throat, and pull the ring box out of my pocket.

Natalie gasps when I let go of her hand and get down on one knee.

"These past few months apart have been challenging, to say the least. But I learned an important lesson—I never want to be without you again. Natalie Clarke, you're my world, my heart. The very breath I breathe. I don't want to spend another day without knowing you'll be by my side forever. Will you marry me?"

Natalie brings her mittened hands over her mouth. Tears are streaming down her face.

Her voice is barely a whisper. "Yes, I'll marry you."

She said yes. I blink back my tears as I stand up and take her left hand in mine. I pull off her mitten and slide the ring onto her finger. It fits perfectly. Then I pull her close and kiss her. I don't even realize we've drawn an audience until they clap and call out their wishes of congratulations. Natalie looks down at the diamond on her finger.

"Alex. It's the most beautiful ring I've ever seen."

"It was originally my mother's. I had a jeweler in St. Petersburg redesign it."

Movement catches my eye, and I look up. Sitting on a branch in a nearby tree is a Cardinal. I look to heaven, knowing my mother is sharing the moment with us.

"I love it." She wraps her arms around me.

I lift her from the ground and kiss her again.

At this moment, everything is perfect.

In my arms is the woman who will soon be my wife.

Natalie

After the proposal, we listen to a few more carols before climbing back into the carriage. We sit close, wrapped in each other's arms. It's as if the rest of the city is silent—there's only Alex and me. The reality of what happened is still sinking in. Alex asked me to marry him. I'm going to be his wife.

As the carriage ride comes to a close, I see Viktor standing outside the car. His head is down, and he's looking at his phone. When he hears us approaching, he lifts his head and gives Alex a questioning glance. Alex nods in response. Viktor's serious demeanor cracks, and he smiles.

"He was in on this, too?"

"I couldn't have done it without him."

When we get to the car, Viktor slaps Alex on the back. "Congratulations, boss."

"Thank you."

"Congratulations, ma'am."

Viktor hugs me, and I swear I hear Alex growl.

"Ma'am? What happened to Natalie?"

Viktor doesn't answer, but his smile tells me all I need to know.

When we get back to the apartment, I take Alex's hand and lead him to the bedroom, where I remove his clothes before doing the same with mine.

"Lie down. Tonight, I'm going to take my time with you, Natalie."

And he does.

Slowly and passionately, my Dominant, my fiancé, makes love to me.

Cutting through the most beautiful dream I've ever had is the sound of my phone ringing. I wake up momentarily confused. Alex grumbles next to me. I'm slightly annoyed when I roll over and reach for the phone. Who would call before dawn on Christmas morning? When I look at the screen, I see my mom's number. I debate sending the call to voicemail. At the last second, I swipe the screen to accept the call.

"Natalie?"

"Yeah, it's me."

Why is she calling me at four a.m.?

"There was a—" She doesn't finish her sentence before she bursts into tears.

"Mom?"

Alex rolls over. "What's wrong?"

"I don't know." I get out of bed. "Mom, are you still there?"

"Ms. Clarke?" A male voice asks.

"Yes?"

"My name's Officer Cooper. I'm with the Northmeadow police department." His voice is calm and steady, unlike my heart, which is beating wildly. "There was a break-in at your family's pharmacy."

"Oh my God. When? What happened?"

"Shortly after midnight. Your father recently had a silent alarm installed. He was notified that the alarm had been triggered."

"Someone broke in? What did they take?"

"It appears the perpetrator was after prescription medication."

My stomach turns. I don't need to ask who did it. I already know the answer.

"Was anyone hurt?"

"Your parents arrived before we got to the scene. There was an altercation, and your father was shot."

My legs nearly give out beneath me, and I clutch the bed for support. Alex is at my side in an instant, steadying me as he guides me to sit down. Gently, he takes the phone from my trembling hand.

"This is Alexander Montgomery, Natalie's fiancé. Can you tell me what's going on?"

Alex walks toward the window. He's silent, listening to whatever the officer is explaining.

"What's his condition?" Another long pause. "We'll be on the next flight out. Please give this number to the hospital and ask them to contact us with any updates." He drops his head against the window.

I'm cold, and my body shakes uncontrollably. As much as I want Alex to tell me what the officer said, I'm equally afraid to hear more.

It feels like an eternity before he turns from the window and slowly walks across the room to sit beside me. He takes my hands while he relays the officer's story.

Dad noticed that the pill count on some controlled substances had been off several times over the past few weeks. Although he already had a security system, he suspected it might be an employee. So, he secretly had a silent alarm installed.

"They were at church for the Christmas Eve service when Stanley got a notification on his cell that the alarm was triggered. He and Charlotte figured it was a false alarm and left the church to turn it off. When they got there, Stanley noticed the employee entrance was propped open. Instead of waiting for the police to arrive, he went inside. A few seconds later, Charlotte heard a gunshot."

According to the officer, she got scared and crouched down in the car. When she heard the metal door slam off the brick building, she tried to peek out the window, but all she saw was the back of a man running away.

"The police arrived within minutes and called for an ambulance." Alex rubs my hands gently as he speaks. "Your father sustained a gunshot to his chest. All the officer could tell me was that he was life-flighted to a trauma hospital in Branson."

Bile rises in my throat. I run to the bathroom, making it just in time to vomit in the toilet. Alex follows behind me and holds my hair. When I'm sure my stomach is empty, I lean against the wall and stare at the ceiling. Alex wipes my face with a warm washcloth and sits next to me.

"Is he alive?" I barely get the words out before sobs wrack my body.

"He's in surgery. The officer said it's going to be touch-and-go."

I drop my head in my hands as guilt washes over me. "This is my fault." If I had said something weeks ago, I could've prevented this.

"Look at me," Alex demands. "This is not your fault. You had nothing to do with this."

"But I did."

It takes a minute to calm myself enough to tell Alex about the night Tommy showed up at the store. The further I get into the story, the more tense Alex becomes.

"I'm sorry. Please tell me you forgive me."

"Of course, I forgive you."

He pulls me onto his lap, and I tuck my head into his chest. Alex rocks me back and forth, whispering soothing words while I cry.

We stay like this until I have no more tears to shed.

Alex

I'VE NEVER EXPERIENCED PURE RAGE BEFORE, BUT ALL I see is red when Natalie tells me how Tommy dragged her into the store and forced her to give him pills. He laid his filthy hands on what wasn't his to touch.

It takes every ounce of self-control I possess to remain calm while she finishes her story. Her heart's hurting enough. I don't need to add to it by acting on the rage pulsing through my veins.

Once her crying subsides, I help her up.

"Let me make you a cup of tea."

She doesn't respond as I lead her down the hall into the living room, get her settled on the couch, and cover her with her favorite blanket. Her eyes are filled with so much pain. It nearly brings me to my knees. But right now, I have to be strong for her.

"I'll be right back."

I call Viktor and quietly relay the information. "Book three tickets to Branson on the next available flight."

"I'll be up in a minute." He hesitates before asking, "Boss, is she okay?"

I know he's grown fond of Natalie after all the time they've spent together. I look to where she sits, tears silently streaming down her face. "I don't know."

"Take care of your girl. I'll handle the details," he says and disconnects the phone.

Viktor has become more than just a trusted employee. He's also a friend. If he says he'll take care of it, I can be confident, knowing this is one thing I don't have to worry about. Next, I send a text to Maxim.

Me: We have a problem. Call me on the secure line.

While I wait for his response, I finish making Natalie's tea and bring it to her.

"Thank you," she whispers, taking the cup from my outstretched hand.

"Viktor's making flight arrangements." I brush a curl from her face. "He'll be up as soon as he has the tickets."

I get a text and check it quickly.

Maxim: I am heading to my office now.

"I have to make a call. I'll only be a few minutes."

I don't want to leave Natalie's side, but I have to talk to Maxim. The phone is already ringing when I get there. I hurry to my desk and lift the receiver.

"What is wrong?" Maxim asks, his voice cold and severe.

He knows I wouldn't ask for a secure call unless there were extreme circumstances. I relay every detail I was given by the police and the information from Natalie.

"Is her father alive?"

"So far. But the prognosis is grim." I rub the back of my neck.

"And they have not arrested Thomas Moore yet?"

"No," I growl. The rage I thought I had under control rushes through me once again. "The security cameras were down. The police are going through the crime scene looking for evidence."

"Send me his picture. I will get things in motion." His keyboard clicks in the background. "Irina is already packing, and my jet is being fueled."

"I wouldn't ask—"

"I know. We will find Thomas, and he will pay." The line goes dead.

I drop my head into my hands and grab my hair. I promised myself I'd never cross that line—never ask Maxim to step in like this. But there's also never been anyone I've loved so much that I'd want to kill another for hurting them. I'm at war inside myself.

"Alex."

I hear Natalie's soft voice and look up. She's standing in the doorway, eyes puffy and red, and wrapped in my blanket. I push up from my chair and go to her.

"Viktor's here."

I hold her petite frame against me. "Let's go find out when we leave."

"I didn't think you'd go back with me after the way my parents treated you."

I freeze mid-step and put my finger under her chin, forcing her to look at me.

"None of that matters now. Stanley and Charlotte are your family, and they need you—they need us, and we'll be there."

Her eyes fill with tears again as she lays her head against my chest. "Thank you, Sir."

"You don't need to thank me. That's what family does." I take her hand. "Let's go see what Viktor has for us."

Tommy

I JUST NEEDED A FEW PILLS, THAT'S ALL.

They were supposed to be in church.

Easy in, easy out.

I had the bottle in my hand. I was just about to grab the pills when Stanley came in.

"Tommy? Is that you?" he called from the door. "What are you doing, son?"

I didn't think. I pulled the gun from my waistband and pointed it at Stanley.

"Don't come any closer."

His eyes moved to my other hand, where I held the bottle of Oxy. Recognition came across his face.

"You're the one taking the pills."

"Shut the fuck up," I yelled. "Move out of my way, and this can all be over with."

"Thomas, let's talk about this. Just put the gun away and—"

Everything happened so fast.

Stanley took a step towards me. I didn't realize I had pulled the trigger until his body fell at my feet. A pool of red quickly formed around him.

I shot him.

I'll never forget his eyes, the way they stared at me, blank and lifeless.

And the blood.

There was so much blood.

The bottle fell from my hand.

All I wanted was a few pills. Now I've killed someone.

I ran for the door to the only person I could think of.

Natalie

Viktor got us a flight at eleven. It doesn't give us much time to pack before we have to leave for JFK. We'll be cutting it close, but Alex is confident we'll make it on time.

On the way, Alex calls Brandon to let them know what happened. Lana wants to talk to me, but I can't handle talking to anyone right now. Alex promises her I'll call her as soon as I can.

Thankfully, we got through airport security in record time, and before I know it, we're en route to Missouri.

"Try to close your eyes," Alex encourages me.

"I can't. Every time I close them, I see Tommy pointing a gun at my father." The nightmare I've been having for months is now a reality.

There's no longer a blank face. I know who the gun was aimed at—my father. I put my head on Alex's shoulder.

"He must've been so scared." Tears slip down my cheeks.

"Don't go there, Natalie," Alex says softly.

Although I nod, I can't stop thinking about it. My dad's been shot. My parents and I haven't spoken in a month. I don't know what will happen when we get to the hospital. Will Mom even want me there? What will she say when she sees Alex with me? So many questions keep going through my mind. So many unknowns. I'm thankful I won't have to wait much longer to get the answers—one way or another.

We finally land, and the feeling is surreal. Viktor and I came through this same airport a few days ago. When everything was okay. I'm thankful Alex and Viktor are here to take care of everything. All I can do is smile when appropriate and nod when spoken to. How did things change so quickly?

Alex leads me out of the airport, where Viktor is waiting in a rental car. None of us talks as we drive to the hospital. The only sound is the dinging of Alex's phone with an incoming text. He checks it and types a quick return.

"Is that Lana and Brandon?" I ask.

"Uh-huh," Alex mumbles, distracted by another incoming message.

I turn my attention out the window. Although nature has provided a beautiful Christmas backdrop, I only see the heavy snow load that the trees' branches are forced to carry. It feels much like the weight on my shoulders right now.

"We're here," Alex says, his tone somber.

A war rages inside me. I want to rush in, hold my father's hand, and know he's still with us. But I'm struggling with anger and hurt. How do I reconcile my feelings? I don't have time to answer that because Alex is already out of the car, giving my hand a light tug.

My body moves of its own accord, following Alex's lead. He doesn't let go of my hand as we enter the hospital and take the elevator to the ICU floor. This part of the hospital is quiet and filled with the heaviness of lives hanging in the balance. As we round the corner, the waiting room comes into view. Mom sits in the far corner. She looks weary and alone.

"Mom," I say softly.

She raises her head, and tears begin rolling down her cheeks, but she does not move toward us.

"We're here. You aren't alone now."

As if my words give her permission to move, she walks over.

"I'm so scared, Natalie," she says between sobs.

"I know, Mom. So am I," I say, my voice cracking. "Is Dad okay?"

"I don't know. The nurse said they'd update me when he's out of surgery."

"He's still in surgery?" Panic rises.

He's been in there almost all day. Something must be very wrong.

Mom turns to Alex. "I'm so sorry."

"No apologies necessary, Mrs. Clarke," he says, taking her hands in his. "We're here now, and we'll face this together."

We wait for what feels like forever until we finally hear footsteps on the tiled floor that are coming closer. I look up and see a tall man with dark skin walking in our direction. He's pulling his surgical cap off. His shoulders slump, and I prepare myself for the bad news.

"Mrs. Clarke?"

"Yes."

"I'm Dr. Fitzgerald. I operated on your husband."

"This is my daughter Natalie and her boyfriend, Alexander."

We exchange handshakes before the doctor motions to the nearby chairs. "Let's sit."

We each take a seat in the waiting room chairs. The doctor takes his time explaining my father's injuries to us.

"Mr. Clarke sustained a gunshot to his right lung. The bullet lodged itself in the lower lobe. The damage caused his uninjured lung to fill with blood, which had to drain slowly," Dr. Fitzgerald explains.

"Because the injured lung wasn't functioning, he was placed on a heart-lung bypass machine for the past twelve hours while we operated. This allowed time for the wounded lung to be repaired and re-aerate."

"Is he going to be okay?" Mom asks, desperation in her voice.

"He's currently on a ventilator. We're keeping him in a medically induced coma to allow his body some time to rest from the trauma. The next few hours are critical." Dr. Fitzgerald pauses.

"Tomorrow, we'll try to take him off the ventilator and see if he can breathe on his own. If he does, that's a good sign."

"And if he doesn't?"

"If he doesn't, we'll be forced to consider a lung transplant. Because of his injury and the amount of blood loss, we'll only consider that as a last resort. So, for now, we watch and wait."

"Can we see him?" Mom asks.

The doctor looks between us. "We can only allow two people at a time."

"Mrs. Clarke and Natalie will go. They're his family," Alex interjects before anyone can answer. "I have a few calls to make. I'll be out here if you need me."

Mom and I follow the doctor to the room. When I look in, I freeze. Dad's hooked up to so many wires and tubes I can hardly see his face.

"It's okay," Dr. Fitzgerald says as he places his hand on my shoulder. "You can go closer."

I look up at the doctor, who nods in encouragement.

Dad's body is still and pale. He appears lifeless. The steady cadence of the monitor is a comforting sound, letting me know he's still alive. Dr. Fitzgerald checks Dad's monitors and makes a few notes in his chart.

"We'll watch him closely tonight, and I'll be back tomorrow to wake him up."

"Can he hear us?"

"I believe he can. Talk to him. Let him know you're here."

I move closer to the bed and grab Dad's hand—it's warm.

"Daddy, I'm here." Tears pour down my cheeks when there's no response.

What did I expect? Did I think he'd hear my voice and open his eyes? Mom walks over and puts her arm around me. I rest my head on her shoulder and allow my tears to fall.

Mom and I whisper to Dad for the next few hours, hoping that wherever he is, he hears us and knows he's not alone.

Alex

WHILE NATALIE AND HER MOM VISIT STANLEY, I GO back outside to search for Viktor. I want an update. I find him standing a short distance from the walkway where people meander in and out of the main door. Even though his back is to me, I see he's on the phone. When I walk up to him, he nods, acknowledging my presence.

"Keep me updated," he says and disconnects the call.

His face shows no trace of kindness. "Maxim's in the air. He's called some local contacts who've dispatched a team and are in Northmeadow now."

"Have they found Tommy yet?"

"They checked cameras near the pharmacy and know he got away on foot. They tracked him for a few blocks but lost him when he entered the woods."

"Dammit." I pace back and forth.

"We'll find him, Alex."

"Did you have any luck with the other part?"

"Yes. Ms. Campbell wasn't happy that my phone call interrupted her Christmas dinner. At first, she refused, but after some insistence, she relented. Everything's been taken care of."

"Good." I'm done taking chances with Natalie's safety.

"Get back up to her, boss. I'll let you know as soon as I hear something. He can't stay hidden forever."

I take a minute to gather my thoughts before returning upstairs. Before going to the waiting room, I check with the nurses' station to see if Natalie and her mom are still with Stanley. The nurse informs me that Charlotte is in the family room and has asked to see me. She points me in the right direction, and I walk down the hall.

Although the door is cracked open, I knock.

"Come in."

I step into the room and close the door behind me.

"Please sit for a minute, Alex. We need to talk."

I take a seat across from the hospital bed where she's reclining.

"I was exhausted. The nurses insisted I come in here and try to rest." She shakes her head. "I don't know how they expect me to do that."

"You'll need your strength for when Stanley wakes up."

"Alexander," she says and fidgets with her fingers in her lap.

I see where Natalie gets that habit from.

"Stanley and I were wrong about you."

"Mrs. Clarke, we don't have to do this right now."

"Yes, we do. And please call me Charlotte." She sits up.

For the next half-hour, we discuss everything that's transpired over the past few months.

"We've known Tommy since he was born. His mom left him when he was a toddler. She never told anyone who his father was. His Aunt Delia raised him. He and Natalie grew up together. Everyone just assumed they'd get married. We never knew why they broke up. Tommy told us one story, and Natalie told us nothing. She just stopped coming home." Charlotte wipes the fresh tears that are falling.

"Stanley and I have always lived in Northmeadow. It's all we know. First, we lost Michael." Her voice catches on a sob. "Then Natalie refused to come home. We were scared. We just wanted things to go back to the way they were. We never saw this coming."

"It's okay, Charlotte." The devastation on her face is too much. She's alone and hurting. I get up and walk to the bed. "May I?" She nods. I sit beside her and take her shaking hands in mine. "Natalie and I are here now. You don't have to go through this alone."

"We listened to Tommy and believed his lies. We were so unfair to Natalie and so wrong about you. Can you ever forgive us?"

"Already done. I want you to know I love your daughter very much."

"I see that now. I hope it's not too late to fix things with Natalie."

"It's never too late," I reassure her. "And when Stanley recovers, we'll have a lot to celebrate."

I hope our happy news will give Charlotte something positive to hold on to.

"Yesterday, I asked Natalie to marry me, and she said yes."

"My little girl is getting married." She brings her hands to her mouth in surprise.

Taking the phone from my pocket, I open the photo gallery and show her the pictures from yesterday.

"Natalie looks so happy." Charlotte smiles through her tears.

"When Mr. Clarke wakes, I'd like to ask him for his—"

She stops me mid-sentence. "You already have our blessing."

I know how important it is for Natalie to have the love and support of her family. I hate that it's taken a tragedy for this healing to happen. I wrap my arms around Charlotte. My move catches her off guard, and her body remains stiff briefly before she relaxes and returns the hug.

"Would you mind walking me back to my husband's room?"

"I'd be glad to." I stand and offer her my arm.

We walk down the hall in companionable silence. As we near the room, my phone starts ringing.

"I have to take this. Excuse me, please."

I watch as she steps into Stanley's room before I answer my phone.

"Viktor?"

"We got him, boss."

"Where is he?" I ask as I pick up my pace, heading to the elevator.

"I have the address. Maxim just arrived. He and his men are waiting for us there."

"I'm on my way down."

I hang up and text Natalie.

Me: I'm going to book a hotel room for us. I'll be back in a little while. Text me if you need anything.

I can't tell her where I'm really going.

Natalie: Okay. I love you.

Me: I love you, too.

When I get outside, Viktor's waiting at the main entrance in the running car.

"In an old fishing shack."

"How did they find him there?"

"Some girl named Ash something."

"Ashlynn. Natalie's supposed best friend." My hand pounds the car door. "What did she have to do with this?"

"Ashlynn saw Maxim's men at the motel and stopped them. She explained who she was and that she knew where Tommy was. She brought them to him," Viktor explains. "I think she's trying to make amends."

"It's the least she could do for all the pain she's caused, Natalie."

I don't know where Viktor is taking us, but it's far from civilization. Finally, we turn onto a gravel road and drive for a few more miles until a small wooden cabin comes into view.

"Where the hell are we?"

"It's a safe house. It belongs to one of Maxim's contacts."

I'm amazed at the lengths Maxim's reach goes. Viktor barely has the car in park before I open the door and jump out. Maxim steps out the front door as I approach.

"Where is he?" I'm anxious to get my hands on him, to instill the same fear in him that he caused Natalie. Then, I'll watch the life drain from his eyes.

"Alexander." Maxim places his hands on my shoulders. "First, you must calm down."

He stops me from entering the building. When I look at him, I see he's the picture of calm. He's dressed in a perfectly pressed shirt and black pants. How is he so put together right now?

"I need to see him. He needs to pay for what he's done."

"And you will. But first, we need to talk. Come with me."

We walk away from the building instead of going inside.

"I'm going to kill him."

"Alexander, you have never taken a life before. It changes you. You do not have to worry about legal implications. I will take care of that."

He stops walking and turns to face me. His eyes are cold. It's something I've only witnessed once before. They're dark and tell the story of a man who's seen the worst humanity has to offer and who's done things that aren't spoken about.

"You need to worry about what happens here." He puts his hand on my heart. "That man hurt your submissive. He tried to kill her father. So, it is only right that I give you the choice of taking his life by your hand. But you need to understand it *will* change you. It is a decision you can never undo."

I haven't thought about what happens after or how I'll explain to Natalie that I've killed someone. I've only considered the hate I'm feeling and the vengeance I wish to extract.

Suddenly, every high and low I've experienced since yesterday rushes to the surface, and a primal yell explodes. I sink to my knees and drop my head into my hands.

When I look up, Maxim stands before me. His face is void of all emotion.

"I want to see him."

"It is time. Let us go."

Viktor's waiting in front of the door. When he sees us approaching, he opens it and steps aside, allowing us to enter. The inside isn't what I thought. Bright lights illuminate the room, but you'd never know it from the outside. The windows must have a privacy coating on them.

Inside, there are no walls. The only piece of furniture is an old wooden chair, and tied to that chair is Tommy. When I step closer, I see Maxim's men have already taken a turn with him. His nose is broken, and one eye is swollen shut.

He raises his head and meets my stare. "Well, well," The asshole has the nerve to snarl at me. "Looks like the man of the hour is finally here."

His cocky attitude pushes me past my breaking point. I pick up the pace of my strides and punch him in the gut. The air leaves him in a whoosh, and he struggles to catch his breath. This is my moment. I can snuff the life out of this bastard for what he's done. I turn my back on him but make no move to walk away.

"You should die for what you've done to Natalie. But I've decided to give you one chance. First, you will turn yourself in and plead guilty to all charges. Then, you will waive your right to a hearing and accept the sentence you're given." I turn to one of Maxim's men. "Give me your gun."

He looks at Maxim, who gives his approval, before handing it to me.

"Otherwise." I walk back to Tommy and point the gun at his head, my finger on the trigger poised to shoot. "You die now."

There's a long pause before realization washes over Tommy,

and his shoulders slump. The only way he's walking out of here alive is if he turns himself in.

"Fine, I'll do it."

I lower the gun and pull out my phone to dial Officer Cooper's number. When the officer answers, I put the phone on speaker. Tommy identifies himself and makes arrangements for where and when he'll turn himself in. Then, I disconnect the phone and hand the gun to Maxim before walking out. A few minutes later, I watch Maxim's men drag Tommy from the building and push him into the back of their car.

"Come, Alexander," Maxim says. "I'll ride with you."

Viktor trails the car that's transporting Tommy to the assigned location. After being ejected from the vehicle, Tommy is abandoned to await the arrival of the police. We watch from a nearby vantage point, ensuring he upholds his end of the bargain. Otherwise, his life is over.

When the officers arrive, Tommy's handcuffed and shoved into the back of a police car. Officer Cooper looks around like he can sense he's being watched. When he finds no one, he returns to his car and drives away with Tommy in the backseat.

It's only then that I'm able to breathe again.

"That was a brave decision that only a man of great integrity would make. I am proud of you, Alexander."

I don't know how to respond, so I say nothing.

"Let's get you back to the hospital."

On the long drive back to the hospital, I call and reserve a hotel room.

Natalie

Mom and I are sitting in Dad's room when my phone rings.

"Is this Natalie?"

"It is."

"I'm Office Cooper. We spoke last night."

"Yes. I remember."

"I wanted to let you know that Thomas Moore is in custody."

"He is?"

"Thomas contacted me about an hour ago and confessed. He also turned himself in and waived his right to a trial."

I struggle to wrap my head around the information. "Thank you for letting me know."

"Don't hesitate to get in touch if you have any questions."

After wishing my father a speedy recovery, we hang up.

When Alex finally returns, I tell him about the call. "Do you know something about this?"

"Be thankful he's in custody and don't overthink it."

Now, I'm certain Alex had something to do with it, but I can't figure out how.

We stay until visiting hours are over. Mom refuses to leave the hospital, opting to remain in the family room. Alex and I say goodnight and promise to be back first thing in the morning.

The next day, we're gathered in Dad's room with Dr. Fitzgerald and his team. Dad's vitals were stable through the night, so they're moving ahead with the plan to remove the ventilator this afternoon. Alex wraps his arm around me, holding me tight.

The room is silent, except for the soft murmuring between the doctor and the staff. They adjust Dad's IV and remove the tube from his throat. The monitor keeps a steady rhythm, but his eyes don't open. Dr. Fitzgerald assures us that Dad's breathing on his own and that we've crossed a huge hurdle.

As the hours pass with no improvement, it becomes increasingly more difficult to take solace in the doctor's confidence. I lay my head on Alex's shoulder.

"You should try talking to him, Charlotte. Maybe if he hears your voice, it'll encourage him to wake up."

Mom moves to the edge of Dad's bed. "Stanley, can you hear me? It's time to wake up."

We wait and watch, but there's no change.

"Stanley, I said it's time to wake up." Her tone is more forceful.

"Mom. He's not going to want to wake up if he's being yelled at." I laugh, and Mom cracks a smile.

This time, when Mom looks at him, her features soften. She takes his hand and begins stroking it with her thumb. It's the first time in many years I've witnessed her showing Dad affection. "Stanley, I need you to wake up," she says quietly. "Our little girl got engaged. She's here with her fiancé, and they want to tell you all about it."

I look at Alex, who's standing next to me. "How does she know?" I whisper. Before he can respond, Dad begins to stir. "It's okay, Daddy. Take your time."

"I'll let the nurses know he's awake," Alex says and hurries out the door.

A few minutes later, Alex returns with a nurse and Dr. Fitzgerald. The room is a whirlwind of activity as they take Dad's vitals and assess his pain level.

"Do the police—" Dad tries to speak, but stops to catch his breath.

"It's over. Tommy turned himself in. He's going to jail."

"I saw Michael. He told me I've been wrong about how I treated you." Dad reaches for my hand. "I'm sorry."

I'm unable to hold back my tears. Thank you, Michael.

I kiss Dad's cheek. "I forgive you."

It's been three days since Dad woke up. Because he's stable and no longer needs all the services of the ICU, he's being moved to a step-down unit. Dad's lung sustained significant damage, and he has a long road ahead of him, but Dr. Fitzgerald is optimistic that he'll make a full recovery.

This near tragedy repaired my relationship with my parents. They've finally accepted that Alex and I are together and have given their blessing for our marriage. My mom even bought bridal magazines from the hospital gift shop to start planning our wedding.

Alex and Dad have become co-conspirators on something.

They spend hours every day on the computer whispering to one another. Whenever I ask what they're looking at, I'm told I need to be patient.

The night of the shooting, Mom came to the hospital with nothing but the clothes she was wearing. Mom hasn't left Dad's side since the night of the accident. The nurses have been giving her scrubs, but since Dad will be in the hospital for quite a while, she needs her own clothes.

Alex and I are making the two-hour round trip to pack her a

suitcase. I hope we make it back to the hospital tonight. School goes back next week, and then I'll only be able to visit my father on weekends. So, I want to spend as much time with him now as possible.

We're making good time and will arrive in Northmeadow right around lunchtime.

"Why don't we stop at the diner and grab something to eat?" Alex suggests.

"That sounds good. It'll be nice to eat somewhere other than the hospital café."

The diner's parking lot is packed. Apparently, everyone else in town had the same idea. Knowing how gossip travels, I prepare myself for the onslaught of questions that are about to occur.

Leslie, the diner's owner, spots us as soon as we walk in. She doesn't waste a second before coming over. "How's your dad, honey?"

"He's doing okay. Anxious to get home."

She leads us to our table. "I couldn't believe it when I heard Tommy Moore shot him. Mrs. Smith was in yesterday. She told me Tommy was after drugs."

"What happened was a tragedy. Thankfully, Dad's on the mend, and we can put this behind us."

I don't ignore the comments about Tommy. I refuse to take part in town gossip.

"Well, let him know we're all pulling for him." She hands us our menus. "I'll be back in a minute to take your order."

"Well done, baby girl. You handled that like a pro."

"I've had years of practice."

Alex excuses himself to use the restroom. While I wait, I look over the menu even though I already know what I'm ordering. The shadow of someone approaching comes over my menu, and I look up. Mr. Meadows is standing over me. I can't deal with anything else right now.

"May I?" He gestures to the empty chair.

"Alex will be back in a minute."

Despite my warning, Mr. Meadows sits anyway. I put the menu on the table in front of me. His actions put me on high alert.

"I'm glad I ran into you today. We need to arrange for you to come by the school and clean out your office." He sits back, a satisfied look on his face. "Figured you wouldn't stick around very long."

"Clean out my office? Why would I need to do that?" That doesn't make any sense.

"Your resignation was handed in, and your contract was paid in full."

"Resignation?"

"We've already started the process of hiring your replacement."

I'm about to ask him what he's talking about when Alex returns.

"Excuse me. I believe that's my seat."

Mr. Meadows stands chest to chest, like he's ready to challenge Alex. But there's no comparison between the men. Where Alex is tall and well-built, Mr. Meadows is short and overweight. Even more noticeable is the confidence Alex exudes.

"It was lovely to see you, Ms. Clarke." Mr. Meadows shoots me a cocky grin as he walks away.

"What did he want?"

I stare at Alex, who's sitting across from me, looking at his menu.

"Did you buy out my contract?"

"Yes."

"How could you? We talked about this."

"Natalie." Alex reaches across the table for my hands, but I pull away.

"No." I push my chair back, nearly knocking it over in my hurry to get up. "You know how much this job means to me."

"Sit down," he says in a low tone.

"You took it away from me without even asking."

I grab the sides of my head, which is now pounding. The walls feel like they're closing in on me.

"I have to get out of here."

"Natalie, wait," Alex calls after me.

With hurried steps, I reach the door and go outside. I don't know where I'm going or how to get there. I just need to leave. Alex quickly catches up and takes my hand.

"After what happened, you can't stay here any longer."

"You went behind my back and ended my career without asking me." I pull my hand from his. "My staying here and working—we agreed on it. Those kids depend on me. Leaving without warning, without saying goodbye, could ruin all the progress they've made. I can't believe you did this. Just go."

"You don't mean that. Let's go somewhere private to talk."

Our argument in the middle of the diner's parking lot has caught the attention of several bystanders.

"You should've thought about that first. This is over." Slipping the engagement ring off my finger, I force it into his palm. "I want you to leave."

"Natalie, please. Let's get in the car and—"

"Red."

It's the one word I hoped I'd never have to use. Alex freezes as soon as the single syllable falls from my lips. Although he says nothing, his eyes reflect the horror he sees in mine. We're frozen in time. Both of us are afraid to move, fearful of what comes next.

I know the moment when what's just happened hits him. His shoulders fall, and he walks away. As angry as I am, I can't watch him leave. I turn my back to him and listen to his retreating footsteps.

I will myself not to change my mind, but I'm losing the battle. His name is on the tip of my tongue, but when I spin around, he's already in his car, driving away.

Alex is gone.

It's over.

I keep my emotions in check long enough to call a cab.

Thankfully, it's a short ride to my parents' house because I can't hold back the tears much longer. I pay the fare and slowly drag my feet up the sidewalk and into the house.

After closing the door behind me, I slide down the wall, and the dam lets loose. Tears pour down my face.

I've been so naïve, thinking that a small-town girl with nothing to offer could have a man like Alex. I talked myself into believing he was different. That he truly respected my boundaries. What a fool I've been.

Desperate for someone to talk to, I call Lana.

"Hello?"

"It's me."

"Is your dad ok?"

"He will be."

"Are you okay? You don't sound like yourself."

I search for the right words, but there are none, so I blurt, "I called my safeword and told Alex to leave."

"What? Why?"

"He knew I said no, and he did it anyway. He ruined my career," I say between sobs. "I don't even think he cared."

"Nat, you know that's not true. Alex was scared, too. He did what he thought was necessary to protect you."

"He went too far."

Svetlana is *my* best friend. She's supposed to be on my side, but she's defending him instead.

"Listen, I have to go. I have to get some things and get back to the hospital. I'll talk to you later."

I hang up without giving her a chance to respond. Lana tries to call back, but I send her call to voicemail and turn off my phone.

Once again, I find myself alone.

Alex

I NEED HER TO LISTEN TO ME. TO TRY TO UNDERSTAND from my viewpoint why I bought out her contract. When she told me what Moore did that night, I realized Natalie could've easily been the one lying in that hospital bed. I was terrified.

Red.

She calls her safeword.

I already did enough damage with the contract. I can't ignore her safeword.

Walking away isn't easy. It's the hardest damn thing I've ever had to do. I'm leaving a piece of my heart standing alone in a parking lot.

I drive until I'm far enough away that I won't be tempted to go back, and then I pull off the road. Grabbing my cell, I try to buy a plane ticket, but I can't go through with it. I can't leave Missouri.

Instead, I drive back to Branson and get another hotel room. Until I figure out what to do, at least I'll still be close to her.

Once I get settled, I call Brandon.

"Hello?"

"I fucked up. Natalie safeworded. She left me." Then something unfamiliar happens—tears fall.

"What happened?"

"I bought out her contract and handed her resignation to the school district."

"Shit, Alex. I thought we talked about giving Natalie the freedom to make her own choices?"

"That was before her psycho ex almost killed her father." I cover my face with my hand. "What do I do now? I can't go after her. My hands are tied."

"You really dug yourself a hole this time."

"I was terrified and reacted. I realize it was too far now, but I don't know how to fix it. I need to get her back. I don't want a life without Natalie in it."

"Where are you?"

"I'm in Branson. I can't leave."

"Let me talk to Lana, and I'll call you back. We'll figure this out."

<h1 style="text-align:center">Natalie</h1>

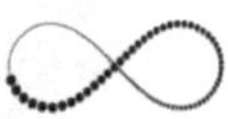

WHEN THE HOLIDAY BREAK IS OVER, I VISIT Ms. Campbell's office.

"Is there any way you'll reconsider and allow me to keep my job?" It's a long shot, but I have to try.

"I'm sorry, but that's not possible. The district already hired a replacement." She hesitates a moment. "May I say something personal?"

"Of course."

"I know you're disappointed. Angry even. But I also understand why Mr. Montgomery did what he did. Only a man in love with a woman would have gone to such lengths to keep her safe."

She's trying to comfort me, but I can't reconcile Alex's words with his actions.

"Can I see my students and say goodbye?"

"Unfortunately, you're no longer an employee, and I can't allow that. Why don't you write them each a note? If you leave them on your desk, I'll ensure they get them."

"Thank you. I'll get the office cleaned out and be on my way."

"Natalie."

"Yes?"

"Please use me as a reference when you're looking for another position. I'm going to miss you. But I know you're destined for greater things."

When I get to the office, I spot a cardboard box on my chair. "I guess that's for my things." The problem is, everything I put in here was for the students, not me. I can't take this stuff away from them. I move the box off my chair and sit. I fight back the tears as I write a personal note to each student, assuring them they'll be in good hands.

The letter to Mary is the hardest to write. We were supposed to meet with her parents next week. I have to trust I'm leaving them with enough tools to navigate the rough waters ahead successfully.

My heart is heavy as I walk out of Northmeadow High.

Another chapter in my life has closed.

Over the past few weeks, Dad has had a few setbacks. He developed pneumonia in the damaged lung and returned to the ICU for a while. There were some scary nights, but finally, he's on the road to recovery. Dad will be in the hospital for a while longer to ensure the infection fully clears up. Even still, the doctors are amazed at his progress.

Unfortunately, this ordeal has taken a drastic toll on his body. Dad's very weak and, at this point, can't walk. They've started physical therapy in the hospital. Eventually, when he's discharged, a mobile therapist will come to their house a few days a week to continue his treatment.

Mom will have her hands full, caring for him and keeping the store running. I can't leave her to handle all that alone, so I decide to move home. It'll be easier if I'm there to help out.

Marshall's been helping me pack all afternoon. "I'm gonna

miss you here, kid," he says as he loads the last of my things into the car.

"I never thought I'd say this, but I'm going to miss it here too."

"I'm sorry things didn't work out with that guy. But, hey, if you're ever free, I'd love to take you out."

"That's a very nice offer, but I'm going to have to pass."

"Can't blame a guy for trying." He gives a slight shrug.

I reach out and hug him. "Thank you for everything."

"Keep in touch." He smiles.

Marshall turned out to be a good friend. I wave goodbye as I pull out of the parking lot, unsure if this move is a step back or a step forward.

Natalie

I'M HAVING LUNCH WITH MY PARENTS IN DAD'S hospital room.

"Explain to me why you broke off the engagement?" Dad asks for the millionth time.

"Alex bought out my contract even though we agreed I'd work for five years. He made me lose my job." I feel like a broken record. "We agreed on this months ago."

"That was before," Mom says. "I think the circumstances are different now, don't you?"

"No." I take a bite of my sandwich.

"And you haven't heard from him at all?" Dad asks.

I can't tell them about our contractual relationship and that I safeworded. I ended it. There's no reason for Alex to call me.

"I think you should try to call him," Mom says. "Talk to him. Give him a second chance."

"Says the person who didn't want me with him in the first place."

"We were wrong about him. That man loves you."

Even if that's true, he crossed a line. I've resigned myself to the fact that I'm probably meant to be single.

Mom has remained in Branson so she can be near Dad. But I've had to return to Northmeadow to keep the store running. We've been gone for weeks, and there's no food in the house. The first thing I have to do is restock the kitchen. What I hoped would be a quick shopping trip has taken over an hour. In every aisle, I'm met with people asking questions about Dad wanting to know what happened and why Tommy would do such a thing. I can't wait to get out of here.

As I near the house, I see an unfamiliar car parked out front. "What now?" I pull into our driveway and shut the car off. Maybe if I wait a minute, they'll leave. But instead of going, they get out.

I glance in the rearview mirror and almost can't believe my eyes. I throw the door open and jump out. Lana runs over to meet me and squeezes me in a hug. Brandon stands to the side, watching us.

"What are you guys doing here?"

"We're here for an intervention. Can we come in?"

An intervention? I don't like where this is going.

"All we ask is that you hear us out," Brandon says. "If it doesn't change your mind, we won't say another word about it."

"Okay." I agree. Although I'm confident there's nothing Lana can say that will change the situation.

Opening the trunk, I grab a few grocery bags. Brandon gets the rest, and they follow me into the house.

"Just put them on the table."

I put the perishables away before asking, "Can I get you guys something to drink?"

"Water would be great," Brandon says.

I grab three glasses and fill them with ice water. Lana helps me carry them into the living room, where Brandon sits on the couch. She hands a glass to Brandon and takes the spot next to him. I choose the chair across from them, hoping this will be over fast.

"Alex is miserable," Lana says. "And you aren't much better."

Dark circles stain my face under my eyes from not sleeping. I'm exhausted from managing the store and driving back and forth to the hospital.

"It's been a rough few weeks. But, it'll get better, eventually."

Lana looks at Brandon. He responds with an encouraging smile.

Sadness comes over her face. "I need to tell you a story. It's not something I like talking about, but you need to hear it."

Whatever this is, it's very important to Lana.

"I'm not sure where to start. So, I guess I just say it. Papa is the *pakhan*, the boss of a group in the Bratva."

"You expect me to believe Maxim's in the Russian mafia?" I laugh at the absurdity of the idea.

"Yes," she says without a hint of amusement.

"And I thought there wasn't anything more you could tell me about Maxim that'd surprise me. But what does that have to do with Alex?"

"I had a sister," Lana continues, a far-off look in her eyes. "Jelena was five years older than me. She was smart and beautiful. I wanted to be just like her. I was ten years old when she was taken."

"We were walking down the street when two men jumped out of a van and grabbed her. We were holding hands, and they ripped her away. Jelena yelled at me to run and not look back." Lana uses the back of her hand to wipe the tears from her face.

"I had no idea. I'm so sorry."

"They were traffickers. Papa searched day and night, but even with all his connections, it was too late when he found her. She'd already been sold and killed. Since then, Papa has used his position in the Bratva to fight the traffickers. He couldn't save Jelena, but he has saved many others."

I'm stunned and don't know what to say.

"It's made him very overprotective of me. When I approached Papa and told him I wanted to come to America to study, he went crazy." She laughs. "He wouldn't be able to protect me here, which was unacceptable to him."

"I'm sure he was terrified something would happen to you. But I still don't see what this has to do—"

She puts her finger up. "Hang on. I'm getting to the part about Alex."

I take a drink of my water, trying to be patient.

"Papa didn't want to hold me back, so he arranged for me to stay with a business associate of his who lived in New York. This is where Alex comes in." Lana grins. "My parents and Alex's parents had been friends for many years. Which is how Papa started working with him in the first place."

I readjust my position on the chair. This story just got more interesting.

"Papa's responsible for reintroducing Alex to the lifestyle. He knew that after Alex's Mom passed away, he lost his focus—his direction. The first anniversary of his mom's passing was a particularly bad time for Alex. Papa found him drunk in his room. He was concerned about him and stayed with Alex the rest of the night. The following morning, he told Alex about his friendship with his parents and invited Alex to the club. Initially, Alex was resistant. He wasn't interested in having a sub. But, my papa can be persuasive, and Alex finally gave in."

"That's how Alex got involved at Fire and Ice." The pieces are finally starting to fall into place.

"It is. Fast forward a few years. The businessman Papa went to visit was Alex. Papa asked if he would step in and become my Dominant."

The familiar feelings of betrayal creep up. Secrets. I hate them. "You and Alex were a couple?"

"Alex and me?" Lana wrinkles her nose. "He's a great guy, but he's not my type. We were *never* a couple."

Brandon steps in to continue the story. "What Lana's trying

to explain." He pats her leg. "Is that Maxim asked Alex if he'd be willing to be responsible for Lana's safety. To allow her to wear his collar of protection."

"Doesn't wearing a collar symbolize a relationship—ownership?" I'm bewildered and still not sure I like where this is going.

"In some cases, yes, but there are other kinds of collars," Brandon explains. "Lana was young and would be alone in a big city, in a foreign country. She was also a submissive who would be playing at a new club. Maxim wanted to ensure Lana had someone willing to protect her in his absence. A protection collar doesn't represent a partnership but rather a Dominant's commitment to be responsible for another's safety. It also meant any Dominants interested in Lana couldn't approach her without getting Alex's permission."

"So, you and Alex were never *together*?" I really hope the answer is no. I can't lose any more people I love.

"Nope, never a couple. Never played together."

Reaching into her purse, she pulls out a thin silver chain with a pendant hanging from it. Tentatively, I accept it and examine it closely.

"That was my collar. On the charm, you can see Alex's initials and the lowercase p to show I was under his protection."

I remember seeing this. "You wore this when I first met you."

"I wore it for almost six months." She smiles fondly. "I was so lonely until Alex showed me the city and introduced me to his friends at the club. Without him, I probably would have packed up and gone back to Russia. But it wasn't always smooth sailing. Alex can be a bit overprotective. He made decisions for me that I didn't always agree with."

Brandon laughs, a full belly laugh. "Alex and Svetlana became famous at the club for their *very* heated disagreements. Star and Owen had to step in on more than one occasion."

She and Alex still fight like they're siblings.

"The thing is, he saw things and knew things I didn't. It was hard, but I had to learn to trust his decisions. And in the end, he was always right."

"This isn't the same, Lana."

"It is, Nat." She comes over and sits on the arm of the chair. "You may not see the big picture. Actually, I know you don't see it."

"When Alex lost his mother, he gave up. He closed himself off from everyone around him. He was afraid of caring about someone and losing them, too. Then you came into his life, and his carefully constructed walls crumbled," Brandon says.

"All those fears rushed to the surface when your dad was shot. When you told him what Tommy did to you that night, it pushed him over the edge. I'll admit, he made some rash decisions."

"That's an understatement," I add sarcastically. "Alex and I had an agreement, and he broke it."

"I agree with you, Natalie. Alex and I have discussed what happened. He knows he was wrong and understands that he should've approached things differently. Alex is a Dominant, a protector—sometimes to a fault." Brandon pauses.

"He's also only human, and sometimes he screws up. But Alex is a good man. All he was thinking was that he couldn't risk losing you. I know you disagree—"

"Disagree? I more than disagree."

"That man loves you." Brandon's expression changes. The Dominant in him rises to the surface. "Do you love him?"

"Yes," I say softly.

"Do you trust him?"

"Brandon—"

"This lifestyle revolves around trust. Do you trust Alex as your future husband and, more importantly, as your Dominant?"

I look down at my hands. My mind goes back to the first night we met. How I allowed Alex to use a flogger on me when I didn't know him at all—I trusted my instincts.

Over the past year, we've shared many experiences. Alex has never given me a reason to distrust him.

On the contrary, he's always been there for me, even when I didn't deserve him. Finally, I look up and meet Brandon's intense gaze. "Yes, I trust him."

"Get your coats, girls." He stands. "We're going for a ride."

Lana jumps up and grabs her coat, but I don't move.

"Where are we going?"

"This time, you have to trust me." Brandon shoots me a wicked grin as he heads toward the door. "Get up. Let's go."

Lana grabs my hand, and I reluctantly follow. A semi-willing participant in whatever crazy scheme they've come up with.

Once we're in the car, Brandon turns around. "One more thing. You need to put this on." He holds out a blindfold.

"You're seriously crazy. You know that?"

I play along with their game and take the offered blindfold, slipping it over my eyes.

"Good girl. Sit back and relax."

He and Lana share a laugh. I'm beginning to question the sanity of my friends. I try to pay attention to the turns we're taking, hoping to figure out where we're going. But unlike in the movies, it only takes a few minutes before I'm all turned around. We drive for what feels like forever before the car stops.

"You may remove the blindfold now," Brandon says.

It takes my eyes a few seconds to focus. We're at the lake, sitting in the driveway of a sweet little stone cottage. Luminaires line each side of a path leading to the front door.

"It's gorgeous. But what are we doing here?"

"Go knock on the door," Brandon says.

"But I don't—"

"Stop questioning and just trust me," Brandon chastises me. "Get out and go knock on the door."

I leave the car's safety and take a few tentative steps toward the house. But then I stop, unsure if I should keep going or turn around. A car door opens.

"Keep moving forward," Brandon instructs.

Reluctantly, I continue walking and find myself at the door.

I RAISE MY HAND TO KNOCK, BUT THE DOOR OPENS before I get the chance. Alex stands in the doorway wearing jeans and a dark blue T-shirt that clings to his muscles. Despite every-thing that's happened, I'm still drawn to him. My gaze travels up his body until it meets his eyes. The usual sparkle in his blue eyes is gone. All I see is sadness—loneliness.

"Come in before you freeze out there." He steps aside, and I walk into the house.

Before closing the door, he waves to Brandon and Lana, who drive away.

The inside looks like it was recently remodeled. The quaint country feel of the cottage is mixed with modern touches.

"Do you like it?" Alex asks nervously.

"It's beautiful. But what are you doing here?"

"I bought this for us. It was going to be a Christmas present. This is part of why I came back early, but you were in New York."

He bought this for us?

"This was supposed to be our home while you finished your contract. Then I thought we'd live in the city and use this as our vacation home."

My mind is struggling to keep up with what he's telling me.

"Natalie, I didn't mean to hurt or betray your trust. That was never my intention. After you told me what Tommy did to you, and then seeing what he did to your father. I was scared. I couldn't take any more chances. I was terrified of losing—"

"I know."

"Can we sit and talk?"

I follow him into the living room and sit on the couch. When I look closer, I notice the small, personal details like the framed pictures of us sitting on the mantle over the fireplace. My favorite blanket from his apartment is folded over the back of a chair. I'm not sure what to think. I have so many questions right now, but I have to stay focused. We have some serious issues to discuss.

"Natalie, when we signed our Dom/sub contract, I had every intention of keeping my emotions out of it. I wasn't looking for a relationship and thought putting an end date on us would protect us both. But the closer that date came, the more I realized I didn't want to let you go. I fell in love with you and couldn't imagine my life without you in it. I still can't picture my life without you."

Alex stands and starts pacing, his nervous habit of choice.

"I understand our falling in love complicates everything. But we agreed I was staying to finish my contract, and then we'd reevaluate our next steps. Alex, as your submissive, I put my full trust in you. But then, you went behind my back and crossed a line."

"I overstepped a boundary and screwed up. I can't argue with that. I was wrong, and my actions forced you to use your safe-word." He comes back and sits next to me. The expression on his face is pained and wrought with regret.

"That's a position I never wanted to put you in. I was wrong, and I'm sorry." He hesitantly reaches for my hands.

"I forgive you." I place my hands in his. "But where do we go from here? Is it possible to try again?"

"As a man and as your Dominant, the last thing I wanted to do was hurt you. I want to be the one you can always count on and always believe in. The only thing I can do is ask if you'd give me another chance. Let me prove to you that you're everything to me. That I'm worthy of your submission."

"I didn't think there was an option to try again," I whisper.

"I put you in that position, baby girl. That's on me, not you. Whether we move forward or not is your decision."

I know his apology was genuine, but I also don't want to let him off the hook that easily. Instead of answering, I get up and walk to the window. "I'm sure the view of the lake is stunning from here."

"It is."

I stand silently, looking into the night for a few minutes before slowly turning to face him. "I guess we have some renegotiating to do."

He raises an eyebrow. "You have the floor, Ms. Clarke."

I return to my place on the sofa next to him.

"As your submissive, I agree to place my full trust in you to make decisions in my best interest. However, where my career is concerned, we will discuss everything openly. My voice *will* be heard. You will not make any decisions behind my back."

"And as your Dominant, I promise to be the man you expect me to be. I will honor the trust you place in me. I'll work to prove myself to you every day. I promise I'll never again break a boundary we've put in place together. I'll always listen to you before making a decision. But when the final decision has been made, I need to know you'll trust me enough to accept it."

"No more secrets?"

"No more secrets." Alex agrees.

Without warning, he slides from his spot and kneels before me. "You make me a better man, baby girl. Will you agree to be my submissive?"

"Yes, I agree."

He takes the ring from his pocket. "Will you still marry me?"

Alex is the strongest and most honorable man I've ever known.

Is he perfect? No. But he's perfect for me.

He owns my heart.
He's my soulmate.
"Yes, Sir. I'd love to marry you."
He slides the ring back onto my finger.
"Mine," he says as he pulls me against him.
I place a kiss on his lips.
"Always and forever, Yours."
THE END

Surrender was only the beginning. Now everything they built is about to be tested.

Continue Alex and Natalie's story in *His Fight*.

Find Tara's Books Here

About Tara

Bestselling author Tara Conrad writes where passion meets peril, crafting dark, spellbinding romances that blur the line between devotion and destruction.

Inspired by the haunting brilliance of Edgar Allan Poe, her stories reimagine Gothic tales with modern sensuality and power.

Within her pages, heroines rise unbroken, villains fall beautifully, and the darkness always tells the truth.

When she isn't writing, Tara travels with her husband, meeting readers who have found pieces of themselves in her worlds.

She believes love isn't always light. Sometimes, it's found in the dark. 🖤

Dear Reader,

Thank you to everyone who's come on this crazy journey with me. I'm so thankful to have Alex and Natalie's story back and that I was able to improve it to reoffer it to each of you. I fell in love with Alex and Natalie a long time ago. I hope you've come to love them as much as I do.

This brings me to ask you, the reader, to leave a review. Reader reviews are crucial to Indie authors. The more reviews a book receives, the more visibility the retailer gives it. Your review doesn't need to be long unless you want it to be. Thank you in advance for each review.

Acknowledgments

There are so many people who have been an integral part of my writing this story. First and most important, my husband, George. You believed in me long before i believed in myself. You've been my rock throughout this journey and have held me up when i was unable to stand on my own. You dried my tears (on more than one occasion), and you celebrated each success with me. i can't believe how many things have changed in one year. Finally, we have Alex and Natalie's story back where it belongs. i love working side-by-side with You. Thank You for Your love, support, and endless patience, especially as you listened to revision after revision. i love You more than words can say. i can't wait to continue this writing journey and every other journey in life with You.

To my children, you have been my cheering section through this whole writing process. I love that you all come to my signings to support me—it means the world to me. **George**: Thank you for finally agreeing to take one of my pens, even though you have more than enough pens. I do appreciate your support and encouragement. I can't wait until we publish your book, too! **Jacob**: Your tech skills have saved me more than once. I wouldn't have a website or any other digital form if it wasn't for you. I'm so proud of you. **Kayla**: Your critiques and edits are something I'll never forget. Literally will never forget—I saved the pages, and they will be part of my book wall. Thank you for always being willing to read and give me your critiques. I love you, Sweetpea. **Rebekah**: Your unwavering support helped make this all possible. You always saw the rainbows when all I could see were clouds. I love you, princess. **Jonathan**: Thank you for loving my daughter and for coming on this crazy ride with us. One day, I'll make enough to employ you as my merchandise manager. I love you and can't wait until you make yourself an official member of the family.

Max: You taught me some of my first and most important lessons in writing. You asked me to take my hurt and put it on paper—that changed my life. Your encouragement and support mean the world to me. I'm proud to call you my teacher and friend.

Jay: You've been with me since almost day one. You've been through my successes and failures. You cheered me on and gave me pep talks when I needed them. I can't wait until your book is born.

Norman and Nancy: Your friendship and beta reading helped shape this book into what it is today. I value the friendship I've found in you both.

Dr. C: The inspiration and brains behind Dr. Fitzgerald's character. You literally saved Stanley Clarke's life with your rock star trauma surgeon skills.

Paul: As a professor, you are the toughest there is, but that toughness comes from a place of wanting to see your students do their absolute best. At the beginning of my classes, I thought I was giving the best. But with each assignment, you asked for more. You forced me to dig deep inside myself, to get out of my comfort zone. Your influence has allowed me to grow as a writer. I can't thank you enough for the lessons I carry with me today. It's been a bumpy road, but I'm loving every minute of it. I'm honored and privileged to now call you my friend.

Last but certainly not least, **Greg**: As soon as we all heard your audition (yep, the whole family listened to it over a tray of pizza), we knew you were meant to be the voice of this book. Thank you for taking a chance on a new author and a new series. I'm so happy you've brought *Her Surrender* to life.

Human Trafficking Resources

National Human Trafficking Resource Center 1-888-373-7888
TTY 711
Text HELP to 233733

ONLINE RESOURCES

www.dhs.gov/bluecampaign

polarisproject.org

humantraffickinghotline.org

www.ingramcontent.com/pod-product-compliance
Lightning Source LLC
Chambersburg PA
CBHW051205190726
48288CB00006B/1826